MY NAME IS SAPPHO

MY NAME IS SAPPHO

A novel by

Martha Rofheart

G. P. PUTNAM'S SONS
NEW YORK

*Library of Congress Catalog
Card Number: 74-79665*

SBN: 399-11400-9

PRINTED IN THE UNITED STATES OF AMERICA

To Bill Targ, who said, "How would you like
to write the story of Sappho?"
And to John Schaffner, who believed that I could.

Author's Note

Willis Barnstone, in his introduction to his own excellent translation of a number of Sappho's songs, says, "In Sappho we hear for the first time in the Western world the direct words of an individual woman." This is a startling statement, a true statement, and a meaningful one for my particular readers. For this, though I hope it does not show too awkwardly, is a feminist novel. Let women remember that nearly twenty-six hundred years ago, on the island of Lesbos, there was, for them, once a Camelot!

In the poetry of Sappho there is not one hint of eroticism; there is none, either, in the prose of Plato. How is it, then, that "platonic" love has come to mean something pure, spiritual, and intellectual, whereas "lesbian" love carries a connotation of lasciviousness? Plato loved boys all his life; Sappho loved girls for a part of hers; neither practice was frowned upon under the mores of the world in which they lived, before the Judeo-Christian ethic, before Paul of Tarsus, before Puritanism, and before Freud, Jung, and the rest. I have tried to present that ancient world as I think it was.

The facts of Sappho's life are spare; we know her birthplace and her approximate birth date; we know the names of her father, mother, brothers, husband, daughter, and her intimates. We know, too, that she, though a woman, was twice exiled for political reasons under the rule of the Tyrants. From her own poems we read that she reached an age where her teeth fell out, her hair turned white, her limbs stiff, and a thousand wrinkles covered her face; her tomb, now destroyed, was visited for centuries by tourists to Lesbos. The legend of her leap to death at Leukas for love of the beautiful Phaon is now dismissed by most historians; I have turned the tables, as it were, in my story. Phaon, described in legend as a lowborn ferryman, may or may not have existed; I have given him the only existence he might have had in an aristocratic world, that of some kind of performer, a cross between Nijinksy and a modern rock artist.

Much of my story is fleshed out by invention, but the background facts are true, though they must be ferreted out in many, many volumes. The Greek period we term "archaic" (seventh to fifth centuries B.C.) is not visited as often in literature as the later "classical" period, though in many ways the archaic world is more interesting; it is lively, burgeoning, inventive and full of color.

My characters, except for a very few, were real people. Pittakos was one of the Seven Sages of antiquity, as were Thales, Solon, and Periander; much is known of these men. Alkaios' character leaps to life from the pages of his own poetry, as, of course, does Sappho's. The love affair of Charaxus and Doricha-Rhodopis was one of the most famous romances of several centuries. The other people in this novel are created from their shadowy existences in the poems. There is no evidence that Atthis was Alkaios' sister, or that Gorgo was Pittakos' daughter, but who is to say they were not? Andromeda is addressed in Sappho's poem as "daughter of kings"; since there were no kings then in Greece, I have dreamed up her African origin.

To those scholars of the period who may read this book, I wish to admit several author's licenses. The woman I have named Phaedra has been, by some historians, called Drakon's sister; I have made her his wife. War chariots were seldom used in post-Homeric times; I have used one in the fifteen-year-old war in the Sigeum. Herodotus says that the iron spits dedicated by Rhodopis were at Delphi; I have placed them at Naukratis, the scene of her meeting with her lover. Where there is conflict in ancient writings, I have gone with Herodotus; he has so often been proven right by archaeology.

The bulk of Sappho's work was burned, along with many other pagan writers' work, in 1038 by the Church of Rome. We have only fragments remaining. These have been imitated ad nauseam by the nineteenth-century Romantics, who, for the most part, sacrificed imagery and meaning to cadence. Those who can read the Greek originals will know the flawlessness of both cadence and thought, which most translations have destroyed. If one would learn (or relearn) the Greek alphabet and sit down with a Greek-English dictionary, one might find the literal meanings. (For instance, a line is translated, "An impalpable fire courses through my body." The literal words of Sappho are, "Thin fire runs like a thief through my veins. . . .") For those without the patience and curiosity to do this, I recommend the Barnstone version, or the stark and unsentimental version of Miss Mary Barnard, published in 1958. It will then be seen that, after Sappho, it was not until Emily Dickinson that the melodic bolt was hurled again at the heart.

The few Greek words I have used seem to be explained by the text. *Kittabos* was a game of chance, involving some skill, played with the wine lees left in the cups (messy as it may seem!); *agora* is translated "marketplace" but was more of an open-air forum; *amphora* was a large stoppered vessel for wine or oil; *himation, chlamys* and *chiton* were garments worn by both men and women. Since there is no *c* in the Greek alphabet, I have used *k* in proper names rather than the more familiar Latin spellings. The sound *ch* is always pronounced as in "chord."

It is not known how or when Doricha was given her nickname, "Rhodopis." The word might be translated as "Red" rather than "roselike," as I have decided. The dignity of her character as it emerges, at least in my story, implies that "Rhodopis" was meant as a compliment to her beauty, rather than as a reference to her coloring.

A note on geography: We are told that the coastlines and positionings of the islands of the Aegean have changed greatly since the sixth century B.C.; earth tremors and erosion have taken a strong toll. I have tried to describe these islands as they were described in ancient writings, and not as they are today.

*My name is Sappho. My song surpasses the
song of women as Homer's the song of men.*

—Antipatros of Sidon

Contents

BOOK I

. . .Mitylene, 612 B.C.

(Told by Sappho,
singer of Lesbos)

Chapter 1

I was born in the loveliest month, the month of May, the flowering month, in the first year of the forty-second Olympiad, or so I am told; I have never been good at figures and dates.

My father was named Skamandronymos, after the Skamander River of the Troad, where he was born; his friends mostly called him Andros.

My mother, Kleis, came from Ephesos, on the Asian mainland. She looked Pelasgian, of the old race that was here before the Hellenes came; we are all mixed up now, especially on our islands. Mother looked like the old paintings from Crete in its days of glory; black, black, black of hair and snapping eyes, and cream for skin; her shape was small and sweetly made, curving to delicate hands and feet; I remember her well. Besides, they tell me I am her image, if I keep well out of the sun so that I will not get dark.

My father was tall, like one of Homer's "brown-haired Achaians," with light eyes, and my brothers Charaxus and Larichus are fair as well; Erigyus, the youngest, was a perfect little Cretan, shorter than the others for his age, and dark, almost russet-dark, with eyes like raisins.

I was jealous of each of my brothers when they came along, thinking myself forgotten. The first two I got over quickly, and delighted in, playing with them as though they were puppies; when the third one came, poor little Erigyus, Mother went away to the gods, and I was long forgiving him. It was not his fault, of course, and I was old enough to know better. It was a hard birth, for it was twins she bore, and the other child died with her.

Erigyus was a tiny shriveled thing that wailed thinly all the time because he was too weak to suck; Father himself used to squeeze goats' milk from a sponge into his mouth, and, thus cosseted, he hung on to life, finally. Father looked up once, though, and caught the old nurse, Eurydike, staring at the baby and making the sign against the evil eye. He was very angry and dismissed her with a year's wages, though she was a slave, really, and many men would have done worse. He told us later that in Sparta and Athens and such uncivilized places, and even in our own hills here in Lesbos, where the folk are ignorant, that such a child would be put to death or exposed; they think it is only half a person, without its twin.

I was not born here, at Mitylene, but in a smaller place called Eresos; it stood sheer above the sea on a high hill, where the winds were wild and chilly in the winter season, and father thought it unhealthy. So, soon after my birth, he brought my mother and me here to live at Mitylene, and I never knew Eresos for home, though we kept the house in good repair and sometimes visited there, in the heat of summer. As a child I thought it very high above the world, like Olympos; sounds from below came strangely, faint but very clear, the breaking of the waves, a horn at sea, or, from the valley side, the lowing of lambs or a single note from a shepherd's pipe. The nearer air about the house was filled always, or I remember it so, with the humming of bees; Eresos was famous for its honey and its barley, though I never saw the golden fields of it ripe and moving like a yellow sea, for we were never there at harvest time. I remember the walls about our dwelling, blinding-white in the whiteness from the sea-light, and the house, white, too, but cool and dark within, shaded by the tall cypresses and sycamores that grew all about. My brothers and I used to climb in those trees and swing in the branches, dangerously, for there was rock face below, and we were punished for it, though only the boys were beaten. They took it out on me later, though, stealing away with some village boys and leaving me alone and crying; odd, what sort of thing one remembers, and for so long! I remembered, too, how they used to tease me for my looks, calling me a little peasant and a hill girl.

Though we island folk are a mixture, as I have said, the hill people, who have not intermarried and are said to be the older inhabitants, are all Pelasgian, plain to see. They are the poorer sort and have no say in much of anything, rarely coming into the cities, except to sell their wares, if they have any; mostly they scrape a bare living from the soil or hire themselves out as servants to those of us who are more fortunate. So, of course, looking like one of them is not greatly admired in this day and age, even though the race was a noble one and once known all over the world for its arts and skills. Even now you will sometimes find, in a poor woodcutter's hut, a sample of carving with a charm and liveliness to take your breath, even though its creator has done it quickly, in his spare time. And father took us always to see the village dancing, at rite times; in all the world you will not see such grace.

Mostly the wealthy in Mitylene who are dark, like me, and show the old blood, will go to great lengths to hide it, putting white lead paint upon their cheeks and dyeing their hair yellow. Myself, I have not cared; there is pride to be had out of anything, if one wishes to make it so.

When I was growing up, and seen to have many gifts from the gods, there were sometimes spiteful taunts from jealous fairhaired dumplings who could not arrange their robes without tripping on the folds and who had voices like crows. I was able to shrug these jibes away, knowing myself clever and talented; my brothers' teasings were light and merry, and I knew they were fond of me.

Once, though, when I was just beginning to leave my childhood, about the age of ten, there was an incident that bit deep, and has kept me under sunshades all my life, for fear of the truth of it, underneath. A tiring woman, Athenian, young and blue-eyed, trod on my new, birth-gift lyre, cracking the tortoiseshell and spoiling two of the strings. I cried out in anguish, and she turned on me swiftly and snapped, "Be still—you misbegotten black bitch!" I stood still, in horror, staring, and the flesh creeping on me. Anger rose deep in me, but I kept it within. I never told, for I knew that she shared Father's couch sometimes, and I was shamed. She was only one of many and was married off early and he forgot her, but I did not. She had rosy, translucent skin, and I was hateful and cruel to another much later, who resembled her. May the gods forgive me for it in time.

One might say that I never knew Mother; I adored her, of course, we all did; even my young brothers, who were little more than infants while she was still with us, ran laughing to her upon her slightest glance, and hung about her, playing with her bracelets and stroking the gleaming folds of her beautiful robes. She had that elusive thing called charm, a kind of perfume upon a woman.

Father, too, never took another wife, though he was still quite a young man when she died. He had concubines, a few greedy and sly and unworthy of him, and that same blue-eyed one who had hurt me so, but these did not last long with him, thank the gods, and most of his companions were sweet and good, with intelligence beyond their stations, and beauty, too, of a higher sort.

To tell the truth, I was never sure who was or was not his concubine, unless she gave herself airs. Father kept a large household, servingmen and maids, teachers for us children, scribes, entertainers for party times, gardeners and charioteers, and old crones who never did a lick of work but mumbled toothlessly in corners or sunned themselves beside the wall of the garden; he was softhearted, Father, only going to the slave market to rescue some poor maimed creature that would be bought cheaply for the saltmines otherwise, to labor hard and die there.

There were slaves in our house, of course, as in all houses, but they were for the most part inherited or given as gifts by friend or kinsman; sometimes a poor man would offer himself or his child for sale, because he was so set about by misfortune, and these my father would buy, training them to whatever work they could do best, and putting them on wages later. But, as I have said, he would not visit the slave marts; he had strong feelings about this, and taught us all to feel the same. "Look," he would say, "think what makes a slave—war, or a free person captured by those who trade in it, pirates or worse." And he warned us all, my brothers and I, never to go alone to any stretch of deserted beach or stray far into the woods to gather flowers. "For that is how they are taken—these unfortunates put up for sale—if not in battle. They are no different from you or any other . . . except that the gods were not with them. . . ." And his gray eyes looked inward, brooding, and his face in sad, long lines. "Some," he said, "some of those I have seen standing naked on the slave platform and in chains . . . some of them were princes or princes' children at home. . . ."

We listened, round-eyed and taking it all in; still we were curious. Our cousins and playmates chattered for days before a slave ship was expected; they would go, with all their families, in wagons or covered litters, and dressed in their best, as for a feastday. So we, too, and I especially, for I was the oldest, got it into our heads that we were missing a treat, and sneaked off to the waterfront wharf on a slave-sale day.

We kept off to one side, mingling with the common folk, for we did not want to be seen and reported on to Father. It was as he had said, a degrading spectacle—the poor boys and girls, men and women, chained at ankles and wrists, and naked as the day they were born, and folk coming close, and climbing up onto the platform to get a closer look, or even a feel. The prospective buyers slapped buttocks, kneaded muscles, and even squeezed scrotums, to see if the merchandise were sound, while their womenfolk, behind the curtained litters, giggled. One coarse fellow pinched a young girl's nipple till she cried out, and the trader ran over and slapped her quiet.

That was how we got the Nubian girl that became one of Lesbos' greatest dancers; I saw her standing, straight and proud, like any statue, not looking to left or right, her disdainful face like a carven dark plum, purplish in its shadows, and ran home fast as my legs would carry me, to beg Father to buy her. He asked me why, not chiding me for going to the mart, but gravely, as to an adult. "Because she was the daughter of a king where she came from . . . or even a king herself," I gasped out, remembering some dim tales of the Amazon peoples. He smiled, and took my hand. We bought her, and she cost next to nothing, for the trader showed his hand, all swollen and infected where she had bitten it; besides, in Lesbos, the folk do not like her dark color, fearing, perhaps, their own kinship, under.

She did not bite my father, when he came to lead her away; he had had her chains struck off first thing, and had the sense to bring a snow-white mantle to clothe her, with a gold clasp for the closure.

The trader had said, with scorn, that she was dumb as well, never crying out when she was beaten. She walked off with us quite meekly, though her face showed no sign of pleasure, fear, or interest. Her wrists and ankles were all chafed and raw from the chains, but she took no notice, taking the garment from my father with a grave nod. She did not drape it as we would, like a mantle and pinned on one shoulder, but tied it in a complicated looping under her breasts, leaving them bare; they were like shallow hills, conical, with a deep valley between, though I think she was not much above my age, and I was still flat as a boy. I did not know where to look, for I had seen only the quickly hidden breast of a suckling mother before, or a glimpse of a flute girl's flaunted charms when we peeped in on a drinking party once through a hole in the drawn curtains. I had, true, seen some old statuettes, from Crete, I think, showing the Mother Goddess with her bared breasts and flounced skirts, but it is not the fashion here anymore. But, as Father has said, all lands have their own customs; where the girl came from it was no doubt the only way to dress. The gold clasp she put in her hair, right in the middle of her forehead; the hair was short and thick, curled all over like the wool of a sheep, with a dusty look.

She was not dumb, though, for when, at home, food was placed before her, she made strange clicking sounds, seeming to come from her throat, and inclined her head in a kind of gesture of thanking. Nobly bred she was, too, for she did not fall upon the bread and cheese like a wolf, though one could see that her mouth almost watered at the sight. It was plain that they had starved her on the slave ship, deeming her worthless.

Praxinoa, Father's companion, a gift slave from a Korinthian guest, took the new girl, after she had finished her meal, into her own apartments, and bathed her and dressed her in a pale-blue chiton, in the Greek fashion, draped and girdled and tied at the shoulders; her wooly hair, too, she oiled and sleeked, binding it back and up with a purple ribbon. The dusty look of her had all vanished and her skin shone with a hint of copper; she was thoroughly alien, but utterly beautiful. She walked gravely to my father and prostrated herself before him, touching her forehead to the floor; when she rose, she pointed her hand to her chest and made another of those clicking sounds. It did not sound like any language at all, and we could make no sense of it, but she repeated the same sound again, and again pointed at her chest; clearly she was telling us her name. Larichus, who was very young then and easily overcome, giggled; the girl flashed a look of scorn at him, and repeated the sound again, and again pointed to herself. Father motioned Larichus out of the room; the rest of us still stared. Then, for a wonder, Praxinoa repeated the sound, or nearly; in Korinth, where she had come from, there are many nations mingled and slaves from all over the world. Praxinoa then said her own name, slowly, and pointed, as the girl had done, at herself.

The girl smiled, for the first time, showing white, white teeth, and, wrinkling her brow, attempted to say Praxinoa's name; it was a good thing Larichus had been sent out already, for what came out did not sound much like Greek. The girl tried again, though, several times, each effort a little closer. Father said she must be from a hill tribe or a forest people, where the language does not make use of the tongue, teeth, and lips, as does ours, but of some throat muscles that we do not use. In the end she learned our language, and not too slowly; none of us ever mastered hers.

"Clearly," said Father, smiling, "we cannot say her name. . . . What shall we call her?" He spoke mainly to me, for I had urged him to buy her.

I thought for a bit. "Could we call her Andromeda?" I said. "Because you struck off her chains. . . ."

Father smiled again. "So you would have me a hero, little one . . . like Perseus—instead of just a man with money to buy another human . . ." And his face looked sad and older than his years for a moment. After, though, he stooped quickly and kissed me on the cheek, holding me close. "It shall be as you say, little Sappho, little bird . . . we will call her Andromeda."

And that was Andromeda, daughter of kings. Drom, my friend, Drom, my teacher. Drom, my beloved enemy.

Chapter 2

I have said that I was not sure who of the women of our house were Father's concubines, and this is true. He did not have more than one at a time and usually their days with him were brief, and he married them off decently to good providers, unlike some men of the town who sold their cast-off girls like so much used clothing. He was not so continent as Thales, the mathematician-philosopher, his great friend, nor so profligate as Pittakos, the soldier-statesman, who kept, quite literally, a houseful of girls, though he was married to one of the island's loveliest women.

My brother, Charaxus, used to point them out to me, Father's favorites, though Charaxus was still a child. Perhaps he saw more than I; indeed, I cannot doubt it, for my eyes were on inward things and my head in the clouds. I learned most of my worldly knowledge in those early days from Charaxus; he was sharp, and spent much of his time with wharf boys and sons of fishermen or shopkeepers. Such boys know everything, for they hear all the news first, getting it from sailors off the ships that came in to port from far places. Father knew of these lowly companions, but did not forbid it, only enjoining Charaxus to be wary, to carry no valuables or coins, and to keep to populated parts of town. "After all," he sighed, "a boy cannot spend all his time with girls . . ."

For a little war had been waging for a weary time now, a chronic war with Athens, over some lands in the Troad, and all the young men of our class of an age to go were there, fighting. Or, as Father said, more likely camping out and seeing what sights there were to see. But Charaxus was still too young for campaigning, and, though we had cousins in plenty among all the noble families, there were few boys among them, and those few, babies still. Thales, nodding sagely, said it was a sign of inbreeding, but Father laughed and said, no, it was simply a whim of nature. Those two were forever arguing and disputing, back and forth, thus and so; one could see they enjoyed it more than wine.

So all my brothers had to take their lessons with me; normally it would be the other way around, and a girl lucky to get her scraps of knowledge off the boys' dining table. But it was not so in our house, for I was older and an apter pupil at all things besides. After a while my aunts and uncles, some of them, began sending their daughters to us, so that our house became a kind of school, really. For Praxinoa was there; besides being most accomplished at all manner of music and dancing, she had the command of many tongues, could read Old Greek, and write a beautiful hand, whether with stylus on wax or pen on Egyptian papyrus.

Which brings us back to the matter of Father's concubines. This was not really the word for Praxinoa; she was much more than that from the first. I truly thought Father might have married her, had she not been a slave. Once I said this to Charaxus, and he, looking sly, shook his head. "No," he said. "Father would not mind that. . . . It is that she was a courtesan, a common whore, really."

I was shocked, but he laughed (he was then at an insufferable age) and said, "Silly—don't you know all Korinthian girls are whores? They have to offer themselves in the temple to the first comer . . ."

"What temple?" I whispered.

"The Temple of Aphrodite . . . it is an old custom, outlawed everywhere else—or just about." He frowned, thinking; he did not know as much as he pretended.

"That is just gossip from your street boys!" I said. "You do not know for sure . . ."

"Oh—you think not?" he cried. "Ask her sometime!"

But I never dared; instead, when one time we were alone, and no one listening, I asked Father. He looked sad, as he often did, or so I remember him, and said, yes, it was true. There was a great temple there at Korinth, with groves and courtyards all about, and wooded places, with an image of the goddess upon a pedestal. "But she is old—very old—that goddess," he said. "Not the Aphrodite that we know at all. It is an Eastern image—and so obscene that it is veiled always. . . . It has been the custom for long years, centuries I guess . . . the girls, when they are of an age for it, must go to the temple and sit before the shrine. The first man who takes her hand and gives his offering to the goddess—that is the maiden's first lover. . . ." Bitterness crept into his voice. "It might be a filthy sailor with the dirt of six months' voyage still on him . . . or a brute . . . or someone with a disease raging within. . . ."

We were silent for a moment; I was shaken to the core. Then I stammered, "But—but surely not—not noble girls? . . ."

"Yes," he answered, with a thin smile. "But they are ringed about with servants and governesses, and sit within a covered litter, while the priestesses make their bargains . . . no filthy peasant for them! It is a corrupt custom," he said, his eyes far away. "It served once, in antiquity, to remind us of our mortality, and our debt to the gods . . . for early man knew nothing of his origins . . . and had little capacity for reason. Such customs have been outlawed in most civilized places. . . ."

"And—Praxinoa?" I asked, timidly.

"She was more fortunate than most," he said, "though she was a girl of the people. Her father, a poor peasant, without an obol to his name, but with a soul beyond his station, brought her in himself, and stood beside her, holding a thick club to frighten the worst sort away. When a clean, well-dressed traveler set foot upon the shrine courtyard, that good father went up to him and begged him to take his daughter. She was beautiful, and the traveler was a decent man, so he did. He paid the father good cash for her afterward, too. . . ."

"Was that traveler—your friend?"

"Yes . . . Pyrrhus of Salamis—a good man. He educated her in all the arts, perceiving that she had many talents, and intelligence as well as beauty."

"But—why did he give her away?"

My father sighed, heavily. "He was very old . . . even on that day he first saw her, he was old enough to be her grandfather. When your mother died, Pyrrhus saw that I was lonely, and he himself was ailing—no longer able to hold converse with her, much less . . ." And his voice faded off. "He died two years ago. . . . And I think she is happy here. She is a natural teacher—born for it, one might say."

"But yet . . . you would not marry her? . . ." My voice must have held a hint of censure, for he looked down at me and said, "No—but not for that reason . . . that she was slave—and offered to the goddess. I do not love her, that is all. And she, too . . . Praxinoa does not love me—or any man. Perhaps she has reason . . . one cannot read another's soul. . . ." And something in his tone warned me that he would say no more. So, in a way, I was no wiser. I did not know what they had been, or were, to each other. Lovers, friends, master and servant?

At any rate, she was much to me, Praxinoa, and to all our kindred. She was accomplished, kind, beautiful, and nobler in her presence than a born aristocrat. Her face was proud and a little stern; her limbs were long and there was much grace in all her movements; her hair was of such a bright gold color that she wore it covered, always, when we went out in public, so as not to attract attention of an unseemly sort. Her instincts were of a gentlewoman, no matter her origin; I have never seen anyone show her disrespect, though everyone must have known she was a freedwoman.

She managed our household, Praxinoa; truly it was so. Looking back, I see that she never ceased from early morning to the evening hours; she supervised all the training of the servingmaids, teaching them to sew, and to bake and broil. Those who were cleverer she showed the arts of tiring hair, and oiling and bathing, and the draping of clothes, and such things. She bought all the produce for our table, arranged for all the feasts and parties; there was nothing she could not turn her hand to. And besides this, she taught me the rudiments of my musical knowledge, for she could play several instruments; I quickly got beyond her, and Father hired other, more expert, musicians for my teaching. But this was my special talent, music, singing, and the making of songs; Praxinoa had a little touch of them all. She was my first dancing teacher, too, after Mother; I was quick at this and loved to learn new steps, being small and light-limbed, but Drom was better. She could bend her dark body as though no bones lived under the flesh, and leap beautifully, high, high into the air, a sight to take your breath. She never learned to pluck a lyre string, though her fingers were longer and slenderer than my own, and I am said to have "musician's hands." Nor could she ever sing, Drom; her sounds were always croaks, though after she learned our speech she could speak it pleasantly and in the proper cadence. Drums of all kinds she could play to great effect, and used them in her dancing later, much as a flute girl will accompany herself in her intricate steps. Father got a teacher for Drom, from Lydia, a woman who had been renowned all over the world in her day, but was getting too old to perform regularly; he had seen that Drom was gifted beyond any of us girls and boys.

All Lesbos dances and sings; we are known for it as Sparta and Athens are known for their games. No noble person is without knowledge of some musical instrument, and one who cannot foot it nimbly is counted worse than a cripple; there are prizes every feastday and everyone takes part. From the time I was four I won them all for my poetry and singing; until Drom came along I had a small collection for dancing, too.

Not everyone can write as legibly as I; Father made me spend hours at my tablets, saying that my poems must be written down by me as I myself have composed them, so they will not be distorted in later years by other singers. "For you have great gifts from the Muses," he said. "I would not have them lost to the world that comes after. . . ." I was a little awed, for it was extravagant praise, and Father has, in most things, a prudent speech. And so I worked hard and diligently, and I think I may claim to have the finest hand in Lesbos for writing. He made me write them all down, too, my songs, even those that I found fault with later. He said they would read well, even without their music, though I wept inside to think of them alone, voiceless, dead things on paper rolls. Years after I was glad of it and thanked him, in my heart; for in my old age these same dead rolls of paper were a sort of joy to me, when my voice croaked like Drom's, and my fingers were too stiff to make the strings sing.

I must speak now of my family, that is, my uncles and aunts, cousins and so on; we were related, my brothers and I, to most of the ruling class of Mitylene, and even of all Lesbos. None of my mother's kin were on the island, but my father had a brother, Erigyus, for whom my littlest brother was named; his wife was called Kassandra—my Aunt Kassie. It was the fashion still, and had been for at least a generation or two, to call girl children after heroines of Homer—that is to say, personages of antiquity. So there were several Helens, none deserving the name for beauty or distinction, a Hermione, a Penelope, and a Nausikaa. This last was a daughter of Aunt Kassie, and my first cousin, near to me in age. We girls, unkindly, used to giggle at poor Nausikaa, for in Homer she is called "the white-armed" and this one was as freckled as a thrush egg all over and plain as a wooden churn paddle. Homely she was, but homey, too, and comfortable to be with, as long as one wished to talk of nothing and not think at all; she had no talent except for cooking, and later grew very fat on her own sweet concoctions. I was fond of her, though, in a way; she was kind and good-natured, with no malice, and got what she deserved, a husband as round and good and solid as she herself, and a brood of seven children, all of whom lived. My songs will live after me, but in the end, they were all I had, cold comfort for the longing that consumed me always.

Then too there were my cousins, once removed, Telesippa and Mnasadika, that we always called Dika, and their small brothers Hippias and Hermias. They were children of Drakon, the wealthiest man in Lesbos, and my father's cousin. His wife was notorious, no better than a common whore, or so Charaxus said, though I thought her very beautiful; one never saw her close to, she was remote with all us children, even her own, so that most of their days, and nights, even, were spent at our house. Her neglect of them was shameful; all her time was taken up with painting her face and gilding her hair to please her latest lover. Her name was another out of legend, Phaedra; as the years went on, it became more and more apt, for each new man friend was younger than the last. Perhaps it made her feel younger, too; I should have thought it would be the other way around.

I had some boy cousins away at the war, sons of Uncle Erigyus and Aunt Kassie; I did not remember them at all, for the war had been going on since I was five years old. Aunt Kassie was no Spartan mother though; just the sight of the littler boys playing with wooden toy swords could reduce her to tears. In fact, that is how I remember her always, with eyes that looked reddened and a lip that trembled; when she was not wringing her freckled hands, she was plucking at something with them, pleating the folds of her skirt or picking off some invisible lint. Her hair was forever coming down from its knot, and hanging in untidy wisps about her face; there was always something awry about her person, a broken sandal strap, a lost girdle, a missing brooch, and sometimes, quite often, a scattering of beads. I remember us children scrambling frantically in corners and under furniture to retrieve a last gold bauble from a broken chain, while Aunt Kassie stood wavering in the center of the room, wringing her hands. It is a wonder to me how she ever produced the placid, docile Nausikaa; her daughter got nothing from her but her freckles.

I liked her, though, Aunt Kassie; we all did. She was kind and good under her nervous twitchiness, and, though she herself was incompetent at all things, she applauded all others' accomplishments; there was not a mean bone in her.

She always accompanied her daughter to our house for lessons; they came by covered litter, with four strong slaves to bear it, for Aunt Kassie was terrified of the streets, with their market stalls and peasant vendors, and the noise and bustle that all the rest of us loved, the inner city, the heart of Mitylene.

Aunt Kassie claimed that she came to our house daily not for the lessons that Nausikaa shared, but because she felt it a duty—to be a mother to "poor little Sappho and her brothers." Not a day passed but she did not weep for the passing of Kleis, whom we had all but forgotten, in the way of children. Indeed, she so upset us at times, especially little Erigyus, who had not known Mother, but was a nervous, sickly boy, that Father threatened to forbid her the house if she did not stop. For weeks after, she went about with a finger to her lips to remind herself not to speak of Kleis, but it did not last; soon we were able simply to close our ears to her lamenting. Even Erigyus got used to it in time.

She was no mother substitute, Aunt Kassie; one could not tell her anything at all, or even show her a bruised knee. Praxinoa was the one we ran to, all, with our childish injuries or our vexing disputes.

No girl of Lesbos is really innocent; we have too many servants and slaves from the outspoken hill folk or from other countries, far away, where the customs are different. And Charaxus knew a lot from his low companions and told me all, boasting. I knew from a child how babies were got, and how born, and I knew also that boys and girls were shaped differently and the reason for it. But my time of women came upon me early; much earlier than any of the others, my cousins and girlfriends, and I was totally unprepared. I thought with horror and anguish that I was bleeding to death from somewhere inside, shamefully. It happened in the bath, with no one about, for the old bath woman had gone out of the room to fetch something, oil or powder, I have forgotten.

I watched the bathwater redden slowly, going from pale pink to coral and deeper still; I had a strange feeling, too, deep down in my belly, a pain, but not quite, more like a fist that closed inside. At first I waited, terribly frightened, to die; I could not move. Then I heard the thwang of a harp string in the next room, where Praxinoa was tuning it, and called out to her, feebly, as though I were already close to death. She heard me, and came quickly, seeing at a glance what the trouble was.

"It is nothing, little bird," she said, soothing. "It is natural—a thing of women, come early to you, poor love . . ." And swiftly she explained, using words that a doctor would use and calming me by her cool theory, the while she raised me up out of the red water and wrapped me about in a soft woolen towel, placing a folded napkin between my legs, where the blood still flowed. Afterward, she ordered my bath emptied, and fresh water brought to her own tub, a pretty thing from Lydia, all painted with dolphins and sea creatures. She did not put me into it, though, but sponged me off, and washed me clean with her own hands, putting me to bed after with a drugged drink to make me sleep. I wonder sometimes if any mother could have done as well.

After that, though, and especially just before those monthly periods, I would dream, horribly, in the night, and wake screaming, remembering nothing of the dream but its horror. Praxinoa was always swift to come to me; she must have slept with one ear alert. She would sit on my bed and hold my hand, speaking softly close to my ear until I fell asleep again.

Once, though, the dream was so clear that I remembered it, all filled with winged black things, like the furies that pursued Orestes; I had been reading late, the old tales. She talked long to me that night, telling me to remember the dream and not forget, and make it work *for* me and not against. "Make a song of it, little one . . . and we will devise a dance to go with it . . . the dancers in fluttering black, with wings . . ."

It was long before I quieted, and she slipped into bed beside me to take me in her arms. When my sobbing ceased finally, I raised my tearstained face to hers and kissed her on the lips. "Oh, Praxinoa . . . I love you," I whispered softly. "I love you . . .

love you . . ." And then I must have dozed, and half-wakened, still breathing heavily. I heard her say softly, "Not yet, little darling . . . not yet . . ." And under the words was something —something that I sensed rather than heard. Something akin, but only barely and most delicately, to the sly looks of the street boys, the looks that undressed one. Or more like, perhaps, the strange intimacy one saw in the eyes of two well-dressed youths exchanging love tokens in a shadowy corner.

My head lay on the soft swell below her shoulder; I felt it rise and fall, too quickly for sleep. I felt, too, a queer feeling in my loins, hot and liquid, but very small and faint. I was vaguely disquieted, and pretended sleep, breathing slow and snoring a little. After a bit she disengaged herself softly from under me, and left, going back to her own room. I was wakeful still for a little, then my pretended sleep became real.

That was the last nightmare I remember. Out of it two things were born. One was the famous Dance of the Harpies, from which I got my name, given to me by the people, my name so dear to me, The Black Lark. And the other—the hidden thing—well, one must begin sometime.

Chapter 3

It is no good trying to explain the making of music and of songs, any more than a painter or sculptor can explain his art; they are god-inspired, we say, and let it go at that. Of course, no educated person truly believes in the gods anymore, though none but Father and his friend Thales express this in words. Father says the gods are simply an expression of man's feelings, his fears and delights. But one must not offend them, he says, for that is an offense to one's inmost self. This is easier for a poet to understand than the things that Thales says about our beginnings, for they are very strange indeed. But then he is a mathematician and an astronomer, and is forever studying charts and watching the stars as they move. I will not speak much of him now; only that in ancient days he would have been put to death by his fellows, and they would have said later that the gods had done it to punish him for what used to be called *hubris*—which means getting above oneself, defying the gods, or whatever. Even nowadays, in backward places, that might happen. But here in Lesbos, or in other civilized parts, he is revered as a powerful thinker, or dismissed by fools as a harmless eccentric.

At the time I am speaking of now, Thales was not with us; our teachers came and went, for they were the best in the world and were in demand everywhere. At this time, when I got my folk name, there was staying in our house a very famous musician named Arion, from the court of Periander of Korinth. He had invented several new instruments, added two new strings to the lyre, and made many other innovations.

Now, from a baby, I could get a pleasant sound from any instrument that was handed me, and make a song from a blown petal or a droplet of rainwater trembling upon a leaf. Is this *hubris?* Perhaps it is, when I say it—but it is no more than the truth. But there is more to music and the making of poems than this. One must learn as much as possible from all those who have gone before, even if, in the end, one discards much of the learning and invents one's own special style. I have studied all of Homer, for instance, and know most of it by heart, though I will never write in the same meter, or with the same meanings, even. Hesiod is my most unfavorite of all the old poets; there is not a note of music in him; he does not deserve the name of singer! And what he says is horrid, all maxim and moral, and warnings and rules; if a farmer could read, he would do well with this Hesiod, who knows little more than the tilling of the soil and the best season for plowing. Also, he hated women, Hesiod, which makes me very angry. But Father says to be easy about it, he was only a rustic, that lived in a bitterer age and a more barren soil than ours, for which we must be thankful.

Archilochus is a marvel! I love to read him, though his music has been lost, and perhaps, too, the words have been changed a little. Certainly the meters are crude, in view of what we are learning today—but his feelings are intense and frank, full of passion and unquenchable energy. What a man he must have been! I am sad that I never knew him.

I have digressed; a fault I mean to never give way to in my songs. I was speaking of Arion, who knows, Father says, more about music than any man alive. Certainly there is nothing he cannot play upon with skill, even a peasant's pipe, for he has made long study of them all. Of course, even he says one must have the ear first. I have studied hard with him, hours a day of practice on harp and lyre and kithara, and all the others, for I would surpass all; it is my constant dream. I have not mastered the drums and cymbals, or the wooden clappers that Andromeda uses in her dancing; Arion does not think much of this kind of cadence, and Drom herself does not understand how she accomplishes her sounds; the best I can do is imitate her, as yet rather badly. But I have got something else from her, a rhythm that I use in my poems; a new thing, with an uneven, but compelling beat, and an odd charm to it. When I perfect it, it will be the best way to express the deep emotions that are born within the heart.

We worked hard on The Dance of the Harpies, Praxinoa and I, but without Arion it would never have happened as it did. Always singers have sung alone, to their own accompaniment, or perhaps one other, in the bardic tradition, as Homer sang, after the legendary Orpheus. But the unskilled folk sing together, and dance together, too, as we have seen them at the sacred rites. And workmen sing together, and sailors as they pull on the oars.

Arion has borrowed from this and invented a kind of chorus of singer-dancers, with leaders at their head, me for the singing and Drom for the dancing.

We used as many girls for the chorus as could carry an air and not stumble over their own feet; we could not leave out Nausikaa even, though most of the servingmaids had more grace. Boys we had none; they were all too small, except for Charaxus, and he had no talent. But I found a use for him, anyway. He was the plagued Orestes himself; all he had to do was lie cowering on the ground throughout, until my vanquishing song, when the Harpies fled and he rose up, saved. Will you believe it? He gave himself airs after, as though he were the whole show! Boys are like that, I have found, in the main, and men, too. One must just put up with it sometimes.

I sang the small bird, whose song, straight from Apollo's lips, conquered the evil spirits so that they slunk away forever, banished from the earth. Of course, it was my own song, and the best I had written so far; it is famous still.

The whole thing was a great success, and we were invited to repeat it at the Festival of Dionysos; indeed, it has been done every year, though lately I have not taken part, for my voice has lost some of its power. But in those days it had great charm and sweetness and a true tone.

Arion was the first poet that I knew, for he was a poet as well as a musician; his songs were sung all over the world. They had a wonderful rollicking quality, and were often sung at feasts and drinking parties, and folk would rise and dance to them, for they set the feet to tapping. He was usually drunk himself, Arion, or halfway; the smell of stale wine clung to his clothes and his very hair. But Father said I must not wrinkle my nose or make any sign that I noticed, for Arion was very sensitive and would have refused to teach me. So I used, always, a very strong perfume, one smell killing the other, as it were, when I was near him. Indeed, after a lesson, Andromeda used to hold her nose at *me!*

Arion was round as a barrel, too fat to dance to his own music, and with a round face punctuated by lewd little eyes and a wide lascivious mouth, the very picture of a libertine. But, as far as any of us could see, his only vice was wine; he never showed the slightest interest in the servingmaids, or the boy servants either, for that matter, and he had never taken a wife. His voice, though very pure, was higher in pitch than most women's; it was whispered that he was a eunuch, but of course we did not know for sure. Charaxus claimed to have seen him in his bath, and that there was nothing there. We did not believe him, though; none of us girls was quite certain what a eunuch was, but Telesippa said, if there was nothing there at all, how could he make water? Which set us all to giggling—all that wine had to come out somewhere! We were great gigglers in those early days; it comes of being so much to ourselves, with never any boys about except children.

I say never—which is not quite true; occasionally the young warriors would come home on leave. We girls were shy of them, though, even of our own cousins; they were lordly, disdainful beings, and went mostly in pairs, with their arms entwined or holding hands, and never once looked our way.

There was one youth, though, who came to our house to pay his respects to Father; Antimenades was his name and he was no kin of ours, but son of a close friend of Father's, now dead. This young man was not like the others; he wore no scent and did not curl his hair, and went very plain, in a clean white tunic, and wearing his breastplate and sword. He had a broad, good-natured face, and his hair did not need curling; one can always tell the real thing from the crimped. He was very dark, and burnt darker by the sun, showing the old blood, like me. We smiled at one another for this likeness, feeling a kinship of our own. He was big, though, and a little clumsy, as though he had forgotten the way of houses; I think, indeed, it may have been so, for he had been campaigning for six years, and this was his first time home.

Lessons were over; it was near twilight and Father asked him to sup. For a wonder, none of my cousins were with us; it was my first look at a young man, and I had him all to myself! After, at Father's bidding, I played to him and sang, one of my own songs; it was a love poem, and not very good, I know now. Too sweet it was, and a little sickly, for I knew nothing at all of the subject. The melody was true, though, and the cadence, and he praised it after. "Your song is almost as beautiful as you yourself, Lady Sappho. . . ." None had ever called me Lady before, and I was much pleased. The other compliments I discounted; he could not have been very discriminating, having been among men so long.

He read my thoughts, for he said, "There are girls everywhere

. . . and my brother is a poet. You did not think I meant what I said. . . ." I colored, and was silent. Father said quickly, "How is Alkaios? He was just a small boy when I last saw him. . . ."

"Oh—Alkaios is much the same . . . clever and brilliant, and the handsomest man in the army. . . ."

"Yes," said Father, "I remember—he was a very pretty child. How is his health? I had always thought him delicate. . . ."

"Oh, he has grown out of that," said Antimenades. "Soldiering has hardened him somewhat. . . ." His eyes looked odd for a moment as they met my father's look, as if there were something else that he wanted to say. Finally he said, "He bids me greet you, sir . . . he would have come, but he is confined to shipboard." He laughed a little then, shaking his head. "He is always into some mischief, Alkaios . . ."

Next day Antimenades took us down to the harbor, my brothers and I, to see the warship close to; civilians are forbidden to harborside when the fleet is in, but, with a soldier vouching, one can always get a pass.

It is a brave sight, a war fleet; I would never have believed ships could hold so many men. Their decks were dark with them, swarming like flies, and even up into the rigging, among the sails. They crowded to the rail, waving at us, and catcalling at sight of me.

"So many!" I said. "And all confined to the ship—like your brother?"

He threw back his head and laughed. "No—but they cannot all have leave at once," he said. "They must wait their turn . . . someone must man the ship. . . ."

I could not see how any more could be crowded on it, but said nothing; I felt ignorant enough as it was.

"Look!" And Antimenades pointed. "There is my brother." I followed his finger, eager to see this poet, who was also the handsomest soldier in the army. "Where? Which one?" I cried.

"There—at the rail. See? He is waving—the one in the purple tunic."

I looked, and saw him. But he was not close enough; from where I stood he looked much like all the other youths I had seen about the town, slender and fair, and with his arm about the waist of another boy. I felt a slight disappointment, and turned away.

Chapter 4

There have been no kings in Greece since the days of the High Kings of Mykenae and Troy, which we know much of from Homer, and of Old Crete, which we know only from legend. All this was long, long ago, and the mists of time have all but hidden it; after the fall of those High Kingdoms came an age that was dark and full of ignorance, when Northern barbarians swooped down from the hills and laid waste to the whole land. In those days the art of writing was lost, and few bards sang; there is little to tell us how those people lived. Father said there must have been petty chieftains, many of them, warring constantly among themselves, until all simmered down, and gradually cities came into being, and became the seats of government. Cities, I mean, like Athens, and Sparta, and our own Mitylene. Of course there are many more, all over the Greek lands; I cannot mention them all. But Father says that in the course of history and the passing of time those chiefs must have wearied of war and some few banded together in certain places and shared the ruling of the people. So have our cities grown up, under the rule of certain families bred to govern; in Mitylene, Father said, there were once thirty who shared the governing, then twenty, and then twelve. This seems a reasonable way to run a city, for no one person has all the say in it, and councils are in constant meetings, and many educated minds are put to the task of running the state. Of course, when one is born to it and is part of this ruling class, as our family is, it may color our way of thinking. If I were a peasant girl, I might perhaps feel different; one must always try to put oneself into another's place, though it is difficult.

As I have said, most of the ruling families are born to it and have inherited the work of government; it is not so easy to become a member of the council of nobles otherwise. Still, Pittakos has done it. He was little more than a farmer from Thrace in his beginnings, and his crudities show in many ways. Father has called him, with a laugh, a "soldier of fortune"; still they are friends and Father much admires this man, so unlike himself. Though I have known him most of my life, I find him a little frightening, Pittakos.

He looks as one might imagine one of the old chieftains from the north to look; he is big and broad and wears a great red beard, unbarbered and rough. His hair and beard are like flames, shooting out in all directions, like the ancient pictures of the sun god, Helios, that was before Apollo. Even his face is red, and the hairs on his arms and hands red-gold; he does not use pumice, and seems to enjoy looking like a beast. Perhaps he knows it frightens people; perhaps it is the secret of how he has risen from his low position. As I think it over, though, I know this is not so, for I remember his eyes. They are deep-set and piercing, of a very light blue; one might fancy one could see clear through them, they are of such pale color, yet they seem as well to look through anything they rest on. This is the most frightening thing about him; one imagines he can read minds.

I bring up this man, Pittakos, because for many months and even years my father, and my uncles Erigyus and Drakon, along with other dissatisfied nobles, had been meeting with him, sometimes openly, sometimes in secret. We children all knew something was afoot, but not in any sort of clear way. I have never been clever at politics anyway; I have gone, always, by my heart, and by my sense of justice. But I will try to explain something of what had been happening.

The old order, of the ruling nobles, which is, in effect, the rule of a group, had been giving way, with or without violence, to another kind of government, where power rests in the hands of one man. This was true in Athens, where a man called Solon had seized control and set himself up as Tyrant; he announced it was for the good of "the people." Father says the Tyrants have passed some good laws, and helped the lower sort of folk in some small ways, but that such a one-man system must depend on the emotions of the mob, really. Everyone who has ever attended a festival can see how frightening this can be; great hordes of people, feeling as one, swayed by a word or a glance, and drunk without benefit of wine. The same thing happens when the army parades in all its glory of banners and prancing horses and ribboned chariots; one sees hundreds of grimy faces wet and streaked with tears and glowing with a mad ecstasy, and, under, a ferocity that is wilder than a beast's. It has always been a sight of horror, truly, to me; I come very close to fainting.

In Mitylene, too, we have a Tyrant, or leader, though the nobles still have some say in the making of laws. His name is Melanchros, and I was too young when he came to power to know how it happened; Father says, though, that such things always happen by a trick of some sort, a cunning stroke, timed well, when heads are busy other places. So I believe it must have happened at some point early in the war, where this man Melanchros took advantage of a laxity somewhere.

I have heard Father and Pittakos talking, many times, when they thought me to be uncomprehending; but I played my harp very low and listened; secrets are sweet and sweetly dangerous, especially to the young. The nobles, all of them, conspire, it is clear, to somehow pull this man Melanchros down; they are simply waiting for an opportunity. I must say they have waited long, for I seem to have been listening to such talk half my life; Pittakos urges action of a violent nature, but the others rule against it always, being milder men. Somehow I feel that he will win, in the end.

When I hear what Solon has done in Athens, I tremble with fear and anger lest it should happen here. This Solon was a noble, but somewhat impoverished; he was also a poet, so-called, though he had no talent but for bombast and rhetoric, an artificial style the Muses frown upon. Still, this bardry served him well; he found he could sway the mob with it. Father says one must give him his due, for he felt great and unusual sympathy for the poor and the unfree, passing many just laws in their favor.

I am not concerned with that, however; one is always thinking of oneself, it must be admitted; this is human nature. In Athens he passed so many laws curtailing the freedom of women that one might imagine that he hated us all!

He made a law forbidding women to go out at night except in a carriage or carrying-chair accompanied by an escort bearing a lamp or torch; what kind of mischief could he have thought they would be up to? One could hardly wish to walk the dark streets alone in any case—but to forbid it! We heard of a case where a lady, distracted, and not trusting her slaves, ran out seeking a missing child. She knew where to look, and found the child, but night fell before she arrived back home with him; she was arrested forthwith and tried before a jury. The outcome was that all her privileges were taken away for three years, and she was fined a huge sum as well. Not that the Athenian women have any privileges really; they have always, says Father, been treated like cattle, for breeding only, the men being taken up wholly by their friend-youths or by courtesans. But Solon has made it all even worse for those poor creatures. (I am speaking now of respectable women and girls—the other kind have a fine time of it!) He made laws forbidding women to wear expensive clothes or carry baskets above a certain size. He abolished the dowry system, in a sense, though he permitted sums of money to be exchanged by the parents of the wedded couple; he simply forbade the bride to bring more than three dresses with her to her husband's house! So—of course—if he did not love her, that husband, he might never buy her any more! Imagine never having more than three changes of clothes—I think that I would die!

Also Solon decreed that a man may have all the mistresses he wishes, and even bring them into his home, but a woman who takes a lover can be sent back to her parents, dowryless and in disgrace, and not permitted to remarry. Of course highborn women who are promiscuous are looked upon with disfavor everywhere—but here, at least, they are not yet legally outcast.

He has also made all forms of prostitution lawful, and licensed even the lowest sort; I can imagine, with all that competition, that many a poor bride lies alone in her marriage bed. Father says it affects even the poor peasant girls, for their young men can buy favors for very little elsewhere, if the respectable maidens wish to remain maidens. I am truly sorry for all the Athenian girls; Father says their lot has always been hard, even before Solon. They are not educated at all, and learn nothing but sewing, weaving, and spinning. How dreadful to have songs within, and no skill to sing them or write them!

When I hear tales of the rest of the world and how life is lived there, especially by women, I thank the gods, truly, that they let me be born on Lesbos.

In the East, of course, women are kept locked up, and are only one among many wives; if ever they are let out at all, they are veiled completely from head to toe. There are many strange customs in this world, that is plain, and all so different.

Drom has told me, now that she can speak our language, some of the ways of her people, for instance. She comes from a far land, though she cannot explain where it is; she knows nothing, of course, of geography, and has little sense of distance, being what we Greeks would call a true barbarian. Her home was deep in the forest, a very old forest to hear her tell of it, with huge trees and immense ferning plants and much swampland. She was, as I thought, the daughter of the king there, but he must have been a very little king, for the tribe he led was scanty, by our standards. When I asked her how many people were of it, she held up both hands, fingers extended, six times. And then there are many other tribes in that same forest; they do not trade or communicate, though, and do not even speak the same speech, close to as they are, sometimes barely a stone's throw away. All the tribes are sworn enemies, with their own sets of gods and rites; they fight constantly, it is their way of life, hunting animals for food, and their fellows for sport. And a cruel sport it is, surely, for that is how she was taken and sold into slavery. Though these peoples do not trade with one another, they traffick with the Egyptians, who are longtime slavers.

Women's lot is no worse there than men's; all live in what we would term a state of ignorance and fear. Their wild gods, mostly made in the images of animals, rule their waking moments, and every act is done to propitiate them, sometimes even human sacrifice. Father says that has been true in all primitive cultures, even our own, long ago, when the world was young.

One of their woman gods is the Earth Mother, in the form of a snake, whom our Pelasgian ancestors worshiped also in the dim past; another is the moon, with a name I could not pronounce. The Amazons, a race of warrior women, held the moon for their goddess, so I thought Drom's tribe might be an offshoot from this long-dead people, especially since she could draw a bow and hit the target as well as any man, and had made herself a deadly slingshot. She shook her head, though, saying they were not warriors, the women of her tribe, only that they had learned to hunt along with the boys when they were children. She had been taken before she came to womanhood; a blessing, really, for she lacked the ritual scars that her people inflict at the Rites of

Women. I thought of the other Nubian slave woman, older, but proud and silent like all Drom's kind, that I had seen in the agora, carrying her mistress' market basket upon her high-held head, and the long, raised, ropey welts that marked each cheek, three to a side. Tears welled behind my eyelids and I leaned over and kissed Drom's smooth brown face; startled, she turned her head suddenly and our lips brushed, a strange little fire running through me. She had never been kissed before; they had not the custom. I showed her how it was done, taking her head between my hands and kissing her, lingering upon the mouth. But the fire had gone; we were children still.

In the summer my little brother Erigyus died. For weeks he lay abed, sweating and shivering, complaining thinly of pains in his back and behind his head. The heat was savage, and no breeze blew, the shipping in the harbor all becalmed. We could not go to Eresos as usual to escape it, for he could not be moved. We all suffered; how much more he! He was dreadful to look at toward the end, for he had wasted away to bare pitiful bones, his head large above his shriveled frame, his face gray.

They said there was an epidemic among the poor children that lived near the waterfront, brought by an Egyptian ship that lay, kept over by the unnatural calm, close in to shore. The physicians said it was a disease well known in Egypt for long years, that took half the child population each season; in Mitylene more than a hundred died, all under the age of fifteen. Father wept that he had let the boys play with the wharf children, blaming himself. Pittakos, raging, and fearful for his own son, who lay ill, too, called curses down upon the tyrant Melanchros for dealing with Egypt. But Father shook his head sadly, saying that it was the will of the gods, for what Greek city could survive without the Egyptian trade?

Pittakos' son, Tyrrhaeos, his only child that was from his true-wed wife, Chloris, lived, but he was left crippled, one arm shrunken and one shoulder higher than the other. Still, he was lucky, for most of those who lived after the disease struck them lost the use of their legs; I felt grief for all those of the poorer sort in particular, for they had no calling left to them but that of beggar. The wealthy are at least taken care of in their affliction.

The day Erigyus died was the hottest I ever remember; the air was stifling, odors hanging upon it, and flies buzzed low, gathering in thick black clouds above the little body where it lay. The professional mourners all came with large fans, charging extra for it. My poor small brother lay dressed all in white; the wreath of flowers on his head turned yellow and dry before an hour was up. Because of the heat and the smell, he was carried to his burial place next morning before sunrise. We walked behind, all of us of the household, the dust already rising whitely about our feet and powdering our black robes.

I took my harp and sang, low, a lament that I had written; it was not perfect, being written in haste, but everyone wept to hear it, some of the mourners scratching their faces and tearing their robes, too, shrieking. It was horrible to hear above the music, but it is the custom, and they like to give a lot for their death-money. We of the family kept a seemly quiet, cutting our locks of hair and laying them upon the little body. Once I heard Aunt Kassie sob, chokingly, smothering it with her hand. But that was at the end, when Father threw the handful of earth, for decency, before the gravediggers finished their job. I thought of Antigone, scrabbling in the dry dust of Thebes to gather the forbidden dirt to cover her slain brothers. Would I have dared? Would I have dared, and done it, and suffered death myself for it, to defy a Tyrant?

I thought about that all the long way home in the straggling procession. For we too had a Tyrant now, here at Mitylene. So far there had been no drastic change in our lives. But what if someday? . . . I pushed the thought away. Perhaps, someday, if needed, some god would send me the strength that I feared I did not have. I prayed silently for my brother, and his journey across the Styx, and I prayed, too, that all would be well forever, in Mitylene.

Chapter 5

In the fall after Erigyus' death, when the harbor was busy once more, the white-capped waves sparkling in the ever-changing sea, and the air clean again and fresh in the nostrils, there came one day a sudden rough wind whipping from the north, rattling the door latches and snapping the little leaf-barren branches from the young trees—and with it, as if she commanded it, came Gorgo.

I shall never forget it; Pittakos' deep voice booming in the courtyard and his great fists hammering at the door, for we had shut everything up against the wind. There he stood, huge and red, and a little angry, a few raindrops, just beginning, darkening his red robe at the shoulders. (He wore the color often, though it did not become him.) In one hand he held a rope, leading a horse; upon it sat a girl, astride, laughing. At first glance she looked to be naked, for she wore only a kind of boy's tunic, slit all the way up the sides and clasped round with a belt at the waist; her legs, indeed the whole length of her, gleamed white, and her arms were bare to the shoulder, though the weather was raw. I had never seen a girl go astride a horse before, and certainly not one so shamelessly clothed as this. My eyes went round and wide; she saw me and laughed again, closing one of her own eyes in a rude wink that was somehow merry, and made me laugh, too. Then she swung down from the horse's back, throwing her leg over and showing everything she had. We had all crowded into the courtyard, curious, and Charaxus gave a low whistle; swiftly she turned and cuffed him, expertly, on the ear. He held it, just managing not to cry out. She walked with a kind of a swagger, bold as a cockerel; we all stared, even Father. As I looked closer, I saw Pittakos in her face, the eyes above high, wide cheekbones pale and icy, and the tight-braided hair of the same red. "Go with the girls, Gorgo," said Pittakos, shoving her.

The girl followed us into the women's quarters, looking wary, and walking tiptoe, as though she were afraid of breaking something. Praxinoa offered her a seat; she sprawled in it like a boy, uncaring, her legs apart anyhow, and her hands hanging like hams. I saw with a little shock that her feet were filthy; she wore no sandals and her tunic looked as though it had been on her a month. I brought her some watered sweet wine, for courtesy, and some small honey cakes. She spat the wine out on the floor, making a face. "I like it neat!" she said, but grabbed up a handful of the little cakes, cramming them all into her mouth at once. She spoke a kind of Greek I had never heard, harsh and angry, though I could just understand her words. She spoke on, her mouth full, and crumbs falling from it. I got a little angry myself and said, "Have you been taught no manners, then?" I suppose I sounded very prim, for she looked at me with hurt eyes, wiping her hands and swallowing hurriedly. I spoke again. "Where have you come from, then—an animal's den?"

She grinned at me widely, the cakes all being down by then. "I guess so, little doll-baby," she said, with a good humor. "Sparta . . . that's where I was raised. You don't get many cakes there . . . and mostly we sit on the ground."

I was all at sea; I heard voices belowstairs, Father and Pittakos, and strained my ears to hear, but could not make out the words.

She saw that I listened and said, "They will be talking about me. Old Pitt is asking your father to take me to live here. . . ." She grinned again, watching my face. "Don't faint. I only bite when I am whipped." And she turned her head; a long mark, old and deep, ran like a snake from somewhere under her clothes at her back, ending above her jawbone.

"Old Pitt? . . ." I asked, uncertainly.

"Pittakos," she said, her look like a knife. "He's my father."

Well, I thought, *I suppose he has bastards everywhere.* She was watching me, and must have guessed what I was thinking, for she drew down her brows, scowling, and said, "My mother was his true wife—before this one. A Spartan lady she was—but not Spartan enough, for she died birthing me. . . ." She shrugged then, and laughed. "I suppose they killed her. . . ."

"Who?" I asked, startled.

She shrugged again, her face hard. "Those who were there. . . . They will always save the child, if it is a hard birth. I have seen it many times. They will cut into the woman . . ."

I was horrified, and covered my face with my hands. I thought her inhuman, this Gorgo that was named after a monster. But when I raised my head again, I saw her eyes were wide and bright, swimming with unshed tears.

She reached for the wine cup again, and took a long drink, not spitting it out this time, but swallowing hard and blinking. After, she wiped her mouth with the back of her hand; the tears were gone, and her face was hard again. "I hate them," she said. "They whipped me every time I wrestled. . . ."

"Why?" I whispered.

"Because I won." She saw me staring still, and said, "Oh, not with the girls—that is a show only, and they do not care . . . but a girl is not supposed to win over a boy."

"But," I said, "how did you? Surely they are stronger . . ."

"I fought dirty," she said, grinning. She reached for the amphora and poured herself another cup of wine. I looked around for Praxinoa, but she had gone. She had left us alone, for tact, I suppose. I watched Gorgo drink. *Great Zeus*, I thought, *she will be drunk soon, even though the wine is watered.*

"I ran away," she said, "but they caught me. . . . They put me in a dark room. For hours I stayed there, with nothing to eat and only some brackish water. . . ." She made a face, remembering; for a moment she looked like the child she was. Then she went on. "When they thought I was weak enough, they sent a big boy in—a man, really, I guess, or nearly—to work his will on me. . . . I think there was a whole line of them waiting outside, for their turn." She laughed, a harsh sound. "When they saw what I did to him, they must have been scared off . . . that one—he is only half a man now. . . ."

"What did you do?" I asked, fascinated and in dread.

She kicked her foot out suddenly, hard. "Like that," she said. "I knew where to aim . . . even in the dark. And I kneed him too—for good measure." She held out her hands, the fingers clawing, and raking down. "His face cannot be very pretty either. His boyfriend will not look at him. . . ."

I must have looked greatly puzzled, for she said, "Oh, they do everything there . . . in Sparta." She almost spat the name. "They have no sense of decency."

"But . . . rape!" I cried. "Surely they would not—"

"Oh, no!" she said. "One must go virgin there to the marriage bed. Worse!" And she said a word I had seen written on wharfside buildings, but never heard, except once, when Charaxus sniggered and boasted, saying that he himself—but I did not believe him, and put my hands over my ears.

"How did you get away?"

She shrugged, lifting her shoulders. "They sent for Old Pitt. Said a girl like me was a disgrace to the state. Incorrigible, they called me. . . . I'll give him one thing, Old Pitt. He laughed when he heard what I'd done. 'Good girl,' he said, and gave me this." She held out her arm. On it was a massive gold armlet, very expensive it must have been, with letters cut into it. I leaned close to read. "Gorgo," it said.

"Why did they give you that awful name?" I asked. "Why did they name you after a monster?"

She looked hard at me. "No monster," she said. "I am called after one of Sparta's greatest queens . . . Queen Gorgo. She is famous everywhere."

I shook my head. "I have not heard of her," I said, "and I know much history. . . ."

"Well, everybody knows of her . . ." she said, trailing off. Then she lifted her head. "What monster are you talking of?"

"The Gorgon. Medusa." I said. She looked blank. *Gods! She has learned nothing*, I thought. *Does not even know the old tales. A true barbarian.*

I explained. "Medusa was a monster of a race called Gorgons. Her face was so terrible to see that any man, looking, would be turned to stone."

She grinned. "I shall have to practice."

I laughed back at her, liking her suddenly.

Chapter 6

Father said yes to Pittakos, as I knew all along he would, and Gorgo came to live with us. I say "came," but she simply stayed; she had no possessions except for the clothes she stood up in, and those little better than a beggar girl's. So she must be outfitted from the start, like a newborn babe, and taught her first steps as well, one might say. It was not easy, and she was more teacher than pupil; a very strong will she had, Gorgo, and a stubborn nature. She never learned the art of draping her own chitons; they were bunched in lumps anyhow, making her look as shapeless as a sack of barley, and she uncaring. And hitch up her skirt she would always, as though it hampered her; and never could Praxinoa break her of it. Now and then, on occasions of formality, when some fine person came to call, or we were asked to go in procession for some god, or light sacrificial torches or another such thing, she would wear seemly robes to the ground, but she contrived always to trip over them and stumble, making everyone laugh behind his hand; it did not vex her at all, she would simply wave and wink, grinning her wide bad-boy's grin. I suppose she had no feel for fine raiment, having gone so long half-clad. But then, so had Drom, in her own land and her early years; still, though Drom had her very own way of wearing them, and her own style of pleating and tying, she was always pleasingly done up, using our Greek clothing to create a charming difference. No—Gorgo was like none other; she was not even boylike, really. Her roughness was never tamed; a lion cub will never make a housecat.

None of us girls, my cousins and I, or Drom either, had played games at all, except for knucklebones on a rainy day, or a turn at Drom's slingshot or bow, which none of us could master. Gorgo changed all that; soon we were running, leaping, throwing the discus, playing with balls of stitched leather, boxing, and wrestling. Father forbade my brothers and boy cousins to take part along with us, young as they were, and would not let us go naked, as they do in Sparta; except for that, one might have thought our flat roof in the women's apartments to be a true gymnasium.

Looking back on it all now, I think it did us all a world of good. Telesippa, a plain, bony girl, so pale that the veins showed blue at her temples, put on a little flesh, and color glowed new and bright in her thin cheeks. She had very long legs and could jump farther than anyone else; it made her proud and she gained a kind of presence and lost her shyness; one forgot that she was homely. And Nausikaa fined down, though she was never slender; she seldom won at anything, but being good-natured she did not care. I think she enjoyed being under Gorgo's thumb for a change, instead of her mother's. Aunt Kassie, indeed, nearly swooned at her first sight of us; Praxinoa had devised tiny kilts and breastbands, but, truth to tell, they did not cover much. Dika and I were both small, and well-matched, nearly evenly, though I ran faster. It improved my wind, too, which any singer needs; on the whole, we all profited. Besides, it was rather fun; we had been such dainty creatures, reared to seemly ways and mincing steps. It was good to know that we were the equal of any boy our size; though it was forbidden, I sometimes wrestled Larichus, who was my weight, though four years younger, and I always brought him to a fall. Gorgo was a good teacher, better than the one the boys learned from in the town gymnasium; of course, he was an army reject, or he would not have been in Mitylene at all. One must be fair. None of us ever wrestled Charaxus on the sly; not for fear of losing, but for fear of his roving hands, that liked to get hold of interesting parts. He was made that way, Charaxus, and could not help himself, even with his own sister. He tried it once with Gorgo; she broke his wrist.

Actually I did not wrestle very much, except for a kind of exhibition, like a dance; there is much skill to it when it is properly taught, and I am always interested in learning a new thing. The danger, though, outweighed all with me; once, wrestling lightly with Dika, who was ever my only match, being small-made, I fell carelessly and sprained my thumb. It terrified me, for I saw that it might easily have been worse; if I had lost the use of any part of my hands, I think that truly I would die, for without my music I am only half myself. Or so I thought then, in my youth; even now, in age, when the cold months make my fingers stiffen, the agony of not plucking the strings is worse than the pain of my sore joints.

Father used to come sometimes and watch us at our games, saying it was a fine sight, all us young girls in our health and pride. "It is a good thing, that," he said once to Pittakos. "One good thing out of Sparta . . . for the exercise makes the girls' bodies supple and strong for later . . . for when it comes time for childbearing. The danger is less . . ." His voice trailed off and his eyes grew sad; I saw he thought of our mother and her untimely death. I was sad, too, for him, and sadder still to know that I had almost forgotten her, my pretty, laughing mother.

Gorgo could not have got much out of our girls' games, truly, except that she had all the say in their managing; none of us was any kind of match for her, except for Drom, who was of a size, and hardier than the rest. But those two had a kind of enmity from the first; their competing looked real, as if it were war they waged. Gorgo, indeed, would not even watch Drom when she danced, though it was a sight of beauty; always she would look down at the floor or out the window at the empty sky, shuffling her feet or cracking her knuckles, the rest of us all shushing her.

Once, though, when they two had wrestled to a fall, Gorgo pinning both Drom's shoulders to the floor and sitting astride her naked hips, her red hair loose and falling over them both like a mantle, I saw a long look pass between them, hard and cool, and, after, a little shade of a smile, each to each. I felt a strange stab in my chest, disquieting, and turned away. Always, after that, when they two boxed, measuring one another, bodies glistening with sweat, or wrestled, with limbs entwined like snakes writhing, dark and white together, I looked away, not knowing why. I could not crack my knuckles, not having mastered it, but pretended to be listening inward to the Muse, my eyes on nothing, or fingered my lyre, my head bent to it. Once, on a blinding-white day, I remember, and all of us sitting under a canopy to ward off the sun's rays, except those two, Gorgo and Drom, striving thigh against thigh, panting, in the cleared place for the match, I turned aside, seeking, blindly, for something, a roll of papyrus, I think; I saw Praxinoa watching me. Her eyes were large and moist, thoughtful, with a look I could not read; that evening, in the cool, before I slept, she brought me a whole new honeycomb on the plate beside my slice of bread. It lay there pure and perfect, as if the bees had just made it, a small slow trickle of the amber honey just beginning at one side. My mouth watered, and I looked up, shy; she had used to limit my sweets, Praxinoa, to keep my skin smooth. "For once," she said, smiling small. "It was such a long, hot day . . ."

She left me, and I ate it all, greedily, while the tears brimmed over my eyelids and ran down my face. I never knew why I cried; the honey was delicious.

Chapter 7

That winter, our troops were fighting in a place called the Sigeum; a runner brought a thick, rolled message to Father, from the youth Antimenades. I did not know its contents, but guessed it to be something of import to our aristocrat faction, something to do with the conspiracy that was always going on, for Father rolled it up again small, without speaking of it, except to say that the war seemed to be at a standstill, neither side making any headway. The scroll was long and contained much more, but that was all he said, except that the youth had asked to be remembered to me. "And here," he said, holding out a scrap of parchment, "is a letter for you, Sappho . . . it was inside with the other." I took it, wondering, my very first letter it was.

Quickly I scanned it to the end, looking for the signature, expecting to see Antimenades' name. But it was signed, with a showy curling flourish that I could just make out, "Alkaios." I bit my lip, puzzled, and looked at Father. "It is from the brother, the poet," he said. *Gods!* I thought, and bent close, excited, to read the writing, for it was careless, and slanted upward on the page.

Strange to say, it was written in verse, like a song; a beautiful thing, I have it by me still. It was only a kind of greeting, full of flowery compliments, but clever, very clever, using a meter I had not heard before, his own. It began, "Violet-crowned, honey-smiling Sappho . . ." I thought back to the day I had visited the wharfside with his brother. Was I wearing a wreath of violets? Probably, I often did, and it had been the spring season. But what far sight he must have, to see it from the deck! And I shook my head; surely I was not smiling, never with all those rowdy sailors watching! It was a figure of verse, to flatter, that was all. But I *was* flattered, and very pleased, my heart beating hard and a little tingle, pleasant, running over my skin. I raised my head and spoke to Father, lying. "I will take it to my chamber—to read when I have more time—it is difficult to decipher. . . ." I felt jealous of the missive and did not wish to share it.

And that was the beginning; we were friends before we met,

Alkaios and I. That very night, alone, I sat up, making a verse-
letter to answer his, and go back with the runner to the front.

All that year we exchanged letters whenever we could, and
always in meters of different kinds, each of us showing off to the
other. He was a fine poet, no question, as good as I myself. His
words were full of grace and wit, gossip from the battle lines, and
with much heart, too. There were many lines praising this one
and that of his comrades, for bravery and high prowess, or
lamenting the fallen in verse to break the heart. Some songs I hid
away; those that were of drinking, and of the women that
followed the camp, and of loose night living, for I did not think
Father would think them seemly for a girl to read. Mostly,
though, he wrote of his captain, a youth he named as Patrokles to
his own Achilles; it was a subtle compliment, for he showed thus
that he knew I knew my Homer. I was very jealous, for I knew also
that Patrokles and Achilles were comrades-at-war and very close,
some said lovers. It will seem strange, my feeling, for I had not met
Alkaios even; but I had met almost no young men at all, and I
was half in love already, and dreaming about him every night.

And still the conspiracy against our Tyrant Melanchros went
on; all of us young people knew about it, and felt the thickening,
though much more secrecy was maintained. I was no longer
allowed to sit, playing my harp, when Father had his visitors;
they came in covered litters, one at a time, after dark. We heard
whisperings and an occasional louder word, incomprehensible,
quickly cut off, from Father's private apartments; we did not
even know who it was that gathered there, or how many. Once I
heard a woman's low voice, oddly familiar; I looked around for
Praxiona, thinking she would know who was there, but I could
not find her. She was not in the tiring room or belowstairs
ordering the next day's tasks, and that night a servingmaid
brought me my bedtime plate.

It seemed clear that it was she, indeed, whose voice I had
heard; I thought it strange that she would be involved, for she
was only a freedwoman, after all, and not native to Lesbos either.
But much was strange in those days, as I look back on it, and all
of us young people making wild guesses; we were told nothing by
our elders, for our own good, of course; it was dangerous games
they played, in their curtained rooms.

Another letter came, in the late spring, from Alkaios; I

remember it particularly, for he asked me to receive his tutor and friend, a man named Melanippos. ". . . and he will relay all my news, for I am weary of telling the tale . . . and truth to tell, weary of this dragging war, as well . . ."

I did not know when to expect the man, but that same day he came, sending a slave before, for courtesy, and to give me an opportunity to ready myself for his call. I was quite nervous; I had never received a man before, but, more than that, I wanted to impress him, the friend of Alkaios. I changed my chiton three times, going back finally to my first choice, a saffron garment with no sleeves; it was the newest fashion, just off the boat from Sardis, patterned all over with white roses, and filmy, with a texture crinkled into wavy lines that had been wrung into it while it was wet. I fancied the new tiring slave clumsy and slapped her, to my horror, snatching the ribbon from her and binding my own hair with shaking fingers. The day was hot, or perhaps my exertions made it seem so; my face in the mirror looked pale and sickly, and I longed for some red paste to color it like a great lady's. I was pinching my cheeks hard and biting my lips, when Gorgo put her head in at the door, astonished. "Get back to the roof!" I cried. "I am receiving!"

"Who?" she demanded, standing stock still.

"My gentleman . . . Oh, never mind! Go—please!" I had heard the sound of a chariot at the gate; I almost wept in my anguish. I could not bear that he should see her, all sweaty, with her dusty bare legs below her little kilt.

She stood a little longer, for spite, and grinning, rubbing one bare foot against the other. The gate clanged; I implored her with my eyes, silently. She shrugged her shoulders, stuck out her tongue, and vanished up the stairs. I had barely time to tuck the mirror out of sight among the cushions before the servant ushered Melanippos in.

I stared, forgetting my manners. I might have let it go, I thought; at any rate, he was wearing enough paint for the two of us, and some left over, and his tunic, violet-colored with gold embroiderings, and finer than anything I owned, was transparent to show his flesh. He was tall and reed-slender, with a languid air, and he sighed as he took the hand I held out to him, brushing the tips of my fingers with his lips. After, he fanned himself with an ivory fan, as though the effort had fatigued him.

It was difficult to guess his age; as I have said, he was painted, and his hair, of a pale gold color, was cunningly combed and curled close to his head and bound with a gold fillet. He wore no beard; though that was not the fashion; I remembered that he was a teacher and that such men often went close-barbered. These things and his slim body gave him a look of extreme youth, even boyishness, but beneath his eyes were purplish pouches, powdered over, and the eyes themselves looked old. I decided he must be thirty years, at least; in those days that seemed a very great age, indeed.

His look of infinite weariness, if feigned, was nonetheless constant; his movements were all of them slow and measured. He stood with his weight upon one leg, throwing the other hip into a graceful curve; when I offered him a seat, he took the couch, half-reclining, leaning upon one elbow, and looking at me from under one raised eyebrow. He still had not spoken a word, except a murmured greeting.

I cleared my throat and spoke, finally. "You had a letter from the poet? . . ."

A tiny smile lifted the corners of his mouth, briefly. "Dear girl," he said, "I will read it to you and gladly—when I have wet my dry lips. I have come clear from the other side of town in a dusty chariot . . ."

I was dreadfully embarrassed that I had not thought of it, and clapped my hands for a slave to bring wine. They must have all been upstairs watching the games, or in the kitchens guzzling, for only an old woman came, grumbling and shuffling. She pretended not to understand, cupping her hand at her ear as though she were deaf; she had been in our household since before I was born and took liberties. Mostly we winked at it, and let her putter about with a broom or doze in a corner. I saw he was amused, in his lazy way, and I began to redden, half-rising; from behind the curtain Praxinoa came, with two servingmaids bearing large trays. "Permit me, Lady," she said. "Here is the wine and fruit you ordered. . . ." Then she was gone before I could thank her.

Melanippos looked after her, helping himself to a cup of old Chian; I saw that he did not water it. He drained it quickly, not even gasping, though it is very strong, and said, "That is Andros' freedwoman? . . ."

"Praxinoa—yes," I said. Then, all in a rush, and fervently,

"But she is much, much more . . . she is everything to us . . . housekeeper, tutor, friend. Indeed, I do not think the household could exist without her." My tongue had loosened and I felt easy, suddenly. "Would you believe it! I had forgotten the wine . . ."

He looked at me and smiled; it was as though he had taken off a mask. "But you are a great singer and maker of songs . . . you are not supposed to worry your head with such things. . . ."

I was much flattered and decided to like him, never mind his womanish looks. "You have heard my songs?" I asked, wonderingly.

He bowed, managing to do it without rising. "All Lesbos knows The Black Lark," he said, pouring another cup and raising it in a toast. "You will not join me?"

I shook my head and reached for the larger amphora, with the wine already watered. "I prefer our own island wine," I said. "It is sweeter and not so strong. . . ." But even as I sipped it, I felt my eyes water; I was unused to it, having drunk mostly milk or barley water, except at feast times. I remembered my duty and said, "Please take food . . . some cheese perhaps, or fruit?"

I saw his weary eyes slide over the table; everything was there, a perfect repast. "It looks most dreadfully toothsome," he said. "But I never take anything before the evening meal . . . must watch my figure, you know . . ."

"But"—I blurted out, astonished—"you are so very slim . . ."

"Well," he said, tossing his head like a bride, "I work at it. . . ."

He picked up an olive and ate it, carefully removing the pit and placing it on the edge of the tray. "Perhaps," he said, "I might take home some of those little salted fish for my cat? . . . I keep a cat, you see . . ."

Well, I thought, *who does not?* In the lower kitchen or the courtyard somewhere, for catching mice. He must have read my expression; he laughed lightly and said, "She is a very special cat . . . like black marble, with eyes blue as gems. I had quite a time smuggling her out—she is Egyptian . . . there they worship the little creatures. . . ."

I stared. "You have been to Egypt?"

"Oh, often," he said. "One of my ships is due back from there this week, if the winds hold . . . with a fine cargo of raw cotton from up the Nile. . . ."

He was a trader, then. I had thought he looked too wealthy for a pedagogue. I spoke politely. "The himation you wear . . . such a fine cloth . . . is it woven from cotton, then?"

"Oh, no," he said, shaking his head and taking up a piece of the stuff and fingering it delicately. "No, this is silk . . . very rare. From Kos, where they have learned the secret. It is got from a worm, you know . . ."

"A worm?" I said, wrinkling my nose.

"Yes . . . I do not pretend to know exactly how it is done . . . but the worm spins a fine thread to wrap its eggs . . . they get the silk from that wrapped thread, somehow. . . ." And he shrugged his shoulders. "But—you have not said—may I have the fish?"

"What?" I was confused. "Oh—but certainly—for your cat . . ."

He was already busily wrapping them; he took three, whipping out a cloth from somewhere hidden, and tucking the little bundle into a pouch he wore hanging from his belt. "I call her Isis—for the Egyptian goddess of love . . ." I thought he looked quite fatuous—and all over a cat!

He went on. "She is breeding, my little Isis." He smiled slyly. "One cannot know how they will turn out; she slipped away one night. They may have dreadfully common blood—but, if they are pretty, I will be glad to make you a present of one of the litter."

He looked as if he were conferring a great honor. I could not see how to refuse, though, in truth, I could not imagine making a pet of one of the scruffy things. "Thank you," I said. "I would like that." I thought a moment, remembering what he had said. "And are they truly worshiped there—in Egypt?"

"Oh, definitely. But"—and he waved his hand, flopping it from the wrist weakly—"they are nothing at all like the beasts we are used to here in Mitylene . . . they are—well, you will see!"

"But I had thought it such a high civilization," I said. "Primitive tribes worship beasts as gods."

"Oh, well," he said, waving that hand again, "you know what the Egyptians are . . . it is a very old culture. I believe they think—or used to, at any rate—that men are descended, in the beginning, from cats. . . ."

"Oh, not very likely, that, I should think," said I.

"Well," he said, "If one begins to examine any of the old religions! Even our own . . . my dear—that swan and egg bit, with Leda!"

"Well . . ." I said, frowning a little as I thought, "there are some interesting ideas—not religions, I mean, but ideas. Thales —he is my father's friend and a very great thinker, I believe— Thales says he has evidence that life actually began in the sea. He says that according to his reasoning—he is a mathematician, too—the whole of the earth was water once, and no dry land at all. . . ."

"Oh, my dear," said Melanippos, "you know how ridiculous that is!" And he leaned forward, for a wonder. "Why, then . . ." he asked, shaking his long white forefinger at me, "why then, my girl, are we not born knowing how to swim?" He leaned back upon the cushions again, looking triumphant.

For courtesy, I forbore to argue, saying only, mildly, "Well . . . I am sure that Thales can explain that, too. . . ."

He flopped his wrist again, idly. "Well, you know what these new philosophers are! According to them, one can figure out the universe by adding up numbers . . . myself, I think it is no more than another sort of magic. . . ." And he gave a wicked little smile.

I saw then it was pointless to discuss serious matters with him; not that he was frivolous, but one felt he had been through it all before in some dim long-gone youth. His worldliness made me shy, and awkward, too; I had been a maiden always of neat movements, but I spilled my wine twice, making purple stains upon my yellow skirt. I shifted, changing its folds, to hide it, but I saw by his eyes' quick malice that he had seen.

He lifted his cup again to his lips; I saw with a small shock that his fingernails were not quite clean, a thin gray line showing at the tips, though they were well clipped and he wore many rings. As he set down his cup, empty, he said, "I will read you Alkaios' letter now. . . ." He took from the roll case he carried one small scroll; I saw it had the same purple cord as the ones I had from the poet; Alkaios must have bought a whole bundle of the stuff! He read it to me in a plodding sort of voice, flat and thin. Even so, it bubbled with wit; I found myself translating it into a song as I listened. It was all about some battle or other, full of clashing swords and war cries, and, after, the dead stillness and the slow black curve of vultures in the sky; one could almost smell the smoke of the sacrifice, and under it all, the sweet sickly smell of the death-rot. And after the pure flawless, awesome words came the one blithe message that ended it: ". . . your Alkaios is safe, my dear, but not his arms . . . they hang upon the improvised Temple of Athene, for the enemy to gaze upon with triumph . . . Zeus give them joy! Bad luck—I shall have to buy another shield, and spear, as well . . . but I could not run fast enough with their weight upon me, so I shed them . . . and sit here alive to write a song about it all . . ."

I laughed, quickly, and then said, musingly, "He ran away. . . ."

"Do you think him a coward, then?" asked Melanippos.

I shook my head. "No, for I should have done the same. But I do not think I would have had the courage to write thus about it. . . ."

He rolled up the letter again. "Well, he cares nothing for life's conventions, Alkaios. He is his own man."

He looked down at the bundle of scrolls in his case, selecting one after a moment and handing it to me. "That is a likeness of Alkaios. . . . I believe you have not truly met? . . ."

I took it eagerly, murmuring that indeed I longed to know what manner of youth he was, such as could be determined by a picture. I saw the head and shoulders of a young god, done in some reddish chalk, with all the shadows and contours rubbed in, most cunningly, so that he looked as if he might smile, or speak. I exclaimed aloud, "But it is so very real . . . one might almost believe he breathed! Except that he is so fair. . . ."

"Oh, he is fair, indeed, Alkaios . . . this is the boy to the life, though I say it myself. Of course, it is only a sketch . . ."

I knew then that he was the artist, and marveled. "Were you then his sketching master?"

"Well, you might say so . . . but it is the art of sculpture that I teach—or used to. Nothing professional, of course." And he tossed his head again, half-deprecating, half-proud. "I have some skill, and thought to pass it on to others . . . truth to tell, his brother is the finer talent."

"Antimenades?" I must have sounded surprised; he raised his eyebrows at me.

I was confused and a little ashamed. "It is just that I thought him a soldier only—and somewhat clumsy . . ."

"His hand is not," said Melanippos. "His hand has much power with the clay and the stone." He shook his head, sadly. "If only he would forbear to copy the ancients . . . one cannot say the same thing twice."

I saw he was serious, finally, and leaned forward eagerly. "Well—but one can . . . and always it will be so. It is that one must not say it in the same way."

"That is what I meant," he agreed. "You have put it well . . . of course, words are your medium. . . ."

I saw that he fingered some other scrolls, and knew he wished to show them too. "Are there other sketches there?" I asked. "I would like to see all. . . ."

He handed them all to me. "They are all of the same subject—you will see that they are lifelike. It is not the fashion, so I will gain no renown . . . but it is how I work. These are sketches for a statue—I have already begun on the clay."

They were all fine; one I put aside quickly, for it was full-length and naked. I felt strange and guilty, as though I had come upon the young man Alkaios in his bath. I saw from the corner of my eye that he looked amused, and picked it up again, as if idly; I did not want to be thought prudish or ignorant of the world. Still, I could not control the red color that crept up from my neck.

"You may have that one if you like," he said, slyly.

I do not know why I felt so odd; all the god statues in our garden were undraped. But then I did not know them, nor was ever likely to; besides they were stiff and conventional and one could not imagine them alive. I composed myself and said, in what I hoped was a cool voice, "I would prefer one of the heads, if you can spare it. There is so much detail and so perfect . . . I would feel I knew Alkaios truly. . . ."

"Well," he said, squinting at the lot, "this one, perhaps." He passed it over to me; it was not the finest, but good enough; I took it and thanked him.

He was still looking down at his rolled-up missives. "Lady Sappho," he said, "there is a letter here—for your father—for Andros." He lowered his voice, looking about him as though there were spies behind the curtain. *Sweet Aphrodite,* I thought, *and is he also of the conspiracy?*

"My father is in the garden, I think . . . it is his day for checking his accounts. I will take you to him." I rose.

He frowned a little. "Who is with him?"

"Only his clerk," I said. "And perhaps he has gone by now."

"Well," he said, with an air of risking all, "let us go, then. . . ."

It was as I said; Father was just then finishing his afternoon's work, putting the wax tablets and the counting board into the hands of his clerk and bidding him good day. Our garden was large and cool, shaded by the branches of almond trees, and covered, too, at the end where Father sat, by a canopy of coarse white linen; there was a little pool, too, where red fishes swam and a dolphin-shaped fountain made soft laughing noise. I saw that Melanippos was no stranger to the place, for he strode forward along ths narrow curving path and did not once look down.

Father looked up; he had been pouring wine; now he set down the amphora hard, so that it tilted, and spread a stain upon the cloth. *Gods,* I thought, *the man will suppose that all of us in this house have trembling hands—What ails Father?* For he had risen quickly, consternation in his thin face. Only for a moment he stared, then ran forward and embraced Melanippos, setting his cheek against the man's painted one. "Zeus!" cried Father. "Is it 'Nippos? Where— How many years has it been then? . . ." I could swear there was a brightness in Melanippos' eye, like the wet gleam of tears, then he cleared his throat and laughed a little. "Too long, Andros—fifteen years? . . ."

"More, I believe, my friend," said Father. "More." And then, for a wonder, they embraced again. "How has it been with you, my 'Nippos?"

They had forgotten me. I watched them as they talked, seeing my father in a new way, seeing him young and careless, with all the small lines of care smoothed and gone. It was some little time before they remembered me, standing aside; they laughed again, and swiftly the explanations were given, my father nodding, his eyes not leaving Melanippos' face. And the man finished, his voice low, ". . . and so I have come to cast my lot with you . . . it has been long enough I have withheld. . . ."

"The gods reward you, 'Nippos, my dear. . . ." I had never heard Father speak so intimately to a man, and looked in wonder, but he was very grave and seemly.

I sat quiet till they had spoken all, going apart from them that they might be private, and bending to watch the red fish swimming round and round, like prisoners, in the pool.

When they had finished, Father called me to bid Melanippos farewell; I thanked him for his news and the picture he had given me, and held out my hand to him.

Father looked after him in silence, not speaking until the sound of his chariot wheels had died away. "We were at school together," he said. "he was the fairest youth . . ." And his voice was sad. "He is much changed . . . only the gray line of the clay beneath his fingernails remains."

I showed him the drawing. "He has given me this, Father . . . it is Alkaios."

Father looked long at the face in the picture; a brief smile indented his lips at the corners. "Alkaios I have not seen since childhood . . . but this might be a portrait of Melanippos himself, years past. . . ."

I must have looked my disappointment, for Father said, "Oh, I have no doubt it is a true picture of Alkaios . . . it is simply that something in all beauty is the same, little one. . . ."

We were both silent for a moment, then he said, "'Nippos—he is nephew to our Tyrant, Melanchros. Yet is he coming over to our side. It is an act of daring, and took much from him, the deciding of it. . . ."

I said nothing, except to nod. Father said, fingering the bit of papyrus in his hands, "I trust you, Sappho, to be silent on this. . . . This I hold is a list of those from the front lines who are with us. It was drawn up by Antimenades; they promise to come home next leave, two weeks hence, and help us pull down the Tyrant."

"Father," I said, "is Alkaios' name there, too?"

"No, child," he said. "But he is always a rebel in the ranks—always in bad odor with authority—his brother has told me. So he will not be with these, since he cannot get leave." Suddenly he smiled. "You will have to wait till the end of the war, my little bird . . . may it come soon. . . ."

Chapter 8

Of course it had been happening gradually all along, but it seemed a sudden thing; life had been easy and gracious in Mitylene, and I, whose head was busy with music and song and pleasures of the mind, had been blind to the small changes in the life of the city. Of course, I no longer ran wild in the streets with my brothers; I was a young lady now. Also, I was much at home, as I have said, for my cousins studied at our house, and it was they who traveled the streets, and not I. I had heard Dika and Telesippa talking in corners, breathlessly and with excitement, about the latest ordinance of the new government, or gossiping over some small scandal, but I heard them with half an ear only, not taking it in.

As I look back on it, it was not till the Festival of Flowers that the changes were truly brought home to me. It was held in the early summer days, when everything was in bloom, and the streets were piled high with cartsful of cut flowers of all kinds, the fragrance nearly unbearable in its beauty; the agora was filled then with all the folk for miles around, come in from the country for this day to lay their flowery offerings upon the altar of Demeter. One must go on foot, for the ways were too crowded to take even a litter; I had always loved this day, for it lacked the abandon of the Dionysia or the lewdness of the Aphrodisia, and folk seemed fresh and gay and newly born.

It had been our custom each year to end the day at sundown in my Uncle Drakon's house, where a fine party of family and friends, feasting and dancing, would go on till midnight at least, and even the smallest of us children were allowed to stay up for it.

For a week before, the maids were busy sewing and bleaching cloth, for one always wore snowy white garments; there was an air of festival already, for none was at her proper work, and every corner was taken up by someone preparing a length of linen or gilding a sandal. I was fingering my lyre and dreaming, as usual, amid the turmoil one day, when I heard my name. It was my father's voice, speaking to Praxinoa. "But there is no pass here for Sappho!" I looked up, and saw him turning over some little squares of papyrus that he held. Praxinoa's hand went up to her mouth and her eyes went around; for once she had forgotten something. "I am sorry, Andros—we will go today."

It was then that I learned of the new rule demanding that everyone must have a pass to show after sundown; one must go in person to get it, too, and pay for it, according to one's standing; the price of mine was a hundred obols, an outrage.

As I went with Praxinoa into the city that afternoon, I saw all the many changes that Melanchros had brought about; it seemed to me that they had happened overnight. At each street corner was a detail of half a dozen boys, some as young as twelve years of age, in breastplates of some hard metal and helmets, too, and each one carrying a spear. Across their chests, upon a broad ribbon, were the words written, "City Guard of Mitylene." One grinned at me and waved, pulling himself up to attention again in an instant; I recognized one of the wharfboys that Charaxus used to play games with not long ago. So that is why my brothers were always underfoot, I thought. I had wondered at their idleness and discontented looks. Praxinoa whispered that Melanchros took these guards from the lower sorts; they were meant to keep down crime among their own kind. It was a good idea, but of course it did not work out that way. These guards, an army of sorts, really, were permitted all kinds of liberties, giving themselves airs and being officious, and it grew worse later. I remember, even that day, we were stopped twice, our way barred by crossed spears, and identification demanded. Praxinoa, who carried her manumission papers always, showed them, explaining that I was the lady Sappho, daughter of the noble Skamandronymous, Member of the Council. The guard who took her papers scanned them, and handed them back, passing us on; of course he could not read. She spoke calmly and without rancor; I should have flown into a rage!

I saw, too, that each vendor who plied his wares in the agora had a number nailed to his stall or cart, a license to sell. The licenses had to be paid for, of course, the money thus collected being used to benefit the city, but I pitied the poor folk who made their livings at selling, for many could not afford it and were put out of business. The prostitutes who hang about the temples were all licensed, too, scraps of parchment, numbered, pinned to their special conical hats, the badge of their trade. Even the crouching, maimed beggars on the temple steps wore numbers; I wondered what had happened to those who could not pay!

The passes were bought in the Temple of Hera, the largest in the city. It was much changed; I stared in wonder. The walls were all lined with sellers of bread, cakes, salted fish, and sweetmeats, even into the inner rooms; the smell was enough to make you faint, all mingled, and under the food odors, the sick sour smell of sweat. The place was dreadfully crowded; more guards went about, pushing people into lines, for there was a long wait for passes to be issued.

Mostly the lines were for people getting trade licenses; the one we stood on had only three people ahead. When it was our turn, the clerk who took down my name and weighed my money looked startled. "You need not have waited, Lady," he said, fawning all over himself with pleasure at the sight of our rich clothes and the heavy purse that I handed over.

I drew myself up to my full height, not very much, it is true, but it sufficed, for he looked cowed. I said, "It's is only fair to go by turn."

He spread his hands, shrugging, "Fair? What is fair, Lady? Any of these"—and he gestured to the others in their lines— "would step ahead if they had the price. . . ."

I said nothing, but thought of the woman I had seen, standing near the end of the longest, slowest line, a child at her breast, and another whimpering at her skirts; she had a face of antique beauty, deep-socketed eyes under a noble brow, the mouth straight and wide and a little stern, and all the features burnt dark by the sun. She must have come in from the country for the festival; one does not see such faces in towns. I gestured, speaking again to the clerk. "Which line is that one—the long one?" I asked.

He looked where I pointed. "Oh, that. That is the line for the sacrifices. They bring their children to sell for the altars. Only girls, of course . . . but they fetch twenty obols. It is a fortune to a poor farmer—and brings back the old piety besides. A very good thing. It used to be the custom years ago before the city went soft and used dolls for the fire. . . ."

I was horrified, and stared, unbelieving, at the man, the flesh creeping on me; I heard Praxinoa's breath catch on a little gasp. "Come, Sappho," she hissed beside my ear. "Come, do not listen."

"Wait," I said, still staring at the clerk. "You mean—they give their children to be *burned?*"

"Not *give*, Lady . . . *sell* . . . they sell them. Our leader asked for voluntary sacrifices . . . but there were no takers. The old days are gone forever. . . ." He must have noticed then the look on my face, for he said kindly, "It does not hurt them, Lady—they are strangled first."

"Strangled—" The word caught in my throat. "Your leader, you said. Who is your leader, that has done this thing?"

"Why—Melanchros, of course."

"He is a beast—that man," I said. "A beast, no better—"

I felt Praxinoa's hand, hard, on my arm. The clerk's face changed. He looked down at me, lowering his voice. "I could take you in for that, Lady. . . . I would—except that I know you, and have sung your songs. But better hold your tongue around here. They are not all as soft as I am. . . ." He beckoned me close, almost pleading. "Look, Miss Sappho—begging your pardon—look at it this way . . . how many of those children do you think would live another year anyway? There is famine everywhere. . . . For each one that is sacrificed, there are maybe three others saved—by the money they bring. And,"—he looked earnest—"I told you before, we don't take any boys, except if they're crippled or deformed and won't make soldiers. . . ." I felt movement behind me, and saw the clerk's eyes go to whoever had come up in the line. He raised his voice, giving me a hard look, for show. "Move on, now, citizen . . . you have your pass. I can't stand here talking all day."

Praxinoa tugged at me, and I went, blindly, not looking at the line of sacrifice. But behind my eyelids I carried the image of the dark young farm woman, like a sorrowing Niobe, with the babe at her breast, faceless, voiceless, soon to be dust.

Chapter 9

I saw the Tyrant Melanchros once only, at the Festival of Flowers that he had profaned with child sacrifice. Though he was surrounded by the young men of his guard, armored and armed with javelin and spear, he was himself a sight to inspire pity more than terror. Old he was, old enough to be my grandfather or more; his body was flaccid under his royal robes and his face sagged wearily, like a hound's, beneath his gilt wreath of office. I sang for him and he praised my song, and asked for another. I gave it to him, and changed the course of history in Mitylene. After, they called me god-driven, but it was not so. I simply sang.

I had known, of course, that I would be expected to make a song for the festival; there was always much merrymaking at Uncle Drakon's house, with scores of hired entertainers and many illustrious guests. Even in former years, I had been brought up from the children's room to play for the company; this year, like most of my cousins, I would be promoted, as it were, to the banquet hall, for I was counted a woman grown, or nearly. For days I had been composing the music, trying it over on my lyre; the words I had already in my head, a hymn to Demeter, and another song as well, which I kept secret from everyone. Once Telesippa came into the room where I was practicing and listened, a frown on her long oval face. "That is a strange air," she said. "It is so harsh, somehow, almost discordant . . ."

"It is not finished yet," I said, and crossly. "I do not like to have my work criticized before it is ready."

"Well, forgive me for being alive!" she said sharply, wounded by my unkind words. "Genius at work!" She turned quickly and walked stiff-backed out of the room, her sandals slapping loudly on the tiles. I was sorry, for I had always been fond of her, but truly I am not fit to live with when I am hard at work. Most people know it and avoid me at those times, or ignore my bad temper, but poor Telesippa lacks understanding, having no talent of her own. I am not being cruel; it is simply the truth. She never learned, and much of her life must have been hard, for she wed another artist. But I am ahead of my story again.

I had prayed for rain to all the gods, for when rain fell out of season, it was taken as an omen that Demeter was pleased and wanted no sacrifice; Father said, though, that it had never happened in his lifetime, and so of course it did not happen that summer either. The day of the festival dawned bright and clear, the sky cloudless, the sea as calm as the rainwater caught in a bucket. When they burnt the little boats filled with seabirds, the smoke went up in thin black columns and no wind blew the stink shoreward; the altar sacrifices, too, those darker rites, did not pollute the air, but rose straight to the goddess; the folk counted it a sign of good fortune and the gods all smiling. But all the same I smelled it, somewhere inside, and could not take food, my head ringed round with pain like a tight black band.

The smoke hung in the air most of the morning, high overhead, like a false cloud, then slowly drifted out to sea, and we saw it no more. All day we stood in the courtyard, watching the folk making merry in the streets, singing and dancing, weaving in an intricate pattern, one behind another all in a line, holding in their hands a long rope of flowers that writhed like a snake. The cymbals clashed and the pipes made shrill melody; one could not hear the voices raised in harmony.

All the faces looked bright and happy, sated; this day all the poor might eat their fill, for bullocks were slaughtered and lambs, and only a small portion given to the goddess, the rest distributed to any who stretched out his hand. All manner of fruits were piled high in huge baskets at the streetcorners, for the taking, and the bakers' doors thrown open; in all the temples free wine was dispensed, though it was well watered and there was not much drunkenness. It was counted a happy day, but here and there, among the crowd, I fancied that I saw a woman's face, shadowed and stricken, clouded by an inner sorrow.

Near sundown, when we went to the house of Drakon for our private feasting, the streets were nearly deserted, fallen flower petals thick under our feet, the rinds of fruit slippery among them. The young men of the city guard were rounding up a few stragglers, pushing them out of the gates homeward, speeding them with curses and crude jests; thick clouds of flies hung over flung half-eaten bones, and sometimes a knot of street dogs fought for them, snarling. At one corner we saw a small detachment of guards, laughing, go among the mongrels and spit them, howling, upon their spears. It had not been this way in past years; the revelry had gone on all night, in seemly fashion, booths for eating set up, and slave-workers detailed to clear away the refuse.

Three times on our way we had to show our passes, though it was not far; Drakon's house was ringed about with city guards, lounging against the walls or leaning upon their spears. We heard later that they had been sent to all the nobles' houses, to keep order, it was said, but between ourselves we whispered that it was to spy.

Inside, there were already many guests; indeed, it looked as if all the aristocracy of the town was gathered there, in our kinsman's house. Some there were who looked like another sort, to my mind, overdressed and garishly bejeweled, even to the men; I remembered that many nobles were now in trade, and doubtless picked up many foreign customs on their business voyaging. Besides, I saw my Aunt Phaedra, glittering like a golden image, and the other ladies striving to emulate her. It was a vain attempt for them all; she was truly surpassingly beautiful, though she was got up like a temple prostitute; even the tips of her breasts, showing through the transparent stuff of her upper garment, were gilded. Gorgo, behind me, gave a rude whistle; I jabbed her hard with my elbow, and she behaved herself when presented, except for her goggling eyes.

Phaedra's paint was cracking already, for the room was hot from the heat of the hundreds of candles, but from a little distance one could not notice. Still, I resolved, as her face swam close in courteous embrace, to seek out something better than white lead to put upon my cheeks when I needed to hide my years. She left a smear of red, too, upon my forehead, for she was taller; my father and brothers she kissed full upon the lips and pressed her body against theirs. Charaxus, I saw, liked it, but Larichus went pink as a girl and looked as if he might faint.

Aunt Phaedra was a snob, too; she looked right through Praxinoa as if she were not there, though Uncle Drakon bowed as to an equal. And at the sight of Drom, in all her dark alien beauty, she turned to me and said that the slaves' supper was set belowstairs. I came close to Phaedra then and spoke low, saying that Drom was free (Father had drawn up her papers first off, for my sake) and that she was my good friend. "Besides," I said, "she will dance later. . . ."

I heard Gorgo's voice, rough and quite loud. "What did the whore say? That her mother was a slave from Kos? . . ." The heart swelled in me for her bold loyalty, but I shushed her all the same, for I saw Uncle Drakon's face, drawn down in stern lines, like an angry Zeus; I did not want to be in the way of the thunderbolt.

My father leaned close to his kinsman, whispering. I heard Pittakos' name, and saw Drakon nod, and look hard at Gorgo. His eye would have withered anyone else, but she just stared back, laughed, and began to pick her nose. Myself, I nearly went through the floor, but I saw my father's lip twitch; his eyes slewed around to Drakon's, and I heard again, "Pittakos . . ." The lordly Drakon put up his hand to hide his wintry smile. I remembered Pittakos' habits then; nose-picking was one of the nicer of them.

I saw a thin trail of fallen yellow rosebuds, and followed them with my eyes; they led, of course, to Aunt Kassie. She had fastened them in her hair, as was the custom, but of course they did not stay fastened; Father had said once that he marveled that her head, even, stayed on her shoulders, or her legs did not come unhooked from her body. She stood, with uncle Erigyus and Nausikaa, in a far corner. They all three had a look of apology, somehow, like poor relations; one felt they would be happier in the servants' hall. It was odd, that, for they were as well-born as any folk there; I put it down to their unworldly hearts, and my own heart went out to them. I threaded my way to them through the crowd; the air was stifling with the perfume of flowers and the headier scents of musk and myrrh, though the windows were all thrown open and slaves waved great fans above our heads, accomplishing little more than to disarrange our hair.

They looked so gratefully at me that I was exasperated with them and wished, almost, that I had not bothered. "You needn't have come to us, you're so popular, Sappho—" Aunt Kassie began.

"I—popular?" I said. "Why, this is the first time I've been allowed into the hall . . . we are all equal here. Except for Aunt Phaedra, of course . . . she is snubbing everyone in sight."

Nausikaa's eyes went round and wide. "Oh, no," she said. "I have just now seen her—kissing a young man who does not even wear a wreath!" She meant, of course, that he was not an aristocrat, for there is a custom that denies the wreath to one lower born.

"Well, he is a man, after all," I said, meaning mild mischief. Aunt Kassie tittered, and Uncle Erigyus put his hand up to hide a smile, but Nausikaa looked puzzled. *Is it possible,* I thought, *that she does not know the gossip?* I decided it was, poor Nausikaa. She warmed my heart, though, for she looked at me, beaming, and whispered shyly, "You are the prettiest girl here, Sappho—I swear it by Aphrodite—the prettiest of all!"

"She has been at the paint pot," said Gorgo, behind me, in a louder whisper. I turned to give her a withering look, which did not wither her but made her grin. Truly, she is impossible! I could not deny the face paint, but I thought I had been subtle about it and that no one would notice. I raised my chin and said, "Well, Gorgo—not everyone wants to look like a sweating horse!"

Her grin got wider. "Horse you will never be. A prancing pony maybe . . ."

I was stung, for I was wearing my new slippers from Chios, with heels; hard to walk on, but they added two inches. I was still shorter than anyone but Dika, and even she had grown a bit lately. When I was older and with more assurance in me, I did not mind my lack of stature, but in those early days, I suffered deeply that I had not a goddess look.

Gorgo nudged me. "Nothing personal, little doll-baby . . . I like you the way you are. I don't agree you're the prettiest"—and she shrugged—"but that's a matter of opinion, right? No bad feelings?" I nodded, though there was a silly lump in my throat and I could not speak. That was the nearest thing to an apology I ever heard from Gorgo.

She brushed past me, dragging Drom by the hand, and jostling everyone as she went. It was unthinking and a little cruel, for it called attention to them, and Drom would have been better off without it. She had that cool, impassive face still, but I fancied she must be suffering agonies of shyness; after all, she was the only person of her color there, outside of slave help. She was dressed richly, like the princess she was, and there was no

mistaking the status we had given her. Still, one who has stood
naked in the slave mart does not like to be stared at, and I felt for
her, with all these hostile eyes upon her once again. When she
had danced for them, they would all love her as we did.
Nausikaa must have felt as I did, for she whispered, "Shall we go
after them, and rescue Drom?"

"Someone had better," I said. "Gorgo is headed for the dining
room . . ."

Aunt Kassie gave a little gasp, and began to wring her hands.
Of course, any well-bred person knows that one does not make
for the food right away at a feast; it is just not done. One waits
for a signal from the host. "Come with me," I said to Nausikaa.

What a sight! The dining room was magnificent, with tall
branched candelabra, the couches set out, each with its own
three-legged table before it, heaped with delicate small foods
from far places, fish eggs, salted nuts, cheeses, little raw sea
creatures in their shells, sprinkled with ginger, all the lovely bits
for nibbling with the unmixed wine that is taken first as a toast to
the goddess. The flagons were set out too, crystal from Syracuse,
sparkling and clear to show the purple and amber of the various
wines. There, on the center couch reserved for a guest of honor,
sprawled our Gorgo, her mouth stuffed and bulging; as we
watched in horror, she tried to force some morsel between
Drom's lips, and Drom shaking her head and trying to rise. I ran
over, angry as a hen partridge that has been caught in the rain,
with Nausikaa behind me, quivering like her mother. The whole
scene was ridiculous, and myself a part of it; this knowledge, and
the fear that some of the company would witness it, made me so
full of fury that I almost bit my tongue to keep from shouting.

Gorgo looked up, surprised. "What's up? Is the roof falling?"

I forced down my shouting voice that wanted out of my chest
and said quietly, through my teeth, "Get out of there! Get
up—this minute! You are rumpling the couch!"

"What matter?" answered that idiot from Sparta. "The food is
here—and I'm hungry. That's what it's for, to eat, isn't it?"

I was speechless at her stupidity; surely she had learned
something at our house! A hand touched my arm gently, and a
voice, Praxinoa's, said, soft, "Easy, Sappho . . ." She came
forward, putting out her hand to Gorgo, and pulling her up.
"Straighten the cushions and put the food back in its place. We

do not eat at a noble's house until the proper time. We do not make spectacles of ourselves either; wipe your mouth. Be quick about it, before someone looks in . . ."

"Well," began Gorgo, "I didn't know . . ."

"Well, you know now," said Praxinoa, calm as Athene. "If, hereafter, you do not know the custom, watch the others, and do as they do. Now," she said, as she swiftly put the whole couch and table to rights, "I think you girls should go into the courtyard. It may be that others will follow your example. Everyone is crowding the hall—it is almost impossible to breathe . . ."

She was right; the courtyard was cool and fresh after the cloying fragrances of the inner rooms; a fountain played, in uneven tinkling, for a little breeze blew. There was no need yet for torches; night had not quite fallen and the light had that special underwater hue that occurs only between sundown and moonrise, pale, bluish-green, but very clear, so that everyone and everything seemed to stand still in its radiance, all edges sharply defined as though by a pen.

There was a little knot of people before us, seeking the peace and the air; mostly girls they were, my cousins, and others that I knew by sight. Soft chatter came from them, like the noise of birds when the shadows gather. As I watched, two detached themselves from the group and walked apart; not girls, but my father and the artist Melanippos.

Nausikaa, with Drom and Gorgo, joined the girls, Gorgo's harsh Spartan speech rising suddenly above the feminine babble, and I went forward to where my father stood, eager to make conversation with the artist, as he was the first of my acquaintance.

He was much mellower this day than when I had first encountered him; I think they two had been reminiscing, for they wore fond, dreaming looks. "Ah, the fair Sappho," Melanippos said, bending over my hand; truly the red on my cheeks and lips must have done wonders!

We exchanged a few pleasantries; I asked him whether this strange and special evening light was not most interesting for an artist; he replied, with none of the flippancy that I had observed in him earlier, that it would be wonderful to paint, if one had the colors. "But," he said, shaking his head sadly, "such colors have not been discovered; we cannot imitate the subtleties of nature's moods. . . ."

I frowned, thinking. "Could not one mix them—the colors—to get the effect? . . ."

"I have tried that. In all sorts of ways. But they are stubborn, our dyes and paints, and will not mix well. Resin makes them lumpy, and vinegar cracks after . . ."

"I see," I said. "Perhaps there is some form of oil, such as we use in our face paints and perfumes—"

"Oh, no!" he exclaimed, as though horrified. "That would never do!" And he flipped his wrist again in his own peculiar way. "A work of art to smell of musk or nard!"

"But it need not," I persisted. "Don't you see—it would depend, would it not, upon the oily base that was used . . ."

Father put his arm about me, drawing me close. "My little Sappho is a great one for argument," he said, smiling.

I drew away, aghast; I had always thought myself a very amenable person. "I *never* argue, Father! But if I have an idea which might work, why should I not voice it?"

I saw a little look pass between them, the sort of complicity that the old always betray toward the young; I resolved then and there that I would never give way to that, when I had come to my own fullness of years. I shrugged then and smiled. "Well, it is no matter," I said. "I was simply interested, that is all . . . and the light I spoke of is nearly gone anyway. . . ." And indeed it was so; there was a pearly look in the garden, shading to gray, and objects had begun to blur softly at their edges.

I turned aside a little, feigning an indifference I did not feel; I had been spoiled, somewhere along my life's burgeoning, and thought quite highly of myself and the powers of my mind. I looked to the group of maidens clustered about the fountain; it broke apart a little as Gorgo left, still dragging Drom by the hand. *Oh, oh,* I thought, *let us pray Praxinoa is on the lookout!* But, in the space left vacant, a face swam to me across the little distance; pearlier than the pearly light it was, and stopped my heart. In such a moment, time stands still; it seemed forever, but was an instant only. The instant passed, and I saw her clear; she was only a little maid, ten years at most, but beautiful as the dawn, or as a rose, or as the foam-born Aphrodite rising new from the waves. One might liken her to anything. What can I say? She was written from that time upon my heart.

I could not speak, but Father said, asking Melanippos, "Is that the little sister? She has the look of Alkaios when I saw him last . . . when he was still a child. . . ."

"Yes," said Melanippos, "and nearly as willful as he. Quite a handful in the rearing, I can tell you . . . for the task is mine." He looked, for the moment, like a fussy nurse, or like Aunt Kassie, about to wring her hands. Then he tossed his head, in his own way, and said, "Very bright for her years, mind you . . . and nearly as good to look at as Alkaios himself, but . . ." He raised his eyebrows, eloquent. *Nearly,* I thought. *What can this Alkaios be?* I opened my mouth to speak, and then I saw she saw me. Our looks met; her eyes were large and wide, like any child's, of some lightish color, uncertain in the fading light. But they were the eyes of a woman, secret, wise, and knowing. I was the first to look away. A trifle breathless, I asked her name. "Atthis."

Atthis. I tried it over in my mind. "A pretty name," I said. I did not know then how often I would write that name, how many times sing it.

Melanippos bent toward me. "She thinks your name uncommonly pretty also, and would love to meet you. . . . Will you do us the honor? . . . For I am her guardian, she has no other . . ." He spoke as he led me toward her.

"I hope I may hear you sing, Lady," she said, taking my hand. Her face swam still, grave and mysterious, on a level with my own, though she was so very young. Her hair was pale, very pale, and she wore it straight, falling to her waist, and caught in a chaplet of roses, baring a broad white brow. The light was almost gone; near us a slave lit a torch, which flared suddenly, bright as noon. She smiled; one of her milk teeth was gone, at the side, making a child-gap. A small sprinkle of freckles ran across her nose, and her collarbones showed sharp and delicate, standing out above her first low-cut dalmatica. I smiled and pressed her hand; the mystery was gone, and the magic flown. She was only a little girl, like any other, but prettier.

Chapter 10

The lighting of the courtyard torches was the signal to begin the formal feast. We were assigned our couch partners, for each was designed to seat two persons. I had been given Melanippos; he bowed to acknowledge the honor. I, too, was pleased, for there were not men enough to go around, and most of the other girls had to pair off two by two. I saw, with some satisfaction, that Gorgo had been separated from Drom; instead, Praxinoa was seated with Drom, and Gorgo had drawn Nausikaa, who looked already a bit uneasy, as who would not? I could not help but smile, they were as unlikely a couple as one might imagine. I looked about for the little Atthis, but Melanippos whispered that she was banished to the children's room, along with all the young boy cousins, and my brother Larichus. Charaxus was allowed in, and was seated with Telesippa; I knew he was disappointed, for he had been eying all the pretty painted older ladies; 'Sippa was rather less than voluptuous, and the only one of all us girls he had never pinched or pawed. *Serves him right,* I thought, *the little libertine!*

I saw Pittakos for the first time; he was lolling, as like his daughter as could be, among the cushions of Phaedra's couch; his hairy face was nearly in her lap, but she did not seem to mind, and, indeed, was twisting a curl of his head absently around her finger, while her seeking eyes roved among the company. Drakon sat, like the king of the gods, erect and correct, beside Pittakos' wife, Chloris. This foursome seemed curiously well-matched, for the lovely Chloris was exquisitely cool, her manners flawless, her profile perfect, and her clothes easily the most tasteful in the whole room, though the simplest.

The center couch, kept for the guest of honor, was still empty, and voices buzzed, wondering. Suddenly there was a loud blare of trumpets, and as suddenly silence. A detachment of civil guards marched in, their brass-bound boots making clanking noise upon the marble floor; there must have been at least twenty of them, marching stiffly, and fully armed. Astonished heads turned, and all eyes were on the wide doorway, for this could herald only one personage. I knew him at once, though no one had ever described him; the look of power was upon him, no matter that he was corpulent and had to be carried in a chair of state. The look of power was there, and its sister, corruption, too. One saw everything in his eyes, the weariness of old lust, long since satisfied; the avarice that narrowed the lids; the greed that watered them and made them blink. It was Melanchros, the Tyrant of Mitylene, the usurper, the overlord, the enemy of every noble in the city. His arrogance was boundless, for he did not bother to show it. When Drakon, as was the custom, bowed low before him, he dismissed him languidly with a wave of a fat, ringed hand, and smiled affably. But for those eyes, he might have been any old granduncle, tolerated for his wealth. I learned later that he had commanded that the couch of honor be left empty in every house that he might choose where he wished to confer his presence.

Beside me, Melanippos, under cover of the general confusion and bustle that attended the Tyrant's appearance, snapped his fingers three times. A young slave boy appeared, beautiful; he must have served as model as well. He spoke very low, Melanippos, still he was so close to me that I could not help but hear most of what he said. "Hurry," he said, "go to the house of—" I missed the name. "Just four houses down. Tell them to make ready the women's gear and the—other things. Make haste—while there is time—tell them the feast is about to begin and who sits in the couch of honor . . . go!" The boy nodded, and went without a word.

I think no one had seen except me; Melanippos leaned close and said, for my ear alone, "Forget what you heard, Sappho—for the sake of the city. . . ."

I was puzzled, of course, but when he put his finger to his lips I forbore to speak or ask any questions. I had a strange feeling of stifling, as when one feels a storm is coming; I wished they would begin the libations, so that I might wet my dry lips, at least.

Drakon rose. He raised high the huge golden goblet. "To the Mother," he said, in the voice one uses for such moments, solemn and intoning. He tipped the goblet to pour the customary few drops as offering, but his hand must have shaken, for a dark pool, like blood, spread, widening, upon the white marble of the floor.

I could not help but wonder how the dancers, later, would manage to avoid slipping in it, for of course no one could dare to wipe it up, it was Demeter's drink. Drakon then drank himself, a sip only, passing it first to Melanchros, who took a long draught. It was passed along the nobles' couches, the men drinking only, a long business, and all in silence, for one must not profane the ceremony. I saw now why the smaller boys and girls had been banished; a whine or a fidget, and the whole would have to be done over.

After, the slaves appeared to pour the strong wine for each diner; still one must wait. I stole a look at Gorgo; even she had not reached out for the goblet. There are holy moments, even in Sparta, though I would not have thought it from her tales.

Drakon gave the signal, and we all raised our cups. "To the guest of the house, who is sacred . . ." It was a formula only, but I only raised it to my lips; I would not drink to that man!

Then my father rose; I saw, as if for the first time, how tall and straight he was, and beautiful as a god. "To the city," he said. "We are all her children." And his eyes swept the company briefly before he drank; there was a look in them I could not read. I drank then and deeply, too deeply. I coughed and choked on the fiery liquid, Melanippos pounding me on the back and laughing. Through the tears the strong stuff brought to my eyes, I saw that everyone laughed; I nearly cried in earnest. Melanippos, leaning close, whispered, "Good—you have created a diversion . . . the moment is not yet . . ." I had no idea what he meant, but was grateful for his kindness. "The toasts will go on," he said. "Remember—a sip only at a time. . . ."

The toasts did go on, it seemed forever; I cannot remember them all, except toward the end. My Uncle Erigyus stood up; he was always a timid soul, but that day he looked as strong and straight as Father, and in his look was the same strange meaning, under. "To the old ways—to the days of honor and justice!"

"I will drink deep to that," said the Tyrant, though he stayed seated still. "And I propose a further toast." He raised his cup, and spoke, loud, though his voice was thin. "To the old ways—in truth! To the new days of order—the new justice! To the old pieties brought back, to the old religion, and the old sacrifices! To the sacrifices of blood!"

I felt the color rise up from my bosom, flooding my face;

perhaps it was the wine truly, I do not know, but I set my cup down hard; the sound was loud in the stunned silence that his words had made.

I saw, as in a dream, the bloated face turn toward me. "Drink," hissed Melanippos in my ear. "Raise the cup . . . the time has not yet come!"

Still, as in that same evil dream, I could not. I could not move; it was as though my arm was weighted.

The Tyrant stared at me; the watery eyes above the sagging cheeks held menace, or so I imagined. "You do not drink to my bidding, little singer?"

There was a little silence; Melanippos pressed his fingers, hard, about my arm. I nearly cried out, but still I did not move. I saw my father's face, frightened, and found my voice, speaking to him.

"Father, I am sorry. I am unused to these ceremonies . . . and unused to the wine. Our gracious guest must forgive me. . . . I would keep my poise for my singing, later. This last toast is too much for my stomach—it cries out for food. . . ." The Tyrant Melanchros stared at me, suspicious. Perhaps my youth came to my aid, for I must have showed the wine's effect; perhaps he too felt its effect, being old. At any rate, he did not catch the double meaning of my words. He smiled. "Well, well, child—you are excused. . . . Little maids have weak heads . . . and we do not want to miss your song, for it has brought us here tonight." He wagged his pudgy forefinger at me, playfully. "But," he said, still smiling, "the song had better be good . . ."

"I hope so, sir," I said, and bowed my head, as if in maidenly modesty.

The moment passed. Under cover of the slaves removing the wine and bringing in the first course, Melanippos whispered, "Good girl!"

I cannot remember what was served; it was, after all, many years ago. I presume it was everything of the most expensive and rare, from foreign lands, and the best that Lesbos has to offer. I never like to eat more than a bite before I sing; it is bad for the voice. Though, after, sometimes, I am famished.

I remember, though, that Melanippos was most solicitous, picking out the choicest slices of roast kid, paper-thin, for my plate, and the whitest mushrooms. The feast went on and on, as they always do, and much wine was drunk. Melanippos had none, nor did I, for I already felt that which I had had already. He had called for a beverage, brought to the feast by himself as a gift, and cooled in a bucket of snow from the mountaintop. It was called beer, from Egypt, and the first sip was refreshing, so cold it was and crisp on the tongue; after, when the snow melted, which it did very quickly, I did not much like the taste, slightly bitter and strong. It was pretty, though, honey-brown with a white foam on top, and bubbles rising; he said they were air, most amazing to see.

I noticed, with nausea, how much the Tyrant ate; one could hardly fail to see, for two slaves attended him alone, running to fetch bowls of water and napkins so that he might wash his hands. Most people use two fingers to eat, delicately, and wiping them after on lumps of barley bread; he, Melanchros, was greasy to the elbows; even Gorgo never managed to do that! There were plenty of ivory spoons at every place for the more liquid fare, but he disdained them, even going in with his hands into the soup bowl for a bit of shellfish or a baby squid. I caught sight of him with one black tentacle still hanging from his lip and nearly vomited; it made me think of a cat I had seen with a mouse tail not yet swallowed. Melanippos sniggered behind his napkin and whispered, "Strong stomachs—that's the thing tonight!" I nodded, but truly my humor had deserted me.

Finally the meal came to its end, a weary business, and all the little tables were removed, and the floor in the center cleared for the entertaining. I began to feel the little flutterings inside that all performers get before their time; often and often have I wondered why we do it! It is a form of Hades; still, applause is sweet.

I knew that I would be the last; already I had renown enough to do the final turn. The flutterings would go on for an hour or two at least, before my suffering ended. And then, too, I had extra fears this night; with trembling hands I raised the cup and sipped the beer, bitter as it was and gone flat, too. But it was better than a dry mouth, for a singer.

There were jugglers first, from the Persian lands, doing wonderful things with brightly colored balls, keeping them in the air and moving constantly, and never once letting them touch the ground. Then came some graceful acrobats from Lydia;

completely naked they were, without even loincloths. Somehow, one did not feel shame, their faces were as austere as priests at a shrine. At the end, a rope was stretched tight, high in the air, fastened between two columns, and, forming a sort of pyramid of bodies, one climbed to it upon his fellows' shoulders, and walked the whole length! This was a marvel of skill and balance and must have taken years of training; everyone drummed heels and clapped palms, shouting words of praise, and many coins were flung onto the floor in payment for the pleasure. After, for something extra, a little dog was led in, and he, too, walked the rope. He got across perfectly, but, on the way back he fell, a long way down; a high yelp, and suddenly cut off; his back was broken. I felt sick, and could not watch the wrestling that came after. I hated it anyway; great squat hairy brutes from Thrace, throwing each other with loud thumps and gouging at eyes, gurgling and growling like beasts; Melanippos said it was all for show and no one ever got hurt. Most of the company liked it and laughed until the tears came; I cannot see why men should imitate animals. Bad enough the other way around, and the poor dog meeting death for his effort.

But I am squeamish anyway and have always been; besides, my insides were in knots by then, it coming close to my turn. First, though, there was a wonderful Eastern fellow, wearing a turban and long rich robes with hanging full sleeves. It had many pockets and folds, for he produced all manner of things from it, to our delight. Appear and disappear they did, rabbits, doves, flowers, seemingly into the thin air. It was skill, too, of course, and not really magic, but one could not see how it was done. At the end he approached me, bowing low, and, reaching out, took from my bosom a tiny bouquet of violets. The dew was still on them, shimmering droplets, as though they had been gathered that moment from the dawn-wet ground. I gasped in wonder; it was near midnight! "For the Black Lark," he said. He could not, being a foreigner, have known my folkname, or that they were my favorite small flower; it was a compliment from my Uncle Drakon, and I smiled and bowed a little bow.

We heard then the sounds of flute and cymbal; it was time for the dancing girls; then Drom would dance, and then, at the last, I would sing. Slaves had swept the floor clean, but had not dared to touch the spilled libation; one could see from the dark gleam upon it that it had not yet dried. Drakon gave an order, and someone brought in a white goatskin rug: I pitied the poor washerwomen who would have to try to bleach the wine out, hours of work in the sun.

The dancing girls came in; I had never seen such a crew! For one thing, their robes were long, trailing the floor; surely one of them would trip and spoil everything. Also they were the tallest women I had ever seen, and, for the most part, uncommonly slender, though their long robes were girded up, making thick pouches at their waists.

I wondered if they were meant to be comic, like clowns; one in particular was awkward in her movements and could not keep time. They wore Egyptian wigs, black and thick, shoulder-length, and cut in a straight line across the forehead, and I never saw so much paint; Phaedra was clean as a wisp of hay beside them! I turned to Melanippos. "Are they Egyptian?" His mouth twitched, but he nodded. Well, I had never seen any—but I certainly did not think much of their beauty standards. Come to think of it though, they did have those broad square shoulders and flat feet one sees in Egyptian work. I had always thought it a stylization. Dance they could not, either; on Lesbos the simplest maiden has more grace, untaught. They were out of step with one another, and the music might have been a wind blowing for all attention that was paid to it. No one at the high dais, where the nobles sat, seemed to see anything amiss, however; perhaps they were all used to this kind of thing, being traveled people.

I grew quite bored and also was finding it difficult not to laugh at the thick awkward one; I looked about me, noticing that Drom had gone to change into her dancing dress. My breath grew shorter, as it always does; from experience I knew it would be all right again as soon as I struck the first note on my lyre. But until then—well, one must just endure it, or stop performing altogether. Someone came up behind me, quietly, Drom. She was wrapped all about in some gauzy stuff, so as not to show her costume before the event, and she had brought my lyre and the plectrum that I like to use to save my fingernails from breaking on the strings. As I took it from her, I felt the slippery sweat from her hand; of course she feels it too, the terror of the god-inspired. I pressed her hand; "Aphrodite with you!" I whispered. "With you also," she answered.

I never invoke the Muses, as most performers do; Aphrodite is my special goddess, and it is to her I pray always. The cymbals crashed, one last time, and the dancers sank to the floor, prostrating themselves as is the custom, and waiting for the applause. It was a mere scattering, for courtesy. Strange, though, the dancers did not withdraw but ranged themselves in a row behind the high dais; they must have had special permission. *Well,* I thought, *that is Drakon's business, not mine.* But, with all the city guard lounging upon their spears, the guests, and the young folk that had been summoned to see the entertainment, the hall was uncommonly crowded. Actually, of course, that is better for the performer; he has more communication with the many than the few.

The drums began, softly, for Drom's appearance; all about the room slaves were quietly lowering the lights, snuffing out some of the candles to create a softer atmosphere.

It is difficult to describe Drom's dances; they are tribal, for the most part, devised from the rituals of her birth land. In one she is a many-colored bird, for instance, clad in a costume of feathers, and done to the music of the flute, low and softly wild, with many twirlings and leapings. In another she is a beast of prey, clad in skins, and with a drumbeat under, louder and louder still, until she is killed by an arrow and dies. It is a chilling and moving thing, the noble creature in its wild freedom, the fear, the death. After, as she sank to the floor, there was a moment of silence, a tribute, then much clapping and shouting.

After a short interlude, when the music played, our own Greek music, she appeared again, this time in a flounced long skirt and cropped jacket such as the women of our hills wear in the dance. She wore wooden clogs and used clappers in her hands, most cunningly; it is our own island dancing that has come down from Crete and the old mainland too, and familiar to all, though none can do it so well as this foreign creature, Drom. The applause was deafening, and she had to do it over again.

My palms were sweating, and I kept rubbing them on a napkin; I must have trembled, too, though I did not realize it. Melanippos leaned to me and said, "Is this just ordinary singer's nerves, my dear? You must be suffering agonies. . . ."

Suddenly I felt I must say something to him, in case the worst should happen. I whispered, very low, "It is nerves, certainly . . .

but not all. It is—I have a new song. . . . Now that the time is
near, I am frightened to sing it. . . ."

"But will you not give us the Song of the Black Lark?
Everyone is expecting it. . . ."

"Yes," I said. "That will be first . . . but then I have written
another—I think that man will call it . . . sedition. . . ."

His eyes leaped suddenly with some unknown fire. "You are
sure?"

I nodded. He snapped his fingers, loud; that same slave boy
came, and he whispered, low and long, gesturing toward the wall
where the row of dancers stood, some twenty-five of them, I saw
now.

I think that no one else noticed, for all eyes were on Drom, and
the lights were low, but I saw the boy go over to the thick,
ungainly dancer and whisper in her ear; she nodded, and patted
something under her girdle, passing the word to the next one,
and on down the line. The very last one handed the slave boy
something from under her robe, something that gleamed; the boy
tucked it into his loincloth. I wondered, dimly, but the dance was
over now, and it was my time.

As in a dream, the faces all swimming before me, I let
Melanippos lead me forward to the center of the room, carrying
my lyre; a chair had been placed for me, backless and easy to
work in, directly in front of the Tyrant's couch. I began to tune
up; a hush fell. The last thing I saw before I began to sing was
the face of Melanchros, Tyrant of Mitylene, beaming broad and
with the grease of the feast still shining on it.

I gave them the Song of the Black Lark, beloved all over the
city; three times they demanded it, and at the last all the voices
joined in. My nervousness had fallen away, as I had known it
would. I felt borne up on wings, as though I were indeed that
bird. Some Muse was in me, but also a god was there, making me
brave. For all my fears had gone.

When that song was finished, I gave them some sweet love
songs, light and gay; I remember the lovely face of the child
Atthis, rapt. It drew me, and I sang the last small song to her. It
was almost an improvisation, though it had been going through
my head for a while. A little thing of no consequence, but with a
sweet catching air; about the red apple high, high upon the
topmost bough, that the pickers had forgot. How sweet the apple

that none could pick, for none could reach it . . . none till now . . .

That was the end of the little piece, and I looked straight at the child-maid and bowed, with my hand over my heart. She was covered with confusion and blushes, for all looked at her, knowing her honored. I had already the greatest reputation in the islands and that is no more than the truth. Cruel it was to single her out, perhaps, but some naughty god had prompted me; at least that is what I told myself then. And what harm to point out her beauty to all? She was certainly beloved of Aphrodite; never had I seen such a fair maid, and still a child, with all her coltish graces stiff and sweet upon her.

I waited, very still, for complete silence, as all true performers know how to do. It came; I struck one loud note, like a crash, that reverberated through the hall, its echoes coming back from the walls. Now was silence indeed, and awe. I stared at the face of the Tyrant, long and hard. I am only a small dark little singer, but his eyes dropped first. He fiddled a bit with the folds of his robe, and said, fussily, "Well, get on with it, child—you have another song? . . ."

"Yes," I said, and solemn. I struck another note, higher, and began to play softly, speaking over the music. "This is a song for the city," I said. "It is a dirge. . . ."

Never had I heard such stillness; I think truly that no one breathed. I did not sing the song's words, but spoke them, low. Still, all the words were heard, make no mistake.

It is long ago and the song has never been sung; nor have I set the words to paper as I spoke them then, so I have forgotten the song in its entirety. But it went something like this:

"I am a baby girl and voiceless, but my dust will cry out forever . . . let Sappho speak for me, since I never had time in my short life to learn . . . to the fire was I given, to the fire was I lost . . . weep for me, women . . . weep for me, girls . . . weep for me, the pure in heart, for Demeter, a mother herself, did not demand this sacrifice of blood. The tyrant demanded it . . . and paid for it with the gold of Lesbos . . . the fire is too good for him . . . Cry out, my dust . . . cry out forever . . . Weep, weep, weep . . . till the seas overflow . . . till the sacrificial fires are quenched . . . O weep!"

I plucked the strings once more, a long, harsh thwang, and then was still. The torches flickered, the only movement. I stared, but saw nothing, knowing that my death stared back at me.

Suddenly the thin voice of Melanchros rang out, high as a flute note, but loud in the stillness. "Seize her . . . seize the traitor!"

I saw the young men of his guard run forward, their spears held before them; one's hand reached for my throat, I felt it, the fingertips just grazing it, before he went down, looking surprised, a dagger protruding from his chest at the side. All was confusion, shrieks and the spurting of blood. I had some dim notion that all the city guards were killing each other; I could not make sense of it, for upon the dais no one had moved, but sat like statues.

Suddenly I realized that all the guard lay dead upon the marble, and their spears in other hands. I watched one of the dancers wipe a bloody dagger upon her hiked-up robe; beneath the robe her legs showed thick and hairy. Another snatched off her Egyptian wig and mopped the bloody soles of her feet. *Her* feet, I said—but of course they were men, soldiers all, the promised contingent from the army. No wonder they had shown so clumsy in the dance!

The hall was a shambles, corpses sprawled among the overturned tables and the spilled wine; it looked as if a war had been fought. And of course it had. And won. I looked to the dais. Melanchros was on his feet at last; I counted more than a dozen daggers sticking from his body, like a boar that has been cornered in the hills. Each had had his turn at the kill; still, he was not dead. I saw one of the dancers, the most awkward one, draw a stolen spear and thrust it through the Tyrant's stomach. He swayed, but did not fall. I heard a voice I knew, and had heard all evening beside me, cry, "Mine . . . he is mine!" And Melanippos, that dainty, fastidious creature, plunged a dagger into the sagging throat, beneath the folds of the chin. The Tyrant turned his pale eyes upon this last assailant, reached out his hand, feebly, as if to touch him, and whispered, the words bubbling, "My boy . . ." His eyes still upon him, the Tyrant sank slowly to the floor. The eyes still stared, but there was no life in them; he was dead. Melanippos turned away. His face was grim, set in lines terrible to see, but, even from the distance where

I watched, I saw the tears, glittering like gems, in his eyes. I remembered then; the Tyrant Melanchros was his uncle. Perhaps, once, long ago, he had held the little nephew on his knee, giving him a bright chain to play with, or a bit of honeycomb for a treat.

Chapter 11

They cut the Tyrant's head from his body and set it above the Temple of Demeter, and hung his poor corpulent body upside down and naked in the agora. Charaxus went to see it and jeer, like all the other boys, even those who had been his personal guard. I thought it was a sickening thing; none of us girls went to the marketplace till the crows had picked it clean. None, that is, except Gorgo; her father, Pittakos, had given the order. Maybe he was right, and a symbol had to be shown the people. But it was never the nobles' way.

Still, his tyranny was over, and the rule in the hands of good men and just, that were voted on in council. I made note in my head that no woman's vote was counted; for now I let it go, but meant to make issue of it later, when I was older and come into my inheritance.

I remembered little, after, of that night of terror. Isolated things, like pictures, remained in my mind. Gorgo, snatching a dagger for herself and stabbing again and again with it, her face like her namesake's, the Gorgon's. The young man beneath her stabbing hand was long dead and his face empty and innocent as a child's. Drom wresting the dagger from her and hurling it into a corner, and Gorgo sobbing loud, staring in horror at her hands, held out before her, covered in blood, like red gloves. The happy, excited face of the little Atthis, running to climb into the arms of the dancer-soldier, her brother Antimenades; he was, of course, that thickest-set one, and I should have recognized him; there was nothing womanish in that face! Praxinoa, calm, leading all the sobbing women from the hall, and giving them juice of poppy to still their cries and make them sleep. Aunt Kassie in a faint, and my brother Larichus vomiting. Father and Uncle Drakon, like bowing jointed dolls, each trying to seat the other in the couch of honor, while Pittakos walked up beside them and sat there himself, picking his nose!

Father, after, like all the others of the council, was not at home much, for many laws had to be changed and many of the old civil customs brought back. They retained the civil guard, but took away their arms, teaching them instead to patrol the dark streets and the low haunts near the waterfront. I said their arms were taken away; this was not quite so. They were issued clubs and daggers, but were ordered to use them only in self-defense; they went in pairs only, never alone, and carried horns to warn of crimes or to summon aid if it was necessary. They were paid well, and many of those poor boys who might have grown up pickpockets or cutthroats found it more lucrative to work for the city law.

The beggars were banished from the temple steps and housed in workhouses or outlying farms; this, however, was not so successful, for they were not used to doing any sort of labor, even light, and felt their calling had been taken from them. Father sighed, and said social ills could not be cured in a day. Prostitution, too, could only be vaguely regulated; there will always be men who exploit unprotected women, and women, too, who would rather do that than beat linen on the rocks or serve at table. They could not be driven from Aphrodite's Temple, for this would have flouted every old custom of our religion; for decency, though, they were forbidden to lie with their customers within the temple walls, and must go into the grove instead. Now, at least, a decent woman might visit the goddess and worship without shame!

Not the least of the improvements is that perhaps the end of the war may be near. The Council of Nobles has voted to sue for peace with Athens and to ask for a mediator, acceptable to both cities, to settle the dispute. All Mitylene waits for Athens' answer!

Little Atthis has joined the group of girls that study at our house; in particular she takes her lessons with me, for it is song and music that draws her most; for a beginner she shows some talent, but her beauty distracts me. I find myself staring at the golden line the light from the window draws about her body as she sits before it, her head bent to the harp; when the breeze blows her soft unbound hair so that it brushes my cheek, I tremble. For she is young, so young; too young even for the small caresses that the rest of us girls play at as we lie idle among the cushions of an evening, dreaming of love. I speak of it as if it were now, days of innocence, days of flowers, days of sweet longing, free of pain. Would I have them back again, those days? Only the gods know. I look now, years after, at my old hands, hands that have written immortal lines, held warm flesh, dropped thirsty dust upon the dead; I see the twisted, knotty, swollen veins, and remember the pale branching of *her* mortal veins, delicate below her palm where the thin wrist begins; thin wrists, blue veins, living pulse. Atthis.

Would I have them back again, the days of my youth? One wonders what accidents have made us as we are. Or was it fate, *moira*? Thales has said that it is useless to wish to live one's life over, for it would be no more than a repetition. We are what we are.

I am no philosopher, or even much of a storyteller; I am a poet. I suppose, truly, on thinking, I would like to have each instant again as it passes; there is never enough time, nor has ever been, to savor life to the full. The gods felt that, I am certain, or they would never have chosen immortality.

I wonder now why I have digressed. Is it to put off the telling of what happened next? Or is it that I do not quite remember the sequence? There was much confusion just then, in Mitylene, and inside myself, my inner self, as well.

As I have said, we were all waiting for the end of the war; none of us girls was old enough to remember life without war somewhere in its background. It was a page unwritten, in a book one cannot even guess at.

The nobles of Athens and our own city agreed to end the struggle, with as much decency and honor as possible. They put it to the vote, in both cities, as to who should mediate the chronic quarrel; the man they chose, in the end, was a choice that to me was a strange one. For he was the most famous of the Tyrants, Periander of Korinth; I should have thought Mitylene, at least, would have had enough of such men, having just got rid of one in a bath of blood. However, he was agreed upon, and accepted the position of trust, and journeyed to the Sigeum, where the armies rested, with no more than a trickle of a stream, mostly dried up, between. One imagines them exchanging sallies, and even songs, across the gap, bored as they would be with the waiting. Or, who knows, perhaps they crossed over, under cover of night, each to each, making friends. They were all Greeks together, after all. That was what was so silly about the whole thing, to us girls, at least.

The young men who had pulled down Melanchros, the soldiers that had posed as dancing girls, went back to wait out the peace talks. We were sorry to see them go; such a novelty they were in our manless lives.

I had grown quite fond of Antimenades; we had talked much, of art and music and song—and Alkaios, always Alkaios. Antimenades had taught me many of his songs, those that he had written earlier; he had a deep voice, but true, and easy to follow. The songs were good, though light and superficial, for Alkaios was only a child when he had written them. I learned them the hard way, practicing and polishing, to surprise him when we would meet, finally. It was difficult to get Antimenades to open up at all about himself; at first I thought him secretive, but he was only shy.

Melanippos showed me Antimenades' sculpture, warning me not to tell, for Antimenades himself would show it to no one, thinking it worthless. Far from it, to my way of thinking, and I could not but tell him so, and praise it. His teacher scolded him for imitating the ancients. Why not? They were better than the sculptors of our day, no question. And Antimenades had added something of his own, as all artists do, if they are true to themselves; his figures were real, close to life, but nobler, with movement in them and no stiffness such as one sees nowadays. He was much pleased, and asked, stammering a little, if I would sit for a head in clay; it would take only an hour at most.

I cannot say that I admired the result, really, though everyone exclaimed that it was me to the very life; I had not known that my nose had an upward tilt, or the back of my neck two little hollows. Of course, one never sees oneself from all sides. He had painted it, as a potter does, baking on the glaze after; I thought he had made my skin too brown, but when I held my face beside it and a mirror up to both, I saw it was the exact shade. I resolved to use the almond bleach faithfully after this; often I forgot.

When the young men went back to the Sigeum, some of the elder statesmen went, too, along with that Periander of Korinth; Athens, too, would send its emissaries, to make treaty. My father went, and Drakon, and a man named Myrsilos, and, of course, Pittakos. He was always in the thick of things, somehow. This Myrsilos was an upstart, really; he was only second generation of his line on Lesbos, and it was whispered that his grandfather had been a slave. I very much doubt this, for he had great wealth; I think it much more likely that his forebears had been slavers, a far worse thing, to my mind. I say this because much of his wealth came from saltmines that he owned in Thrace, and these, of course, are worked by slaves, who mostly die, for the life is very hard. Also, it was known that he owned slave ships, making regular runs to the African lands, and stopping at all the islands to sell off stolen merchandise. It made me shudder, for maybe Drom had come to us on one of his ships! I knew him by sight only, but he had an evil face, drooping nose and loose lips, and eyes that were hooded like a hawk's. I could not imagine the other nobles tolerating his company, but Father said he was clever and sly, and that such shrewd men are a great asset when one is dealing with the enemy.

Uncle Erigyus did not go, but moved into our house as protector and head, with all his family and servants. Strange to say, Uncle Drakon took Aunt Phaedra along; perhaps he did not trust her, though I should think there would be better pickings in a whole army than here, where men are as scarce as rooster's eggs! So we were rather crowded in our house, large as it is, for all Drakon's family were with us too, including some tiring women to serve them.

It was rather fun, actually, like a continuous party. I did not get much work done, for inspiration does not often come to one in the middle of a crowd. But, all of us being there together, we had lessons only sporadically, as if we were on holiday, though Praxinoa gave the smaller children an hour every morning at writing and sums, while it was still cool. The rest of us practiced our various skills and arts as best we could, trying to find unoccupied corners. After Antimenades left, there was quite a craze among us for drawing and working in clay. Melanippos came every day, or nearly, and taught us the rudiments of these things, bringing little Atthis for her own lesson with me.

I think, also, that Father had asked Melanippos to look in on us; he had more sophistication than Uncle Erigyus, who, for instance, still thought of Charaxus as a little boy. Charaxus, who had one bastard already belowstairs, and another kitchenmaid boasting that she felt a kicking in her belly!

At first I felt that I was another reason for Melanippos'

appearances; I was, after all, the first to have known him, and I had a high opinion of my charms. Except for Dika, who was much like me, but quieter, I was much the prettiest girl; one could not count Atthis, she was still only an awkward child, and his ward, besides.

Of course, I cared nothing for him in any sort of meaningful way, thinking him womanish and almost an ancient; still I was piqued to find that it was Telesippa who had caught his eye, that shy, plain maiden who had nothing but adoration to offer. They were much together, after lessons, holding hands in corners and walking in the gardens.

He was old enough to be her father, but she bloomed in his attentions like a flower that opens to the sun. He did much for her; he had exquisite taste in all things, and taught her how to dress and wear her hair. In later years she was often called "the beautiful"; it was no more than a certain distinction and style she had, ever, but he brought it out.

I think we were all a little jealous; he was the only man about, after all, that was not a kinsman, never mind his fine-drawn looks. Their names were a problem, Melanippos and Telesippa, so long, so alike, and with the same rhythm in the speaking. Gorgo, with her unerring sense of the ridiculous, called them Nip and Sip; we stuffed pillows in our mouths all one night to keep from giggling.

For it was hot that summer; hot, so hot, even the perfumed nights brought no relief and only made us giddy. We slept on the roof, we girls, all in a row on pallets, like wounded on the deck of a warship that is limping home through the waves. It is an odd simile for me to use, that, for as yet I had never seen such a sight; but as I toss my mind back into that summer, somnolent, waiting, unreal—we were wounded, all of us in our flowering girlhood, pretty, soft, laughing, wounded things. Life was seeking us out with its long fingers, and the merest touch brought the gift of pain. Or so I remember it now—my long gone maidenhood.

Too hot it was for sleep; sometimes we would lie talking, laughing low, till the first streaks of dawn showed and the little wind we called the breath of Apollo blew. There were a lot of us, besides our household, distant cousins, friends from across the city, staying for the night; I have forgotten now all their names,

but many were pretty and gay, or pretty and pensive, and all
were very young.

We used to talk of sweet silly things, a new perfume or a new
dress, a dance step, a wedding, our own bridegrooms, as yet
unknown. We whispered secret knowledge, too, blushing in the
dark, and sometimes lying close and kissing, exploring with our
hands, tentative. Or we would pretend to be bride and groom, on
a wedding night, not knowing much of what went on, and
giggling all over again.

I was lying with a girl named Hermione, I remember, on her
pallet; she smelled of roses always, and her hair was crisp and
curling to the touch. I put my fingers into it, twisting, and pulling
her head downward to my breast; I felt her lips, soft as a bird's
wing, and gave a little moan. Suddenly I felt her being yanked
away, and heard Gorgo, harsh, "You want to know how it is
done? This is the way!" And she threw her hard body down upon
mine, pressing hard on all our lengths, her mouth bruising me
and her teeth cutting into my lips. Her hands were rough and
demanding, and my flesh shrank from them; I went still as a
stone. She flung me away from her with a curse I had never
heard, "Well, doll-baby—and here I thought you'd been wanting it!" She sat back on her heels, looking down into my face;
though the moon was dark, I could see her teeth shine; she was
laughing!

I got up onto my elbow, pulling my fallen robe up to my chin
and my tattered dignity around me. I lifted my chin as high as I
could. "Have you been watching your father, then?" I said,
nastily. It hit the mark; I think she hated Pittakos, really, for all
they were so alike. There was a charged moment; I could feel her
looking at me. "You *are* a bitch, Sappho . . . I was only doing
you a favor. Next time don't ask for it!" And she was gone. The
silence under the silent stars was so thick you could feel it. Of
course everyone had heard.

Soon after, the rains came, the heavy rains that the gods send
to wash the air and break the heat wave. We had no need to
sleep on the roof, for the nights grew cool and pleasant, and our
giddy moods were blown away. We all, our great household, got
back to our work and our lessons, and had no more night visitors
among the neighbor maidens; they had their own home duties,

too, of course, though some did no more than spin or sew. Also I think that ugly scene had sobered us all; we had been drunk on our own innocence, and now there was, sadly, a little sliver of shame.

There was still no word from the Sigeum; not even a runner with a message or a private letter. Nothing was posted, either, in the agora, though we went every day to look at the temple doors. The city crier, too, called the hours, and that was all; no news. There was nothing for it but to wait.

I was restless and a strange mood was on me; I could not make songs by day, and I could not sleep at night. My monthly courses came, and made me very ill, indeed; I had to get into bed with hot compresses to ease the cramps, a thing that had never happened before. When it had passed and I got up, I felt shaky still, and wrung with nerves; a vase, dropped by a housemaid, and shattering on the floor, could make me burst into sudden tears. And still I could not get to sleep, often till dawn; next day I went about with heavy eyes, red and swollen.

One night, lying alone and staring through my window at the moon and counting the stars, I threw the coverlet from me and rose. I tiptoed softly, not wanting to wake anyone, thinking to mount to the roof, breathe the air, ease my aching head. It was chilly; the floor was cold on my bare feet; I threw a robe about my shoulders.

From the time that she had come to us, Drom had slept in the small antechamber off my own; I went very softly past her bed. The moon had not yet set; I glanced down to make sure I had not disturbed her. In a shaft of thin light from the latticed window I saw that her bed was empty and rumpled, the coverlet thrown back. I smiled a little; she had gone outside to relieve herself; she would never use the little chamberpot. I went on past, warily, and climbed the stairs.

It was quite cold already on the rooftop; we would have an early autumn. I shivered, but the air was good; the stuffiness had almost left my head. I looked up at the stars; so close they seemed. I might have reached up my hand and touched one; for the first time in weeks a song flared briefly in my head, as quickly gone; I would think about it later. For another moment or two I stood, breathing deep; then I turned to go. Something caught my eye, dimly glimpsed to my left, some movement. I froze, staring.

A cloud passed from the face of the moon, making a brightness where I looked. I saw a heap of tumbled clothes, colorless in the silvery light; a pallet on the ground, left over from the hot nights, and upon it, prone, two bodies, dark and pale, strained close, the limbs writhing like snakes. Wrestling! Drom and Gorgo! And in the cold dark. And naked. And then it came to me, in shame and flame, the heat rising slowly from my heels up to my head. No. Not wrestling. I do not know how long I stood there, it seemed forever, and time stopping; then I turned, blindly, and went stumbling down the stairs, holding hard to the rail as if I were drowning in a dragging sea.

There was someone in my room; Praxinoa, holding a saucer of oil, with a wick floating in it, a night light, very small. I could see her face dimly above it, long shadows thrown upward, making her wraithlike and insubstantial. "You have seen them?" she asked, softly. There was a great tenderness in her voice; I wanted to weep. "It has been going on for a week or two now . . . I could not see how to tell you. . . ." I nodded, dumbly.

She set down the night light on a little table beside my bed, and slipped her robe from her shoulders, shrugging it to the floor; it lay in a soft pool about her feet. She was beautiful; even in the small light one could see the cool length of her, perfect, edged with radiance, an Astarte; so beautiful the breath caught in my throat. "Come to bed," she whispered. "Come to your bed, little sweetheart . . ."

She drew me down beside her, slipping her arms around me under my robe. I knew that my face was wet now with tears against her shoulder; she made soft soothing noises and stroked my hair. "Which of them is it that hurts you? . . ." she asked tenderly. "Drom, is it? Or Gorgo?"

"Yes . . . no . . . I do not know. . . ." And I sobbed, miserably.

"You are jealous of their love. . . ." She kissed my wet face. "You taste of salt," she said, and I saw she smiled a little smile. "Stop weeping, my darling . . . stop . . ." She reached her arm above her head, loosening the pins from her hair; it fell about our two bodies like a golden mantle, sweet-smelling. I shuddered as her hands touched me.

She was my first teacher in all things, and in this, too.

I knew the aching, and the wonder, and the release. I saw the face of love, but its eyes were turned from me. Behind my own closed eyelids I saw the pale wide woman's eyes of the child Atthis, and, merging as in a dream, the unknown cloudy eyes of Alkaios.

BOOK II

Pyrhha

(Told by Alkaios,

soldier-poet)

Chapter 1

This war is a bore, no question. Perhaps they all are, all wars, never mind what the poets say. For I am a poet myself; I can make verses, sing songs, play a martial air to set the blood to tingling. It is my calling; why not?

When I first came here, to the front, I was fourteen, and lied about my age to get into the army. Now—if I could think of another lie to get out, without disgracing myself any more than I already have—but that is impossible. At any rate, the whole business is coming to an end any day now, or so the rumor goes. It will be a limping end—but an end, thank the gods. Already the nobles of our side and the other, the Athenian, have set sail with a mediator, and will negotiate for peace. Let us hope the peace will go faster than the war, or I shall be stuck here, in Homer's land, to the end of my days!

That is the thing that drew me, you see, the grandeur, the glory of Homer . . . the liar! For this barren plain, where I sit sweltering or shivering, and writing when no one is looking, is the very site where once golden Troy stood in all its splendor. Very likely the splendor was a few mud huts and a puny castle on a rock, and its treasure a few bagsful of dusty gold and some poor starved skinny women. Ten years they spent here, our hallowed Greek forefathers; cattle stealers, rapists, butchers, heroes.

They at least, those old boys, knew what they were fighting for; plunder, pure and simple, and the destruction of another race. We are accomplishing the same thing, in our own way. Like locusts, we have laid waste the fields; there are no crops, no pastures, and no animals left to pasture anyway. For a honeyed fig, any boy of Sigeum city will sell you his sister, and she herself will lie down all night for a barley loaf from the army stores. Of course, it is off limits, Sigeum city, but it makes no matter; any soldier can find his way there without even tiptoeing, and the commanders wink at it. Outdoing the old heroes, our armies have been in this place for fifteen years, and discipline is slack by now on both sides.

I have said they knew what they were fighting for, in the old days; the great liar-bard blamed Helen, to stick in a little romance. She was no more than a wayward whore, and Menelaus her cuckold. Agamemnon was a brute, and Achilles— well, he had his heel. I am what you might call disenchanted; so are we all, though no one but me says so.

Why are we here at all? And why are the Athenians? We are not even fighting these people of the Troad, though we are destroying them, no question. We are fighting each other, year after weary year, for a foothold in an alien land, a trading post, a free passage up the Hellespont. Who needs it? Is that what civilization has made of us—merchants? Such is progress. Nothing.

Our fame will not even live after us, for there is no bard to sing his lies. I am the only poet around these parts, and I gave up war ballads after the first year. (I have now been here four.)

True, when I got here, I was all afire; the clash of swords was music, and every camp follower a Helen. I loved a youth, my captain, named Phenius, and we swore to be Achilles and Patrokles, inseparable in war and love. He was killed in the skirmish I ran away from; I left my arms on the field, and, unburdened, escaped. So the Athenians got my weapons, and his, too, to hang upon their temple walls, and his lovely flesh rots in the stinking war furrows. I wrote a beautiful lament, and wept thin, salty tears; our affair, like the war, had gone on too long; there was no savor left, even in the mourning.

So many have died in the high days of their youth; glazed eyes staring blindly at the white, god-blinded sky; pale, bleached bones of the living, laughing comrade, picked clean by the mercy of the vultures' beaks; the beating black wings loud in the battle hush, waiting, waiting. So many have been torn and maimed, patched up, shipped back, to rot, living, on the temple steps and the agoras of Mitylene and Athens; to scrabble in the street dust for the coin thrown from the flawless white hand of the innocent maid, to stink in the nostrils of the perfumed adulteress. The glory of war. I drink to it.

There was a little girl, a native of these foothills of Mount Ida, where we make camp. A little girl, about the age of my sister, Atthis, but no longer pretty, if she had ever been. How many times had she been raped? There was still a little life left in her

when I ran the last of the fellows through; I heard her moan
softly under his death cry. He was only a common soldier though
he was one of ours, so they did not kill me for it, but put me in
chains for a month. She must have come timidly, begging a crust
of bread from the golden warriors; had they sung the songs of
Homer, too, around the hearthfire of her home?

And the Athenians are no better; maybe they are worse,
depending how you look at it. They caught a pretty boy of ours,
an armor bearer, gently bred, and sent part of him back. They
made a eunuch of him; a deaf eunuch, for they sent the ears, too.
O, the high wars. I drink to them. But I grow maudlin; I would
drink anyway, the wine is the only good thing in this army.

Well, there you have my war songs. An end to it, Alkaios—get
on with your story.

When I first set foot on these shores, I gaped in wonder; I was
a raw lad, of course, and did not think. In all the vast plain of
Troy and the mountains behind, there was no shred of green,
though it was spring, and rainy, too. High, high, upon the very
peaks of Mount Ida there was a little scrub of trees, low slung
and white with snow. But below, and stretching before us, the
newest contingent from Mitylene, there was nothing at all but
gray mud, and, in the hollows, black mire. When one looked
closely at the ground, where it had dried, it was all dented and
hollowed, full of potholes and furrows. The prints of horses and
men, if one looked very close, and the deep ruts where chariots
had gone. A battlefield. For years a battlefield. A wasteland; for
a hundred years nothing will grow there. Perhaps, I fancied,
nothing had grown there since the days of the old heroes.

I spoke of it to a veteran of five springs; he said, shaking his
head, that no, when he came there was still some grass upon the
hillsides, but the skirmishes had killed that, too. I made him
curious, and he asked around, of those that had been there from
the first days of our war. They were hard to find, naturally; who
survives so long? Except generals and the like, and they are not
so readily available for questioning. Finally, though, we found
one, a rough fellow with one side of his face all knotted and
pulled together, scars crisscrossing his cheek and one eye
half-closed. One of the knives on a chariot wheel had caught
him, where he lay fallen in its path; he thought himself lucky to
be alive and grinned with the good side of his face. "Yes," he

said, "it was all green, rolling hills and valleys, and little gurgling streams. A lovely sight—till we got at it . . . and then . . ." And he jerked his thumb toward the Athenian camp and spat, for luck. So time heals all, I thought to myself. When we are gone, sheep will graze here, and shepherds will sing of a night around the fire to keep up their spirits against our battle ghosts. And children will play lightly at war with wooden swords, and cry over who has to play the losing side. After we are dead and gone. I do not like to think of that; it makes me thirsty. I pray to Zeus I will not pass with a sword in my hand, but a wine jug.

I am always confined to quarters, for some reason or other, some breach of conduct, or so it seems. I have not once had leave in all these years—no, I take that back. I *did* get leave, last year, and made it all the way home on shipboard. But a sea voyage, when it is calm, is a tiresome thing, especially when the ship is literally swarming and one cannot have a moment to think or a corner to call one's own. So one must invent ways to pass the time. The food was loathsome, after the first week or so, the bread rock-hard and moldy, too, and the meat rotten, except for the maggots; our fresh water gave out, so there was nothing but wine to drink. I do not complain of that, but, with boredom and lightheadedness, I was indiscreet, and made mischief; we were in sight of land, our last night out.

I was roaming the crowded decks, alone, unable to sleep for the snoring and the smells; there was just enough moon to see my way about. Behind a great coil of rope, I caught sight of two figures, naked, writhing, in a posture natural or unnatural, according to how one thinks of it. One was my sergeant, a brawny brute, hateful, who had gone to his superiors with many a tale of sodomy and made trouble; here he was, caught in his own trap, as it were, to put it crudely. I crept up, unnoticed, for he was occupied, to say the least, and tied their four ankles together with a bit of red cord I had upon me. You can imagine the scene; they could not, that pair, positioned as they were, summon enough agility to untie themselves!

Of course, they had not seen who did the tying; I might have got away free, except that they caught a young boy, with the smooth milky cheeks of a maid, and frightened eyes, and accused him; they were about to flog him. I had seen such floggings before; it takes much to endure one, he might even have died.

What could I do? I confessed. It is unlawful to flog a noble, but there went my home leave. I sat it out on shipboard, and never set foot on shore.

I have disgraced myself over and over; half my time has been spent on latrine duty or in chains. Most of what I have done is just disinclination for war work; I have not always made willful mischief. First off, being familiar with chariots and horses, I was assigned, in my very first skirmish, one of the few war chariots; the wheels have flashing blades attached, deadly things. When I saw I was likely to hit someone with a wheel, I swerved, and went the other way, out of the battle. I begged off that time, saying the horse bolted. Next time I was mounted, and given a fine war-horse that had seen many a battle and was used to the blood-smell. He did my fighting for me; I sat atop him, sword undrawn and stiff with horror, while he reared and trampled, reared and trampled. Afterward, I vomited, remembering the mangled things beneath his iron-clad hooves. That earned me my first latrine job; it is supposed to strengthen the stomach.

I suppose it did; after a bit I killed my first man. If I had not, he would have had me. He looked surprised; they always do. I would rather run, but it is not always possible; sometimes the way is blocked. So, one fights, one stabs, one slashes, one kills. It is war. One grows used to it, shocking as it may seem. After a while, fear goes, too. In the midst of battle, my only fright is that I will perhaps slip in the blood or the spilled guts.

I should have liked to have gone home with those twenty-odd that pulled down Melanchros; the whole idea of dressing up as dancing girls was mine, and I reaped none of the benefits. For, just at the last, and leave due next day, I was caught off limits. As I have said, usually they wink at it, the commanders. But with me they do not; I am so many times over an offender. I did not even have my fun off limits; every girl I picked was a hag by candlelight, and I wasted obol after obol paying them off, and ended up with a street boy. I might as well have stayed in camp!

I should have liked to have met the little Sappho, too, after all these months of exchanging letters; they are singing that song already—the one that precipitated the fall of the Tyrant—already, here in camp, so far away! It is a wonder to me always how such things can travel. Of course, they are back now, the soldiers that dressed as women; Antimenades says they do not have the song quite right, either words or music, but the gist of it is clear. A brave girl she must be, indeed. And a great artist, too—for he let her finish the song, Melanchros, before giving the order to seize her.

Strange—I feel some sadness at the dreadful end of that man. I remember him, the uncle of Melanippos, as wise and learned and sensitive beyond other folk, before he came to power. Of course, I was only a child; perhaps it is that he paid some small attention to me, and I, an orphan, was flattered. In my mind's eye I see him, benign and balding, with a baby's skin and fastidious manners, and only running a little to fat. The power he seized was his ruin, and it is so with all such men. One has only to look at the famous Periander of Corinth; his vices are marked in his face for all to see. They say he is ninety; certainly he looks it, his face crisscrossed with wrinkles and a palsy shaking him like a small constant wind. But still he can control the shaking, on occasions of state, and his orator's voice shows how he can sway men when he wishes. Close to, there is evil in his face, carved deep; but behind the eyes is something else I cannot put a name to, sorrow, shame, a begging look. He killed his wife, it is said, in a fit of mad jealousy; he had loved her to distraction, and, after, would not part with her body, but kept it, rotting, in his chambers, embracing it and begging it to come alive again. They say the great singer, Arion, finally, quieted the mad murdering lover by a song, and Periander suffered the body to be burned and the ashes buried. Melissa was the lady's name, a soft whispering name, and poor Periander consulted all the oracles of the dead to bring back her soft whispering shade. She had been a lady of purity and honor, innocent of the foul suspicions he put upon her; he suffered dread remorse, begging her forgiveness from beyond the grave.

There is a strange tale told; of course the man was mad with grief for years. It seems that finally, at Epirus, in a grove of oaks, the shade of Melissa appeared to the old women that served the oracle there. This shade, they said, was wringing her hands and shivering, saying that she was cold; she had no clothes, she said, for the dresses that had been buried with her ashes had not been burnt formally on the funeral pyre and thus had no existence in the world of shadows. As proof that it was really she who spoke, she said some words that only he would recognize, for he had said them to her the night of her death. "The oven is cold when I bake my bread in it," were these words, a wild accusation of her indifference. The tyrant fell into a fit, frothing at the lips and beating his fists upon the ground. When he came out of the fit, he determined to give his Melissa the finest wardrobe in Hades. Every woman in Korinth, he determined, should contribute. Cunning he was, though; he suspected that these women, when called upon, would give their second-best, their old clothes, in fact. He hit upon a brilliant piece of strategy; at the festival of Hera, the women all dressed in their finest, his servants went among them there assembled, and politely but firmly stripped them to their undergarments making a huge bonfire of the beautiful clothes, and the priests, as the flames leaped high toward the heavens, dedicated all these to the long-dead Melissa.

The women were enraged, but their husbands smiled behind their hands; it was the first public display of the new strictures that Periander had put upon extravagance! Those gentlemen laughed on the other side of their faces, though, when he took away their surplus gold to build a colossal figure of himself to ornament the city!

All of this tale may be just that, a tale; such stories spring up about such men in high places. True it is, though, that he was much hated by his own people, in spite of his long reign over them; he never went anywhere, even among us, who had asked for his services, without a large armed bodyguard.

Well, they are all here now, our elder statesmen, their noble faces a little reddened and roughened by the sea voyage, and all their wrinkles showing white from squinting into the sun; Drakon's high nose is peeling from the wind, the salt, and the bright rays; the little Sappho's father has fared well, bleached streaks shining in his light brown hair—a handsome man. She does not take after him, though, the poetess, for Antimenades has brought me a head of her, which he has modeled in clay and glazed in bright, lifelike colors; he has copied it from one she sat for, but, amusingly, has left an opening in the top of the head, where the hair is drawn up into a knot, the braids forming two handles on either side.

I shall use it for a wine amphora, and drink from it only Lesbian wine, though I shall tell her it tastes of ambrosia. Truly, if it be a likeness, and my brother swears it is, this little maiden is charming. Not beautiful, perhaps, by our dull Greek standards; there is nothing straight or stern about this face, it is all curve and movement. The chin is tilted forward, small and a little pointed, and the nose tilted too. Skin like old ivory and black, black hair. The brows arch thinly above large dark eyes, which she has lengthened in the Egyptian manner with powdered kohl. The upper lip has a little curl to it, and the lower lip is full, a mouth for kissing. I ask my brother what shape she has; he begins a gesture of description, known to all, and then stops, reddening under his sun-dark skin, and dropping his sculptor's hands. "She is," he mumbles gruffly, "a small-made lady. . . ." I smile to myself; she has not a lady look. Well, it will have to wait. If all goes well, we will meet before my next letter reaches her.

There are innumerable meetings of the nobles, both sides, the old men talking, talking forever, thus and so, back and forth; we of the armies shout taunts across the narrow trickle of dirty brown water that is the River Rhodius. We have no heart in it, none of us wants to fight any longer; upon the opposite shore is many a pretty youth. Friends and lovers there are among them, maybe, if the world were otherwise than old and foolish. One, a black-shocked boy with hair growing wild like long grass, but with a lithe and slender length to him, is fishing in the scant waters. He pulls out a longish fish, red along the gills, and holds it aloft, laughing; he has probably been at it all day, there is little else to do. He sees me watching, and our eyes meet across the small distance. He cries out, "Here, beautiful—catch!" He throws the fish; it falls short, flopping. I run to pick it up, saluting him.

"My thanks," I cry. "What is your name?"

"Mennius."

"Alkaios, here," I called back.

"Have you wine?" he asked. "Here we have nothing but that filthy Egyptian brew. . . ."

"I have wine in plenty . . . but I cannot throw it so far," I answered, laughing.

He squinted up at the sky, cupping his hands and looking to the reddening in the west, where the sun would set soon. He looked back at me. "It will be a dark night . . ." He jerked his thumb to the left. "The stream narrows to nothing . . . just a bit on up . . ."

"I catch your meaning," I said, cupping my own hands. "I will be there. . . . Do you like Samian? I have a jug, almost full . . ."

He made a gesture of clasping his hands above his head, and grinned. Even from here I could see his teeth were very white. Then he tossed his wild hair back and ran off, up the slope.

I looked after him, smiling; then I felt eyes upon me. My brother Antimenades stood beside me, looking heavy and dark, as he can sometimes. He had heard it all.

I shrugged. "What of it?" I said.

"And if you are caught?"

"Then I am caught—like this fish." I held it up, laughing. "And fried like it, too. . . ." I put my arm across his shoulders. "Come—share it with me, brother. We have had nothing but dried goat for weeks."

He shook his big head. "What will I do with you? . . . Well, it is your life, after all."

"Or my death," I said, gaily. "It is all one."

We shared the fish, Antimenades and I, baking it in clay as we had learned from the natives. It was fresh and white, flaking to perfection; with a barley loaf he had brought from home, only a little stale, it was a feast.

In the dark of the moon I crept down to the riverbed, carrying the wine jug and a rushlight sheltered by my cloak. I followed the stream to its narrows, and there he was, waiting, the black-haired youth. There was barely a yard of water between us.

"You brought the wine," he said. "So I shall make the leap."

He jumped over, and sat down beside me; I handed him the jug first, for courtesy. Even in the weak light of the rush I held, I saw his eyes were green as a cat's.

We finished the wine, and, after, lay side by side, watching the stars wink on, one by one.

When the sky grayed with the first hint of dawn, we made our farewells. "Well, dear enemy," I said, "and shall we ever meet again?"

"I hope it may be," said he. "But if not, my next drink of Samian shall be to you. . . ."

I was not caught. But neither did I see him again. It is a large army, the Athenian.

Chapter 2

We had had a commander in chief; naturally, every army does. But I, for one, had never seen him; such men generally do most of their fighting on paper, and usually turn out to be so honorable in length of years that they are decrepit. Such a man was our Mausanius; I saw him finally at the ceremony where he gave up his command, his horse and his sword. The thing was done in full sight of the whole army, drawn up in battle array and standing at attention. I think most were as uncomfortable as I, nobody knowing what moment to cheer or to boo, in a manner of speaking. The poor old thing had a certain battered dignity, in his breastplate and helmet that looked as though it had been taken down off the wall somewhere after thirty years; I remember as a child a shield with the very same boss at the rim, hanging with its sword-mate over the hearthplace in my grandfather's house at Pyrrha.

He was handing over his command to a man named Pittakos, a much younger man, vigorous as a red bull. He had been chief of the conspirators against Melanchros, and, in gratitude, the Mitylenian council had voted him into the job. A pity we were bringing the war to an end, and not beginning it! One might well imagine this one dragging Hector at the heels of his chariot round the walls of Troy, or, if one looked close, inventing the wooden horse as well! One had only to look at him once to read him; he was a mixture of brawn and brain, but vulgar as a Thracian farmer. No matter, he was clearly cast in the heroic mold, rude and crude. I fancy Agamemnon just such a man, red-gold and hairy, with little light eyes that miss nothing. I was standing in the first ranks, next to the platform where he stood to receive the sword of office. My eyes were just on a level with the floor; one look at his feet made me retch. His sandals were new and gilded, but his toes were cracked in black creases and his heels were grimy with the dirt of years. At least, I thought, he will not die Agamemnon's death; if he has a wife she will not murder him in his bath, for clearly he never takes one!

The ceremony was long and boring, as they all are; I found myself remembering all I had heard of this man. He was much respected by all the nobles and invited into their homes, filthy feet or no. And he *did* have a wife, the wealthy and beautiful Chloris, and two legitimate children. His heir, by Chloris, was a young boy still, severely crippled by the Egyptian bone disease; he had a daughter, older, by a Spartan wife that had died. It was the Agamemnon setup, but there was never a whisper of scandal about Chloris—no lover there to aid and abet! It was the other way around, or so they said; Pittakos had a houseful of concubines, like an Oriental, and his bastards ran wild in the streets and peopled the cypressed hills.

There was a subtle change about; one could feel it, somehow. The atmosphere was charged differently. I had been musing, not listening, like everyone else, I guess. Suddenly we were all ears; Pittakos was talking. He was merely thanking his peers, saluting the army, invoking the gods and so forth, but his voice was different from other voices, harsh, with a husky undertone, and a little sibilant; if it had been another man, one might have laughed, for he almost lisped. No one did, however, but listened gape-eyed. He was challenging the Athenian commander to a duel!

Again—it was right out of Homer; the man knew what he was about! But, after, there was a shocked silence. For this Athenian, a man named Phrynon, was one of the most famous pankratists in the world. This was a comparatively new sort of sport; a mixture of boxing and wrestling, and demanding great skill and agility, besides an iron strength. Phrynon had won every contest of this kind in the Olympian games since the sport had been initiated, that is to say, at least three times.

Naturally, the Athenian commander took him up on it, amid loud cheering from his own side; the contest was agreed upon. There were some few long faces among our own nobles, needless to say, much clucking and shaking of heads. But I had been close enough to see the man Pittakos' eyes; I knew he had something up his sleeve (though of course they wore none, both were stripped to the waist).

The contest was set for a week hence; everything takes forever in the army, except dying. Bets were taken on the outcome; even in our own ranks the odds were very long against Pittakos. I had taken his measure, though; he certainly had the strength for it, and the two were evenly matched in weight and roughly the same age, somewhere just under fifty, one would guess. Besides, as I say, I had seen his eyes. I put ten thousand drachmae on him; of course it was just on paper, but I would have to pay up later if things went the other way. My comrades laughed, and would not take my advice. "What wine cask were you sleeping in?" jested one. Antimenades, even, looked shocked. "The man hasn't a chance in Hades . . . he might even be killed!" And he leaned close, saying, "Look, Alkaios, you can take it back . . . the man has never boxed before, or wrestled, much less together . . ."

But I stuck to my hunch, keeping quiet under the taunts.

The day of the contest was like a festival; a great wooden platform had been set up, with ropes around it so they could not push one another off, and the floor sanded to smooth it out. At the last moment Phrynon complained of this, saying it made the surface slippery; so it must be scored over with knives, criss-crossing cuts, to roughen it.

The platform was in a little depression, with sloping low hills all around, making a kind of improvised amphitheater. Both armies were spread out, up to the very tops of the hills, swarming like ants; I had not realized before how much humanity had been packed into this small piece of the Troad lands.

Phrynon appeared first, wild cheers rising from his Athenian ranks. We, on our side, were silent, except for a few muffled groans. The fellow was huge, muscled all over; a giant. His upper arm bulged larger than my waist! It was a gross sight, and no sculptor would want him for model, but in its way it was impressive. Huge calves, the chest of a bull, and a thick corded neck that made his head look small as a fist. He smiled and turned himself about, raising his arms to make the muscles ripple, and showing his knotted back; he held his hands up, fisted, as big as boulders.

When Pittakos appeared, a gasp went up from both sides, and then, suddenly, a huge guffaw. He was carrying, buckled upon his left arm, a shield; in his right hand he held a trident, such as fisherfolk use. One of the nobles came close, Drakon I think it was, and whispered something, low. Pittakos' face did not change; he stared through the man. "No mention was made of weapons," he said. And, turning to face us of his own side he said, "I am descended from Poseidon. . . . Would you laugh at the god?" Truly one could not laugh; he had a face to command, I'll give him that.

Well, all the nobles from both sides dithered back and forth like a gaggle of geese, whispering among themselves, and pulling long faces. But there was nothing they could do; he spoke truth, and nothing had been said of weapons. So, finally, Drakon gave the signal, and they began.

I say began; Pittakos did nothing, while Phrynon circled round him, coming a little nearer each time, and he turning in one spot, with the shield hiding his body, and the trident acting as a sort of staff. Phrynon made a couple of tentative swipes with his fist, but always Pittakos stepped back; the boxer could not get in close enough to land a blow.

Suddenly, so suddenly that we could not see how it was done, Pittakos ceased turning, and let the other man come in behind him. Phrynon's arm was going out for a stranglehold, when Pittakos turned suddenly, whipping a net out from behind the shield and casting it, covering Phrynon and drawing it in as one would a caught fish, the man flopping onto the platform, and all the net gathered in one of Pittakos' hands, rendering the fish helpless. He raised the trident then and plunged it down; a terrible sound went up from the Athenian side; we were too stunned to utter a word or a gasp. At first it looked as though he had pinned Phrynon through the body, but he had simply secured the net; his assailant could only writhe within it.

Pittakos swaggered away from his fallen foe, coming to our edge, where we watched aghast, and drawing a dagger from his belt. "Well, boys," he said, "what will you? Shall I finish him off?" Then, after a pause, came a great roar, half laughter, half triumph, from all our Mitylenian ranks.

"The fish is caught!" cried Pittakos in a loud voice. "Shall I throw him back to my father?" He meant Poseidon, of course, and every man of us got it and laughed again.

"Or shall we eat him for supper?" cried Pittakos.

"No . . . no! He is too tough!" came a loud shout, followed by more guffawing. "Throw him back . . . yes, throw him back!"

Pittakos stood laughing, feet apart, arrogant and bold. He saluted us, raising his hand, and a cheer came, too, of course.

Then he walked away, turning to face the Athenian side. "You have heard the judgment! Poseidon has spared him! He is still yours. Take your champion! But take care . . . I want the net back without holes!" And, so saying, he saluted us again, stepped down, and made to walk away through our ranks. Of course the men were wild with glory and would not let him, but raised him onto their shoulders and carried him through the camp, cheering loudly and calling him "Old Pitt."

It was a name that stuck. Later, when I met his crazy Amazon daughter, she said with scorn that she had invented it; but for me the name was born then, the day I won ten times ten thousand drachmae.

That night I was drunk without benefit of wine; drunk on my own good fortune. To this day I never pass a body of water, however small, without tossing in a coin to Poseidon.

Chapter 3

Well, the war is over. It is, after so long, almost a letdown, and our side has not come out of it very well, except for that brief glory of Pittakos' cheating victory. For Periander of Korinth, the mediator, decreed that each army should keep the lands they were now holding; we happened to be on the downswing at the moment, though territory had changed hands constantly over the years.

The Athenians had been holding the Sigeum, and Sigeum City, though not very strongly, so they were given that part; with it, of course, went the right of passage through the waters of the Hellespont, and a trade advantage. We got nothing but that dry mud of the Troad where we were encamped; at least it was Homer's land, and I wrote a war ballad to cheer us up—my last.

Actually, except for the utter devastation of the place, it was a great deal of territory; once it was cultivated again it could be colonized and become a thriving city. I wished I could be given license to dig there; some of our soldiers had found, not very far down, in the potholes, ancient bronze weapons, and broken bits of pottery with the antique look. Clearly, this land we held was the true site of old Troy of the tales. However, my word is less than nothing, for I have distinguished myself, to say the least, in the worst sort of way. But it is a pity, for much could be learned from this sad, disputed soil. However, I am not the man for it; they will build another city here, on top of the old one. A strange thought has come to me; this is an old, old world. Maybe beneath all our cities are others, lost forever, and our lives are all lived on other men's, that have gone before.

Perhaps, someday, long, long after my time, someone will do this thing, dig up this soil, find the lost Troy, find out how men lived aeons ago. Probably, when it has happened, if ever it does, we will find men have not changed much, if at all. A sad thought, and sobering. I will not think it often. While there is wine, and roses, sweet air to breathe, blood pumping in the veins . . . and love, it is enough. So will I live, while life is in me, make songs when the gods send them, and love when the heart leaps.

Because of Pittakos' exploit of courage and cunning against the Athenian champion, the Council of Nobles has offered him a huge tract of this Trojan land that has been given us. He shakes his head, though, and says he wants no more than the rest of us. When he is pressed, he says, finally, laughing, that he will take for his own however much he can cover with a throw of the javelin; in sight of us all, he throws. It is a fair throw, but one can erect only the smallest of villas upon the area it encompasses. However, he cannot be persuaded, and says he will reserve his bit of land for a playing field for those of Lesbos who come after us, when we have made our colony here. And he says, too, scratching at his wild red beard, "Also we can sink a pool for bathing, paved with mosaic, and depicting sea creatures . . . I shall call it the Place of Poseidon." He has a head on his shoulders, that Old Crack-Toes, and a way with the soldiers, too. He is their only hero, of course, for all the rest are dead in this dragging war. Men need to worship a little, most of them, and the gods are not often available. So, Old Pitt, Old Crack-Toes, wily Pittakos, will have to do for now.

Drakon was my father's friend, and some of the others, too, the father of Sappho among them; I will be let off my misdeeds, for once, and go back on the first of the ships to set sail for home. My heart swells; it is long since I set foot on the dear land of Lesbos.

The peace is signed and seal set to it. We are polishing our gear, so as to make a brave show when we reach home. We none of us have much left; it has been a long war. My arms that I left behind in forfeit for my life have been replaced by a poorly crafted shield and a sword that will not cut through butter, and my sandals are in shreds. I have made friends with some of the natives, though, and one shoemaker presented me with a beautiful pair, soft kid like cloth. I wanted to pay him, but he shook his head; there were tears in his eyes. After, someone told me he was the father of that raped dead child that I had avenged; I wept, myself, then, spotting the beautiful leather of the sandals. I asked her name, the little one, and was told that it was Myrrhina. I made a song for her, a lament, sweet and sad, but short enough to carve upon a burial urn. My brother made the urn, spending much time on it, and carving in the words below. He pictured the child, beautiful, unsullied, being greeted by Proserpina in the realms of death. Her parents transferred her ashes to it, from the plain jar that had held them; it was the finest thing in that humble home. Years later, I passed that way again. True, it had greened over; there was a tiny town there, and called Myrrhina. The urn stood on a pedestal in the center of the small agora. And so she had given something to the world, after all, the poor butchered child. It is not everyone who has a town called after her. In fact, she is the only one I know. Another sobering thought. I must stop thinking.

We set sail for home on a bright blue day, cloudless but with a good brisk wind behind us; still, it was long hours before we lost sight of the mired black battlefield. I watched it till it was no more than a thin dark line of mist, fading. When the gods had wiped it out, as a master does a child's smudge that has been put on the canvas faultily, I went forward, and stood watching the waves parting before the prow. They were blue, bluer than the sky, those Aegean waters, and topped with white foam, forever pure and forever changing. Small wonder the ancients had dreamed an Aphrodite born of this beauty, this evanescence, this clear sea-foam. Once, when we dipped low, and a great wave came up above the rail, I reached out to take some of this stuff of beauty upon my hand; it vanished at my touch, leaving not even a trace of moisture. I have held the goddess in my hand, I thought. So briefly, and all we can have. The long war has left me sad and sick. I turned my thoughts to home.

I heard a step, soft, behind me, and a man came to stand beside me, watching the waters, too. It was Andros, the father of Sappho. I glanced at him, nodding, not wanting to stare; he topped me by a head, a true Hellene. His profile was long and straight, as the sculptors love to mold; one does not see them often, these faces. I thought to myself that the daughter must take after the mother, for I saw nothing there that resembled the girl's head that my brother had done.

He turned to me, holding out his hand; I took it, touching my forehead to it in courtesy and custom. "You have grown well, Alkaios," he said. "I remember you when you were just so high . . ." And he measured off a place somewhere around his knee. We both laughed.

"I am not as tall as I would have wished," I answered. "I am nearly eighteen. . . . Do you think I have time yet to grow?"

"Well," he said, smiling, "I am sure that it is possible. But you are a good height and well made. I am too tall. When I was a boy, it made me awkward, and I got the habit of stooping, making myself look round-shouldered. It had to be beaten out of me in the gymnasium. Even now, sometimes, I forget and do not stand straight."

"Did you know my father, sir? I cannot remember him well, or my mother either, but Antimenades says he was nearly a giant."

He smiled again. "Antimenades was a small boy. All grown-ups look enormous then. Your father was about your size, as I recall. Your mother was almost his height—tall for a woman."

"Yes," I said. "Atthis will be like her. Even four years ago, when last I saw her, she was leggy and long as a colt, and she was then about six years only."

"Yes," he answered. "Atthis is already as tall as my Sappho, who is a woman grown, fifteen years, and a half more to go to make sixteen. . . ."

I could not keep my face from lighting. "Oh, I am glad to hear it! It is how I have pictured her, your daughter." I hesitated a bit, then said, "You know we have been sending letters back and forth? And all in rhyme? I feel as though I knew the maiden. . . ."

He nodded. "I knew," he said, and smiled again, a little wryly. "I knew, but she keeps them hidden, locked up in a chest, like treasure. I suppose to her they are; you are the only poet she knows, except her teacher, Arion, and he is an oldish fellow and fat as well. . . ."

"I think she has great gifts, and so have I told her. . . . That she is small, and pretty, and gently bred is like honey on the cake." I looked into his eyes, straight. "I have not seen a girl of good blood or decent habits in four years; it is a long time. Yet I hope you will permit me to call upon her when we reach Mitylene."

He clapped me on the shoulder, laughing. "She will be at the docks, for sure, to hug me, and, from the shelter of my arms, to spy you out."

"You are kind, sir. My reputation is not all it should be in this army of ours. . . ."

"I know you the son of a dear gone friend, and will welcome you," he said. We stood in silence for a little, watching the waves break in their endless patterns. Suddenly he cried, "There— there it is! Homer's 'wine-dark sea' ! " I looked where he pointed, to our right, and spreading in an arc before us across the way of the ship. The waters were dark, almost as though a line were drawn between the light blue of the true sea. As we came closer, I saw they were purplish, like the unwatered wine of the darkest grape.

"Yes," I said. "I, too, have wondered about that phrase in Homer . . . but, sir, I have come this way before, and I have not seen it thus. Always the waters have been clear, blue like the sky, or sometimes, near shore, greenish because of the grass that grows there. . . ."

He pulled at his beard, thoughtfully. "Perhaps it is something that appears only at some seasons. Clearly it is caused by a growth under the surface, a purple coral, or a strange plant of the sea. . . ."

"It could even be some sea animal, tiny and multitudinous, that comes here to spawn," I said. "There are many creatures in the sea . . . we know so little of it." I shook my head. "I have not seen it before, that is certain."

He said, "I must speak to Thales about this. He will know. For he has made much study of the oceans, believing, as he does, that life sprang from the water in its beginnings." He turned to me. "Do you know this philosopher?"

"I know his name, sir, and his fame." I smiled. "My tutor and guardian, Melanippos, does not think as highly of him as most men do."

"Well," said Andros, and smiling too, "Melanippos was always a romantic . . . he will not hear of sciences or practical things."

"That is odd to my ears," I said. "I have always thought him the worldliest of men."

"That is a mask he wears," said Andros. "I have known him when we were boys. . . . He hides his heart well, 'Nippos."

"I have never heard him called that," I said.

"Well, his name is a mouthful, truly, like my own."

I remembered then the name he bore, Sappho's father. Longer still and hard to say as well. I tried it over on my tongue, softly, not realizing I spoke aloud, "Skamandronymos . . ."

"Yes," he said, smiling, "I was called after the River Skaman- der. I was born upon its banks, though I cannot remember, for I was brought early away to live my life in the city. The river is somewhere hereabouts; I have been watching for it."

"I know it, sir. I have seen the mouth of it, where it pours into the sea. It is ahead, though, I cannot remember how far. But first we must come to a shoal and cut over to shore. . . . Its waters are very green," I said, surprised at myself that I remembered.

I heard a heavy tread behind us, and a hard hand fell upon my shoulder. I turned and looked into the icy Agamemnon eyes of Pittakos.

"I have not yet met this young man," he said, in his harsh Thracian speech. "Alkaios, is it not?" I nodded, a little afraid of him; I do not understand this feeling, but most men have it when they first encounter him face to face.

"I have heard your songs, though," he said, with a certain grace that I did not expect from him. "You have genius . . . like our Andros' girl." He stared at me; I felt that those eyes looked through me, a strange feeling. "They call you coward," he said, and waited, still staring.

Well, it was all or nothing with this man, plain to see. I would not cringe before him. I shrugged, lightly, my eyes still upon his. "I am alive," I said. "If life holds no glory—death holds less."

His eyes moved first; that cannot have happened often. He sighed, heavily. "You speak truth, young Alkaios. There is no glory—except in songs. . . . I have tried my hand at some myself. . . ."

I had heard his poems. Poor things they were, without charm. He had turned again and was looking hard at me, a look like a knife.

"Yes," I said. "I have heard them sung about the fires."

He was silent for a long moment. Then he said, "And think little of them, eh?" And he threw back his head and laughed loud, clapping me again on the shoulder. His touch nearly felled me, but I braced my feet and stood.

"You are no coward, either, Alkaios. You please me. A good enemy is better than a bad friend." It was one of those sayings of his that men have repeated often, but it was said first to me, on the deck of a warship, going home.

Chapter 4

We dropped anchor at the mouth of the Skamander River, by orders of Pittakos; he said we would get fresh water there, and a new supply of grain. It had not been the custom on other journeys, though, and I knew he had done it for Andros, that he might glimpse his birthplace. These were the things that endeared him to his peers, and offset his vulgar habits and his neglect of his person. Most of us Greeks are fastidious to a fault, but Pittakos was forgiven much; it is not often that a man will delay a war-tired army on its homeward way, for the sentimental yearning of a friend.

It was a beautiful valley, the place where the Skamander flowed; it had no look of our rocky, sun-washed Greece; we might have been in another country, softer and kinder, with a dryad behind every tree.

In fact, I found one; we camped there, on land, with the ship harbored at the river's mouth, and sang songs around the campfire after our supper. From the village nearby, folk crept up, keeping their distance, to listen. I caught a glimpse of a slender girl, shy, with long yellow hair; when I sang my song, I made it a song of light love under the moon; a sailor and his lass. After, when I walked toward her where she stood, she did not run away. I have forgotten her name, but she was sweet and young and a maiden still; I was sorry for this after, and gave her a gold armband of some value. If there should be a child, he would have a start in life, and, if not, it would make a fair dowry for her. Folk in these backward places would not shun her in any case; she had been honored, in their eyes, by a brave warrior.

I think that most of us, sick as we were for home, regretted leaving that pleasant valley of the Skamander; the stretch of open sea before us was treacherous and rough, the worst part of the journey. I myself am not afflicted with seasickness; it is a gift from the gods, surely, this immunity, for those who do not have it look as though they would rather be dead. There are no cabins on a warship, only canvas shelters; beneath them, men lay like flung seaweed, sprawled in twisted postures, and green as the weed, too. It was hard to look at them without feeling a deep nausea. I kept to the open decks, even though footing was precarious in the high winds; the ship tossed and pitched like a living thing in agony. I held onto the rail and sucked in the air; I took little food and much water, without wine. I forget who had told me this, but it worked, always. The only other man I saw in my walks about the deck was Old Pitt; he was hardier than I, even, grinning as he swabbed down the decks. There was no one else to do the work; all the able-bodied seamen were needed at the oars or for the steering. I took a broom, too, and helped, though the slime and the vomit turned my stomach; I could not let this man get the better of me. We did not speak much, but he had my measure and I his. In those days, I almost liked him.

There was nearly a week of this bad going; suddenly, within the hour, as though some god had snapped his finger for a signal, the clouds lifted, and floated away, out of sight, and the blue-white sky and sea blinded our unaccustomed eyes. Like sleepwalkers, the men rose, one by one, staggering to the rails to gaze about them, wonderingly

"Poseidon has gone to sleep again," said Old Pitt, grinning wide. "He had a little nightmare, but it has passed." And he pulled off an armband and threw it overboard. "Thanks, Father Poseidon," he called into the sudden calm.

Others followed his example, coming out of their daze, and grateful. We were all ravenous, falling like wolves upon the food the cooks brought, and getting a little tipsy from the wine, our first in many days.

The sea was like glass all the rest of the way; we sailed into home harbor happy as children, crowding the rails to get a first glimpse of our dear Lesbos. It was high noon, and we had to shade our eyes; the red tile of the rooftops was bleached to pale coral in the bright sun, and the city shone white and gleaming, a god-city. Mitylene. Home. The tears ran down my face and all I saw was a white blur. My throat ached; I realized suddenly that I was shouting at the top of my lungs, lost in all the other shouting round me.

We waited; the waters were deep here, and the ship could come right in. When we were close enough to the dock, the sailors began grinding at the winches to let the landing plank down. The hinges were rusty, and it took a while. The mist in my eyes cleared and I began to see the folk upon the docks, waiting. I picked out Melanippos, with my little sister, Atthis, and two other maidens. One was tall and thin, so thin that she looked as if she might break in two, with a long face and a beautiful long neck; it was the only beautiful thing about her, but she had style and a look of breeding. I saw that her eyes were for him only, 'Nippos, and did not even look our way; he held her hand in his, and occasionally whispered close to her ear. I chuckled to myself; I had never thought he would be drawn by a woman, so set in his ways had he been always. But he had chosen well; she was just his sort, one not for all shoppers.

The other maid was Sappho, no mistake. Even had I never seen the likeness of her, I would have known. She was the kind that drew all eyes, never mind that she had not the promise of perfection of my sister. Tiny she was, and alive with grace; even standing still, she seemed to be in motion. Piquant and vital, and wearing a rainbow of colors; on anyone else her clothes would have looked all wrong, but they suited her, and she knew it, clearly. Even the small sunshade she held above her head was rainbow-patterned and edged in gilded fringe. *Aha*—I thought— *she does not want to show her dark blood, the old Pelasgian witch-blood; she will shade herself to look like an ivory doll.* She glanced my way; even at that distance I felt our eyes meet and hold. I do not know what she saw; I have been told that I am handsome. But I saw my fate, and my heart leaped to it, rejoicing.

It was as her father had said; she ran to him, and he swung her off the ground, holding her close. Thus held, above his shoulder, her eyes veered over to me, seeking. I could not see her lips, but I knew they smiled a little, before she dropped her eyes, and hid her head upon her father's chest. Those eyes were startling, looking exactly like the eyes one has seen painted upon old Cretan pottery, large and round, but almond-shaped, tilted at the outer ends and set very far apart, fringed with unbelievably long black lashes. I looked down at Atthis (I had not very far down to look) and compared. Atthis' eyes were cool and level, mysterious in their depths, though she was no more than a child; a misty gray-violet they were in color, like my own, with a swimming look. I have been told we are much alike; for just a second I hoped not, looking into her eyes. I cannot explain the feeling, and it was gone as soon as it had come; she smiled her child's smile, and prattled her child talk in my ear. My brother, beside me, swept her up, flinging her over his shoulder like a sack of meal, and she shrieked with laughter and pleasure as he carried her about among our kin and friends.

There were so many; some that I remembered dimly, and some that I had forgot. So many girls! And all looking beautiful, even those who were not; so dainty in their fine clothes, so clean and fresh, and smelling of flowers. No dirt, no knobby elbows, no hollowed cheeks and begging eyes. A deep pain constricted my chest, remembering the poor starvelings of Sigeum City that I had known, and those others, in worse case, that had come right down into the tents. The girls of my youth, the ravaged girls, the spoiled and used-up Helens; with dry eyes I wept for them, looking upon all this lovely innocence.

We felt, all we noble youths, bewildered and strange, shy of our home that we had so longed for, and looking like some sort of animal pack that has been let into the yard. Most of us tried to hide it by banding together, ignoring the girls and their glances; a youth named Philomelon, whom I had never even known for a night, came up and slipped his arm about my waist as I stood talking to some of my kinsmen. I shrugged him off, but I was sorry for it; I knew his feelings.

I must have greeted a hundred people that day; tired and hungry as I was, and weak from the voyage, without my land legs back, I could remember almost no one. Melanippos, of course, was my dear friend, almost a father, and we embraced with tears, it had been so long a parting; his girl I remembered only by that first sight, she had a way of fading, until one came to know her well. She was some sort of cousin of Sappho; there were many. A plump, freckled girl with a sweet smile, a tiny dark one, resembling Sappho, but without the fire, some small boys, all lit up alike at the sight of us, their heroes. There were aunts, too, and one I took to be, though later I discovered she was not. I do remember her, for something struck sparks between us.

It was not exactly dislike, for she had a goddess beauty, and I am susceptible. I even remember her name from that first encounter, Praxinoa. She had a proprietary air; perhaps that was the thing that put me off; toward all the girls she showed it, a little, but in particular toward Sappho. It was as if she owned her

. . . and I had marked her out for mine, Sappho. A silly thing, that, for who can hold quicksilver? But I was still young then.

I remembered Gorgo, too, and the other eyestopper with her. Gorgo was the image of her father, Pittakos; arrogant, red-gold, with the same icy eyes. The other was as beautiful as Atthis, but in her own alien way; a princess out of Africa, I guessed. How had she come here? Amazons, both, clearly—or Ammies, as we called them in the talk of the army; girls that love girls.

They were all bid, those I have mentioned, among others, to a supper party at Melanippos' house—my home, really, and my brother's and sister's. After a little rest, I would be up to it.

I lay down that afternoon for the first time in four years in a real bed, my own, in my own small room in Melanippos' lovely house. It was cool and clean, and so was I, after a bath, long needed. I fell asleep almost instantly, remembering with a smile the wild, bright eyes of Sappho; her voice, which I had not yet heard, sang to me softly in my dreams.

Chapter 5

The shadows were lengthening when I woke, roused gently by the sound of soft silvery chimes. I looked up to see a beautiful youth, smiling, holding high the little set of hanging bells. He had tended me earlier, but I had been too tired to notice. I sat up, yawned, and asked what hour it was. When he told me, I said, "Zeus, then—I shall have to hurry! "

"No," he said. "There is plenty of time. The guests will not arrive till the sun is well down, and it lacks an hour, at least, till setting. . . ."

"Good," I said. "My mouth is dry. Is there a little wine, perhaps? Anything will do . . . something light."

"There is some Lydian, from the white grape . . . my master had me chill it against your waking. . . ." He left the chamber. I noticed he was graceful as a girl, though truly there was nothing girlish about him. He was compact and muscular, with the body of a boy athlete, but too white; one could see he had spent no time in the open gymnasium. The face was too perfect, really, the features so symmetrical as to be a little stern. This was softened by his unexpected coloring, black hair curling close to the head like a cap, and hot black eyes against a complexion still childishly rosy-fair.

I could not place his accent; when he came back with the wine, I asked him where he came from. "Right here. Lesbos."

I stared at him as he poured the wine into a cup. "Your speech is not like ours . . . there is a difference in the vowels. . . ."

He grinned, looking human suddenly, though the teeth were too perfect to believe. He looked at me straight then, but his mouth still curving, and said, "You have never heard it, being an aristocrat. It is waterfront speech, that is all. I am learning, but still it clings. I have had three masters, and have learnt a little from each."

I was intrigued. "And yet so young?"

"Well, I think I am nearly fourteen—but of course I do not know for sure." He paused for a moment, as if pondering how much he would tell me. "My first master was a poor man, the owner of a ferryboat. When my father, who was his ferryman, was drowned, he could not afford my keep. He sold me to a troupe of dancers . . . it was a life I liked. But they were poor, too. When this master, your friend, saw me dancing among them, and offered for me, they could not resist the offer. I guess he paid a lot. They all got new costumes, and a passage on an Egyptian boat. . . ."

"How long have you been here—with Melanippos?" I asked.

"Two years, and a little more . . . he is very kind, and the work is light, just this kind of thing"—he gestured to the serving-tray upon the table where he had put it—"and to hold still while he makes a sketch or works with the clay."

"You are his model, then?" I asked.

He nodded. "He pays me for it, too . . . and sometimes he lets me dance for his guests. I will be good someday. . . ." His lovely face had a look of purpose to it, suddenly. "It will take a long while to save up enough to buy my freedom . . . but he lets me practice—and I am still young."

"You mean to be a dancer?" I asked, surprised. "It is a lowly life. You are better off as you are. . . ."

He shook his head. "Not when you have a troupe of your own—and trained musicians. No, I shall make something out of it. I would rather be a soldier—but that of course is closed to me. . . ." He shrugged and picked up the tray.

"In the gods' name, why?" I asked. "Soldiering is the worst lot in the world."

"Well . . . there is power when you have a weapon . . . when you know it can kill. . . ." His eyes had a dreaming look, like a maiden's in the first rapture of a kiss; I felt the flesh creep cold on me at his words.

"At the killing of the Tyrant," he said, "I was given a dagger, long and sharp, my first. I used it—though I could not get near the man himself. I used it on a guard—one I had known before, when I was a dancing boy, one who had tried something—" He swept me with a look of scorn, as though I had been that man; I had not even touched his hand! He went on. "I killed him, too—my first . . ."

"If you are prudent," I said, "he will be your last. Stay out of political quarrels."

He smiled. "I think you do not take your own advice, Lord Alkaios—from what I have heard."

"That may be." I smiled back, spreading my hands. "We are all as we are. . . ."

He stared a moment. "It is getting near the supper hour," he said. "Will you need me for anything?"

"No," I said. "Send a bath woman." I did not trust myself, one way or another, with this chilling, beautiful boy.

He turned to go, saluting me. "What is your name?" I asked.

"They call me Phaon," he answered, and left, bearing the tray.

I stared at my face in the mirror that stood beside the bath table. Since I was old enough to grow one, some two years, I had worn a beard, but it reminded me of my army life, and I eyed it with disgust; I decided to shave it off. It would be going against the fashion, but why not? I would start a new one. It took a while, and my chin was sore after, and a little red; I rubbed it with an unguent that I found in a drawer, aromatic and soothing. By the time I had dressed, the redness was fading.

I was pleased with myself. I no longer looked like a soldier, with my new smooth face, and long blue robe. I had found the robe in a clothes chest, and helped myself; I could not bear the thought of wearing the short warrior tunics I had brought back in my sea box. I rummaged further, and came upon a gold brooch, shaped like a lion's head, fastening the draping upon one shoulder and leaving the other bare. The color was good against the light blue cloth, for I had been in the sun a lot; the mirror was flawed, and the light dimming, but I saw enough to feel pleased with myself.

There was a scratching, light, at the door, and I called out, "Enter, I am ready!"

It was Melanippos, done up magnificently, as always, in the finest clothes money could buy; I noticed he was going easy on the paint and powder, though. He stood a little way off, squinting his eye at me in his artist's way, and bidding me turn around. "You'll do, my boy . . . you'll do," he said, smiling. "I always liked your face as is . . . without adornment. However" —and he opened a chest somewhere, and took out a little vial—"we must rid you of that plucked-fowl look . . . your chin is too white." He dabbed at it with whatever it was he held. I drew back, shaking my head. "No paint," I said. "It is terrible on me. It makes me girlish."

"Not this," he said. "Just a tiny bit . . . not paint, but something I invented, to match the sun-look, where it has not hit." I let him rub it into my chin, and took the mirror to the window, looking close. It had done the trick, just darkening the skin a little. "You could market this," I said, laughing. "The hetaerae would love it. . . ."

"Not they," he said. "They must be white as snow, it is the fad. . . . I have given some to the games master at the gymnasium, though . . . for the ballplayers, those who must keep their eyes upon the rolling ball, and thus have whey-faces." He gave me a sharp look. "By the way," he said, "watch out for those newfangled terms you're using . . ."

"Which?" I asked, puzzled.

"Well," he said, "around here these girls call each other hetaerae, from its old meaning—companions." And he wagged his finger at me. "You could stir up a little trouble, calling whores by the same name."

"I take your meaning," I said, laughing too. "I thought everyone knew what the hetaerae were—in modern language . . ."

"Not in the islands," he answered. "It is a mainland usage—it will be years before it reaches these parts. . . ."

I heard light speech outside, and feet coming down from litters. "They are arriving! " I cried. I took one last look in the mirror. "Will she like me, 'Nippos?"

"Who?" he asked, pretending. I made a little face at him, and he laughed.

"She adores you already. Your name is always on her lips—she invents occasion to use it."

"Truly?" I asked. I was delighted and it showed.

"Go easy, though, Alkaios," he said, with a sheepish sort of smile. "She is the daughter of my old, dear friend."

It was my turn to give him a sharp look. "What do you take me for?" I asked. "I have some manners, I hope. . . ."

"Well," he said, "tongues wag. . . . your exploits are well known by now. Your liking for a pretty face . . . either kind . . ." And he smiled a sly little smile.

I fisted his shoulder, grinning. "War is war," I said. "I am home now." I stopped laughing and felt myself frown, thinking. "Truth to tell, dear friend—I have known no pretty ladies . . . no ladies at all. I shall probably just stare at her, tongue-tied."

"Take your lyre," he said. "I am sure she has brought hers. It will make speech for you. . . . I will find occasion."

I had spoken truth, for, though I had eyes only for Sappho, I stood silent when we met, looking down at her. She said nothing either, though her eyes were very bright. She held out her hand in courtesy; I took it, feeling it cold, and with a little tremble in mine. So she, too, was full of nerves! I remembered; if I had known no lady-girls, she, too, had known no youths. For this war had gone on all our young years, curse it!

I found my voice, and started to speak; so did she, and our words crossed, canceling each out. We began again, and clashed again; when she stopped, my own voice went on, hoarse as a crow. I do not remember what I said; I faltered and was still. We stared; her long Cretan eyes crinkled and her lips indented at the corners. Together we burst into astonished laughter. She leaned to me and whispered, "Say on—I will be quiet."

I shook my head. "Later," I said, "we will speak later. . . ."

I loosed her hand that I still held, and moved away; my brother Antimenades had come up to stand beside us and to greet her. Grateful for the press of folk that now filled the little hall, I made for the long table and the wine bowl; behind me I heard her voice, talking to my brother, an easy silver flow. I was befuddled, for I rarely feel unease, mostly taking things as they come. I think she had gone to my head a little, for the wine I drank was weak and watery, yet my ears hummed and a dizziness clouded my head.

I steadied myself against the table as I drank; there were a little knot of others like myself, lately come from the war, and shy as unbroken horses. Not many had come, though; it takes a while to adjust. I watched Antimenades, his big paws still swallowing both her little hands, talking easily as I had never seen him do with any woman; there was a little fist of jealousy in my stomach, clenching. I remembered that he knew her well; she had sat for the sculptured head, after all, and they had had much converse. She had a changing face, going from light to deepest dark, fascinating to watch; one could almost tell, across the room, the things of which she spoke. A performer, I thought, a born performer. Well, that is a good thing, after all; besides making the songs, she must put them over, or what is the use of them, they do not reach the heart of the listener. She moved away, lightly, greeting all her cousins and friends, the pretty girls of her youth. They embraced like lovers, all, tenderly and with a sweet passion. *Zeus,* I thought, *are they all Ammies, then?* Well—it makes no matter. What else have they had to do, all these years, growing up? One must learn the art of pleasure somehow. Though again I felt the fist clench, forgetting that I, too . . . Well, men have been thus always. One has to sort one's thoughts out about women. They were very strange to me in any case, these highborn virgins. The girls of the street are simple; they give to men, or they do not, that is all. One knows where one stands. I watched, and kept my counsel, and drank sparingly, for me; I knew that later I would be called upon to sing.

Supper was light, and taken in the gardens; when darkness fell, we were summoned into the large hall, where a space was cleared for the entertainment. I · saw the Nubian girl, or Ethiopian, or whatever she was, the handsome one, part lovingly from the red savage daughter of Pittakos, and go apart into another chamber; they said that she was a skilled dancer, and had left to make ready. I studied that wild one; I had heard her name, Gorgo. Named for a Spartan queen and, as well, for a monster; I smiled, for both were apt. I could not bear her; I do not like mannish women, and this one, too, had her father written all over her, not the most charming of lineaments, to my mind. *Poor girl,* I thought, *she is awkward as a bear.* Sappho, fingering the strings of her lyre, was distant with her, I noticed, not smiling back when she grinned whitely, and bending her head to her instrument, listening for the true tuning.

Melanippos had always a feeling for gracious presentation; all was done without formality, and in a light and casual manner. He bade the servants snuff out the candles at each couch and bring in great tall ones to illuminate the center of the floor; there was a flourish of drums somewhere hidden, and a hush fell upon the company. A high flute sound was heard, and a figure came in, walking gracefully and slowly into the light, playing softly upon the flute. It was the slave boy, Phaon, gleaming white as one of the candles, for he was naked. A gasp went up; he did not turn a hair, but wore a haughty face, waiting for silence. He had taken the flute from his lips, and stood still. When not a whisper or a sigh was heard, he spun, suddenly, many times, a dizzying sight, leapt high into the air, as if he wore the sandals of Hermes, and fell to the floor, bowed before his master. Melanippos waved his hand, a signal for the dance to begin; the boy handed him the flute, and danced, in silence. I have never seen such dancing; he had no more bones than an eel! He gave us the Phyrric dance, back bent into an arc and rolling, handstands, spinning upon the head, and much else that I cannot, in truth, describe. It was a marvel of skill and endurance; I applauded with the rest, after, but there was no heart in him, no soul showed. This is my private opinion, and not shared by many; he became one of the greatest dancers in the world, after. Still, to my mind, he was cold as an icy stream from the mountains, always. But even I saw, then, so early, that remarkable craft, and, of course, the beauty, godlike and possessed.

After, the notorious Phaedra, wife to Drakon, summoned him to her couch to bestow a favor. I saw her eyes, painted blue upon the lids, and heavy, flicker over him where he stood. She smiled, and held out a purse, embroidered, and filled, I suppose, with gold coins. He did not take it right away, but, smiling and a little cruel, twisted on his rolled loincloth, bowed, and took it from her jeweled hand, brushing his lips across her palm. He knew, even then, where to strike and where it hurts most. She colored, whore that she was, and fumbled with the folds of her gown. *Cruel child,* I thought, *beautiful as you are, and talented, your arrogance will play you false one day.*

Next came the dark dancer girl, swathed in particolored veils, even to her head; drums played, and she moved to them, swaying and bending, slow, solemn. I leaned over to Melanippos, curious. He said she was a former slave of Sappho's household, but freed now, like most of Andros' servants; they called her Andromeda, because, as he said, smiling, they could not pronounce her name, so outlandish was the sound.

I began to watch her, fascinated. All the heart that was missing in the performance of Phaon was there, in the body of this girl. Excitement, valor, joy, all were expressed by that brown creature made of flame; she was herself a work of art, fashioned by the gods. I knew, of course, this was not so, that long, harrowing practice had made her what she was, as all artists are made. She was unique, able to do all manner of dancing easily, and more besides, her own invention. I never came to know this girl; she had been of Sappho's household, and a friend, but now estranged. I never knew the reason; also I think she feared and hated men, had perhaps been mishandled on the slave ship that brought her to our shores. This is only a guess; as I have said, I admired her from far away. Indeed, this was the case, always, with most of Lesbos; except for Gorgo, throughout the years she seemed to have no intimates. Aloof she was, and imperturbable, except for her genius, which she gave freely and from her heart. Our island folk dislike and fear the dark barbaric alien, from some old instinct; in her later days, though, she was much admired, and only a few of the most ignorant made the evil eye sign after she passed, behind her back.

It was my turn now; I had been so engrossed in that Andromeda that I had forgotten to be nervous. It came upon me suddenly, while I sat tuning my lyre; my mouth was dry as old earth, and I called for wine.

Everyone laughed, and my nervousness fell away. I gave them first a drinking song, funny and with a little edge of sadness to it, the last notes wobbling drunkenly, a purposeful device; they cheered, and I had another swallow, making them laugh again. I knew I had them, then, but did a war ballad, just to make sure, and a dirge to follow; it never fails, and there was not a dry eye in the crowd, as we performers say. I glanced Sappho's way, and fancied I saw a little mocking smile play about her lips; she knew the tricks, too, of course. She had been singing for company all her life. I bowed to her where she sat, all in white maiden's wear, looking as fragile as a moth; I sang my next song to her, a love song, but pure as the rain, unlike my usual stuff. It was a subtle compliment, and she rose, after, and walked toward me, holding her lyre.

I gave her my seat, bowing again, and going off to a round of applause that warmed me. I sat some little way off, but close enough to see her face as she bent, fingering her strings softly; clearly she was thinking, intent on her song. My heart nearly stopped; she took my meter, not her own, and, improvising, made a little song in answer to mine, a perfect thing. The folk in the hall were not ignorant; they recognized what she had done, as easily as a bird sings, or so it seemed. I had never known anyone before who could do this thing, on call, as it were. Truly, a god had spoken at her birth. I marveled, and went forward to kiss her hand. The audience loves that sort of play between artists; it lets them in on secrets, or pretends to.

She sang song after song; they would not let her go. I noticed that the doorways were filled with serving folk, and, beyond, common villagers crowded the courtyard to hear her. I had heard this of her singing, that it drew the world within earshot, but how they knew of it was impossible to tell; I think Aphrodite whispered to them.

She gave them the sad and shocking piece that had offended the Tyrant and brought on his death; talk about tears! I thought some of the women would tear their robes and rake their cheeks as for a death! A great hush fell then, and she tuning up again, to prolong the suspense. I heard then the first notes of the famous Black Lark Song, soft at first, and gathering fire and passion, mounting ever higher. I knew then that, however much I had heard it before (for it was much sung by all the singer folk), I might never have heard it till now. It was not her voice alone; it had a little husk to it, and was not nearly so pure as she believed. It was the kind of witchery she had about her person, and the supreme and indescribable artistry with which she made the song and sang it. She was still a girl, but I have never heard her equal, then or after. She struck up the song again, and all joined in, for everyone knew the words. At the end, the lesser folk had crept right into the hall, through the doors, and had to be shooed away. There is no tribute like it, for an artist. I saw her cheeks were red as fire from excitement, and her great eyes sparkled like jewels. I led her from the dais, holding her hand, and giving both our lyres into the keeping of a slave. The skin of her palm was so hot that it almost burned mine; I led her outside into the cool of the evening, in the garden.

I never let go her hand; we walked and walked, round and round the little gardens, among the scent of roses, heavy on the night air. And we talked and talked, as though the dams of speech had burst and we were lost in our own flood. My eyes were on her face always, a pale almond color in the moon's light, and my hand in hers.

I do not remember the things we spoke of; music mostly and verse. We were starved, each for each, for neither of us had

known before another true poet. Never mind her charm and
beauty; she was like a part of myself, lost and now found again. I
think she felt it, too.

I cannot remember either, how long we walked and talked; it
must have been close on midnight when we heard Melanippos'
voice, with a little curl of humor in it. "Children," he said, from
the doorway, "all the guests are gone . . . weary and seeking
their beds. They are waiting for you, dear girl . . . Praxinoa and
the little yawning slave . . ."

"Oh, gods!" she cried softly, her hand, snatched from mine,
flying to her mouth. "Is it so late?" She turned to me.
"Good-night, Alkaios . . . sleep well. . . ." And she was off,
hurrying into the house.

Sleep well I did not; I was too full of her, my thoughts going
round and round, dizzying. It was now I who burned, hot-flushed
and giddy as from wine; I had taken none for hours!

I had not thought to ask her when we might meet again. It did
not matter; I knew I would be on her doorstep at first light.

Chapter 6

Days of roses, days of music, days of Sappho. As I look back upon them now, they seem to merge and become one long innocent morning, warm and still and cloudless . . . the morning before life.

We had found our voices, both, and talked and sang at one another forever, trying out words and verses, plucking strings. We walked in her father's garden, holding hands, moving through the dappled sunlight as in a dream. Or we sat side by side upon a stone bench staring together at the playing fountain and the little fish that swam ceaselessly in the pool, till the shadows fell and the stone of the bench struck cold upon our flesh. Then she would sigh, and start a little as if wakened, and rise and bid me good-bye; it was time for her supper. Sometimes I was asked to stay for a meal, but we were never unsupervised after dark; she was accounted too young yet for true courting. At least I told myself this, hoping that it was not that I went untrusted. I bore myself well, I *will* say, never doing more than gently touching her hand, though, truth to tell, her nearness made me tremble. I had to make up for it with some wild nights, with whatever wild love I could find; I was too young to burn alone.

I used to wonder what she did with her evenings; all those girl cousins and friends, so loving— Did she play at life's night-business with them? I was not really jealous—I counted it the play of pretty puppies, but I wondered.

One day she told me in a poem, or I took it so.

I came upon her in her upstairs music room, trying over some notes on her little harp, and frowning. "I have the words," she said, "but the music will not come. . . ."

She tried some more notes, then struck her hand across the strings, making a harsh thwanging sound, and laid it aside. She raised her great dark eyes, thinking, and said the words of a little verse; I remember them still.

The moon and Pleiades are set.
Night is half gone and time speeds by.
I lie in bed, alone.

Then she turned her eyes upon me; my heart beat wildly
against my ribs. I went and placed my mouth on hers, softly. Her
lips were cool, and trembled a very little under my own.

I moved away, for I knew the house alive with people, and
looked into her eyes. "Write it down, dearest—and keep it till the
music comes. . . ."

"The music will come," she said. "I know it."

Later—years later—she expanded the song, and with the most
wonderful music. It became very popular for lonely lovers, and
was often sung. I grew very tired of it; it was written, in those
later years, for someone else. But this little, vulnerable bit of
song—this was for me.

Antimenades and I were both accounted old enough, and were
admitted to the Council of Nobles, being sworn in at the first
postwar meeting. It was a sad little ceremony, in a way, for there
were others, young comrades of ours, home from the battlefield,
that had been invited to join as well; not one showed up.
Someone said, Melanippos, I think, that perhaps they were all
too busy playing, drinking and the rest, making up for lost time,
as it were. But he said it with a wry smile, and we all knew it for
a lame sort of excuse; after all, who plays as much as I—and I
was there! I could not help but mark that Pittakos was not
present either; nor was that crafty Myrsilos. No one mentioned
it, but there were long faces all about, and worried looks. I hoped
it was nothing but coincidence. Well, we would see at the next
meeting, the following week.

Melanippos' Egyptian cat, Isis, had her litter—on silken
cushions, no less. They were nicer than might have been
expected, seeing that the whole thing was an accident, and only
the gods knew who had sired them. Our island cats are half-wild
creatures, big and ugly; in Greece cats have not been bred to
houses, and are only tolerated to kill vermin. Isis was a tiny,
delicate thing, fine-boned, with a triangular face; two of her
kittens resembled her, but with a different coloring, tiger-striped.
Sappho took one, and I the other, thinking that we would mate
them when they grew older. After all, I said, it is the Egyptian

way! Indeed, according to Thales, the whole royal house of
Egypt should be idiots, or worse, seeing that they have for
centuries married sister to brother, in their custom. He says that
makes a dangerous watering down of the blood; 'Nippos says that
he suspects they use substitutes, and give it out they are close kin,
for he has been there many times, and all the royalty are very
shrewd and clever. It sounds a place of fable; I am longing to
visit it! Meanwhile, we are trying to teach our little cats to walk
at the end of silken ribbons; if they roam loose they will be
mangled by the Greek roughnecks.

About their pet names we have had quite an argument, our
first. I had not known my Sappho had such a flaring temper; I
am glad, in a way, for it makes her more human. I had been
treating her like a perfect little goddess. My own fault, for I am
struck numb by her great talents, and at a loss, anyway, as I have
said, for I do not know how to behave with highborn maidens.
She got her way about the names, of course. I had wanted to call
them Hero and Leander or something else out of myth, but she
said such names were too fancy, the sort of thing a courtesan
would think up to prove she was knowledgeable. I refused to
anger, but only laughed and said she might call them whatever
she liked. "Boy . . . and Girl," she said, very proud of herself.
"Who else would think of that?"

I shrugged, and said, mildly, that I hoped we had them the
right way round, as it was fairly difficult to tell on such young
things. She gave me a sly look that flicked like a whiplash, and
said, "I understand it does not matter much, one way or another,
in the army . . ." Whew! What had she heard? I thought of the
way these noble girls carried on with one another and nearly
gave her as good as she had given. But just in time I remembered
I adored her and bit my tongue. One needs a bit of patience with
this filly, plain to see.

I see now as I write that the long innocent morning was
already coming to an end; shadows were forming, clouds blew in
little wisps across the sky; there was even a distant rumble of
thunder and a quick flash of thin lightning; nothing ever
happens all at once. I might even make a song along those lines
some day.

Chapter 7

There had been signs, as I have said, but I had not had wit enough to take notice, or to put them together. I think now, fancifully, that the little disagreements with my own Sappho presaged those other events, but that is, of course, a poet's whim. One had nothing to do with the other, and she was merely showing her true colors, as I was myself, colors bright and dark together, as they should be. Pretty palenesses were not for us, then or ever.

I had noted that the Council of Nobles was ill attended, that those two, Pittakos and Myrsilos, were not present. I had seen already the one man to be wily, the other corrupt; it should have disquieted me. I had seen, too, how the ranks of the City Guards had swollen since we came back from the Troad; literally hundreds of veterans had joined. What other trade did they know but soldiering? This was the closest thing to it. Now and then I had seen a wellborn youth's face, too, among the guard, and wondered, for it was not formed for such as they. Also, I had marked, idly, Drakon's gray looks, but supposed him to be suffering from some small upset of the liver or kidney. Melanippos, too, had been wearing an abstracted look; that I put down to his artist's temperament, that is ever high or low, according to how his work is going. I should have seen that Sappho's father wore this look, too, but in her presence I saw no other face. And so the huge thunderclap came unheralded, when it came.

One morning, just after dawn, there came a loud pounding at our doors. I was still abed, for I had had a late night, as usual, but 'Nippos was wakeful and answered the thumps himself, for all the slaves were still snoring; he had always been indulgent.

The hubbub wakened me; by the time I had thrown on a robe and run a comb through my hair, they were already in the hall and sobbing rose, loud, and right on the edge of hysteria. Women! Strange—at such an hour. It was the tall mild one, Drakon's daughter, Telesippa, and her younger sister, Dika, in much disarray, and wailing. One could get nothing from them that was coherent. They had brought a slave woman with them, oldish, that had probably once been their nurse. She had the dark hill-woman look, gone quite yellow now, and her eyes rolled wildly in her head; she looked, truly, as if she might die of fright, and, indeed, after a moment, she swooned, falling onto the marble floor.

The slaves were up by now, crowding at the doors and staring. Melanippos signed for strong wine to be brought. It did not rouse the slave woman; she was still as stone, and the wine dribbled purple over her work garment. The girls swallowed some, though, and their sobbing died down to soft hiccups. Dika, her face smeared with tears, spoke first.

"Dead—he is dead!" She said it over and over, wringing her hands. Telesippa took another long swallow of the wine, and said, calm now, "It is my father—he is dead . . . lying in his bed. Stiff already . . . and eyes fixed wide . . . there is froth and blood upon his lips . . ." At this she began to sob again, but softly. Melanippos took her in his arms, tenderly. "Quiet, sweet, quiet . . . tell us all. Is there a wound upon him?"

"No—no . . . I turned him over . . . nothing."

Dika stopped her crying for a moment and cried, "But there is vomit all about him . . . black and bloody!"

Melanippos' face was grim, suddenly. "Where is your mother?"

"Gone!" cried Dika. "They are all gone—my brothers, all the slaves. There was no one in the house but Euphrosyne, there—" And she gestured to the poor woman, still lying on the cold stone.

"Mother's clothes, too, are all gone," said Telesippa. "At least—it seemed so . . . all the chests are standing open, empty, or with a few old discarded chlamys trailing out—a scarf or two . . ."

"And her jewel box is gone," said Dika. "Can it have been robbers? Have they taken her away—to slay her somewhere?"

Melanippos bit his lip. Then he said, "Come, let us go back and look . . ."

"No—oh no!" And Dika wailed again, terrified.

I spoke. " 'Nippos—let them lie down here somewhere, with someone to tend them. They have had a great shock. You and I will go." And I started for the door.

"Wait—we must take others with us. Zeus knows what awaits

us there." And Melanippos called some of his men to come with us; I saw, among them, the youth Phaon.

The house of Drakon was close by; we walked, or half ran. The door stood open, creaking a little on its hinges in the first breeze of the morning. We walked inside, wary.

It was as the girls had said, empty and echoing, our footfalls sounding loud upon the paved floors. We went through chamber after chamber of the downstairs part; nothing stirred, and there was no disorder.

We climbed the stairs, coming first to Phaedra's chamber; one could tell it from the paint pots, all in disarray, and some tipped over, spilling out their contents; a flask of perfumed oil was broken, the strong sweet smell of musk clogging the nose. It was the smell of Phaedra, but she was not there.

We walked through into Drakon's bedroom; a different smell, horrible. There was no disorder here; it looked like Drakon, neat and austere, everything in its place. Except when one came to the bed. We gasped in horror; no wonder the girls had been hysterical.

His face was nearly black, and contorted, the foam dried upon his mouth, and the eyes set like stones. His night robe was fouled with vomit and excrement, bloody, and the whole bed reeked of it.

It was a hard thing to do, but we turned him all about, stiff as he was. There was no sign of a stab or a blow; I could hardly repress a shudder, for he was cold as ice to the touch. He must have been dead for hours.

"Poison," said 'Nippos. "Clearly, it is poison. . . ."

The boy Phaon came close. "She has done it . . . the woman. She poisoned him."

We stared. "How do you know?" said 'Nippos, grabbing his arm roughly.

The boy gave us stare for stare, cold. Then he shrugged, and 'Nippos let his arm go. "Out with it, Phaon. What do you know of this thing?"

"I am not implicated. But I can put two and two together." He wore a strange look, a mixture of shame and arrogance. "I—was with her—Phaedra . . . night before last. After—a woman came to the chamber—a witch woman, for I have seen her in her haunts, long ago, when I lived among such folk. She

deals in potions and the like . . . love potions, death draughts
. . . deadly juices. I saw her give Phaedra a vial; money changed
hands. They did not know I saw, for I pretended to be spent with
passion, and sleeping. . . . There it is!" He stooped and picked
up something from the floor. It was very small, a little
round-bottomed vial, such as medicines are carried in; the top
had been broken off, and it was empty now. 'Nippos took it and
held it to his nose, then passed it to me, silently. It had a strong
odor of almonds still. "It is true," said 'Nippos. "It is the deadliest
of all poisons. There was enough in here to wipe out a
regiment. . . ."

I spoke, remembering suddenly. "He has been looking ill for
days—weeks even . . ."

'Nippos looked as if he might be sick. "Yes—I, too, thought
him ill. She has probably been trying all kinds of stuff, too weak
to do a proper job. . . . Gods—what horror! I never liked the
woman, but . . ."

'Nippos turned to Phaon. "Will you swear to this thing?"

Phaon turned very white. "Master, a slave's testimony is
counted for nothing . . . unless it is obtained under torture. . . ."

"Yes—yes, you are right. I would not ask that of anyone. . . . I
will sign your manumission papers—then you can testify. But
will you?" He looked hard at him.

Phaon smiled. "I will testify to anything—if I am free!"

'Nippos took his shoulder in a strong grip. "But it *is* true?
Between us. Tell me. I will give you your freedom anyway."

"Yes—it is true. I saw it, just as I said. I did not see her *give* the
poison . . . but I will say so . . ."

"No," said 'Nippos. "The truth will be enough. . . ."

There was much to do, and all in a hurry. The early hours of
that morning are nearly lost to me, for we were torn every which
way by our various duties. The Council of Nobles must be
summoned for an emergency meeting, to deal with this murder of
its most honored member, the body must be tired decently for its
descent into Hades, the woman Phaedra must be found and
brought to justice, and much else that buzzed through our heads
all at once. And as yet we had not even moistened our lips with a
drop of morning wine or taken a crust of bread! Antimenades,
my brother, was away in Pyrrha, seeing to the family estates and

vineyards there; they had been sadly neglected while the war was on, and they were all we three orphans had in the world. So he could not help us, and we missed him sorely, for he had a steady head on his shoulders and broad shoulders, too, for any kind of burden.

The first order of the day, of course, was to get the papers of freedom for Phaon. What a time we had; there was no one at all in the Temple of Hera, where all such law business was transacted; usually unemployed clerks hung about there, idle, and waiting for just such a call. We hurried on; 'Nippos knew of an old scribe, still licensed, but bedridden. He lived in the poor quarter, near the docks; if it were not for Phaon, we might never have found him, for those mean streets are like a puzzle, twisting and winding upon themselves, and not so safe either. He led us straight there, though, for he knew that part of town like the back of his hand. The poor old man, though, when we found him, was weak and shaking with the palsy, though his official stylus still hung on a thong around his neck, for he had never given it up, his mark of pride. We had to guide his unsteady hand, asking forgiveness from the gods for this breach of justice; it was all we could do, and it made the papers legal, and freed the youth to speak in our cause.

We dared not send slaves unattended to summon the council members; it was pure instinct, as yet we did not know anything of what lay ahead. But go we must, ourselves, to each of the twelve houses—well, ten, as it turned out, for Drakon's house was undone, and we ourselves already knew. A slave met us, haughty, at Myrsilos' gate, saying he would inform his master; an odd thing, that, and full of discourtesy, but we had not the time to protest, or even wonder. Pittakos' house was empty of all but a few, another strange thing; his Ammie daughter met us at the door, that Gorgo, with a mocking laughter behind her eyes. She promised to tell him, saying the household was still abed; by now it was near midmorning! Also, we could see behind her the empty chambers, unlit. I had thought that she lived in Sappho's house, being unwelcome in her father's, since she was his child by another and naught to do, ever, with his current wife, Chloris. I said as much to 'Nippos, and he shook his head, saying, "You have me there. I thought the same. Perhaps Chloris has relented. She is a woman of much sensitivity and honor, and with a forgiving nature, too. And the girl is not without charm, in her own rough way. . . .";

Not without charm! I should have thought 'Nippos touched in the head, but that I knew him well.

We had alerted all the nobles, briefly, leaving them, each, with shocked morning faces, and hurrying on, bidding them to 'Nippos' house as soon as they could get themselves into seemly clothes. When we got back to the house, we found that Drakon's daughters had recovered somewhat, though their faces each had that raw, shiny look that comes upon the skin when tears have washed it many times. Telesippa had given orders for food and wine to break our night fast, a welcome thing; I noticed, too, that she had made herself free with 'Nippos' toilet things, for both girls were washed and combed, and wore clean white borrowed robes. Telesippa smiled shyly, and said, "I knew you would not mind . . . we were in such a moil and mess." He kissed her full upon the lips and answered, "What I have is yours, my dear, you know that. . . ." She colored, rosy-pink, looking lovely suddenly. The little Dika bit her lip, and looked at me with big bright eyes; I would have followed 'Nippos' example with this sweet maiden, except that Sappho, if she found out, would have run me through with anything sharp she had to hand. Besides, there was other business more urgent; I contented myself with a smile in her direction.

They had been unable to raise up the old slave, Euphrosyne, that they had dragged behind them; she lay still as the stone beneath her. I knelt down and felt her hand; it was as cold as Drakon's, and there was no beat of blood within her wrist. "Zeus!" I cried softly. "Another death—It is beginning . . ." 'Nippos signed for the body to be taken away.

The two sisters then burst into that womanly wailing that is so exasperating when there is work to do. But 'Nippos was sweet as sweet with his dear, and her sister, too, calling them poor children and wasting time hearing them out about their old nurse and her virtues. I gave a little cluck, for I was worried at this delay; he shot me a glance of dark reproof, and bade me go and greet whoever was at the door. I opened my mouth to protest this treatment—what have we servants for? But then I closed it, getting back my cool demeanor; he was behaving decently, that was all, and I like a raw lad not dry behind the ears.

At the door I had another shock, for there stood Tyrrhaeos, Pittakos' beloved only son, looking weak and pale, holding his withered arm in his good one; I guess it pained him in any exertion, for he was not born so, but had got it in the Egyptian disease a few years back. He was a good-looking boy, save for his deformity; he resembled his mother, fine-boned and delicate. There was a white line of pain around his clear-cut lips; I guessed he had been running, for no litter stood behind him, and no one accompanied him. He signed that he could not speak yet, breathing heavily; I called for wine, and he drank eagerly, sinking into the chair I brought for him.

When he could speak, his news was another shock; we were getting them from all sides, truly, this day! He said that his father had disappeared, he knew not where, after a great quarrel with his mother, that the whole household had heard, though behind their chamber doors words could not be distinguished, and he did not know its import. He said that after Pittakos had gone, in a rage, his mother Chloris called him to her and spoke gravely and with tenderness, saying that she meant to leave her husband, for he had passed the bounds of ordinary affront, and she had borne much. "I cannot countenance this latest move," she said. "You may choose. My Tyrrhaeos, come with me if you will. But I tell you that you choose between love and duty—for your city needs you . . . Mitylene needs you, as it needs all her true sons." He swore he did not understand her, but that something dreadful was afoot, and he had come to warn and to stand with us, the rulers and keepers of the civic right. "She has taken ship in the night," he said, "for the island of Chios, where we have kinsmen of her side. All the household has gone with her, and they have carried off much that was portable, money and gold bars, and jewels . . . it is all hers, after all. This"—and he pointed to the pouch that hung from his girdle—"she has given me for my needs and to help our cause. . . ." It looked full to bulging; I grew cold, not knowing why. Did he know more than he told? I looked at him searchingly, but his face was guileless, worry lining the skin about his fine eyes.

"I saw your half-sister there, at your house," I said. "That Gorgo."

"Yes," he said. "She has come to live there, with her dancer girl. Perhaps the quarrel was in part over her—but I do not think

so. Mother is kind . . . she has never even shunned his
concubines. . . ." He looked up, suddenly mischievous. "They
are all there still, bickering and wrangling in loud voices and
stealing from one another. . . . I hope he has the wherewithal to
feed them, for Mother picked the place clean as a bone. . . ."
We all smiled then, the first smile in that sad morning.

They came then, one by one, all the nobles of the council, with
asking faces, for we had told them nothing as yet. A pall fell on
the company when the dreadful tale was told; it seemed that no
one felt it in him to take action, so shocked they were. Finally, it
was Sappho's father, Andros, who sent a servant to get the death
women for Drakon's laying out, and priests for the rites.

Phaon testified to the thing that he had seen, showing first his
papers, all in order. It was decided that the City Guard must be
called out to search for the woman Phaedra, and charge her with
this murder.

"Although," said Andros, "she has probably taken ship for
somewhere or other. . . ."

"No, I think not, sir," said Tyrrhaeos, respectfully. "For I put
my mother on the one ship that lay in harbor . . . and it has
sailed. There was no sign of any other passenger."

"She may have fled overland, then," I said.

The two young women had been listening at the door, though
it was forbidden when the council met. Telesippa came forward,
timidly, begging our pardon. She said that she thought their
mother might be still in the city, and hiding. "Perhaps it means
nothing," she said, "but at the sight of my father's chamber and
what lay in the bed, poor old Euphrosyne put her hand to her
mouth, and whispered, 'Pittakos!' As I say, maybe it has no
importance. But mother has seen the man often in these last
weeks. We thought"—and here she hung her head—"we
thought, my sister and I, that it was just another of her . . .
flirtations. She has so many. . . ."

"But there was no one at Pittakos' house," said Melanippos.

"My father has not been at home," said Tyrrhaeos. "I swear
it—I would have known. . . ."

"Where do you think he has gone?" I asked. It seemed a
prudent question, but Tyrrhaeos' eyes shifted a little.

"I . . . I cannot say." He seemed to ponder a bit, and then to
come to some conclusion, for he straightened his thin shoulders

and said, "I have noticed that he and Myrsilos are thick as thieves lately. Indeed—though I could get nothing out of my mother—I had a thought, fleeting, that it had vexed her . . ."

We all exchanged looks then, we were beginning to put some pieces of this puzzle together. 'Nippos went to the door and called in Phaon again.

"Will you summon the guard?" he asked. "Take several others with you—armed. And carry your papers, too. One never knows . . ." His voice trailed off, and his face, usually so mobile, wore a stern and heavy look.

We had not long to wait—not even the space of a moment. Phaon came back into the room, quickly, going up to 'Nippos, and speaking softly.

"They are there—outside—surrounding the house. The guard is there, a hundred, at least. I made to beckon to one of them—but they stood at attention, and would not look . . ." Even *his* composure was ruffled; I felt a sickness crawling deep within me, and quickly put down the morning bread that I still held in my hand. There will be no breakfast for any of us today, I thought. Perhaps never. And the thought struck chill.

I had not time to make a jest of it, though one had formed on my lips and was ready to come out. There was a loud noise, as of a great club sounding hollowly at the door. We stood still for a little, wondering how to run, for I think we all knew by then that something fearful was about to befall us. Melanippos, with a sick face, summoned a servant.

"See who is at the door—and ask what is their business. . . ."

Again came the noise, louder, and then a terrible crash as though the roof had fallen in. *Gods,* I thought, *they have torn down the door!* I ran toward the sound, or started to, but 'Nippos caught me by the arm.

"Wait here," he said. "It is best that we stand together . . . unarmed as we are." For in Mitylene no one ever wore a knife or dagger, even in the streets. I thought of the arms that lay rusting in my clothes chest; they would be better than nothing. 'Nippos must have read my thoughts, for he said, with a touch of his old humor, "Forget it, Alkaios. What can any of us do against a hundred?"

He had no time to say more, for clanking steps were heard

upon the stone of the floor, and four—or perhaps six—set-faced warrior types marched in, looking straight ahead and holding spears at the ready. Behind them came Pittakos, at his ease, shuffling and picking his nose, but not, I noticed, smiling. Behind him walked Myrsilos, his jowls jiggling at each jarring step, for he kept time with his soldiers. I saw behind them more guards, and more yet, crowding the doorway, and all holding spear or sword. None of us of the council made a move, but waited.

There was a long silence, then Myrsilos made a sign to the first of the guards behind him. It was a burly brute, full of importance, and he shouted, as though he had learned it by heart, and with no inflection, "You are all under arrest—for the murder of the noble Drakon!"

For a moment none of us could speak a word, we were so aghast at this effrontery. Then Andros stepped forward. "This is ridiculous!" he said, firm and indignant; he never looked so Hellene. "His daughters discovered the body, close after dawn, and ran here, to the nearest house, for help. All morning Melanippos has spent assembling the council . . . for the purpose of making some decision. I myself have arranged for the death women, paying their fees out of my own pocket, for it had to be done quickly; the body is in a dreadful state, and most unseemly. The priests, too, have been summoned. Would guilty people do such things? Or would they flee . . . or hide? As indeed the culprit has done. And I charge you, Myrsilos, and you, Pittakos, with harboring the murderess!"

"What murderess?" asked Pittakos, taking his hand from his nose finally. "There is no murderess . . . the body has been beaten beyond recognition and stabbed in a dozen places. No woman's work, that!"

We were stunned. What had happened? I spoke. "Lord Pittakos," I said, "you and I have shared a sea journey, long and tedious, we two being like the only live ones upon a boat of the dead. I think you know me. I was the first to see the body, outside of those poor girls—and their nurse, who perished at the sight. Melanippos and I, we have seen it. No bruises—for I turned the body over with these own hands. . . ." And I held them out. "There is no blood upon them either—for none was upon Drakon, except that which he vomited up with the bile and the poison. He was full stiff, too, by the time we came upon him—dead for many hours. And there is proof . . . we have it still."

Melanippos drew out the empty, broken vial, still smelling of the bitter almond tincture that was inside it, even now. Pittakos took it, sniffing at it curiously, and looking Myrsilos' way.

Myrsilos spoke. "It is a plant," he said. "An easy thing to do. You are all guilty. Why have you barricaded yourselves from justice? You thought to remove the head noble and seize the reins of power among yourselves. But I tell you you have failed. You will all die. It is the law!"

"What law?" demanded Andros. "We *are* the law, we nobles— here in Mitylene. You have the right, for there are two of you, to demand a trial. But that is all. You have no power at all, except the power of two out of twelve. It is a fraction of the whole."

Pittakos smiled then; he had been saving it, and it struck cold on all of us. *Zeus,* I thought, *and these fools of nobles have made this man their army chief.* As for the other—he does not deserve the right to break bread with us. But that is the way of all good men—they are trusting. And we are undone, and no mistake about it.

Pittakos, still smiling, said, "Andros, my friend, you do not move with the times. The Council of Twelve is outmoded. We want no more of it in Mitylene. Mitylene needs a leader, like Athens, like Korinth."

Melanippos, angry as I had never seen him, cried, "You have helped to pull down one Tyrant—do you want now to stand in his shoes?"

Pittakos shrugged. "Not I." And he thumbed his hand at the other. "Myrsilos. He is our new Tyrant. The people have acclaimed him."

"Who? What people?" I cried.

He gestured to the door, still with that gross thumb. "See for yourself. Just take a look. Look out the window if you fear some treachery, though it would take a word from me. I give the orders for the army—remember? There are some three thousand to enforce my words. Just look!"

I was stung, and walked to the door, dwarfed between the first guards, picked for their brutish size. Still I kept my swagger, though my knees knocked, and I felt as I passed by, the points of their spears move with me. I walked to the street. It was as he said. Hundreds upon hundreds stood armed and waiting for a sign; I could see only to the end of the street, but I knew it was no idle boast; he had them all, all the idle veterans who held him for a hero. Gods, we were duped. I knew then that I had sensed it all along. It was behind my dislike of the man, but I had not recognized my own insight. I came back into the hall and looked at Melanippos. "It is true," I said. "We are undone."

"By treachery!" said Andros, quietly. "Well, men have died in a worse cause."

Pittakos' smile broadened. "Oh, you will not die," he said. "You are all our old friends . . . besides, we want no dead heroes to rise up against us in folk memory. No, you will cool your heels for a little—that is all. Cool your heels . . ."

And he went a little ways apart, talking behind his hand to his ally, that hideous Myrsilos. They spoke for a bit, and we could hear no words. Then Pittakos turned toward us and said, "This is our judgment. You are all, forthwith, exiled, with your families, even to the smallest child, to the town of Pyrrha—it is just far enough away to keep you sweet. You will be permitted four body slaves each, and what possessions can be carried upon four mules. I will not rob you either. Your houses shall be closed and guarded against thieves until your return. Of course, that is unknown. Perhaps . . ." And he shrugged again, and laughed, as though it were a great joke for all to share. "Perhaps it will be never. Who knows? Then again"—and it was Myrsilos' turn to get that icy eye's bend—"then again, it may be our new Tyrant will not wear well either. . . . It is all in the lap of the gods." And, shockingly, his face turned from his ally, he winked broadly at us poor exiles!

Chapter 8

We of Lesbos have a Mount Olympos, too; that is why sometimes the poets among us forget we are not gods. Though, truly, we do not live there; no one can, for it is bare of trees at the peak, and it looks like marble. Sometimes, on a very bright day, the sun strikes blinding sparks from this craggy top, and one must shade one's eyes even to look upon it. At the Festival of Zeus, it has long been the custom to climb this high mountain, though most of the celebrants do not make it, and fall by the faintly marked trails to eat and drink and make what more homely joy they are able. Indeed, it often ends up more like a feast of Dionysos, if you take my meaning. When I was twelve—it seems now so very long ago, for it was before the war—I went once to climb for Zeus and prove my manhood on the way, for I had heard tales to tempt me. Alas, it could not be; I was not yet a man, by any account at all. The tall village girl I had singled out went with me for my look of wealth; she took the purse and shook off my hand, laughing, and ran away. For a wonder, it did not embitter me; I laughed, too. After all, I could have given her nothing but a chaste kiss.

I mention this Mount Olympos of ours because it stands directly along the road one takes to Pyrrha; in fact, one must skirt it, or go over. It is the tallest hill upon our island, and can be seen from quite far away. On the outlying plains around Mitylene, on a clear day, it is visible, looking like a mountain of glass; in winter there is white snow topping it; sometimes, wreathed in mist, only the very topmost point shows, seeming to float, like the breath of a god.

Pyrrha, where we journeyed as exiles, was my home, really. As I have said, all I owned in the world was there; my brother Antimenades had gone there earlier, and taken with him my little sister Atthis. Since our parents died, we had only visited there, for 'Nippos made us gift of his home; both foster father and friend, he was to us three. Now, for once, we could be benefactors

to him, and perhaps to all those others. Actually our estates in
Pyrrha were vast; it was only a matter of readying the many old
villas for folk to live in them in some comfort. We had sent a
runner ahead with the news of what had befallen us; I knew
Antimenades would work hard in preparation for our coming,
and rouse up masons and carpenters, gardeners, and painters.

We exiles had been given three weeks to put our Mitylenian
affairs in order; it seems a generous length of time, but try it some
day. You cannot imagine how much there is to do when one is
migrating, like the birds, but perhaps forever! The women and
girls, I think, changed their minds seven times a day or more
about what to take along; first it was this they could not do
without, then this other! Truly, all the myths about females have
truth in them; it is funny and sad, and then funny again.
Though, in this case, one cannot blame them, really; four mules
are scant bearers for the stuff of a lifetime. Privately, I did not
think that it would come to that or anything like it. There was
that cryptic wink that Pittakos had thrown our way, and besides,
I brooded on plans of my own. We are not, in Pyrrha, more than
some seventeen miles away, after all; it is no great distance, to
one who has been across the seas.

The thing is, we "conspirators," as those vulture-tyrants called
us, were not given much freedom before the time of the journey.
We were closely guarded, each of our dwellings ringed about
with guards, even at night. I had not seen Sappho, and was
pining; I slipped past a guard who was sleeping on the job, but
he woke and I was nearly caught.

Sappho was terrified, and made me swear by Aphrodite never
to try it again. She was right, of course; give these fellows some
power and a weapon and the gods know what might happen;
they are sword-happy, all.

And so we waited, and gathered together our belongings and
chose our servants, and parted from those left behind as best we
could, usually by letter. Pittakos' face was a study in mixed
feelings when he caught sight of his only son among us and
standing with us, ready for whatever was to come; I shall never
forget it. Myrsilos said they might waive Tyrrhaeos' punishment,
but father and son alike shook their heads violently. It was the
only time, then or ever, that I saw a resemblance between them.

So the fine-souled cripple cast his lot with us; after, I fancied that I saw a fugitive look of pride, quickly suppressed, in his father's pale eyes.

We, the disgraced ones, were not even allowed to attend the funeral rites for Drakon, though he was close kin to so many; we watched, each in his own courtyard, the yellow flames leap high and thin, a golden stream going straight to the gods, a good omen, and said our private prayers to help him across the Styx. The day we were sent into our exile was the same day they scattered his gathered ashes into the Gulf of Hiera, a way that we must pass. It was done for the effect, and to point us out for scorn and calumny. But only a few merry-faced urchins shied some clods of earth at us, and that was their way always with travelers of any sort. And so we knew that, under, the folk of Mitylene, silent, were with us, in their hearts.

We went by slow stages, for we were forbidden chariots, wagons, or litters; those highborn among us were mounted, but the slaves and servants must walk, for the four alloted mules were needed as beasts of burden. The older ladies rode on quiet ponies, sitting sideways, with the skirts of their robes gathered round them like Egyptian mummy wrappings, but the young maidens rose astride, in the Spartan way, wearing short tunics and sandals that were thong-strapped to the knee for support. I saw that Sappho's slender legs, from much dancing, were muscled like a boy's; it gave me a little pang of pleasure to look at them, being what I am.

We skirted the mountain of Olympos, of course; it was the only safe way. Some of the winding roads, though, led a little way up the side of the foothills, through forests of pine that filled the air with a scent as keen as a knife blade. Deer ran free there, staring at us, immobile; we were probably the first humans they had ever seen. They would wait, poised on their delicate small hooves; when we neared, they vanished like shades among the tree trunks. One among us, one of the smaller boy cousins, raised his bow and took aim at a speckled doe. "No! Oh, no!" cried Sappho, striking down his arm and turning upon him eyes exactly like the startled creature speeding away. "She is right," said her uncle Erigyus, the father of the boy. "We do not need the meat—and there is no sport in killing a gentle thing. . . ."

Sometimes we went in well-timbered valleys, valleys one would not think to find in Greek countries. It is a barren land, ours, if beautiful. Here there were very Titans of trees, old as time, gnarled and knotted, with great twisting roots, upon which our horses stumbled. It was still green in parts, though autumn was setting in; only in spring and fall is the grass bright with color; summer bleaches it to a dry whitish-yellow. It was, in some ways, a lovely journey, though our hearts were sad and our minds disquieted. Perhaps it was this very element of grief that lent the beauty; I have made the journey many times since, in the course of my life, and never noticed it, but slapped at my mount, fretting to be done with it.

When we rode the twisting paths of the lower hill, we could see, looking down, the Gulf of Pyrrha, from which the city takes its name. It is a large inlet, as such bodies of water go, almost a little sea; its waters, though, were fresh and sweet tasting, and we filled our water bags there.

We made slow progress, as I have said, though the distance was so little; the first night was clear and mild, and we slept in the open, beside a fire, and under a sky thick with stars. The moon hung low, yellow and full, and almost as bright as midday, but paler. I could not sleep, tossing and turning on the hard ground, disturbed by the unnatural light. I heard a sound, soft padding feet and a kind of snuffling; a shape loomed clear, black against the glow of the fire, some wild thing come to investigate or perhaps to prey. I reached out a cautious hand and shook the nearest sleeper, softly. It was Tyrrhaeos; he had not been sleeping either, and rose up on his good elbow. "Soft," I whispered. "Is your spear to hand?"

"It is beside me, but I am awkward with this cursed arm. . . ."

I reached over him, for my own weapon was still bound up in my horses's side trappings; I had hated my army training and so forgot it too soon. Softly I took his spear up, hefting it to test its weight for the throw. The beast stood still for me; it was a clean kill, and almost noiseless. We crept near, where the thing lay on the other side of the fire. It was a mountain lion, of a fair size, its fangs bared in its death agony; it had been drawn, doubtless, by the smell of our little Egyptian cats, both still curled in sleep beside Sappho.

We dragged the carcass into the deep of the bushes, out of

sight, covering it as best we could with broken branches and fallen leaves, for it would not do to alarm the women of our company. I resolved, though, to protest against this sleeping out; next time it might be no one would be awake!

I had no need to argue, though, for the next day it poured rain, with hailstones as big as plovers' eggs. We were lucky to be close to an inn of sorts. It was still only just past noon, and the place was a hovel, no more, but at least it had a roof, with only a few leaks. There was only the one building, and space for us nobles only.

We giggled all the time, in the half-dark and the mustiness, Sappho and I holding hands and happy, not caring that there were no beds and a low, mean fire. The older people among us must have suffered, though, for our clothes never dried, and there was no place to change. Indeed, the only latrine was outside, a ditch dug in the open, reminding me of our military camps. It was not so difficult for us men, made as we are; open the door, raise the tunic, and that is that, and only a little bit of us got wet. The girls were a different matter; finally Praxinoa managed to procure a large old pot; I hoped the innkeeper would not use it for cooking later. In any case, we would hardly be stopping here again, so it was not my problem.

We were packed too close in that place to get to lyre or harp, but those of us who could, sang, to while away the hours and drown out the doleful drumming on the roof and the occasional sharp claps of thunder.

None of us slept that night, sodden as we were, except the small children; we sang softly through the long night, songs long forgotten, and some new ones, too, gifts of the gods in our extremity.

The dawn broke bright, though, the storm had ceased all of a sudden; when we came out of that dank shelter, the world looked new-washed and the smell was sent, truly, from heaven. Birds had taken up our song where we left off. It was a perfect day and very clear; we could see the city of Pyrrha in the distance, white and shining as our own Mitylene, but smaller.

Chapter 9

Pyrrha! Dear gods . . . if each mortal might have such an exile! There was, of course, the bitter with the sweet, as there is always—but never mind. If I had chosen each day as it came, I could hardly have bettered it.

Antimenades came riding out to meet us, his kind, broad face alive with pleasure; Sappho slipped off her horse and ran to him, burying her face in his chest. He might have been *her* brother! Or so I told myself, holding my jealousy in check.

In my turn I jumped down, and little Atthis flew into my arms, laughing as though it had all been a great holiday; surely by now, being close to eleven years, she should have some notion of the import of this enforced journey! I knew her wits were sharp, but in this thing she was like a child of four, a being without heart, as all children are.

She leapt into my arms; I was not Antimenades, and I was tired from long riding anyway; I put her down soon, giving her a pat on the rear end and saying, "Greet the Lady Sappho . . . she is waiting." She had sworn, Atthis, that she adored Sappho, but now she stared, scraping her foot in the dirt, and not putting out her hand.

Sappho smiled. "Dear Atthis . . . you are fresh as a rose!" And she took up the hem of her robe, which she had been wearing for seemliness, as we neared the city, and wiped her face with it; I saw that sweat pearled her skin; the sun was high. The robe had been trailing in the dust and left a little smear of dirt along her cheek; to me it was all the more endearing, an earnest of her sweet mortality. But Atthis bent her head to receive Sappho's kiss upon her forehead; one could not read the child's eyes.

Sappho laughed a little. "Am I then so filthy? Or are you shy, darling?" And she put her hands upon each of Atthis' shoulders, gazing searchingly into her eyes. I thought I saw a little tremor in Sappho's face, but she still smiled. "Well, we will be friends again, my lovely one . . . once I have settled in and all the strangeness gone. . . ." She turned away, gesturing to the others behind her, dismounting now. "Come, Atthis, greet your new playmates, my cousins. Soon we will all be working hard at our lessons . . . all will be as it was. . . ." But the face she turned to me was sad, suddenly.

There was room, as I had thought, on our lands, for all the exiles; in fact they rattled about in the big villas, having been allowed so few in service. After a time we were able to hire some extra help, but not what any of these aristocrats was used to. Once, as Sappho poured herself some milk from a pitcher in the kitchen of the house where they were living, she made a little joke. "See how I am roughing it!" I smiled to myself, thinking of the Sigeum land and the baths that were taken with half a helmet of water, red with rust, and the maggoty meat, the moldy bread, and all the rest. I wondered if she even dressed herself, now, in her "rough" life; then I remembered Praxinoa, and knew that she did not. Nor undressed either; a thought that dashed me. She was always about in those first weeks, that woman, with her mother's face, and her ripe, sensuous body. I found it very difficult to be alone with Sappho, though in Mitylene we had been often left unattended. It was, of course, on Andros' orders; he must have known that to the young such adversities as we had endured at the Tyrants' hands were a hectic flush upon our headlong passions. This is a thought that I have had later, much later, looking back on my youth; at the time I blamed the woman Praxinoa, and resented her presence, so that at times I was rude, as I never am with beautiful people. A strange thought, too, comes to mind; I never desired Praxinoa. I never knew why; she was not all that old.

Though our property is considerable, the lands spreading far beyond the confines of the city, we are not really wealthy, by Mitylenian standards. There are some olive groves, pretty but not carefully cultivated, so that they bear only enough for our own use and a bit over. Our vineyards bring us in some profit, for in all the years since our parents' deaths, Melanippos has seen to them, and they produce a fine light wine that is much prized in Egypt, where he has trade connections; truly he has been a great good friend to us. Antimenades has said that, given the time, he can make our olives trees into something, but 'Nippos advised against it. He said it will be years till a profit could be realized on the olives or their oil, what with the complications that go with such things. I never knew anything of business; all I ever wanted was the means to be comfortable. Antimenades said that is all very well, but someone must do it; gold, once it is spent, is gone forever. He was right, of course; many of the noble families had gone into trade of late. Strange, I never thought where wealth had come from, ours or our friends'; most of our island nobles have lived on inherited wealth for generations, as a way of life. I guess in the beginning it was the spoils of some dreadful war or other, and the winning side wresting all. And from these plunderers we have risen, we learned, lordly, gifted aristocrats. Until the gold runs out, and then we must do it all over again, one way or the other. For successful trading is much the same, a form of stealing, say what you will. Except of course it is not so bloody. Ah, well, it is the way of the world. The changes we can make are so little—not worth aching for or fighting over. But this is the old man talking, that is Alkaios today. Long ago, in the days of my youth, I was the biggest hothead of all, and my cause the only just one. I can hardly remember them, I have striven for so many.

Because the households of the exiles were so small, we were able to be hosts to all of them; each family had a house to itself. We were a small colony, and there were many artists, of one kind or another, among us; the life we led was civilized, but simple, almost idyllic. The normal activities that went with large households were suspended, because forbidden; there was no excess of gold among us, but we wanted for nothing either. I am sure that secretly some of the nobles worried about their estates at home, though Pittakos had given his promise not to interfere or allow interference, and to protect us from having all confiscated; but after all, we had seen already that he was not a man to be trusted. One could only hope, and pray. But on the surface at least all seemed well, and even happy. The older men, such as Andros and Erigyus, found homely occupation about the grounds; Andros cultivated a flower garden, terracing the side of a hill, using stones from the fields to layer it. It did not take long to begin to look attractive; one could visualize it, even in winter. The soil of Pyrrha is, for some reason, blacker and moister than in Mitylene, perhaps because of the gulf waters that wash it.

Erigyus became a very farmer, brown and sturdy, beaming over his cabbages and leeks.

There were a good many young children; Praxinoa formed a school for the smallest among them, teaching them the rudiments of learning. Sappho and I gave lessons on harp and lyre, though I must admit I made a poor teacher, for I had no patience with the untalented. She, on the other hand, would go over and over a phrase with some clod until he or she had it right. It was the same with poetry; she managed to teach meter and cadence to them, all, and even to stimulate some pretty thoughts; I would give up in exasperation and stomp off somewhere to sulk. For of course, in a way, I resented the time she spent at this; I should have liked her all to myself. By the time a month had passed, the watchfulness had let up, and we were allowed to be alone. Winter was upon us, and we could not walk out of doors without warm cloaks, for it was raw and chill in the valley, and windy on the olive hills. Still, we managed some little contact, holding hands, and a kiss or two, snatched and sweet, like green fruit that is tart and leaves an ache afterward. Being myself, I must assuage that ache, somehow. The peasant girls were exceptionally pretty in those parts, but I never went near one of them; I felt it would be a betrayal, somehow, and that I could wait. I contented myself with the adoration of young Hippias, who had hung around me for nearly a year in the army. It had only amused me then, because there had been plenty of other attractions, and I had thought him far too young then; I have *some* code of ethics, after all. But he was old enough now, and most attractive, just growing into manhood, with a soft down on his face that was not enough to shave, and limbs that were lengthening gracefully. He was a cousin of Sappho's (everyone seemed to be, in truth!) and resembled her a little, so there was an extra sweetness in it. And it could not hurt her, after all; he was only a boy.

Melanippos shared the big villa, that was our old family house, along with me, my brother and sister, and those deserted children of dead Drakon and the runaway Phaedra. Dika spent much of her time in Sappho's house, for she was a good poet and singer herself; Telesippa, taught by 'Nippos, learned to work with clay and basked in his attentions; Hippias was their brother, so he was about when I needed him. There was another brother, younger, but he had never turned up; we all supposed that he was with Phaedra, wherever that might be. There were, of course, many others of us, there being nine exiled families in all. But it does not do to name too many; it just makes for confusion. It is enough to say we were a pleasant little group, and for the time, playing at a pastoral life.

It had been hard for all of us, I know, to pick just those four servants that were allowed us; what to do with those others, dependent and vulnerable? I know some families sold the slaves they left behind; it made for ready money. Most of Andros' slaves had long been freed; he sent them from him, with a year's wages; I suppose they settled in some of the smaller hill towns. Phaon, who had been freed recently, asked to be left behind in Mitylene. He said he would find employment, dancing for whoever could afford it, or performing in the festivals. At a pinch, he said, laughing, he could draw a crowd on the wharfside or in one of the taverns, and so pick up a living. "And," he said, "you need a spy at any rate. . . ." I almost came to like him in those days, for he helped our cause greatly in the months that followed. Melanippos gave him a purse of coins, as generous as he could afford; he found some likely boys from the dockside, agile and sharp, and made dancers of them, forming a little troupe. We heard, after a while, that they were in great demand, as a novelty, at banquets in the city. And, more important, they brought us news, from time to time. Risking their lives, merrily, one or the other of them would slip out of the city, past the guards, by night, and come to us, grinning and covered with dust, a message memorized, and would take no fee, but vanished, back into the night. Not one of them was ever caught; they had charmed lives, or some wayward god protected them. They were proper little knaves, no doubt about it, sly-eyed and rough-tongued, but loyal to their leader, Phaon; well, after all, he was one of them in his beginnings.

The news they brought was confusing; the City Guard had grown to great proportions, yet still there were dissenters, demonstrating at street corners, and somehow managing to vanish before they were caught. The song that Sappho had made for the feast, the night of the assassination of the first Tyrant, Melanchros, was sung everywhere, but to different words, revolutionary and a little scurrilous, at least in the versions that found their way to our ears. Other songs, too, were sung, with

rude words. There was one, set to my music, an old drinking song
of my early youth, which was really obscene, about Phaedra; we
had to keep it from her daughters, though it was very funny and
would have quickly caught on. We exiles were well liked here in
Pyrrha; we were all generous, with the little we had, and
courteous and fair, as well, to all; the ordinary farmer folk were
unused to it, from nobles, and were inclined to treat us like gods,
or nearly, and to refuse pay for their services. And people in
small outlying settlements are always independent; they do not
take kindly to the rule of one man setting himself over all. It is a
hangover, I suppose, from the old tribal days, when people met
in council to decide all points; chiefs, warriors, wise men, and
even some venerable old wise women. All the very earliest tribes,
of course, were matriarchies; I suppose there was a kind of race
memory, still, in our island places, where nothing new happens,
year in and year out. Anyway, among these people were many
volunteers, asking to join us, when and if we should ever come to
need them. And so, from the very beginning of our coming, there
was a little rebel band, forming, almost without conscious effort.

We learned, from Phaon's spies, that Pittakos, with Phaedra,
was back in his own house, left empty by his flown wife, and that
his daughter and her friend, Andromeda, had opened a school of
dancing and games; you guessed it, only girls were admitted. I
was shocked at first, but Sappho said, flushing a little, "Well,
why not? No girls were ever admitted to gymnasiums, except in
heathen Sparta!" I could see, though, that, underneath, she was
a little piqued, her mouth clamped tight and her face shut. After
a bit she said, "Wrestling! A silly thing, when you think of it—for
girls! After a certain age, one certainly cannot continue it. . . .
And what is dancing—without music?" They had got the jump
on her, those two, I could tell—and probably in more ways than
one. But I said only, "Darling, let them have their little whim.
. . . It will not last out the father's dictatorship. When we get
back to Mitylene, you will open a wonderful school . . . music
and singing, the arts of poetry and verse . . ."

"Ah, gods," she said, in a little, little voice, "when will that
be? . . ."

"My darling," I said, bending close and taking her face in my
two hands, "and you do not like it here?"

"Oh, Alkaios . . . it is beautiful in Pyrrha . . . and I love

it—your home. And all those I love are with me . . ." She
lowered her eyes; she could act the demure miss very well. Then
she looked up, meeting my eyes with her own, and honest and
frank. "But it is not my home. . . ."

I took her in my arms then, for no one was about, and we
clung together. I tasted the salt on her cheeks. She could always
weep like that; I have never known anyone else who could. Tears
would run down her face and drop from her bent head, like rain
from the sky, and leave no mark upon her. It was a great asset for
an artist—a performer, that is—yet I knew they were sincere,
too. Oh, my wild sweet girl, my heart's darling!

Gods—how sentimental I have grown, with my white hairs. I
sicken myself sometimes. Get on with it, Alkaios.

Chapter 10

As I was saying, we settled in nicely, living our little lives, and plotting our little plots. In fact, it was not long before we had a wedding! Well, it was only to be expected, with 'Nippos' beloved right here in the house with him!

To tell the truth, he rather shocked me, 'Nippos. I had never thought he would marry. He had never even, to my knowledge, cared very much for women at all; besides, he was old enough, or nearly, to have fathered the girl! I had grown to like her well, though I always thought her a little dull. So I was glad to see the marriage come to pass, glad for her and glad for him; besides, it was a delightful occasion for merriment. There is nothing quite like a wedding; it is better sometimes, even, than a Dionysos day! And I had my plans, wicked spider that I was, spinning my web for my adorable fly. I need not name her; she was busy weeks ahead, writing her wedding songs.

The wedding, following custom, was set for late February; this had been done in order to insure that the first child be born the following fall or winter, as in our Greece, the summer months often carry, in their heat, disease and even death. Again, this shocked me a bit; I guess Melanippos meant business, and was not just moved by a sort of avuncular love. I mentioned this to Sappho; we were composing a difficult dancing piece, putting our two heads to it, for neither of us had been able to come up with anything good enough. She set down her lyre and stared at me, prim. I said, jesting, "Oh, come now, you know very well what I mean . . ."

She looked at me for a long moment, and then at young Hippias, who followed me about, as I have said, like a dog. Then she said, with a light wave of her hand, "Oh, 'Nippos has given up all that sort of thing . . . and high time, too!" I said no more on the subject and found occasion to send Hippias away on some small errand. It seemed I had misjudged her, and she *was* jealous. Well, I should just have to keep him out of her sight.

This was an odd wedding, too, in that none of our old customs could be followed, truly. The bride already lived in the bridegroom's house, for instance; and the groom had no mother or father to greet the bride at his door when she came, had she not already been there. It all sounds quite confusing; of course everything among us exiles was a bit awry. We would just have to make the best of it. It was decided that for a full week before the ceremony, Telesippa would stay at the house of Sappho's father; he would give her away, and provide the feast. Then the pair would proceed to 'Nippos' house, to be welcomed by some of the women, who had gone before to ready the bedchamber. Sappho's Aunt Kassie volunteered; she was a silly, sweet, nervous woman; one could see that she was getting herself all worked up for a good cry. The freedwoman, Praxinoa, offered to help; it was a good thing, for poor Kassie was utterly incompetent, and would probably have forgotten the sheets for the nuptial bed!

In all of Pyrrha there were only three good chariots; that is, such as would be fit for ceremonial use. Most folk used wagons or litters, those who could afford it, and all the others rode on mounts or walked; the town itself was small anyway, and could be traversed completely on foot in half a day. These chariots belonged to my brother and me; one, the finest, had been our father's, and could take four horses. We determined it should be our wedding present to 'Nippos; it was the least we could do for that kind foster father. We still possessed a fair stable of stallions; from them we picked a matching four, white, the lead one having a yellowish star upon his forehead. We named him Hymen, thinking it a rare good joke, but when he was called by name, all the other three turned their heads, too. So they became Hymen One, Hymen Two, Hymen Three, and Hymen Four. Weddings are always ribald affairs, but even so, by the time we got around to presenting them to 'Nippos, the joke had worn a little thin. He was always the gentleman though, and smiled politely while Telesippa's pale face went crimson.

Antimenades and I spent a day polishing the brass sides of the gift chariot, and Sappho and little Atthis draped its sides in bright-colored ribbons.

The bride, along with her sister Dika, was the poorest of any of the exiles, for their hell-cat mother had taken everything in their house, even the girls' clothes and sandals, though she was taller than Dika and riper bodied than Telesippa, and they could not possibly have fit her. So the bride went dowryless, and in just the clothes she stood up in. We all saw to it that she looked charming, all the girls donated something for her wedding gear, and a whole chestful over to carry with her to her husband's house.

Nothing of Sappho's would fit her, of course. Sappho was so much tinier, and had already shared out most of her own things with Dika, who was small, too, and about her size.

There was, a little way outside the city, in a cypress grove, a little pool of fresh water, that ran down the hill from a hidden spring; for no particular reason, or one long since lost in the mist of time, it was called Daphne's Pool, and every bride since anyone could remember, had been washed there on her wedding day. It was a kind of rite, held over from the days of the worship of the Mother, when all springs were sacred to her, and no men were allowed anywhere near the place. Two old crones kept it, like a shrine, and they in turn were kept by the city, food and clothing being left for them at regular intervals on the outskirts of the sacred place. I had glimpsed them once, when I was a small boy, warming their hands over a fire of twigs and chanting a tuneless song. They looked to be more than a century even then; I wondered if they had died and been replaced.

Of course I did not see the ceremonial bath, but heard about it afterward from Sappho. It seems the spring had long dried up, and there was just a pool of brackish, stagnant water, covered with dead leaves and stinking. The poor shrinking bride had to strip to the skin, and it was chilly too, it being the middle of winter, and step with both feet into the water, what there was of it. Then the old crones scooped up some in their hands and sprinkled her with it. All the girls giggled, the shivering bride included, paid the toothless priestesses, and flung a warm fur robe over the bride's nakedness. Still, though, they had to wait, while the Mother was invoked, and Daphne, too. Upon which, said Sappho, they all broke out in giggles again, for who could need such a prayer . . . Telesippa was tall as a tree already, and did not need a dryad's beneficence. She needed another bath when they got her home, the poor anointed, for the droplets from Daphne's pool had speckled her with black mud. Praxinoa scolded, saying it was a silly, outmoded custom, and a good thing if the girl did not catch her death in the cold, and give it to her husband, too! "Oh, but Praxinoa, dear," wailed Telesippa, "everything must be right. I want nothing left to chance. . . ." She wailed, poor dear, because she was herself a little old, owing to the war years, to be bedded for the first time; I believe she was over twenty. They were all of them overripe, the girls from Lesbos, and innocent still. But what could be done till husbands were found? They could not very well be lined up like little whores and tumbled; after all, they were delicately bred and proud as blooded mares.

They were all, Sappho included, terribly excited by this wedding. One might have thought they were all getting married!

The ceremony was nearly like a wedding in Mitylene itself, though some things were missing—kinsfolk, for instance. We were a very small band, we exiles. Still, the folk of Pyrrha love weddings, too, and turned out by the dozens, lining the narrow lanes for the procession.

A group of us, young men for the most part, my brother and the nice boy Tyrrhaeos, son of the Tyrant, attired the groom. Antimenades and I had tossed for the part of best man, and I won. We had done it by kittabos, flinging the wine lees, so the jug had to be drained first. We were all a bit tiddly by then, and Antimenades emptied a whole cone of perfumed Egyptian oil over 'Nippos' head; it was the finest stuff, but in such quantity it stank dreadfully, and the whole head had to be thoroughly rewashed. By the time we finished with him we were giggling as crazily as the girls who tired the bride.

He looked marvelous, I must say, our old friend and tutor, not a day over thirty! There was another sacred pool, but we had skipped that; he said he was too old, never mind his looks, for such nonsense. But we had done all the rest. He was robed in spotless new white linen, very fine, with a white wool upper garment against the sun's going down. His close-clipped hair was wet still from its bath, and combed very straight, not curled as is the custom. It was a look that became him well; he looked like Apollo, especially after the flower wreath had been placed on his head and he stood tall in the chariot, with the reins wound around his left arm. I was next, in the second-best chariot, with a pair of fine black horses, very lively. I had to choose my passenger and started to nod to Hippias, as a matter of course; at the last moment, remembering Sappho, I changed my mind and chose Tyrrhaeos. His thin face lit; he had not expected the honor, and so I was glad. Antimenades took young Hippias, who looked sulky and slighted, beside him in the third and last of the chariots. All the rest of the groomsmen either rode or walked. It was a slow bit of parading, for the people watching kept dodging out into the streets and we had to be careful not to hit them; they were waiting for the coins that the groom threw from time to time. Also, being a thrifty stock, they picked up the horse droppings that fell; it was counted the best manure for any kind of growing, and sometimes, too, they dried it and burned it for fuel when wood was scarce.

The chariots and the company following moved so slowly that red streaks from the setting sun were striping us all by the time we drove up to Andros' villa. The entire front of it was covered with anything green that could be found, ivy, bay, fir and balsam, interwoven with the little red flowers of winter, sharp as winking red eyes among the massed foliage. There was a great canopy overhanging the way from gate to door; it looked to be carelessly put up, and threatened to fall upon us, an indignity, but it did not happen. At any rate, Melanippos never looked up, but proceeded like an Olympian, his face very grave. Well, I guess getting married is a serious business. I must say he looked wonderful, without his customary paint and powder. And where had the bags gone to, from under his eyes? I never remember him without them, like a mark of his own, even when I was a child. I guess it was abstinence that had done it, worked the miracle; he drank sparingly now, who had always been first to call for another bowl of wine. I promised myself that I would remember this . . . some day, much, much later, when I too was old. (Alas, I have forgot, and avoid the mirror of late.)

Andros stood beaming, if one might call it that, on so godlike a countenance, in the doorway, holding out his arms to welcome his old friend over the threshold.

Beyond, in the hall, with all her cousins and girlfriends twittering about her, dressed like gay little birds, and smelling of every kind of perfume under the sun, stood the bride, trying to smile and looking dreadfully faint. Melanippos went up to her, in the formal way expected of the occasion, took her hand, and bent over it, lightly kissing it. But I, behind him, heard him whisper, "Courage, sweet—it will all be over soon. . . ."

The smile came through then and she was transformed, a beauty for this one day. She, too, was all dressed in white, and draped in some gauzy stuff that enveloped her from head to foot. Very thin it was, though, and showed her face, all painted prettily red and white, with blue upon the eyelids and fingernails stained with henna from across the eastern sea. Melanippos led her into the dining hall, and they took the central couch, the bridal seat; it was also spread with greenery; I hoped there were no pine needles left among the branches.

On this occasion, men and women were separated, the couches to the bride's side filled with girls, and the groom's half of the hall occupied by the men and boys. The toasts began, getting dirtier and dirtier. The bride was crimson above her maiden white, and, glancing down toward where Sappho sat, I saw she had hidden her face in her hands. Well, it is simply one of those things, the custom, hallowed by time. Rather silly, actually, for the first jokes are always rather forced, not enough wine having gone the rounds to make them seem natural.

There was lyre playing, and songs, then, and the ladies left off pretending not to listen. Sappho sang a tender little verse, which I thought rather inane, but did not say so. It was all about lost maidenhead, lost forever, and so forth, and oh how sad . . . all the older women wept aloud, and it was the bride's turn to hide her face. But then Sappho—performer that she was—tossed her head, running her fingers over the strings loud to command attention, and sang a very funny little number with a catchy air. It was all about what she might liken the bridegroom to. A tender sapling, a slender shoot, a youth with mother's milk not yet dry upon its childish lips. Everyone roared with laughter; it was timed well, after the wine had been passed many times; it was really not as funny as all that. However, as happened with all that little witch's songs, it was sung for years afterward, whenever the bridegroom was a little ripe in years.

I had to follow her, of course. Impossible, in the natural way of things, so I improvised. The song was an old tune of my own, very pretty, even though I myself say it . . . but it was so very bawdy and lewd that all the ladies held hands to their ears and the young boys were sent from the room. And that is saying a lot, because at a wedding, truly—anything goes! I was feeling the wine by then, and verse after verse rolled out, as if inspired.

Finally, Melanippos rose, laughing, and stretched out his hand.
"Stop, please—I beg you. Not even Pittakos could accomplish all
that . . . and I am out of practice!" He had topped both us
singers with that; I had always known him clever. The hall rang
with shouts and clapping hands, and that was an end to the
singing, and a signal for the feast to begin.

I can never remember what there was to eat at a wedding
feast; I always am so drunken by the time the food comes. I am
told it was delicious, all, even though we were in straitened
circumstances. Course followed course, mussels in a creamy
sauce, huge stuffed fish, fowl, pastries, and so on . . . and each
with its accompanying wine. I kept watching Sappho. She sat
with the other women and girls, and she, too, looked my way,
and we raised our glasses to one another, smiling. I noticed that
she drank along with all the others, tasting of each variety, but
not eating very much; I had never known her to take wine in any
quantity; she usually preferred goat's milk, or that honeyed
barley water that children love. Perhaps she was finally growing
up, I thought, and found myself smiling. She saw me, and blew a
kiss, not caring who saw. As for me, I tingled all over, even to my
toes and fingertips.

When the dinner was at last over, and the guests rose to take
their places outside for the procession back to the bride's house, I
noticed that Sappho had put aside her lyre and was holding a
little drum, not much larger than a large man's fist, but deep and
tapering, cone-shaped. It was a curious thing, the first of its kind
I had seen, and strangely decorated, with birds' feathers and
little fur tails from some small dead animals. Her brother,
Charaxus, next to me, saw me looking and whispered, "It is a
beating instrument left over from that fickle Drom . . . Sappho
cannot really play it very well—she must be full up with
wine. . . ."

I eyed him with some distaste; I had never come to like him,
really, though he was handsome enough, like his father, but
weaker in the features, and with eyes that roved, even while he
spoke with one; I suppose he was always looking over the likely
women; he had a name for it already, though he was younger
than his sister.

"Drom? . . ." I said, questioning.

"Oh, you know . . . the freedgirl, black, that ran off with the Ammie, Old Pitt's daughter."

I had not known the army talk had spread so far. But, of course, Charaxus was just the sort who would get friendly with the rougher kind of soldier, and pick up all the dirtier tales.

"Yes," he went on, "poor Sappho was red-eyed for weeks. They used to be like that, she and Drom"—and he held up two fingers entwined—"before Gorgo got hold of her, with the wrestling and all . . ."

I digested that, along with the last course; both were a little rich. I said nothing, but rose to take my place outside in the bridal chariot. I pushed thrugh the crowd, all ready with their baskets of flowers and grain, and climbed up, taking the reins. On the way back, it was the custom for the best man to drive the chariot and the couple to sit on the little low seat behind, trying to duck the showers of barley and roses thrown at them along the way. I noticed, not without a small wrench of envy, that my brother, Antimenades had chosen Sappho to ride along with him in the second chariot. He lifted her up as easily as if she were little Atthis; her long skirt lifted, showing a bit of leg, and there were some few whistles. By now the wine was showing everywhere. She did not even look offended, but laughed and waved to the crowd. *Well,* I thought, *that augurs well; her primness is slipping.*

Strange, though, there were flute girls hired from one of the best houses in town, going before us with some singers and acrobats; they go, always, those girls, with the thinnest, shortest garments, and the traditional bared left breast, and some were pretty as paintings, too; yet no one even as much as noticed them. But let a lady maiden show an ankle, and all eyes goggle! Well, the flute girls would earn their pay later; it was what they were hired for, after all. Most of them did not know one note of music from another!

I glanced behind, while the couple seated themselves; Sappho was getting almost as many rose-peltings as the bride, and the folk were shouting and hailing her. "The Black Lark" they called her. Her fame, then, had traveled ahead of her. I was always fairly popular myself, but more of a poet's poet; she had the folk touch that cannot be learned.

When we reached Melanippos' house, the door stood open;

within its frame stood the mother-by-proxy, Sappho's Aunt
Kassie, her face all crumpled from crying, and wringing her
hands. She stepped aside just in time, for the bridal pair were
making a dash through, laughing, to escape the thrown barley
seeds; they can sting if they hit hard, a whole handful. As a
matter of fact, I got some down my back and had to shake myself
like a wet dog to get them out from my tunic.

At one end of the entrance hall was a little altar, where the
household gods lived; I had not given it much thought before, for
'Nippos rarely kept the lights burning in front of it, not being a
man of religious observance. But, for this day, it was unshrouded
and brightly lit, the little images graceful and charming, in their
old-fashioned way. He led her to the altar; they took, each, a
pinch of sweet-smelling stuff, powdery, and threw it onto the
flames, coloring them like a small rainbow; everyone cheered. He
kissed her then, most tenderly, and reached down to her waist,
unclasping the ritual girdle she wore.

It is the custom for the bride to close her eyes, holding the
girdle, while the groom turns her about three times, round and
round. After, still playing blind, she reaches out to touch one of
the other girls who attend her. The first one she touches is
privileged then to wear the girdle for that night. And the belief is
that this favored girl is destined to become the next bride in the
lot. Telesippa, eyes closed, but smiling, stretched out her hand; I
thought it just grazed Sappho's shoulder, but she shifted quickly
and the hand held another arm. It was the arm of the plump
freckled one, Nausikaa, Aunt Kassie's daughter; at this, poor
Kassie broke into a true storm of happy weeping, and everyone
shouted with laughter and made rude jokes, and Nausikaa's
freckles were swallowed up in her blushes.

Under cover of the din and noise of the pushing of the couple
into the waiting bedchamber, and all the door-spying and
banging and shouting, I edged over to Sappho, who stood
quietly, beating softly upon her curious little drum.

"She touched you first, Telesippa did . . . I saw," I whispered.
"Why did you shrug away?"

"Sh-h-h," she whispered back. "Nausikaa has a boy she fancies
. . . it will give them both courage. Besides," she said, louder,
and straightening her shoulders, "I am not ready. . . ."

The door-banging had tapered off now to a few sporadic

thuds, and the shouting had turned to singing; couples were
sinking to the floor outside the bridal door to keep their vigil
together, chanting between sips of wine from the little flasks they
carried, and moving ever closer. The lights had not been lit, and
only the glow, fading, from the little altar, kept away the
darkness. In the half-light I turned her face toward me, gently,
with my hand; it was shadowy, the whites of her eyes catching
red sparkings from the altar flames.

"Not ready for love? . . . " I said, low, into her ear.

I saw her mouth curve into a little secret smile. "I did not say
that," she said, and banged the drum louder. I pulled her slowly
down to the floor beside me, and we sat with our backs to the
wall, close along our bodies and dreaming. I was aware of sounds
about me, the singing seemed louder; I realized she had stopped
her drumming. Our faces turned together, as one, and we kissed.
I had been kissed before, you understand, thousands upon
thousands of times, before, during, and after love. It was not the
same. This was the before, the during, and the after. The kiss was
long, too long; perhaps we fainted. I found myself on top of her,
crushing her against the stone floor. I felt like a raw lad, all
emptied and a little shamed, our clothes wet in front and clinging
damply, and Sappho moaning. Well, I thought, that was quick,
Alkaios, and you full of wine, too, which usually works the other
way around. I blamed it on her, of course, as men will, and
thought also—Where did she learn to kiss like that, this little
dainty maid? I did not move, but whispered, "Are you a witch,
then?"

She smiled up at me; I could just make out her lips, but she
did not have time to answer. The door of the bridal chamber
burst open and light from a flaring torch lit the shadows. All
around us were stirrings, as couples moved apart and sat up.

The woman Praxinoa came out of the chamber, carrying a
half-eaten quince upon a plate; Kassie, still weeping, but trying
to smile, followed. "They have eaten the quince," said Kassie,
quaveringly. All is well . . ."

Zeus, I had forgotten that ridiculous custom. In the presence of
the bride's parents, and lying beside one another under the
coverlet, the groom unveils the bride (it is all she is wearing, or
he either, for that matter), and the couple then are presented
with a quince fruit on a ceremonial plate, which they must eat,

or at least partly, as a pledge of future sweetness of speech. It takes forever, for speeches go with it as well, and much ceremony. I could not help but picture in my mind the two in bed there, watched over by the two women, one silly, one stern; Telesippa with her long sweet mare's face and Melanippos with his crow's feet and freshly dyed hair, and the covering pulled up to their chins, hiding their bony nakedness. And then to have to bite into the plump fruit and hope it would not spurt juice all over the best linen! And now to lie beside each other and know they must get down to business, for the company will not leave until the sheets are examined and the marriage pronounced consummated. I only hoped they were both well flown with wine to make it easier to get started!

It was Aunt Kassie who carried the torch; even though it wavered, it still gave a fairish bright light. "Hide me!" whispered Sappho, beside me, and I leaned forward, for, like all the other couples, we had sat up in quick guilt; I was trying to pretend to reach for a cruet of wine, but I was not quick enough. I saw the woman Praxinoa's eyes flicker over my shoulder and hold, staring. There was a look in them that I understood and, despite my dislike, sorrowed for; I knew, suddenly, where Sappho had learned her kiss!

She, little minx, was as cool as snow from the mountain. She met those eyes and smiled, smoothing her hair, and looking down at herself in dismay. "Sweet Praxinoa," she said, coaxingly, "lend me that cloth you are carrying . . . We have spilled white wine all over ourselves in the dark. . . . Thank the gods it was not purple!" I was aghast. What a liar! I could never have done it so well. And I have had practice!

Praxinoa handed her the cloth; I suppose it had been used to wipe up the quince juice. She watched silently as Sappho dabbed at the lap of her crumpled tunic, and then handed it to me, with a demure smile; it was too damp to do much good by then, but I dabbed in my turn, feeling the woman's eyes on me all the while.

She spoke then, her voice a little hoarse. "You will catch a chill, Sappho . . . perhaps you had better go home and change. I will come with you. . . ."

"Before the singing is over? I can't leave now! It would be dreadfully bad manners!" Sappho sounded absolutely horrified. "It is very warm here . . . my dress will dry in no time. . . .

Besides, Father promised I could stay . . . and drink deep, too! I am a grown woman, after all!" Then, with a subtle difference that made Praxinoa's face change, she said, "You may go, if you wish . . . I will not need you any more. . . ."

It was cruel, reducing the woman from her privileged status of mother-teacher-intimate, to the role of servant. But it was cruel as a child is cruel, and I forgave her, remembering she was not yet a grown woman, no matter how much she protested it.

"As you wish, Lady," said Praxinoa, and she moved away. Aunt Kassie still hovered, uncertainly, having heard the exchange, the torchlight wavering in her hand. By its light I could see Sappho's face, defiant and a little sulky. "Well," she said, "she is so fussy . . . and Father *did* promise . . ." She picked up the little drum and tapped it again, humming along with it, a wedding song that someone had started.

The interruption had started up all the noise and ribaldry again. Youths began banging on the bridal door and shouting rude things, as are licensed at a wedding, and the girls all giggled and pretended to be dreadfully embarrassed. Aunt Kassie, very distraught, set down the torch upon a little table and moved away, beginning again to wring her hands. As she passed us, I heard Sappho give a little muffled laugh; she picked up something from the floor, and got to her feet, leaning heavily on my shoulder. "Aunt Kass," she called, "you have dropped a hairpin. . . ." And she held it out; I saw that Sappho swayed a little, and put out a hand to steady her. Kassie took the pin from her, looking puzzled, and hurried off, her hands going quickly to her hair.

"Sit down, sweetheart . . . rest," I said, pulling Sappho down again beside me.

Her face was merry and very young. "I remember her so—always," she said. "She drops things as she goes, like a molting bird. . . ."

We sat quietly for a while, both singing softly, our cheeks close and her hand still beating the drum. "I want some more wine," said Sappho suddenly.

"You will get drunk," I said, teasing.

"I want to," she said. "I want to see how it feels . . . I think I like it. . . ."

I got up and found a jug of Chian and two glasses; there was always plenty of wine about at wedding parties, well within reach. After all, this thing could go on all night, depending. If you take my meaning.

I poured it, and handed her one glass. "It is red wine," I said, smiling. "So be careful."

She took the glass, meeting my eyes and not smiling back. "I know it wasn't wine before—silly!" She took a sip and hiccuped. "Excuse me." She took another sip and set down the glass on the floor, turning her face to me. "Just don't do it again—that's all! Or perhaps I *will* get a chill . . ."

"You won't," I answered, putting down my own glass and bringing my lips to meet hers.

I wish with all my heart that I might end the episode there, and the reader think of it as he will, or as I hoped—but alas, it did not happen that way. I am not a writer of love manuals for the student, nor yet a Homer, that can lie so gloriously. I am Alkaios, and I put it all down as it was.

The kiss began, and my head began to reel. But the chamber door opened again, and Melanippos stood within it, framed and tall, a light woolen robe flung over him, and holding out the bedsheet. There was a small brazier within; the red light from it edged his form. On his face was a look half of triumph, half of sheepishness. "Here," he said, holding it out. "It is done. A good night to you all." Someone—I cannot remember who—took the sheet from him, and he stepped back into the chamber, shutting the door firmly.

A babble of excited voices rose as all crowded to examine the bloody evidence upon the sheet, the earnest of a lost maidenhead. I stayed where I was, taking his word for it. Of course we had sprung apart, like all the other couples. And Sappho, dear girl, got the hiccups.

They went on and on and would not stop. They got louder and louder, her face got red, and tears ran from her eyes.

The women came to take the sheet away—to preserve it or whatever is done at such times—a women's mystery. A crowd began to form around us two, and Sappho shaking with each loud hiccup.

"Pound her back!"

"Count to ten!"

"Stand her on her head!"

I did none of these things, but ran for a jar of water.

"Take a deep breath," I said, "and then drink . . . as much as you can." She did, and hiccuped again.

"Take another drink of water," I said, holding the jar to her lips. She drank, deeply this time, and then handed back the jug, looking surprised. A moment. "They're gone!" she cried.

"Good!" I said, firmly. "And now get up and go home—for here is your father. . . ." I had seen him a bit before; I am almost as good a pretender as she.

He took her hand, Andros, smiling indulgently. "She is not used to so much wine. . . ." And he shook his head sadly. "And I am afraid she has mixed it, too. . . . I shall have to instruct her, I see."

He put his arm about her small shoulders and guided her to the door of the house. Before he took her through, he turned to me, and, with great courtesy, said, "I thank you, Alkaios, for your kindness. A good night to you . . . sleep well." And, so saying, he took her to her home.

As for me, I went, swaying a little myself, to my own chamber, falling heavily upon the bed. After a bit, there came a soft scratching at the chamber door.

I went over, tiptoeing, and opened it. It was Hippias. I let him in, and shot the bolt.

Chapter 11

I write now—now that I am old—of young romance and song and our Pyrrhic life, as though it were some kind of sweet soft tale. Truly all our heads whirled with plots and counterplots. And there was violence and death and sorrow with it. The blood in my veins runs thinner now, I suppose, or such fires as we kindled in those days I shrink from now, and like best to remember the warm glow of the long-gone wine within, and the withered flesh without.

But I shall put my mind to it and write as it happened, as best I may remember it and the way that it went, and what thing came first and what after and so on.

During all that time in Pyrrha, Phaon's spies brought us word of Mitylene and the happenings there; it was not really far away, but it might have been at the world's end for us, who were forbidden to enter it upon pain of death. Truly, I think I would have sneaked in anyway, for defiance and for the risk, but that the attractions were too great right here in Pyrrha. Most of the friends I had left in Mitylene were army friends; I was sick to death of anything or anyone that reminded me of those days, and a great many of them, anyway, were under Pittakos' sway and no longer my kind.

The girls of our party were in worse case, for they missed their friends of a lifetime that were left behind, and they missed the bustling marketplace and the wares they could buy from far lands; how often I heard Sappho bemoan that she had nothing to wear! She had robes and cloaks and sandals and scarves by the dozen, and all else besides, but I suppose an only daughter of a wealthy father missed that new present each week. Also, I could feel, too, it would have been pleasant to see the sea, and the harbor, and the ships lying off, all with their fascinating cargoes, and the sight of the outlandish sailors in their strange dress.

Speaking of ships, we had some heartening news, brought in the night by one of Phaon's dancing boys. Myrsilos, that had seized the reins of power along with Pittakos, had grown wealthy and powerful in the slave trade; he was hated, and heartily, by all the folk of the city for this. Pittakos must have needed his money, and was making use of him for his own ends; though Pittakos was exceedingly popular, especially with the young men who had seen service, and with the peasantry, who remembered his beginnings, he was never seen in public with his co-tyrant. (Actually they had, each, their separate titles, self-bestowed. Myrsilos was Tyrant, and Pittakos, Dictator; they mean much the same thing.) Even he, beloved of the people, would not risk his popularity so far. And we heard that Myrsilos himself did not even dare show his face; even his servants were stoned in the street, and the walls of his house vandalized.

. Now, it seems a ship of Myrsilos' was standing in harbor, well offshore; its cargo, human, had been taken off and shipped overland to be sold. The ship was waiting for its return cargo. The crew, pirates really, went up in the hills and captured what they could find, unwary children playing alone; or they bribed some to sell others. Who knows what perfidy the human soul is capable of? At any rate, the empty ship was set aflame by night, and burned to a cinder; a loss of profit to break old Myrsilos' heart. The people banded together, under the leadership of some of the street boys that had been ousted from the City Guard to make way for the army veterans. They waited for the returning pirate crew, the slave catchers, and killed them, every one. All those intended to be sold into slavery were set free, joining the mob and dancing around Myrsilos' house, smashing whatever they could, while he cowered within, behind barred gates of iron. The house and all the outbuildings were of stone, or they would have fired it; even so, all the walls were black with smoke, and nothing was left of the showy gardens. We rejoiced when we heard this, as you may imagine.

We had all supposed that the murderess, Phaedra, was dwelling in Pittakos' house; that news was misheard. She was with Myrsilos, as might have been expected; he was the wealthiest man in the islands of Greece, and she was hardly the sort to care how he had come by it. Her children cared, though, and bitterly. They were all, remember, here with us in exile, except for little Hermias. They set apart a day, and buried her in effigy, digging a grave and putting into it a long bolster wrapped in an old cloak that had belonged to the lady, scattering dust and bitter herbs upon the thing and filling the grave in; Hippias, that dainty boy, did all the digging! They wore black, and heaped ashes on their heads; it was in vain that I reminded them that we had no real proof of her murdering their father—and that, indeed, all our news might possibly be false. Dika said, sharply, "It does not matter . . . a cat is a better mother than she was, ever. . . ."

I wrote verses, ugly but full of wit, if I myself say it, about that wicked team of rulers that had Mitylene, our beloved city, in their grip. The boys of Phaon took them back, by return mail, as one might say, and they were sung openly in all the taverns there, and even in the streets. Sappho felt strongly, too, and tried her hand at such songs, but she failed; there was no anger in her poetry, or rancor; she kept it for her private use. That sounds like a sort of backbiting, but I loved her—even her flaws. We quarreled bitterly, not a few but many times; the kisses afterward were all the sweeter.

The winter passed; at its very end, and none too soon to conform to custom, there was another wedding. It was as Sappho had predicted; she who wore Telesippa's girdle became the next bride, with a girdle of her own. I smile to myself as I remember that, for Nausikaa was far too plump to borrow the one that she had won from 'Nippos' bride. Her groom was a young man of these parts, wellborn, in a smallholder's way; our Pyrrhic families are not much more than prosperous farmers. He was always called Xeno, for he had another of those unpronounceable names—Xenochranaxos, or something like it, I have forgotten now. He might have been her brother; they had identical expressions, smiling, sweet, and ineffably dull; he matched her weight, too, and some over. So beside him, she was a slim little thing.

The bride, and the groom, too, had proper parents of their own to see to things; though the wedding was just as full of ribald jokes and play, the men and girls were made to sit separately throughout the night, the girls at the bridal door and the men at the groom's house. It was stricter in its observance; Erigyus and Kassie were old-fashioned. The night after the actual bedding, the groom, from olden times, has always slept in his parents' house, to give the bride a full night's sleep. This, in its implications, is, of course, a lewder custom than the more modern. One imagines the poor deflowered creature worn out from a dozen or so mountings! At any rate, Sappho and I did not pair off, as we had before; I had been hoping for a better conclusion this time! I am told that she practically ran the whole thing, organizing the singing and dancing of the maidens and chanting outside the door all night long. I know the next day her eyes were redder than the dawn they welcomed. I know also that the songs she wrote were some of the most exquisite of such pieces ever done; the bride was her cousin and dear friend, after all. She was in great demand in Pyrrha after that, at every wedding; the lesser folk do not hold fast to the winter custom, but marry at any time they feel like it, only asking the gods to smile upon them and the goddesses to make them fruitful. She never turned down any bride's request for a song; even the poorest were given her best, though sometimes they paid in garden produce or could pay nothing at all.

With the first stirrings of spring and the spring dances that go along with it, we felt, as one always does, having been confined indoors by chilly rains and sleet, a little stiff in the joints, even the young among us; in our Greek lands we are much used to playing and running and exercise of all sorts.

The folk of Pyrrha have their gymnasium, just a rough sort of open place outside the town, a kind of playing field. They have their games, too, but they have not learned much skill, except at a kind of acrobatics; they have developed this almost to an art, but they know little of boxing, wrestling, running, or jumping. I organized a crude sort of training in these things, and all the young men and lads of our party, and some others, too, of the town, came to the field each morning, when it was fine, to practice.

The girls liked to watch, for the sun and the air and the sight itself, so we wore tight loin-pieces, which hampered us a little. Though privately I think it is not a bad thing, for I have seen many a lad ruined for life, by some stupid accident, unforeseen.

I was a good boxer, light and quick, and I had good speed as well, but Charaxus could always wrestle me to a fall; he had the right mind for it, a little cunning, quick to see the main chance. It served him well, all his life, in many ways; in one thing only he was blind, caught unawares. That was by love, and I, for one, liked him the better for it. But I am way ahead of my story; Charaxus was a raw boy still, in Pyrrha.

One fair morning, the air new-washed by an early fall of light rain, and the sun not too hot yet, an odd thing happened. I had seen the girls' bright eyes and heard them call out the turns, knowledgeably; unusual, for women do not often attend the games, except on some special occasion, to honor a god.

Dika stepped forward, after the field was cleared of us boys, and we sat, panting, and taking turns scraping the oil off each other's backs. She held out her hands in the accustomed wrestler's pose, planting her feet and smiling. Sappho took the place opposite and they began to circle round, watching for an opening. Sappho saw it first and got in the first hold, a simple arm-bend, but it forced Dika to her knees. They were both laughing, but one could see that they knew some tricks. It was something to watch, for their skirts went all awry, and their knots of hair slipped from the bindings and fell about them like dark rippling water. It ended in a draw, neither making the throw; they got up, looking a little sheepish, and straightening their clothes. "It is always like that!" cried Sappho. "We are too perfectly matched. . . ." Privately I thought that, girllike, they had not wanted to hurt or be hurt, as well, but I said nothing, and asked only where they had learned such a skill.

"Oh," cried Dika, "we know much more . . . many games. We used to play them always on the roof after Gorgo—" She clapped her hand to her mouth, looking with wide eyes at Sappho.

"Oh, don't be a silly, Dika," said Sappho. "Give her her due. . . . She was good for something, at least, Gorgo . . . though I think we are better off without her, even at games. She took them all too seriously. They are fun, rather, sometimes, and preserve the wind that singers need . . ." She turned to me, for she saw a surprised look on my face. "Gorgo was a girl from Sparta—Pittakos' daughter . . ."

"I know," I said. "I have seen her."

She gave me a sharp look, then went on. "Old Pitt—she called him that—was good friends with Father once. He brought her out of Sparta, where she had been much abused, and asked leave to board her in our house. He hoped she would learn civilized

ways. . . ." Her face went all merry then, and all the girls began
to laugh.

Setting her features straight, she said, "She did not learn a
great deal—as you may have seen . . . but she taught us some
things. In Sparta the girls wrestle and box and compete in all the
games with the boys. It is the custom. They think it will breed up
heroes. . . ."

I said quickly, "And instead it breeds up Ammies, eh?"

"Ammies? . . ." she said, her brow wrinkling. I heard her
brother, Charaxus, snort behind me, smothering a great laugh.
"Sappho does not know the word . . . she is too prim."

"None of us girls knows it," said Telesippa, with her new wife's
dignity. "Please enlighten us, cousin."

I thought to myself, *So they really are as innocent as they look, these
doll-things.*

Charaxus went a dull brick red, and stared down at his hands,
knuckling them. I decided, *Well—now or never—what's to lose?* I
tried an explanation.

"Well, it is soldier talk, really. The word, you see, comes from
Amazon . . ." They all were still staring; no light had hit their
eyes. "Well," I began again, rather lamely, "Amazons . . . they
were a tribe of warrior women . . ."

"Oh," said Dika, breathless, "I do not think the Spartan girls
really go to war!"

"Well—but, I mean—well . . . women without men . . .
you see?"

"I see," said Sappho, giving me a long look.

"I don't," said silly Nausikaa, not wed long enough to have
gained much dignity. "I don't see it at all. Because, if they were a
tribe of women without men—how did they have babies?" Her
face was a little pink beneath her freckles; I saw for the first time
a little bulge at her waistline, not just fat.

"Well, they are sort of legendary, after all," I said. "One does
not exactly know about them. I mean, some people think they
may have been priestesses of Artemis, and vowed to chastity . . .
with men, that is . . . and so . . ."

Sappho cut in. "My father's friend, Thales, who is a great
thinker, and much traveled and read as well, says the Amazons
were a race where women were in all ways superior, and simply
used the men for breeding—just the reverse of most of the world.

And that they were greatly feared and respected for their prowess and their lore of magic and healing. . . . They are all vanished now. It was long, long ago. . . ."

And her face looked a little pensive.

"Oh, come on now, Sappho," I said. "It is just a word, a rude jest. I mean—someday you will have to learn things of the world. It is simply a word—whatever its origin—that means . . . women who love women. . . ." She looked at me blankly. I spread my hands and shrugged, and spoke again. "Look—women, girls, whatever . . . girls who make love to girls . . . who lie with girls, and prefer it that way . . ." I heard Nausikaa gasp. Sappho flushed. She whirled on me. "And what of the men—and boys . . . who do the same? Is there no name for them? There are enough of them around—" And she flicked a glance at Hippias, who tossed his head, petulant. I could have cheerfully slapped him.

Charaxus saved the day. "There are many, many names, Sappho . . . but they are all too rude for girls' ears. And they are said about the lowest sort, anyway . . ."

I caught him up quickly. "Yes . . . and, Sappho . . . it is just a word . . . usually it means the rough sort of girl, a bit boylike. . . . I just thought she looked it, somewhat—Gorgo. . . . I'm sorry if I offended."

"Oh," she said, her head high, "you do not offend *me* . . . Gorgo is no friend of mine—nor ever was, really."

"And she *doesn't* like boys," put in Dika, eagerly. "Remember the time she bit you, Charaxus?"

"Oh, well," said Sappho. "Charaxus deserved it—he always does. . . ." But she smiled in his direction, and I knew the worst was over, and that she was no longer angry. She never liked, now that I come to think of it, to hear any man speak of any woman, even the lowest, without respect or courtesy. It was different when she was doing the name-calling, man or woman. I have heard some pretty bad names from her when she got her temper up. And that was in the days before she knew any swear words.

I have said that we quarreled; then why is it that I remember her, so many years later, as the one great love of my life? I cannot answer it; perhaps there is something back to back in love and anger, that cannot ever meet, and the pathos of it, looked back upon, is sweet. I truly do not know. We fought—over music, over verse, over meter. We could never work together, there was no common ground. Yet each of us knew that, in all the world, we had no peers, except ourselves. We were gifted beyond all others, and it would be a false foolishness to deny it.

Our only meeting ground was kisses, thousands upon thousands of kisses, lingering and soft. It was spring nights, the scent of sharp opening buds upon the air, warm flesh, and seeking hands. It was laughter, sudden, bubbling, and whispering low, and the secret held breath to keep out the rest of the world. I say—and do not care who scorns—that we two were put upon this earth for each to enjoy each—and only the capricious gods kept us apart.

Her father, the strong and godlike Andros, died, gored by a wild boar in the hills; he had gone, with some others, old as they were, but not feeling it, and telling no one, to rid the hill folk of their homely menace. But a boar needs much strength to be held, when you have it upon your spear, and this was a wounded one, and angry, and all the hunting party were of an age. Andros' brother Erigyus, was pinned against a great oak by the weight of the beast upon his spear; Andros rushed in to aid him, no one else being near, and the maddened beast broke free, and, turning, finished the rescuer.

We all mourned his passing and the waste of it; Sappho lay upon my breast all of one night, weeping her copious tears to bring my tunic to a sopping wetness. She sent away the woman Praxinoa, saying that she had no need of her, being grown, and that I would give her comfort.

And so I did; but that was all, for she never stopped crying till dawn, when she fell asleep suddenly, exhausted. My arm, beneath her, cramped, and I eased it out from under, gently, and she never woke. I watched by her while she slept, and drank a whole jugful of Cretan. When she wakened finally, I was dead asleep, from the long vigil and the unwatered wine. She called me drunken, afterward—but no matter; she was distraught, and could not understand.

Chapter 12

Andros—or Skamandronymos, to give his full, honored name —was much mourned, for he was loved by all, and it was a great waste. Our party lacked a leader now; after Drakon, he had been the one to look up to.

His brother Erigyus became foster father to Sappho and her young brothers. In fact, he, with his wife, moved right into Andros' house; they left their own quarters to the new-made bride and groom. They would be needing more space soon; the bulge beneath Nausikaa's girdle was getting larger.

Erigyus was very unlike his dead brother; he was a worthy man, to be sure, but not a man to follow, except in homely things, such as gardening or supervising the sheepshearing. I do not speak of him slightingly; there are all sorts in the world, and he was likable and honest.

He and his wife, though, now had the full charge of Sappho and her brothers; such people, feeling inadequate, will sometimes be overstrict to compensate. The youngest brother, Larichus, was a child still, just Atthis' age, and a little supervision did not go amiss; Sappho and Charaxus, though, had been given much freedom, and chafed under the gentle restrictions put upon them. Charaxus was forever sneaking out of the house by night and going to whatever low haunts the gods alone knew.

Sappho, too, felt the constraint and balked at it, as she had never thought to do when Andros was alive. She defied the new authority openly, and, at times, in secret also. Erigyus was much inclined to mildness, and tended to believe that all would be well with us exiles; "it will take a little time," he would say, "but be patient—we will be recalled . . ."

He may have been right; the young among us did not think so, and still conspired as best we could, sending messages to Mitylene and receiving our spied-out news. I continued to write inflammatory verse and was gratified to hear that it was taken up by the city people and sung often. A small group of us would meet and plot the death of Myrsilos, or at least his overthrow;

somehow, we never extended our plotting to Pittakos. I think we still felt that, without Myrsilos, he could be controlled. Or, maybe, we feared him.

Our little group of conspirators included Melanippos; a good thing, as I look back upon it, for all the others of our band were young enough to be foolhardy. He came, with his new-made wife, Telesippa, to our meetings; after a time, I could almost see and hear dead Andros in him; he became, in fact, our true leader, a wise and restraining influence. Erigyus would have nothing to do with us, nor would any other of the older members of the former Council of Nobles. Tyrrhaeos, son of Pittakos, was with us, and my brother, Antimenades, Charaxus, and Hippias, with several other young men. Sappho and her two cousins, Dika and Telesippa, were the only girls.

Those two, embittered by their mother, Phaedra's, actions, were all for the Tyrant's death; most of us were content to plan and work for his downfall. Dika even gathered poisonous herbs and made an infusion, asking me to give it to our next messenger to be used when the opportunity arose. "Oh, no," I said. "That is the same death as your father's . . . and we were blamed for that. This time we would not get off so lightly. No, it must be done some other way . . . by a rising or some such thing. . . ." As it turned out, we had not long to wait, though we could never have guessed the way the thing happened.

I must admit now that many of our meetings served as an excuse for drinking deep and staying up all night; we had little else to do. The other two girls went home early, upon Melanippos' insistence; Dika now lived in his house with her sister, and owed him some deference, though her eyes showed that she would rather have stayed. Drinking parties are meant for men, anyway; once, though, Sappho sent her woman, Praxinoa, home, and stayed on; she could be very willful. And so I purposely got her drunk that time, and one other as well. That was twice, and twice I muffed my chances; it humiliates me to recall them.

The first time the poor girl mixed her wines, being an innocent in such things; she was staggering and with a green face; I took her outside, into the air, to revive her. I had a small two-wheeled cart, with a fast little horse to pull it; I thought a brisk ride would do the trick. It did not; instead the jolting made her throw up, all over herself, me, and the cart, ruining the paint. I clucked my tongue at her, like a fussy housekeeper, though I was not in much better case myself. For a wonder she did not lose her temper; I guess she was beyond hearing me, even. She drooped against me, like a wilting flower, smelling of sour vomit mixed with roses, her favorite essence. I could not take her home in such a state; I headed back to my own house, not quite sure what to do. The fountain in the garden was spouting water; the spring floods had started, and it was fed by a mountain stream, running early this year. I lifted her down from the cart, and walked, carrying her, into the spray. It did the trick and sobered her up, drenching us both; she gasped; the water was icy. Her chiton, like my own, was sopping wet, but at least it no longer smelled. She drew her arm back, and landed me a great swat on the cheek; she was wearing a ring, and the stone of it cut me; I have the scar still.

"You are a beast!" she cried. "How can I go home like this? And—" Her face was horror-stricken; she clutched her throat, wailing. "I shall catch a chill—and get hoarse!" It was all she thought of, really, her singing and her songs; I could not help but smile, for I would have felt the same, in her place.

I pulled her close, kissing her sodden, dripping hair. "Sh-h-h," I whispered. "Come inside . . . we will find warm clothes. . . ." She melted against me, turning up her face. "Why did you do it?"

"You were very drunk, my darling," I answered. "It was the only thing I could think of." I expected another blow, but she just walked beside me quietly to the house. I led her to the back entrance, so we would not be seen by whatever revelers still were about; I heard the thin notes of a single flute, wavering. I took her, tiptoeing, finger to my lips, to my chamber.

She was not sober enough to object when I undressed her and toweled her down, wrapping her in a clean dry robe of my own, and she lay quietly on my bed, waiting while I did the same for myself.

She was warm enough when I got in beside her; she had not caught a chill, and the cut on my cheekbone had stopped bleeding. We kissed, in our lingering way, and more besides. But the wine and the wetting between them had done me in; I was not fumbling, but I was very slow, too slow. She was too exhausted, and too young, to wait for me. I felt her go slack, and give a little gentle snore. I covered her, and went into the antechamber to sleep it off myself. I believe, truly, though I have drunk deep often, that this thing has never happened to me, before or since.

The next morning, early, I was awakened by a knocking at the door. I roused myself and went through the hall, stepping over Hippias, enfolded in some youth's arms, and going carefully to avoid the puddles of wine. The woman Praxinoa was at the door, her eyes behind the cool mask of her face frightened. "Sappho is not in her bed . . ."

"No," I said. "I gave her mine."

Her eyes got wider. "I have not harmed her," I said. "She has been sick. Come." And I led her through the hall, and through the antechamber, where my lonely bed showed the imprint, still, of a single body, my own. In my chamber, she looked down on the sleeping girl.

"She ate too many mussels," I said. "They did not sit well on her stomach . . . or perhaps they were not smoked long enough."

"Whose robe is she wearing?" Praxinoa asked.

"Mine," I said. "I gave it to her. Her own was soiled; I will have it laundered."

"I had better take her home—before she is missed," she said. But before she bent to wake her, she gave me a long look from her statue's eyes. "She never eats mussels," she said.

After that, it was difficult for Sappho to shake the woman; she was like a watchdog. If the girl stayed longer than was seemly, she urged her home. If Sappho dismissed her, she returned with orders from the uncle; clearly, I was no longer trusted, if I had ever been.

We took to meeting secretly. She would go home with Praxinoa, docile as any lamb, shut her door, and wait for my soft whistle beneath her window. She would climb down to me, and we would cling together in the soft dark.

Only once again, though, did I lure her to my chamber; it was another disaster.

I had brought a jug of light, sweet wine, brought from Mitylene, one of my last. She liked it for its taste of home, and drank just enough—or so I thought. She went home with me, happily, and swaying ever so slightly, humming a little under her breath.

In my bed I slipped my hand beneath her loose chiton,

stroking upward on her leg. Against her ear I said, softly, and in wonderment—remember, I, too, had had my Lesbian wine!— I said, "Sweet—your legs are just like a boy's . . ." I cannot think what possessed me; I had noticed that she had more muscles than girls have, as a rule, and there was a stiff little stubble, too, where she had let her shaving or pumicing, or whatever, go a day too long; most boys are careless that way; I have always found it endearing. But she leaped out of the bed as though I had stuck her with a pin, pulling her clothes together and glaring down at me; I had purposely lit one lamp only, but I could see her plain, like one of the Furies.

"I hate you, Alkaios!" She stood over me, tears of anger glittering in her eyes. "I hate you! Antimenades wants to marry me . . . but you call me a boy!" A hot tear splashed on my face, and she was gone, running wildly through the night. I was stunned; it was the first I had heard of Antimenades' wooing. She did not marry him, though; perhaps it was just a lie. I never knew.

She got over her tantrum, and smiled at me again, and sang with me, too. But it was a long, long time before we kissed again.

By the summer's end, we were recalled to Mitylene, pardoned by Pittakos, after the death of Myrsilos . . . just as the elder statesmen had predicted.

After a whole year in Pyrrha, I swear—though it will not be believed—when we set foot again on the dear soil of our city, Sappho was a maiden still.

BOOK III

Far Shores

(Told by Kerkylas of Andros, Sea Trader)

Chapter 1

I always like to go about wharfside, mingling with the people, and not making myself known, especially in a city that is new to me, like Mitylene. One gets all the news firsthand that way, and nothing held back out of courtesy or fear; besides, it gives me pleasure to skip all the bowing and scraping and so on that I get at home and among the great that I deal with. All the sailors of my fleet know that I dislike fawning and scraping, and after a bit do not even lower their voices when I come near, but welcome me with easy grins and pass their jug to share. For years now my ships have been more home to me than Andros, the island of my birth.

So I stepped onto the dock at Mitylene one spring day, got up like an ordinary seaman, or pirate if you will, for that is how most folk think of those of us who follow the sea. I went bare-chested, for the air was mild, and in leather trousers hacked off at the knee for ease on shipboard. I was burnt dark by the sun, wherever the skin showed, and wore a long scarf wound like a turban, in the Eastern fashion, around my head, hiding my hair. It was the mariner's uniform, complete with metal rings in the earlobes, except that mine were gold. I looked a proper swarthy Phoenician; only my blue eyes gave away the fact that I was born a yellow-haired Hellene.

Phoenician, I say; there are none of that race left now and the gods know what they really looked like, but one supposes them to have been Semites, kin to the nomads of the desert and the Hebrews of the one god. They were of such importance in the sea lanes once, going even far, far north to those islands shrouded in mist to bring back tin that was mined there; all sailors have come to be called Phoenicians, still, to this day. It is said that they were the first inhabitants of the islands of the Cyclades, of which my own Andros is the largest; largest . . . it is a mere twenty-mile strip, with perhaps eight miles across! At any rate, legend has it that they were driven out by old Minos of Crete; that was long, long ago, before the great earthquake. By other legends, that same earthquake sank a whole great body of land, and all that is left is the line of high peaks, sticking up out of the sea, that form the Cyclades of today. So where are we? One of the legends has to be wrong. We live in a morass of them, truly; I know, for I have traveled far, and each land has its own holy beginning, different from the others, but all amounting to the same thing, a tale dreamed up and sung around a fire at night to frighten off the fear of the vast unknown.

Certainly Andros has no dark people on it; there are not even any Pelasgians, as on the other isles of Greece. We own it, my family, or as good as; all of its folk are our kin, one way or another, far back. Probably a small band of Achaeans or Dorians were washed ashore there, fleeing some old catastrophe, and intermarried and populated the place, with a chief over all, who happened to be my ancestor. There is no hair color darker than honey, and most is as pale as the silk of corn; the children you cannot tell apart, until they grow a little and life writes different stories on their faces.

On Andros the grapes grow wild, the vines clustering and thick as a man's arm; it is impossible to cultivate them all, though much has been tended now for many years and produces a high quality of fine wine, which is our wealth. Once the whole island was sacred to Dionysos, and my immediate ancestors its priests and priestesses; the family must have grown rich in the first times by the offerings brought by the folk, but that is only my conjecture. I know I cannot remember a time when we did not dine off plates of precious metals and wear fine linen and burnished ornaments. As I grew to manhood, though, I saw signs of it wearing thin; our prosperity, like my two old parents, had a look of prideful shabbiness; they were the same plates, polished daily, and the same linen, washed many times. I had visions of another legend, far in the future, of the island of grapes, so heavy with its ancient bramble of vines that it sank into the sea. Besides, I had had an Egyptian tutor, a man who had sailed the known world's oceans, and fired me with an itch to roam, as well as teaching me the number arts he was hired to do. He had one leg only, the other having been bitten off by a shark, or he would be on a deck still, make no mistake.

I was the child of my parents' old age; my youngest sister was twice a mother by the time of my birth. The peace of a house of the aged surrounded me, and, outside the walls, the beckoning, mysterious, eternal sea. I was much alone, but did not feel it; I read, studied, dreamed, and ran wild at the water's edge, fishing, sailing, pulling at the oars.

There was a bit of trade between us and our nearest island neighbors, but nothing to speak of. The grapes rotted on the vine for the most part, and the wine that was made from the others was wasted on the wild, old-fashioned rites of Dionysos.

I feared my loving old parents might drop dead when I announced my decision to go seriously into the trade, for real profit, but they survived. They are alive still, and I am thirty-two, and wealthy beyond anything they ever dreamed. I think, truly, they are a little ashamed of it; my mother still wears the same well-washed chitons, draped in the old way you never see nowadays, and thanks me gravely for the rich exotic gifts I bring her from my voyages, and then puts them away neatly in a chest. My father's wits are straying, and he thinks, sometimes, that I am his father, long dead, a priest of the god, and shyly brings me captured doves for the altar. Ah, well, the gods must love them, my parents, for I cannot even figure up their years!

I have more than fifty ships working the sea lanes, up and down both coastlines, east and west; it pleases me as I stroll about the rough-paved landing, among the crowd of hawkers and sightseers, that no one knows it. Except for my height, I am not even given a second glance, for all seamen dress in this fashion; dockside, they are used to it everywhere. One old granny, though, caught sight of the light eyes in my weathered face, and made a sign against them, hurriedly, pulling her black hood over her face. And a litter, richly embroidered, stopped, evidently at a command from within. The bearers set it down, and stood beside it woodenly, staring in front of them. The litter's curtains opened, just a crack; she was looking me over, a woman, wealthy and bored, seeking a touch of the slums. I stared until the curtains parted, and a face looked out, thickly painted and past its prime, but still beautiful. We exchanged look for look, a long moment; we will know each other again if we meet. But I smiled at last, shaking my head; she was getting on a bit, even for me. Besides, I do not really care for light women; they are too easy, and there is no joy in it. The curtains snapped together, there was a low-spoken order, and the litter moved on.

Mitylene is a city bustling and busy, when one steps onto its shores; from sea, it is white and still, like a city in a cloud, and shining in the light of the sun, a fine sight. As I said, it was new to me; in most of my trading years I had avoided it, and Athens, too, for they two had been at war all this time, and it does not do for a trader to take sides, or try to play one against the other. But there was peace now, and, though the Lesbian wine is good, our Andrian is the best in the world. (I mean to set a high price on it, for it was said that the people of Lesbos are great wine drinkers.) Of course, Mitylene had a Tyrant and all the modern laws; I would have to get a trade license, a nuisance.

It was early, and I had had nothing much to break my fast, only a little Egyptian beer and a rusk of ship's bread; I saw a cookshop, fairly clean, and went in. There was a smell of sausages frying; I called for them, and whatever goes along with them, and sat down on a bench against the wall. The place was dark; there was only the sun coming through the open door and a single rushlight with a feeble flame. Still, it was full up, a good sign. I saw some sailors from my ship, and shook my head just a little to indicate they must not give me away. They know, of course, but just in case. I settled back and looked about me.

There was a group of girls; there was an unmistakable stamp on them, though they were not wearing the conical hats of their trade. Whores . . . at this hour! I was curious enough about it, watching them, about six altogether, sulky in their corner, to ask the cookshop owner when he brought my food.

"Oh, they are out of work, Master," he said low, bowing. Could he tell my earrings were gold, then—or had someone spoken out of turn? I looked at him with a cold eye. "I am only a sailor, like all these others," I said.

"Oh, I know, Master!" And he closed one eye in a gross sort of wink. Well, there had been some sort of leak; I shrugged inwardly. It did not really matter, it was just a whim I liked to indulge.

I held out the price of the food, tripled. "Keep it under your hat, my good man." He took the money with trembling hands. "Oh, yes, Master, certainly, Your Eminence . . ."

I took in what he had said about the whores, and pulled him down to sit beside me. He took a seat on the very edge, leaving a space between us, like a proper-bred young lady that has been taught to keep her knees together; a comic sight, for the man was balding and round as a dumpling.

"How can girls like that be out of work when a ship is in harbor?"

"Well, you see, Your Eminence . . . they don't have licenses," he answered.

"Are they so expensive then, or so hard to get, the licenses?" As a rule, under the new laws, the license is only nominal, more of a way of keeping a check on the girls, seeing that they stay reasonably clean and reasonably honest.

"Well," he said, "they are high—have been for quite a while now . . . but it's not so much that. They could pay, scrape it up some way. It's that they don't want to work under the priests."

"The priests?" I said. "What priests are they?"

"Why, the priests of Aphrodite—at the temple."

"Now, wait a minute, my friend," I said, laughing. "Aphrodite is a women's goddess. There are no priests, only priestesses."

He nodded vehemently, and then shook his head just as hard. "Yes, that's as it should be, of course, but—" And he scrunched his head down and looked around to see if anyone was looking our way. "But the old Tyrant, the one the whores killed, he made new laws, that called for priests, that would have the girls under them and take their cut. . . . And Old Pitt, the new Tyrant— well, he didn't change the laws yet, like for a punishment to the girls, see?"

I was astonished. "You mean—*these* girls killed the Tyrant? . . ." I asked, looking over their way.

"No, no, no!" His jowls shook. "No . . . they were put to death—the ones that did it . . . and very nasty it was, too—"

I held up my hand, laughing. "Slow down, my friend," I said. "I'm just off the ship, remember? . . . And I've never been to this city before. So start from the beginning . . ."

He opened his mouth, but I stopped him, asking for a glass of his best wine, while I listened. "And bring one for yourself, too. Wet your tongue . . . it's on me."

And so I got the story, and quite a tale it was.

It seems the first of the Tyrants to set himself up over the Council of Nobles was a man named Melanchros; that was a couple of years back, while the war was still on. The nobles were all still around, but had lost much of their power and were forever plotting together to get it back and oust this Melanchros. Pittakos—who is called Old Pitt—was one of them then. They finally assassinated Melanchros at a banquet; some of the soldiers from the army did it, sneaking home and dressed up like dancing girls. A pretty funny thing, to begin with. What precipitated the killing was a song sung by a singer they called the Black Lark, a woman. This was getting beyond me, and I stopped him.

"A woman, you say. A flute girl, was it? A whore?"

His jowls shook again, and his eyes looked shocked. "Oh, no! the Black Lark—she's an aristocrat. Daughter of one of the nobles. He's dead now—may his shade find rest . . ." He bowed his head with a new dignity. He had a comic look, but still I was touched, in spite of myself, at his old-fashioned piety. I waited a moment, out of courtesy, then bade him continue.

"Well, Master, it gets a little muddled from now on . . . but I'll try . . ."

"Maybe another glass? . . ." I said. This time he summoned a boy and gave the order. He was beginning to get going on it now; all island folk love to tell a story, and I guess he was glad, too, of the chance to take his weight off his feet for a spell.

I will tell it as I remember it—my own way—hoping not to have left anything out. This first Tyrant, Melanchros, had enforced a number of unpopular laws; unpopular, some of them, even with the people of the peasantry that they were supposed to help, and enraging to the nobility. One of them was the forming of a city guard, made up, for the most part, of ruffians. Another had to do with the licensing of just about everything, a form of taxing. But the real outrage, and even I gasped, to think of it in a Greek country in modern times, was the revival of the old child sacrifice. He tried to make it attractive by paying for the children; of course there are so many poor everywhere that some folk were forced to take advantage of it. It is all very well to say that those same children, girls mostly or crippled boys, would have died anyway, of deprivation; the custom is still a shocking one, in this day and age.

Being a woman herself, this Black Lark singer felt the sacrifice of baby girls strongly and made a song about it, and what is more, sang it for the Tyrant, right to his face! When he gave the order to arrest her, those youths disguised as women overpowered his guards and killed him. That was one down—but the troubles were only just beginning.

After the war Pittakos, commander in chief of the army, teamed up with a man named Myrsilos and seized power. It was very cunningly done, as such things always are; the leading noble was a man called Drakon; he was poisoned by his wife, a woman called Phaedra, or so it is said. The nobles called a meeting to bring her to justice, having proof, of a sort. But apparently she was in with the two joint Tyrants, who had not yet made themselves known. They were able, with the help of most of the army, idle now and ready to follow Pittakos, to turn the whole thing against the nobles. While the council met, hurriedly, their twelve now dwindled to ten, with Drakon dead and Pittakos on the other side, the body was hacked up to make it look like another kind of murder and the nobles were accused of it. With thousands of armed men behind them, Pittakos and Myrsilos had no difficulty. The nobles were exiled to a town called Pyrrha, with all their families, and much of their wealth taken from them.

While the exiles plotted, having spies in the city here, many changes were made by the new government. It is no good listing them all; again, most of them were unpopular. Taxes were imposed upon just about everything; licenses were required for all persons who did anything, almost for breathing! Restrictions and curfews were laid down. It is an endless tale of oppression, it seems.

When the prostitutes' license fees were raised, there was much protest; mobs of girls gathered and did damage where they could, defacing the houses of the government, setting fires, and so forth, all under cover of darkness. Also, it became unsafe to patronize these girls, for they would steal a man's purse while he lay naked and vulnerable, two sneaking in while the third girl had the fellow occupied. It is said that they knifed their victims, too, and worse; some of their patrons, who showed a little fight, got dumped into the sea. Some action had to be taken; unfortunately, the Tyrant Myrsilos went too far. He hand-picked some likely rough boys and made them priests of Aphrodite, and allocated to each a group of girls; instead of the girls giving a pittance to Aphrodite as a thanks offering, which has been done time out of mind, for they work out of her temple, after all, these priests got a huge cut of each girl's take. Naturally, Myrsilos got *his* cut after, as well. This enraged the girls; at the Aphrodisia, the goddess' festival, when Myrsilos came to throw his pinch of incense on the altar, they mobbed him; it was said he was gashed in more than a hundred places, and his genitals cut off. (They have not been found yet; one of the girls who escaped is probably wearing them on a string around her neck, for luck!) The woman Phaedra, who had been living with Myrsilos, got away, though she had accompanied him to the temple; she must have a charmed life. Only a handful of the prostitutes were caught. They were to be burned alive as a sacrifice to the goddess they served, but that goddess, loving her own, sent a heavy rain, and the fire would not take; their throats were cut instead, a quicker death.

So my question was answered, but the wine made the cook garrulous, and I heard the political history of Mitylene! Truly, there has been much ado here—but then such things are happening all over Greece, wherever the population has grown large enough to complicate matters.

The whores are waiting it out; I suppose a few of the more fortunate, who have a private business, one or two lovers of note and substance, are helping the others, for they could not live otherwise. Pittakos is still keeping to that law against custom, still keeping the priest-procurers, and the girls are still keeping up their protest. There is a standstill, as happens in war; I could not help but smile. The cook, though, was very grave; he said the girls will win, for already some of the "priests" have given up, finding no profit in their new calling; they are back in the alleys again, robbing and knifing. He told me to warn my sailors, and so I shall. What a coil they will be in, for sure, no women, and a perilous shore leave! Of course, some of them will make do with street boys; no Tyrant has put a license on *them* as yet! I think no one would dare; it is a winked-at custom everywhere. However, things being the way they are, these boys must come high at the moment; my seamen are paid better than most, but they do not make a fortune either.

The cook told me that all the exiles have been recalled; Pittakos did that first thing, after Myrsilos' death. He has a head on his shoulders, that one; it is obvious that he would wish to keep in the good graces of the aristocrats, wherever it is possible;

no Tyrant can stay in power long without some concessions to this ruling class. Even Solon of Athens has found that out, and mitigated his more stringent laws of late.

Pittakos has reformed the old Council of Nobles, but has limited the number to eight, all elders whom he feels he can control. The younger exiles still plot among themselves and still make what mischief they can. Mainly they are two brothers, one a poet and one a sculptor, but longtime soldiers as well. The woman-poet they call the Black Lark is in it, too—and, strangely enough, Pittakos' only true-born son, a cripple. It does not sound as though they could scare up much trouble, but it seems they have.

Pittakos has borrowed many of the laws from Solon, those that curtail the freedom of women; Lesbos has been famous for many years for the freedom enjoyed by its women, especially those of high breeding. They move about as freely as men, and are taught to read and write, to reckon with figures, and to play instruments and sing and dance; here, the weaving and spinning is left to slaves and servants. Naturally, these girls and women resent any change; the Black Lark is their spokeswoman, being a poet and singer; her songs, all directed against the new laws, are sung openly all over the city.

None of the exiles can have been very happy on returning, for they came back to gutted houses and vandalized courtyards; much of their wealth had been confiscated, though Pittakos had promised clemency; their fields, groves, and vineyards had been shamefully neglected, and all their serving people, free or unfree, dispersed. The wealthy class is no longer wealthy, except for one man, Melanippos, who is in trade, and whose name is familiar to me; it is said that he is supporting all the others.

The first thing the exiles did, those who would not give an inch, was to attempt to bring the woman Phaedra to justice for the murder of her husband, Drakon, of which they had been accused. They had the proof, a vial, smelling of the poison, and found in the chamber, a witness, or as good as, and their own sworn testimony. Pittakos would have nothing to do with it, naturally, for by this time he had married the woman! By Solon's law it was legal, for his wife, a high-minded woman of Lesbos, had left him at the start of his power seizure; Solon's law called this "desertion," and it was enough to annul a marriage.

I must say that, according to some lights, Pittakos has been very patient; my talebearer repeated some of the songs that have been made about him and sung all over; they are, particularly those of the man-poet, definitely treasonous, and horribly vile, though extremely witty. He calls Pittakos "Old Crack-Toes," "Pot Belly," "Wild Pig," and other uncharming names, describes how he eats and smells, how filthy he is of person and habit, and so on. He has had his fun with Phaedra, too, calling her a worn-out whore. One verse I particularly enjoyed; he, the poet, says that Phaedra has been hammered as hard and polished as smooth by her hundreds of lovers, as any old ship's bottom by the carpenters!

This tale is long in the telling; I will make an end, as I remember it. The two brothers, with some other conspirators, partly among the exiles, and partly city youths, actually made an attempt upon the Tyrant's life, while he lay with his new wife, thinking thus to get him off guard. It did not work, for Pittakos was wily enough to post soldiers of his own behind screens in the very bedchamber; I suppose he knew Phaedra would not mind an audience! At any rate, they were caught, the conspirators; they languish in close custody. For a wonder, they were not put to death. The poet, even, has been given writing materials, for a song is already circulating about the whole thing.

There are two other prisoners, also; one, at least, must be tearing at the Tyrant's heart. It seems, though he had disapproved of this same custom when it was revived before, still Pittakos, for whatever reasons, revived the child sacrifice at the Festival of Flowers, paying a fair sum for each girl, or maimed boy, that was brought in. The woman-poet (I have heard her name—Sappho) did not make a song this time, but stood in the line of sacrifice with her own offering for sale. The clerk went cold with fear when he saw who it was, but had the presence of mind to seize them both. The sacrifice was the crippled youth, Pittakos' son! And so they are in custody, too, and all day and night outside the walls of the Temple of Hera, where they are held, a mob, mostly women, chant, "Set free the Black Lark. . . . Let the Lark go. . . . Set free the Black Lark!" And the Festival of Flowers was not celebrated this year; the sacrificial victims were returned, and the poor parents allowed to keep the money as well. Those mothers shout for the liberty of the Lady Sappho;

they have left their homes and the fields where they labor and they sit unmoving, night and day, chanting their demand.

It truly seems a city in turmoil, and not a place for pleasure; still I will stay long enough to make some profit where I can. Perhaps this Melanippos can offer some advice; it is a large city, after all, Mitylene; one cannot just ignore it. The barley bread from Eresos and the honey, too, is famous; it is served everywhere here, or so the cook tells me. It would be a good addition to my cargo; still, it will come high, since it has been brought overland. I must put my head to this problem, for it would very likely cost much more to make the sea voyage around to Eresos itself; it is on the other side of the island. I cannot think what other wares I can come by here; they trade a good deal with Egypt, but so does everyone. There is probably nothing new there, unless a boat has just touched in the last week or so. I must ask. The owner has left me, to tend to his other business; I suggested it, for it was getting to be too much of a good thing, and the tale very long in the telling.

I looked for him; it was very smoky from the central fire, and was dim in any case. Finally I made him out, in the doorway, and started toward him.

As I came near, I saw, in the slanting light from the opening, a look of fear on his face, and droplets of sweat that were not all from toiling over the fire. He nodded his head as he saw me, and turned to someone outside, that I could not see. "Yes . . . here he is, Your Honors."

"Someone want me?" I pushed past, stretching to my full height, which is considerable, and putting on a looking-through-you sort of stare. There was a whole company of young military outside, their hands nervous at their long daggers, which were hanging from their belts. They did not speak for a moment; they were all very raw of years and had to look up at me besides. Finally one, a little bolder, stepped forward about two inches. "You Kerkylas?"

"So my mother addresses me," I said. "From you it shall be 'sir.'" I fingered the long knife at my belt, curved, unsheathed, and with a wicked edge, plain to see. I had got it in the Eastern lands; they had never seen anything like it.

Another one of them spoke roughly, "He wants you, our leader . . . Old Pitt . . ."

I did not move, my hand still on my knife. Another, with something resembling intelligence in his eye, said, "Sir, it is Pittakos, the Tyrant . . . he wishes to see you—about the trade license."

I looked at him narrowly. "I had thought there was some clerk or other who handles such matters. Surely the head of state has better things to do."

He squared his shoulders and looked at me straight; I saw he was very young, not more than fourteen. "Well, sir—Old Pitt . . . he generally likes to do everything himself." His mouth curved. "Nowadays, anyway."

"He's cagey, eh?" I said, smiling. I took my fingers from my knife and put two of them to my lips, giving a low whistle; I heard a rustle behind me in the cookshop. "Well, I will come. I like that. I am cagey too." I counted the guard boys; there were six of them. "Five of my sailors will come with me." I turned and counted them out; they were ready, behind me, near the doorway, big fellows, bearded rough from the voyage, and each with his knife at his belt.

"Well," the boy said, looking uncertain, "there wasn't anything said about sailors . . ."

"They will come," I said, looking down at him, "or you will have to carry me. . . ." I took my knife out, holding it up to the light and feeling its edge. "And," I went on, smiling again, "I have not been carried since I had a nurse. . . ."

I felt my sailors, crowded up behind me; some of the guard boys had taken out their knives, too. A voice, the cookshop owner's, spoke up, high and quavering. "Please, Your Eminences . . . no brawl in my shop! Go with them, sir—I beg you!"

"Well," I said, looking at their spokesman. "What shall it be?"

He stood a moment, thinking, then spoke to those with him. "Put your knives away. We don't want trouble." He turned to me. "All right, sir. He didn't say anything about *not* bringing sailors either. . . ." And he grinned, suddenly; I found myself liking him.

I blinked in the strong sun; it was getting on for noon. "No wagons, no litters, even—we walk?" I asked, looking at the street with its crude paving.

"Well," I said. "Lead on . . . we are guests of the city." I did not fall in behind, though, but walked beside this youth, laying an arm across his shoulder, and speaking low. "I'm curious," I said. "How did you know where to find me?"

"Oh, Pittakos has spies everywhere," he answered.

"But, I mean, how did you know it was I? I do not wear my name around my neck, and I look much like the others of the sea."

"They are *good* spies," he said. I laughed. "Come clean, little rooster," I said. "You were never in the army. . . . How old are you?"

"I am sixteen."

"You are a barefaced liar . . . but even so, the war was a year or so back— How did you get in this business?"

"The guard?" he asked, looking surprised. "What else is there? It's not a bad life . . . I used to dive for coins thrown off the ships; there was a lot of competition. And the good heavy ones, the drachmae, they sank in the bottom mud, anyway. . . . There's better pay in the guard, and always something to eat, even when the money comes late."

"And you always like the work?"

"So far." His head was bent, but I thought I saw a funny look on his face, and waited. After a bit it came. He said, "I wasn't keen on—well, we drew straws and I was lucky." He shook his head. "But I wouldn't have liked sticking my knife in those girls. . . ."

"The whores, you mean?"

He threw me an odd look. "One of them was my sister."

"I'm sorry, little rooster." And I meant it. "So she got it, did she?"

He nodded. "I didn't watch, even. . . . Still—it was better than the fire."

I didn't say anything; there wasn't much to say. We walked along for a bit. "It's a pretty fair walk—Pittakos' house," I said, finally.

"Well, it's right out toward the end of the city," he said. "Not much farther now."

"What do they pay you in the guard?" I asked. He told me. "I'd double that," I said, "and a measure of Andrian each night at supper. How would you like to come to sea? I'd make a place for you on one of my ships." He was a likely lad, one that you take to right off. "Maybe the one in harbor now . . ."

He moved away a little, and looked at me, wary. I guess he saw what he wanted to and no funny business; he just said, looking straight ahead, "I never been on a boat. Maybe I'd get sick."

"Not on a ship of mine, little rooster . . . and we don't stick girls with knives either . . . at least not this kind." I patted the knife at my belt and gave him a rough nudge. I had seen his throat working. He swallowed it, though, and didn't cry, but looked up at me with a grin; his face was still round-cheeked, a little sprinkle of freckles across his nose. "I'd think about it," he said. Then, eagerly, "Do you go to Egypt . . . sir?"

I shook my head. "Not this trip. Touch at all the islands, then down to Korinth, and on to Syrakuse. I've got a ship for Egypt, though. I could put you on her . . ."

"No, sir," he said. "I'd want to go with you. Be more . . . homelike. No, Syrakuse'd be all right. *If* I decided . . ."

"Well, let me know before we sail. Ask at the wharf, they'll know where to find me. . . . What's your name, in case? . . ."

"Makro," he said. It was a pretty common name, but I didn't think we had one on board.

"Well, think it over, Makro," I said.

"Yes, sir. We're here, sir." We had begun to climb some wide shallow steps; a house, huge, stood at the top.

"Pittakos' house, is it? Nice."

"It's his now, sir."

"Oh," I said. "Whose was it before?"

"It belonged to his wife's family. The one that ran off. He's got another now."

"I heard," I said, following him through the doorway. It was broad enough to bring a chariot through. Our footsteps echoed on the stone floors; there were no carpets. We went down an endless sort of hall, doors open along the sides. I looked in them as we passed; most of them were empty, not a stick of furniture, and uncurtained windows looking like blind gods' eyes.

"Pittakos," I said, "he's a frugal man, then? Or is he moving out, maybe?"

Makro grinned his boy's grin again. "He doesn't like this part of the house. No one knows why. I guess it's because of his wife—taking everything and going like that . . . and never a word. No one comes in here even, just some slaves, to sweep and dust."

"A waste," I said, looking about me. It was a beautiful house, with fine proportions and a sense of space and light; one does not see that often, in the islands. We came to a courtyard, once pretty and cultivated. Now weeds grew wild, like a jungle in some other land, tendrils creeping over the ground and right up the house walls. There had been statuary; one could see the marble bases where they had stood, the house gods, but some robber had been there before us. The walkways were cracked and buckled from the heat; no one had repaired them, not for a year or two, nor was the fountain tended. The pool beneath was filled with stagnant water, stinking, with a green scum on top, and dead foliage floated there, barely moving. There was a Niobe and her children in the center, bulky, antique work, the stone all pitted with age and neglect; at first I did not see that we had company, for the statue loomed large. As we rounded the pool, though, I saw two girls—young women really—sitting glum and idle upon the rim, wetting their bare feet in the water, their wiggling toes making a faint ripple on the surface. One was a Nubian and moodily, pensively, beautiful, still as a carving, except for her feet; the other was white—or white and red—her hair was like a flame, the skin almost bluish against it. They wore strange costumes, scantier than flute girls'; still one could see at a glance they were not hired whores, or anything like it. Little tight bands covered their breasts and a sort of loincloth was wrapped about their hips, but the cloth was of the finest, woven stuff, with a design worked in; as we came closer, I saw the pattern clearly, a crescent moon, and small sprinkled stars. They heard us and turned to watch us go past. The dark one did not move a muscle of her face, just stared with those huge swimming liquid eyes her people have; the red one, though, she gave me a long look, cool and hostile, from ice-blue eyes. I laughed; something leaped behind those eyes, and she stuck out her tongue, at the same time putting her hand to her face and pushing her nose up and her eyelids down, a horrid sight, but funny, too. I recognized it as the sort of thing small boys do when they do not like to be looked at. Ammies, I guessed, and shrugged, looking a question at the boy, Makro.

We passed on through the courtyard and through a door, into another part of the house. He said, looking miserable, "That will be his daughter—Old Pitt's . . ."

"Which?" I asked, laughing.

He looked sharply at me to see if I joked, then said, "Well . . . it could not very well be the brown one . . ."

"Why not?" I said, spreading my hands. "We are all the same made—no matter what color. Her mother was a woman, after all."

I saw I had shocked him, but I could see he liked it, too. I had not been wrong to guess he was intelligent. "Well," he said, slowly, "I'll give you that . . ." But then he smiled. "Wait till you see him, though—Old Pitt. You'll understand. . . ."

"I had heard he had a son," I said, looking narrowly at him and waiting. He said nothing about the gossip; I liked that. I went on after a moment. "I heard nothing about a daughter. . . ."

"She is from a Spartan wife he had before—" Then he looked at me, questioning. "They seem about the same in age, though . . . I never thought about it before."

I gave a short laugh. "Maybe the laws in Sparta are different—the marriage laws. Or maybe it's a case of the right hand not knowing what the left does? . . . I could be cruder, but . . ."

He grinned happily, glad to be talked to man-to-man, as it were. "I take your meaning, sir . . . name of Gorgo . . ."

"What?" I asked, a little startled.

"Her name—the daughter's."

"Oh," I said. "A monster's name, or almost."

"She is," he said, glumly.

"She just looked like a girl to me, a little boylike, maybe, with funny-colored hair."

"She's stronger than any boy," he said, shaking his head. "See that fellow up ahead—the one with the humpy nose and blue marks under his eyes?"

I had noticed him; a villainous-looking face, for sure. I nodded.

"She broke it for him. His nose. They warned him about trying anything with her—fooling around, you know . . . And she's not all that pretty either . . ." He shook his head sagely, like a man of the world. "He was lucky at that. She could have broke his leg—or worse. Knows all kinds of tricks . . . wrestling and that . . . dirty tricks."

"Well," I said, "she is the Tyrant's daughter, after all. As you said, he's lucky."

"Oh, she wouldn't tell Old Pitt . . . she hates him."

"But she lives in his house . . ."

"Well, where else?" He shrugged. "She is only a girl, after all. The two of them—her and the dark one—they're trying to start some kind of games school . . . just for girls. Not many takers yet, though. Their mothers won't let them—the girls around here, those that could afford it. Don't like the way they have to dress, I guess—or don't like their daughters wrestling and the rest of it."

"It's the Spartan way," I said.

"Yes, sir. I can't see it catching on here, though. . . . Here we are, sir." We had come to a flight of stairs, marble, and recently scrubbed. I could smell the soap, strong with lye.

The upper chamber where we entered was not all that much more luxurious than the other part of the house. A standing rushlight blew in the wind from our passing, near the door; at the end of a sort of long hall was a raised dais, where the Tyrant sat on a big chair, old-fashioned, with claw feet. Doric style it was; I could just remember one like it, from my boyhood, in my father's audience chamber, but it had long since disappeared. Beside him, on one of the new folding chairs from Lydia, with a sling back, silken, sat a woman, eating white grapes. As we came nearer, I saw she was the woman of the litter, that I had seen earlier, dockside. It crossed my mind in a confused sort of way that this must be Phaedra, but I did not waste much time looking at her, for I was curious about the Tyrant.

Pittakos was a man, all right. I'll give him that. Virility oozed from his pores and crackled along the standing red-gold hairs of his arms and legs, though I knew he was over fifty. He was a man out of legend, an old-time hero, massive as a block of stone. His hair and beard were flame colored, like his daughter's braids, and he did not comb them; they were like copper wires, catching the light. He wore a short red mantle, the wrong red, making one wince, and clasped at one shoulder with a great gold head of Helios, the old sun god; it was like a picture of himself that he

wore. My eyes traveled down his bare hairy legs to his sandaled
feet, remembering the verses I had heard. Sure enough, his toes
were filthy and cracked, with the old dirt grained right in. I
would perhaps have smiled, except that he rose, and held out his
hand to me. Strange conduct from a Tyrant!

I took the hand, pressuring it firmly, knowing what his
handshake would be like; I was not wrong, he was a bone
crusher; I managed to keep my countenance, though it hurt like
all Hades.

"Welcome, Kerkylas of Andros," he said. His voice was heavy,
with a rasp to it, and a thick accent of Thrace.

"You know me, sire?"

"I use no title, I am Pittakos . . . though the army boys have
another name for me," and he laughed, deep and rumbling. It
had a marvelous jovial sound, bringing an answering smile to my
lips, until I saw his eyes. They were small and deep-set, of a blue
lighter than my own, and they pierced through everything, like
little daggers of ice. I nearly shivered, but forced myself to go on
smiling; it does not do to show anything at all of one's inner
feelings to such a man.

"Naturally I know you, Kerkylas . . . the whole world knows
you. It is said you are the wealthiest man in the Aegean, after
Kroesus . . ."

"Many things are said, Pittakos," I answered, meeting his eyes
with as cool a glance as I could muster. "They are not all
true . . ."

"Thank Father Poseidon for that," he said, "or I myself should
be pulled this way and that by contradictions. . . ."

"There is talk," I said, "about all men who are raised up above
their fellows. It is their penalty for eminence. . . . I am not quite
in that category."

"You are well known in the islands, and some of the mainland
places, too. They are not so ill informed, our neighbors."

I saw where this was leading, and did not mean to take that
course. I would not pay higher than the going rate for a trade
license; Mitylene is not so important as that.

"Take my word for it," I said, firmly, "I am not a rich man."

"The word of a trader?" Pittakos laughed again, an ugly
sound now. It was a slur against my birth, and I recognized it. I

saw now why verses were written against him; the man was a boor, no question.

"The word of a king," I said calmly. "My fathers were kings in Andros as far back as there have been folk on it. But," I said, and I waved my hand lightly, "I do not use the title either . . ."

He took my point, and I saw his little eyes chalking it up to my credit. "Priests, I had heard . . ." he said and then sat down, heavily, making the old chair frame creak. From the corner of my eye I saw the woman Phaedra turn at the sound, a malicious smile beginning on her lips. I did not glance at her, but watched Pittakos.

"Priest-kings," I said. "You heard right."

"Well, you are in trade now, no matter what your standing on your speck of an island. And to trade here, in Mitylene, you need a license."

"That depends," I said. "There may be nothing here I wish to add to my cargo."

"You would not say no to . . . say, one hundred drachmae an amphora of your Andrian wine . . . and a contract to buy all you carry? . . ."

I thought it up fast in my head. I am like lightning at it, one has to be, or forget the whole business of trading. Back at him, quick as lightning again, I said, "One hundred fifty."

He stared at me. "You do not have your license yet."

I shrugged. "It may be expensive."

"It costs nothing—in drachmae."

"Oh?" I said, raising an eyebrow. What in Hades was coming? In any case, I wanted one thing made clear, and spoke up.

"One hundred fifty is my price. I can get it anywhere." I was lying, and he knew it. He said nothing, though, and only narrowed his eyes.

The woman spoke, beside him, slow and soft, with just a hint of the shrew. "Better break the news, Pitt . . . get it over."

He turned on her, starting to speak, but thought better of it, whatever he had meant to say. Instead he gestured in my direction. "Kerkylas of Andros. A trader . . . my wife, the Lady Phaedra."

I bent over her hand; it was a little sticky from the grapes and very soft, not really pleasant. I barely brushed my lips over the back of it, a trick I had picked up from the Sicilians. "We have met," I said, looking at her full.

Pittakos stared, then shrugged his bulky shoulders and said in a dullish voice, "No doubt."

"Only for a moment," I said, quickly. "And I did not know the lady's name, then. One could not, of course, forget her face," I said, with a gallantry I did not feel after the tales I had heard.

I thought her eyes had a mocking look, before she let my hand go.

"Well," Pittakos said, heavily, "this is the deal . . . and we will talk about the price of wine later. If you want the license, you must take three passengers—"

"Four!" she put in quickly.

"Yes . . . four." There was a longish pause; his eyes were hooded and I could not read them. "These passengers—not all on one boat, you understand. You have a sizable fleet, I take it?"

"Upwards of fifty," I answered, coolly, exaggerating. "But they are not all in port. Only one, that I command. And they are not passenger boats. The charge will be high, I shall have to shift cargo . . ."

"I understand," he said, wryly. "It will be paid by the city. You have a boat that goes to—say, Egypt?"

"Next week it will put in here, if the winds hold. And I expect another, bound for the city of Babylon, or as near as is comfortable. Nebuchadnezzar is readying his troops. . . . We carry weapons to him, and shields, from the iron lands. My own . . . I mean to make a lazy trip, stopping off at home, and some of the other islands; we are bound for Korinth, and Syrakuse, but the gods know when we will get there. I have no commitments, no cargoes to place . . . just a few pickups. . . . The plan is not feasible—I am sorry. The other ships, yes . . . I will have the masters make room, and they can work their way—have to, in fact—but my ship . . ." I shook my head. "I have no need of more hands on board."

He seemed to take no notice of my words, hearing only what he wished to. "Egypt. Yes, that will be all right for Alkaios—he can make his way there, with contacts from his foster father. I would not strip him bare . . ."

"Why not?" asked Phaedra. "He has stripped you. Your dignity . . ."

"Oh, my dignity! If it is there, it cannot be harmed. If it is not, well . . . then it makes no matter. It is just that I want no more plotting . . . no more intriguing . . . let us have done with all that. They must be separated . . . and then time will do the rest. The city will forget them. . . ." He looked sad, or as sad as such a brutish man can look.

I waited; he seemed sunk into a kind of deep contemplation; even his wife did not interrupt it. Finally he raised his head, speaking to me briskly.

"Alkaios then, to Egypt . . . Antimenades and—the other— will take ship for Nebuchadnezzar's country . . . and the woman will go with you. She has kinsmen in Sicily, somewhere—her mother's people."

I had heard nothing of the last sentence but the word "woman." "Great Zeus, man!" I cried. "I cannot have a woman on my ship! There are no accommodations . . . besides, the sailors think it is bad luck. . . . A woman!" I was speechless.

"You will have to do it," he said. "I must be rid of her. . . . She is the worst of the lot, for they follow her, the people. I must be rid of her."

"I told you," said Phaedra. And she made a gesture of drawing a knife across her throat.

He looked at her with contempt; I wondered what kind of marital bliss they could have. "There have been enough killings. There will be no more." Strange words for a Tyrant! Especially this one, who looked as much like a butcher as one could imagine. However, it was not the first time I had found that a man's outsides do not tell the whole of the story. Suddenly it was borne in on me just who these were, these passengers that he was ridding the city of. The poet and his brother, the woman called the Black Lark—and his own son! I felt for Old Pitt, but still I shook my head.

"I have heard of these folk," I said, "something, at least, of the tale. . . . But I cannot possibly give passage to a woman. You will have to find another ship, one that is used to passengers. My sailors would tear her apart, be she ugly as a crocodile and older than a tortoise!"

Pittakos smiled; I heard the woman laugh, a sly little sound.

"You must have some kind of quarters on board—your own,

perhaps—where she might have privacy of a sort? . . ." he asked.

"I have," I said, coolly. "But I do not mean to give them up. This woman is some sort of criminal, I understand. I know nothing of the politics of this city, and care less . . . but it is obvious you are exiling these persons. Am I to give up my own comforts, on a long sea voyage, for a penniless outcast? Besides, even if she could be protected from molestation, I do not want the responsibility. . . . Where is she to be put ashore? What is she to do? Where will she go? A woman cannot make her way, without means, in a strange country—"

He cut in, rudely. "That is not your affair," he said. "In any case, I am not quite so cruel as you imply. She will be allowed a servingwoman, and a box of personal belongings. . . . I have left her her jewels, they will fetch something, certainly. And she has kinsmen in the city of Syrakuse. . . ." He chewed at his lip, thinking. Suddenly he said, "I will give two hundred drachmae an amphora!"

I heard the woman gasp; I could not blame her, it was an unheard-of price. These people must be a real threat to this Tyrant! I looked at his face, trying to read it, but he could be stony at will. I gave up trying to figure him out. Surely death would be simpler—and he could withhold punishment in the case of his son. He *was* the ruler here, after all. But I shrugged away my thoughts; it was too good a thing to miss—two hundred drachmae!

"Well," I said, "when the hold is emptied, it can be swilled down, and there is a lock, and a door to open for air now and then. She will not be traveling in style . . . but what can she expect? And at least she will be safe . . . well, within reason. I cannot promise . . . Done," I said, holding out my hand. "I will take them. Passage will be one thousand drachmae, each. You are getting a bargain."

"I think not," he said, with a small grin. "But I have no choice. When do you sail?"

I thought for a moment. "Two days should be ample for the unloading, and to make ready the quarters for the woman. . . . Shall we say day after tomorrow, if the wind is right?"

"Done," he said. He turned to the woman. "I shall release them then—tomorrow. . . ."

"No! That could be dangerous," she hissed, "she has a following!"

"I will release them under heavy guard. After all, they must have a chance to put their affairs in order . . . and time is very short for Sappho, two days!" He shook his head sadly. Truly I could not understand him. Had this woman been one of his concubines? I had heard tales of them.

I spoke. "One thing I want understood. She—this Sappho—I want her to know me simply as this ship's captain, that is all. Not Kerkylas." I did not want a desperate female trying to worm my favors out of me.

"What shall she call you then? You do not want her to snap her fingers at you for attention. She is perfectly capable of it. . . ."

"Let her call me Andros, then—"

"No—no . . . that was her father's name! He is not long dead . . ."

"Oh, Great Zeus!" I was losing patience. "Let it be Nikko, that will do." As soon as I said it, I regretted it; Nikko was the name I used on the rare occasions when I visited a brothel or a Temple of Love. My sailors would snicker. Well, it was done now.

"Good. That is settled," he said. "She will be there in two days, dockside."

"At first light," I said.

Phaedra laughed, with malice. "She will hate that . . . she is a late riser."

So? . . . I thought to myself. *She has little choice. I am the captain.*

I saluted them, making my farewells, and turned to go.

Out of pure curiosity, I turned back, and asked, "Are they life exiles, Pittakos?"

"Yes," said Phaedra.

"No," said Old Pitt. "They will return—when I say so—when they are sweetened up again. . . . They are the soul's fire of Lesbos—those four." And upon his brutish face was a look of—strangely—longing.

Chapter 2

We were all stowed away and getting up the sail when the day broke, the day of our departure. It was clear and still cool; a good brisk wind was blowing from the land side, a good sign. I had risen before dawn and was restless, waiting; to occupy myself I had been lending a hand with the loading of some jars of honey and fresh produce that we would need for the voyage. The honey went into the cargo spot; I hoped to sell it for a good price at the first stop. But for that, we were nearly empty and rode high, almost a foot of watermark showing on the hull. It had a pleasant feeling, buoyant and light, but I knew the hazards; we would have trouble holding course in a storm. I had been aboard ship in such a case twice before, bobbing like a cork on the angry waters. Still, this was a fairly new ship, with her own weight, and good caulking; besides, this was not the bad season. We had more to fear from a becalming. I dismissed my uneasy thoughts, and straightened up from the last haul. I had got up a sweat and would have liked to give sailing orders and get a breeze behind me before the sun came full up, but my passenger had not arrived. I cursed the woman lightly under my breath and sat down on a coil of rope to wait.

From where I sat I could see the whole waterfront; a few hawkers were already setting up their carts, and putting out their wares, hoping to get some sailor's last leave money. The cookshop, where I had heard the whole tale of Mitylene, was just opening its doors; the proprietor saw me watching and bowed, beaming all over. Glad to see us go, probably; even though it is profitable, a shop full of half-drunk sailors can be a trial. I waved to him, smiling.

There was not much to look at on the dock; I turned and gazed seaward. I always like to watch the ever-changing ripples that go forward to the horizon; it draws one like the heart of a fire, inside the leaping flames. I was sunk in myself, not thinking any particular thoughts, just dreaming of nothing. I jumped like a hare when a hand touched my shoulder. I whirled around. It was the boy of the guard, the one I had offered a place to. I had forgotten all about it, but, seeing his round face, merry with his own adventuring, his name came back to me.

"Makro—right?" He had brought his belongings, a sad little bundle, knotted together in some square cloth that must have served as a cloak, too. "Come to join up?" I said, and clapped him on the back. "Welcome aboard, then!"

"Thought I'd get here early and help with the rigging. . . ."

I shook my head, smiling. "It's all done now . . . an hour since."

His face fell. "Never mind," I said. "You'll get the hang of the ship soon enough. . . . Sit here beside me." He put down his bundle, but I stopped him, saying, "Better still . . . see that shop over there—the cookshop? Run and get us something . . . I'm hungry as a wolf. Anything will do—whatever's on the fire. . . ." And I flipped him a coin, gold. He bit on it and grinned; then he was gone, running across the paving.

We were munching wedges of fresh bread, hot from the oven, and licking our fingers, which were greasy from the roasted slices of pig that we had eaten already, washing it all down with Egyptian beer, when Makro pointed to a little knot of people that had gathered on the dock below; I had watched them alighting from their litters along with bedrolls and boxes, piled now beside them, and heard their voices, high with excitement.

I turned to Makro, sputtering beside me, and said, "Don't talk with your mouth full . . . swallow first. There is not such a hurry."

When he had done chewing, he said, "That's them! The exiles! He has let them out. . . . What are they doing? Are they going to take ship with us?"

"Only the women," I said. "The other ones go later, on other ships."

"The Black Lark?" His eyes were round. "The Black Lark is coming with us?"

"You sound happy about it," I said, looking at him. "I wish my sailors felt the same. They think women bring bad luck on shipboard."

"Not that one," he said. "Not Sappho. And maybe she will sing . . ."

I shook my head. "I doubt it. Exile is nothing to sing about."

I watched them, busy below me. There were three young men,
and the two women, beside the litter bearers. I spotted the
crippled boy, Pittakos' son, right away, of course, though he was
not much deformed, having a shrunken arm only, and one
shoulder a little high; a shame it was, for he was a likely lad
otherwise, tall and with delicate features and a fine, sensitive
expression. The other two must have been the brothers, though
there was not much resemblance between them. The one who
looked to be older was tall and broad, with a wide, dark face and
quantities of curling black hair, though his chin was shaven, like
his brother's. I wondered if the fashion was catching on; I myself
wore no beard, disliking it because it was yellow and spoiled my
dark sailor's look, but most Greeks still cultivated the small chin
beard, trimmed to a conventional shovel shape.

My eyes lingered a while on the other one; very handsome he
was, short and compact, with an athlete's body, perfectly
muscled. His face, too, was perfect, almost too much so; one
usually sees such faces only on statues. His expression, though,
was like no statue; there was a wild look to him, reckless eyes like
the eyes of an unbroken horse, and a mouth that mocked. I could
almost believe him a little gone on wine, if it were not such an
early hour; he was not, clearly, one to languish in exile, but
would find his pleasure, come what may.

I looked, then, at the women. The small one, young, I took to
be the servingwoman, though she was richly dressed, in peacock
colors; she was moving about among the others, rummaging in a
box, handing out little packages, farewell gifts, I supposed. I had
not yet seen her face. The other was tall, with a still dignity and a
goddess' body, the chiton simple and beautifully draped; her face
was perfect, under a broad white forehead, her head covered by a
fold of her mantle. She carried a small harp; clearly, this was the
poetess.

As I watched, another litter joined them, and a large group of
nobles, too, but walking. These must be some of those who shared
the earlier exile, for I had heard they possessed only a fraction of
their former wealth, all having been confiscated by the Tyrants;
their clothes were good and finely draped, and the men wore the
wreaths of the aristocrat, but they were without chariot or
wagon. One woman, plump and untidy in crumpled linen, but
with a sweet face, emerged from the litter; she was wringing her

hands, and, even at this little distance, I saw the tears running down her cheeks. The lady with the harp set it down and took the woman's hands, smiling warmly.

The whole group, and it was fairly large, was moiling about now; it was difficult to distinguish anyone, they looked, all, like bright-feathered, darting birds, embracing one another and kissing, exclaiming in flutelike voices, and the ladies furling and unfurling sunshades; there was a kind of nervous excitement among them, and tears and laughter mingled.

I saw the small maid embrace a very young boy, and then another, younger still. Beside me Makro stood up, waving and shouting. "Ho, there—Charaxus!" The bigger of the boys turned, waving back, and then all three came shipside, looking up at Makro.

"Ho—Makro . . . you a sailor now?" This was the big boy; he had an impudent face, with a crooked grin.

"From today—yes!" cried Makro. "I have left the guard!"

"I wish I could come with you!"

The girl turned on him, quick as a flash. "What a thing to wish! With things as they are here in the city, and Larichus to care for, and your schooling not yet finished!" She caught sight of someone behind her. "Oh, here is Antimenades!" And she threw herself into his arms. It was the bigger of the two brothers; close to, his face was cheery and kind, a face to trust. He lifted her clear off the ground, holding her close; she squealed like a child. Of course, she was small made, and I could have done it myself, would have enjoyed it, in fact, for I had by now got a good look at her. She was a sweet armful, no question.

He looked up at me, still holding her off the ground. "You the captain?"

I felt Makro, beside me, ready to speak, and kicked him quiet. "Yes," I said, "I am Nikko . . . I command this ship."

"Take care of our little jewel, then. Bring her safe to Sicily."

He scowled at me as though he thought I would not. "Don't worry," I answered. "She's a good ship . . . and there are some twenty others to think of, as well. She'll get us there."

I felt the girl's eyes on me as I spoke, but when I looked at her, they shifted, and she slipped down from Antimenades' arms, and went to the brother, who had come up behind. I saw her reach up and put her hands on his shoulders, looking long and deep into his eyes. He bent and kissed her, a long embrace; she was the first to move away. I heard her say, "Atthis has not come then?"

There was an odd look on him; after a moment he said, "We did not have the heart to wake her. She has been weeping every night . . . it is the first sleep she has had."

"Poor child," she said. "Still . . . I wish you had wakened her . . . the gods know," she said, so low I could barely make it out, "when I shall ever see any of you again? . . ."

"Darling," he said, "don't be sad . . . it will all be as it was. . . . We will be recalled, and all will be as it was. . . ."

She shook her head, though I saw she smiled. "Nothing is ever as it was. Each day is new. . . ."

The big brother still stood, close to shipside, looking up at me. "Is it all right if we come aboard, to help bring the traveling things, and to make our farewells?"

"If you'll step lively," I said, squinting at the sun, above the horizon now. "We want to take advantage of this good wind. . . . I don't like to be hard, but"—I gestured to the woman who still stood surrounded by her friends—"if you'd tell the lady poet that it's time . . ."

He stared at me, and then turned to look where I pointed.

"Tell her yourself, for here she stands." And he turned and brought the maiden toward me. She was very young, and very pretty. Not everybody's style, perhaps, but I had a weakness for dark hair and eyes; I had glimpsed such eyes before, above the veilings of the women of the East, large and bright, tilted at the outer corners. As for the rest of her, she looked moist and edible, like a ripe apricot.

"I have been in error, it seems," I said, bowing. "It is *you* who are the exile . . . The Black Lark."

"Yes, I am Sappho." She pronounced it *Psappha*, the name sounding softer and more sibilant. I have noticed this softer speech here on Lesbos, a pretty accent, with a lilt to the sentences, like music. They all speak so, but she, I found, had a more pronounced difference in her speech than the others, perhaps because she is a performer, and makes use of it.

"Will you come aboard, then?" I leapt down to the dock to give her a hand up. She took my hand; her own was small and warm, and she went up the footholds as though she had been doing it all her life. I saw her eyes, startled, rest for a moment on my bared chest, with its rows and rows of gold beads that hung against it, but she turned away quickly, not to be too bold. I smiled to myself. *She is a proper little lady-girl,* I thought. *She's probably wondering if I am really a pirate!*

They all trooped up then, carrying boxes and bundles. "Wait a minute, little lady," I said. "Pittakos made it clear you would have one servingwoman and one box . . ."

She put her fingers to her lips, her eyes crinkling. "I have foxed him. . . . How can I go so far with one box? Impossible! He has left me nothing . . . no money. I must have my lyres and my drums and the other things . . . I must have a change of clothes!"

"But what is in all of them?" I asked, picking one up. "This must be empty. I cannot allow—"

"Oh, no . . . that is the most precious of all. All my poems are there. They are on paper only, that is why they are so light. . . . Oh, please," she said, putting her little hands together in a pleading gesture. "Oh, please let me have them! I will make room for them by me. You will not be inconvenienced."

What could I do? I let her have them. "You are kind, Master Nikko," she said. Then, in a small voice, "I hope others, too, will be kind. . . ."

"Nikko, is it?" said a voice at my elbow. I have said they had all swarmed over the rail by now. I saw a man, good-looking, in his middle years, with a keen and humorous face. He looked at me hard, shaking his head. "I would have sworn you were Kerkylas himself. . . . I have not met the man, but he has been pointed out to me, and you are his very image."

I started to deny it, but then I saw no one was listening, and put my finger to my lips. It was senseless to make a scene about it, and besides I liked the man, first off. "Let it be a secret between us two—for now. . . . You must be Melanippos, for I have seen you, too. Though I feel you have changed in some way. . . ."

He smiled. "I have been married."

"Ah, well," I said, "that will do it every time. . . ."

We exchanged a few pleasantries, nothing that could not be

overheard, and he, also, enjoined me to watch over my passenger.

"Funny thing, that," I said. "I took the other one to be the poet. She is surely not a servingwoman. . . ."

He rubbed his chin. "Praxinoa . . . well, it is difficult to say exactly *what* her position is. She is a freedwoman, true, but very handsomely educated—"

"Handsome, too," I said, watching her as she quietly supervised the traveling boxes and their disposition.

"Truly?" he said. "I find her rather cold. . . ." He shrugged and smiled. "But each man has his own taste. . . . Praxinoa has been a mother, almost, to those children, Sappho and her brothers, their cousins, too. . . . She teaches the little ones their letters, still. She ran the household—when there was one—" And he gave a wintry sort of smile. "There is hardly a house left, now. . . ."

"That bad?" I said.

"Yes . . . the Tyrants have left them all close to nothing. They manage—but in a way, they might as well all be exiles. . . . They have no life left, of the sort they were used to. No parties . . . no new clothes . . . a servant or two where once were twenty. . . . It is hard, especially for the older ones."

I nodded. "I can see it would be—but perhaps a change will come. . . ."

"Yes . . . Pittakos will relent. He will give them back a privilege or two, from time to time, and maybe give back some of their own to them. But he will do it in a niggling way . . . he is that kind of man. Besides, he will want them always out of power. It is that he fears . . . the power of the nobles."

"Strange," I said. "I thought he was one of them."

"Not in his beginnings, no. He is a self-made man. Such men must always be on guard, or lose all."

I saw he was shrewd, and liked him for it. A trader must be. "This little singer here, he finds her dangerous?"

He looked about us, then said, "Come here to the railside with me; I will explain, briefly . . . Old Pitt wants them separated— all the conspirators, but especially Alkaios and Sappho. He has a great influence on her; alone she would not bother her head a great deal about politics. Except, of course, where the rights of women are concerned. She feels strongly about all the injustices done to her fellows in other places, like Athens, and will not stand still and let them happen here. Besides, she has a very great following among the common folk. She could sway them to her side by a song—and good-bye, Pittakos!"

"She is that good, is she?" I asked.

"Better. There is no one like her for singing and the making of songs in the world. Even Alkaios' fire dims beside her genius."

"You are using strong words, friend," I said. I could not help but smile to myself at the thought of this slip of a girl possessing genius. I had always reserved that term, you see, for the dead great, like Homer. Truth to tell, I did not know a great deal about it then; I had been raised on the bardic song that tells of battles and remote doings of long ago, and the strange wailing music of the East that I had heard on my travels, the kind that hurts the ears. Nor had I given much thought to the plight of women, except when they were mistreated in war; my own mother had always seemed content with her lot.

The exile—or the exiles, for the woman Praxinoa was there, too, after all, though no thought was being given to her—had made their farewells, and the ship was now cleared and we hoisted anchor. The little Sappho was noisy and gay, calling out jests and reminding them of this and that. As we pulled away, the wind strong behind us, I saw the poet Alkaios lean out perilously over the water to blow her a last kiss. She cupped her hands and called, "Take care of Boy and Girl. . . ." A cryptic admonition, I thought. And then, "May Aphrodite keep you, dear one!" I guess she meant him, all right, and wondered. She stood there, unmoving, till the figures on the dock were tiny ants, merging together; when she turned away, I saw her bright looks had vanished and her eyes brimmed wild with tears. In fact, they ran down her face like rain, unchecked; I have never seen anyone weep like that. When she rushed past me to throw herself into her freedwoman's arms, a few of them splashed, hot, on my chest. I wondered what in Hades I would do with these two women on the long voyage. Then I shrugged; it was none of my business, after all. I went forward to take the wheel.

Chapter 3

We were headed for Andros, first stop. With the kind of wind we had, I figured we could make it in three days, maybe two. If, by chance, we were becalmed, I carried twelve oars. Merchant ships as a rule do not carry any at all, but I always like to be on the safe side. And here, among the small islands, one can usually make it to some port or other, even without sail. I had decided to reveal my identity when we reached my home island; it would be discourteous not to invite the two women to come on land for a bit, and my parents had never seen me in this outlandish garb, and would give the whole thing away in any case. Meanwhile, I rather enjoyed the little game I was playing; I am not cast in the heroic mold, and this rough outlaw-adventurer was the closest I could come to it.

I had never had a woman passenger on any of my ships, except now and then as a favor to some visiting neighbor, which would be a matter of a few hours at most. I had resigned myself to inconvenience, annoyance, a disrupting of discipline; I was almost disappointed to find myself mistaken.

For one thing, some knowledgeable person had warned Sappho that close quarters made for seasickness; she refused to go below, and asked that I rig a canvas shelter on the deck, such as I had for myself. "I like the sea air, and the stars," she said. "Besides, the hold reeks of sour wine. . . ." And she held her nose, delicately, laughing.

"Andrian wine is not sour, Lady," I said, laughing, too. "I have none left on board, or I would insist you sample it."

"To me, all wines are much the same," she said, "like a kick from a mule. I have a weak head for them."

I almost gave her a lecture on the mores of wine drinking, but caught myself up in time. What could a mere shipmaster know of the proper wines to drink with what foods, or the amount of water to be mixed? Chances are his head would simply be stronger than hers, from practice, only. So I contented myself with a shrug and a smile.

The woman Praxinoa lay against a pile of cushions most of the day; it was as though she did not wish to look at the water. Some folks are like that; it makes them dizzy if they look down. The other one got her sea legs early; she skipped about the ship fearlessly, sometimes leaning out so far over the rail I had to caution her. She wanted to be shown over the ship, too. "I have never been on any kind before, you see," she explained. If she heard the rude remarks and whistles that greeted her, she pretended not to. After, I had a talk with my men, but it did not mean much; sailors are a rough sort.

She had a nice way with me, too, not too free, but not talking down to me either. And she was a good listener, very quiet when I explained ships and their ways. When she asked a question, her brow wrinkled, and she felt for the simplest words, speaking slowly. Of course, she thought I had no education to speak of. To her, I was a cut above Makro, that is all.

As a matter of fact, I put him to serve the ladies this trip, instead of teaching him the business of sailing. It seemed fitting, since he was Mitylenian and knew the girl's brother. Besides, he was too young, and too awed, to try anything; it was a good arrangement, and left me free for my duties.

I did not wish to intrude, so I took my meal at midday alone, that first day out. At supper, though, Sappho sent Makro to fetch me. "It is silly to stand on ceremony," she said, graciously. "And I am only a poor exile now. . . ." She gave me an enchanting smile, belying her words. "Let us take supper together. And Makro, too—once he has done serving. . . . Here, little one, sit beside me." She patted the cushion that lay on the deck below her folding chair. I swallowed my chagrin; I had brought this upon myself with my playacting. To an aristocrat, after all, there can be little difference between a shipmaster and the rawest new hand on board!

I had rigged up a canvas shelter, quite large; it was warm, even at night, so there had been no need to let down the sides until the ladies retired. There were two folding chairs, and I brought my own from my place on the other side of the deck. I thought Sappho looked at it curiously, it was ornate and obviously quite expensive. I had donned an upper garment, with long sleeves and a closure down the front, clasped with my second-best brooch; it was perhaps not in character, but I did not wish to offend the ladies with my nakedness. Sappho asked me where it had come from. "I have never seen such a garment, except on the hill folk at home, but theirs are made of sheep's wool. . . ."

I told her it was Eastern cotton, layered and quilted in a pattern. "But you are not Eastern," she said. "Your eyes are too light."

"No," I said, and took up the stone jug. "You have said you do not care for wine. Would you like to try an Egyptian drink—a milder brew?"

"Beer?" she said, surprising me. "I have had it before—but I only like it if it is cold."

"Well," I said, "it is not iced, of course . . . but it has been all day hanging on a rope overside, in deep water. I think you will find it pleasing."

Our repast was all fresh, it being the first day out; the woman, Praxinoa, however, ate nothing but a little fruit, and sipped the cool beer. I looked at her and said, "Do you require anything, Lady? I have an excellent remedy for seasickness, not unpleasant."

"No," she said, looking sad, "I am not really ill. It is just that I do not like the sea. . . ."

I caught Sappho's eye, and she gave a tiny little shake of the head, indicating silence, I presumed; I dropped the subject.

We finished our meal. It was just being cleared away as the sun set, always a spectacular sight at sea. We watched without speaking; the blue of the sky changed to purple, streaked with rose, and the sun, flame colored, fell like a great child's ball, into the flaming sea. The purple changed again, darker, almost black, and the first star winked; I heard the little Sappho catch her breath. She will probably make a song about this, I thought, if all the tales I have heard of her are true; this kind of thing is just her style, nature and its wonders, the changing world, dreams and the shapes of dreams.

We sat on, as still as if a spell had been put upon us; soft music rose from the aft deck, and a voice sang. The sailors usually do this, in the evening, when the weather is fine, and the day's work is done.

Suddenly Makro cried, softly, "Sappho—Lady . . . it is your song—the Black Lark!"

"But the words are different," she said, "and it was not written for the harp." We listened till it was over, a soft, slow melody, full of peace. I had heard it often, on the last voyages; it was nice enough, but nothing to write home about, certainly.

I looked at the singer; she was shaking her head emphatically; it was dark and I could not see her face, but her voice, when she spoke, was almost tearful. "What have they done?" she cried. "It is all changed . . . the whole feeling is changed!" She jumped up suddenly. "Praxinoa—which box is my lyre in? The old one that Arion gave me?"

"I'll get it, darling." The woman rose.

I spoke. "Makro—go before, and take a lantern. Look sharp—the last rung of the ladder is missing!" I had not thought they might need anything from the cargo place. No lamps had been put down there, for safety. Thinking about it, I excused myself and went to fetch a small lamp. When I came back with it, Sappho said, "I can feel the strings in the dark, you did not need to trouble."

"It's no trouble," I said. "Besides, I like to see your face. . . ." I could have bitten my tongue, for it sounded presumptuous, from a seaman. *Well, I will tell her in a day or two,* I thought. Meanwhile, she did not seem to notice anything amiss.

She sighed. "It is very beautiful," she whispered, gazing at the evening sky.

"Yes . . . it is," I said. She turned her head and caught me staring at her face. "They have been gone a long while," she said. "I wonder . . ?"

"I will see if I can help," I said, getting up from my chair. "It may be they cannot find it in the dark. I know the place as well as you, Lady, know your lyre. . . ."

But when I got to the hatch, I saw they were coming up the ladder, the woman first, carrying a lyre. I stepped aside; the beam from Makro's lantern showed me her face. I swear I saw a look of positive dislike flit across it, as quickly gone, and the statue look back again. *Gods,* I thought, *have I been offensive? Surely my disguise is harmless enough—nothing to get the wind up about.* A true aristocrat, of course, would not have cared, seeing she was only a freedwoman. I am a strange sort, though, not liking to make enemies at any level. Watching her carefully later, while Sappho tuned up, I could see no trace of that look upon her; perhaps it was simply the sea that affected her. Or maybe I misread the look, the light was weak, after all.

Sappho played; she was a master. She did not truly sing, but spoke in a sort of lovely chant, each word clear to the ear. She was right; I would not have recognized the song, so different it was from the sailors'. Unlike most islanders, I am inept at musical instruments, though of course I have had some training, and can play along with others, if I must. But I lack the ear; words mean more to me, and these words were straight from the gods, in my opinion. The whole tale of Orestes' dreadful passion lay bare, poignant and heartbreaking; yet the song was quite short. The last notes, soaring and triumphant, ended as though cut off; one waited for more, but when it did not come, it was clear that this ending was the perfect one, full of artistry. The last note, truly, seemed to hang in the air, setting up a trembling in the veins. No one spoke.

After, I tried to tell her how good it was, but it was no use; such things cannot be expressed. She smiled, though, and thanked me, as though she had not heard such words a thousand times!

She told me of the whole conception, and of the famous Arion, who had been her teacher then; how it was a story, really, told in song and dance, a new kind of entertainment. "I mean, some day, to make some such of my own. . . . It is a marvelous thing, and most moving to those who hear and see it. One might make up the tale, a new one, and not depend upon the old legends at all. . . ." I saw that she dwelt upon this in her mind, and said nothing, just nodded while she fingered the strings.

I had that strange feeling of a presence or presences, sensed, and turned around, peering into the darkness. All the sailors had crept close to listen. "It is the Black Lark herself," said one. There was that in his voice that sounded as though he might fall to his knees at any moment. I laughed to myself; I had feared for her among these men! I learned later that this happened always when Sappho sang; she had whatever it was that touches all kinds, even the commonest. One could almost believe the old tale of Orpheus, that he could charm the birds off the trees, and tame the wild beasts with his music! It was the explanation for her extraordinary fame, that was indeed already on the way. "I think, Lady," I said, "that your exile will be sweet, for you will be welcomed everywhere. And it will be short; for sure your own city cannot do without you for long. . . ."

"You are very kind, Master," she said, inclining her head gravely.

She played a few more songs, sweet, small things, and very charming, but none as impressive as the first. Then she handed the lyre to her woman. "Put it away, dear Praxinoa . . . I am tired. And I think the air is damp, too—not good for the strings."

"I will wrap it in several layers of wool," the woman said. It was the first time I had noticed her speech; it was a cultured voice, and very careful, without the soft accent of Lesbos. When she left us, I asked Sappho her origins. "She is from Korinth, I think. : . . I think, too, that she dreads to see it again, for it was there that she was sold into slavery."

I thought a moment. "Was she put onto a slave ship?"

"No, I do not think so. But she was taken by sea, certainly . . . wherever it was—before she came to my father . . ."

I nodded. "That is why she fears and hates the sea, then. . . ."

"Yes, I am sure of it. . . ."

She said no more, and I did not ask. Later, when I heard all of the woman's story, I understood her better, though never perfectly.

We watched together as the moon rose, looking like a slice of melon, and paler than the stars. There were no clouds, but the wind still held. At this rate, we would make land by day after tomorrow. She must have been thinking along the same lines, for she turned to me and asked, "What is our first stop?"

"Andros," I said. "In two days, perhaps, or three . . ."

"Andros . . . that was my father's name. Or rather, the shortening of it, but most men called him that. His whole name was very long—Skamandronymos."

"There is a River Skamander," I said, "in the Troad lands."

"Yes. He was named for it, it was the valley there where he was born, the Skamander valley."

"A beautiful place," I said. "I know it well. You have never been there?"

"I have never been anywhere," she said, laughing a little. "But I shall make up for it soon . . . Sicily is very far. . . ."

"Depends how you look at it, Lady," I said, hearing an uneasiness in her voice. "To a seafaring man, it is a short hop. In any case, we will be taking it in stages. You will see something of the world—or part of it anyway. The ship touches down at some few of the islands—and the mainland, too, at the isthmus."

"That is Korinth, is it?"

"Well, in a manner of speaking—"

"The temple there . . . is it . . . do the girls still have to— offer to the goddess?"

"No, Lady," I said. "That custom has been outlawed now . . . there are only temple prostitutes now, like anywhere else. Periander—that was one good law he passed. Most of the Tyrants have one good thing that they did, to make up for all the bad."

She shook her head. "I cannot think that Pittakos ever will have a good thing."

"Well, time will tell," I said. I did not feel like arguing with a young maiden about politics, under a soft night sky; besides, it was about time for my watch.

A silent moment passed; she yawned delicately, putting her hand up to her mouth.

"You are tired, Lady—and I must take my turn at the wheel. . . ."

"Yes, Master Nikko, good-night."

I showed the women how to roll down the canvas sides for privacy, and posted Makro outside their tent for a lookout.

As I went forward, I heard, above the noise of the lapping waves and the wind-beaten sail, their soft voices, flutelike in the night. I smiled, thinking of Fate and the twisting way of it.

Chapter 4

The wind held, as it does in the good season, blowing steadily to the south; all that was needed was to keep the wheel to the westerly side a little, in the direction of Andros. In two days we sighted it, still far away, a mere speck, but I hoped to touch shore by nightfall. It was a beautiful morning, and we were in luck; I ordered a full measure of wine all round, broaching a cask I had held over, red Samian.

Toward noon it grew very hot; I was glad of a chance to come in under the women's canvas shelter and share the midday meal. It was cool and pleasant out of the sun, and the small flapping of the canvas in the wind nearly sent me to sleep. Praxinoa seemed to have got over her listlessness; she had taken over the serving, and had set Makro to cracking nuts, using a ship's hammer and a whetstone.

Suddenly Sappho cried, "You are smashing them all to bits! Give me the hammer!" There was something in her voice that I had never heard, setting my teeth on edge; at the same time I seemed to *hear* a silence. It took me right out of my lethargy, I can tell you; there was a strangeness somewhere, a warning. I still heard the canvas above flapping, and the larger sound, over it, of the sail's creak, but something was amiss; I could not put my finger on it.

Praxinoa dropped a smoked fish into my lap as she was serving me, making a greasy stain on the worn leather of my trousers; little Makro, usually so neat in his movements, tripped over the leg of the standing brazier, and nearly overturned it, a hot coal falling on the polished deck, marring it, and I swore at him, softly; Sappho hit her finger with the hammer and cried like a child. Clearly something had happened to the day!

We finished our meal in silence, none of us feeling very hungry, and each nursing his small resentment. When it was cleared away, I excused myself early, not stopping to chat, and went forward. The men were gathered in a little group; they were not loud, but a dispute of some kind was going on. What in

Hades has infected us? I wondered. I settled the matter, sending all hands to their posts, and taking over the wheel, but still uneasy. The sun was even hotter now, though high noon had passed; my hands were slippery on the wheel; I wiped them, taking off my head cloth for once, not caring, and using it to wipe the moisture from the wheel as well. My hair, loosened from the turban, felt damp and crawly; I shook my head, impatient.

Suddenly I heard a shout behind me, hoarse and frightened. I looked around. It was the mate, a man called Pelagon; he was young still, but I valued him; he had been a fisherman, and knew much of the ways of the sea. As I looked, he pointed up to the sky, with a face of fear. My eyes followed his hand; I shuddered. The sun hung like a lamp above us, a dull dark red like dried blood, with no brightness. Behind it the sky was tin colored. I heard the silence again, stronger this time. I listened, cocking my head. There was no sail creak, no wave sound against the hull; we were becalmed! But not calm as I had ever known it; there was a threat in it, something unhealthy. "Secure the mast!" I called. "All hands to secure!"

Pelagon had disappeared; I saw him on the other side, giving his own mate's orders. The men were moving now, fast, the only movement that could be seen.

I strode aft, trying to look as though this were all in a day's work; the curtains were down at the sides of the canvas tent, and I could see no movement within. I stood away a little and called, softly. A head came through the flaps, Sappho's. She put her finger to her lips, smiling. "Quiet—Praxinoa is sleeping . . . I think it is the first sleep she has had, truly. . . ."

"You must wake her," I said. Something in my tone made her eyes go round and wide.

"Why—what is it?" she asked.

"I don't know . . . the weather is not right . . . best to be on the safe side, anyway. We must take down the canvas. Makro!" I looked around for the boy. He had been sleeping, too, on the other side of the tent; his head poked round it, tousled. "Make haste," I said. "Start getting the canvas stowed away . . . never mind the lady—we'll have to wake her."

My urgency caught him; his face looked a little awed, a little fearful as he rushed to do my bidding. I felt Sappho's eyes; she gave a little laugh. "Your hair!" she exclaimed. "It is like—electrum!"

I grinned; I could not help it, even at such a time. Trust her! Other women have called it corn colored or wheat, or some such fancy—but an alloy of gold and silver! I ran my hand through it, suddenly feeling foolish. It was straight as rain always; flattened by the turban, it must look very strange indeed. "Lady," I said, "only a poet would think to compare it so. It is yellow—that is all—and made lighter by the sun. . . ."

As I spoke, I felt the first stirrings of the storm wind; that same yellow hair, left unbarbered for weeks, whipped suddenly across my face; I spat the long strands out, and said, "There is haste. Wake your woman, and get below, quickly! Take what you can, and stow all away . . . we must clear the decks—for safety!"

"Why—is there danger?" Of course she knew nothing of the sea, and it could not be explained in a moment either—that unnatural sudden calm, and now the little fingers of wind, clawing and erratic.

"Maybe not," I said, not to alarm her. "But we may be in for a big blow. Look at the sky."

When she had seen the unhealthy sun above, she turned a still as stone face to me. "It is ugly," she said. "Does it mean a storm?"

"Hard to say," I answered, trying to read the signs in the sky. The tin color had turned to iron in the north, with a dark cloud, angry and low, just on the sea's rim. "The only time I ever saw a sun like that there was an earthquake after. But that was on land, when I was a boy. At sea it may mean nothing at all." I said it for her; if the sea floor heaved, it could create havoc in the waters above it; there was no precedent for it, and all I could do was prepare for a storm of sorts, and hope that that would be all.

"Get below, both of you," I said, "just in case. . . . If the ship rolls badly, try to keep your boxes from moving about . . . wedge them in under something, and hold on to whatever is solid. I will send Makro to you."

Fear flitted across her face. "Makro knows nothing. He has never been on a ship either. . . ."

"He is almost a man, and stronger. Besides, it may come to nothing. Pray!"

"Who shall we pray to?"

"To Poseidon," I said, "that he will keep quiet. And to Aphrodite, who calms the winds. . . . I must go now. Do as I say."

I saw them down the hatch, and closed the door, not bolting it, in case we could not get to it later; I did not want to trap them there if things got worse. I went forward to the wheel; the wind was getting wilder now, blowing every which way, but the ship was still holding course, of a sort. I stopped the men; they were taking down the sail. "Keep it up," I said. I was by no means certain what orders to give, but still, one must gamble, sometimes. If there proved to be any kind of steady direction to the wind, with sail we could ride the waves; without it, we would toss till the boat fell apart.

It grew as dark as night, but still the wind did not blow strong; there was still that odd heat, oppressive, like a stifling blanket. There was a sudden fierce flash in the sky, jagged and blinding white. On the heels of it came a crack like a whip crack, but loud, louder than one could imagine. Instinctively we cowered; it was over in a second, and we all looking sheepish. Then the skies opened and rain poured, as from buckets, emptying. The whole deck was awash in minutes and I set some of the men to bailing out below; it was not really necessary, but I have found that keeping busy helps, in extremity. I could see nothing at all, where I stood at the wheel; the rain was a curtain of angry gray. Lightning began to play all about us, as though twenty Zeuses were hurling thunderbolts at each other, just missing us, and each with its horrid crack of thunder just behind. *Well,* I thought, *as long as it comes after.* When the two come together, that is the end, or so I have always heard.

The ship was still reasonably steady, not pitching or rolling; I could feel the deck, solid beneath my feet; only the skies went wild.

As suddenly as it had started, the rain stopped its lashing, and the sky, though dark, was not alive with the darting light. There was a strange, still moment of peace, complete; then came the wind. We were in luck, for it blew hard from the north, blowing us at top speed to Andros, and to port. I leaned on the wheel, like a piece of dripping seaweed, and laughed from relief. We would come through it.

I made my way aft, slipping on the wet deck, the wind against me, so that I slanted forward, with its beating hands in my face. I gasped; there was just enough breath left in me to heave open the hatch door. In the light of one lamp I saw them, the two women and the boy, looking very small and frightened; of course they had heard the rain pounding and the thunderclaps, but they had not seen the lightning's flare, for which I gave thanks, silently.

Sappho spoke first. "Is it over, Master? Can we come up?"

"I think the worst is over, yes. The wind is with us—behind, and blowing us to Andros. . . ." I laughed a little, shakily, and said, "Shall we drink a little wine to it—to our salvation? Makro, there is an amphora, half-full, in the drawer there, behind you. . . . You have the bowls—if you have not forgotten where you hid them away from old Father Poseidon. . . ."

We all smiled small and sipped gratefully. After a moment the woman Praxinoa opened a box and handed me a great length of soft wool. "You are soaked, Master," she said. "At least get the water out of your eyes. . . ." I grinned, toweled my hair, and wrapped it around me. It had been hot, but now I was shaking with the cold, and beginning to cough as well. I cursed myself; it was ever thus with me. Any change in the weather and I am fated for some ague or chill; it never fails. Mother always clucked her tongue, saying it was a sign of our island inbreeding, that had weakened our blood stock.

I shrugged off my worrisome thoughts, and *willed* myself not to come down with some inconvenient illness; it must have worked, for the chill left me straight off. Of course, it might have been the wine; I had tossed off three bowls, far beyond my usual ration.

After a bit, feeling the ship steady enough, I said they might come on deck; it was stuffy below, of course, and I could not risk fainting women. "Be careful, though," I said, as I handed Sappho up onto the still-wet deck. "It is bad footing, and we are being speeded along by an uncommonly strong wind."

The sky was still gray and clouds hid the sun, but there was no wildness at least, though the same wind that pushed us along was chopping the waters; it was most difficult to stand steady. I took Sappho's arm in a firm grip. "Forgive me, Lady, but I am more used to this precarious lurching than you. . . ."

"Indeed, sir, I thank you," she said. "It was dreadful there, belowstairs. I thought I might suffocate—before you came to rescue us."

"I am sorry," I said. "I would have felt the same. But it is the only safe place to ride out really bad weather." I was still making little of the force that had shaken us, hoping to keep her calm, and the other one as well.

A sailor made his way to us, holding onto the rail, his face white as bleached linen. He spoke in the rough dialect of Thessaly; I saw she did not understand, and was grateful, for he told me we had lost two men, swept overboard during the first turmoil. I answered in his same speech. "How . . . who were they?"

"Pelagon, the mate," he said, "and Thrasus, my brother. . . . The sailpiece caught them, when we came about to set course. . . ."

I laid my hand on his shoulder. "Gods, man, I am sorry . . . and Pelagon, too . . . good men, both." I frowned and bit my lip. "And I shall have to tell his father . . . poor old fellow—his only son, Pelagon . . ."

He turned away; I saw that his face was working with grief. She is a treacherous mistress, the Lady Sea.

I realized, looking at the little thread of brightness along a cloud, that the sun was only halfway down the sky; it had seemed like a day and a night, but not more than an hour or two had passed. "I must go now and take the wheel again," I said. "The poor steersman I left at it must be chilled through, and soaked to the skin as well. Besides, we are coming in sight of Andros now." I pointed to a long line low against the sea in the distance. "I cannot trust anyone else to take us in." My words were ill omened. I suppose some jealous god had overheard—but this is hindsight. I continued, "You had best go below again for a bit—but keep the hatch open for air. Stay with them, Makro." He smiled and nodded, proud of the trust I was putting him in.

As I left, the woman Praxinoa spoke to me, low, in the Thessalian dialect; I had not known she knew it. "Those men overboard . . . there is danger then?"

I shook my head, meaning it. "No, not now." I should have kept quiet; we are all fools sometimes.

Chapter 5

I was flattened against the helm, the wind behind us was so powerful; I had much ado to keep firm hold of the wheel, much less control its direction; in the end, I had to call two of my men to give me a hand with it.

We were coming close to Andros now; I could see the lights of the beacons, guiding us in, and even the smoke rising and blowing flat, from our own hearth fire.

We were alongside now, about a mile away. The three of us strained mightily at the helm, to take the ship about and head her in to shore. The wind was even mightier now; I never in all my days had known it thus. We were powerless; the ship would not turn! Swiftly I gave orders. The oars were taken, and the men pulled desperately against the gale force; still she did not turn. Three more came to pull with us on the wheel, but my heart sank; we sped past my island, not even coming close. Truly the gods were against us! I sank wearily against my post, and the men to the deck, collapsed with their vain effort. I could not think what to do. I feared to take down the sail; we could be overset and sunk. I feared the sail, too, for the gods knew where the wind would take us; they can be capricious things, the sea winds.

We were blowing straight on the same course the wind had made for us, and it looked to go on till it was spent; it might be morning before the fury stopped. I closed my eyes and pictured in my head my own mapping of these islands. If we held true, in this direction, we would hit Gyara. And hit is a true word, for that island is all rock, and treacherous beyond any in the Aegean ocean. I had taken the ship, and other, larger ones, too, safe into Gyara's bay many times, but not on sail; it could not be done. One must row always, and with a careful lookout; underwater is all reefs there, barely covered, with only one deep twisting channel.

I had to make up my mind, useless task that it was; one might as well throw the kittabos and let the toss decide! In the end it

was settled for me, for I heard the horrid little noise that meant
the sail was going, a kind of tearing sound. Looking up, I saw the
rip just beginning; it would widen soon, and the sail go to tatters;
perhaps, too, the mast would break. The whole must be taken
down, and quickly. I set all hands to the task, and even left the
wheel myself; it was no use manning it, anyway, with that
punishing gale. I prayed we could accomplish it before we
reached the reefs, and so soften the impact, and give us a chance,
even the slightest.

I bethought myself suddenly of my passengers, and ran aft
myself to call them out. All our weight must be aft, there, with
them, I was thinking, as I went, or the ship, when the sail and
mast were gone, would go over, tumbled forward, when the wind
hit us. "Come up," I called, trying to keep the sound of great
urgency out of my voice and yet make them understand a little
and take care. "Come out—and hold hands! Keep together! Stay
close to the hatch and hold on wherever you can. We may toss a
little, or scrape the reefs . . ."

Makro, frightened, stared at the sailors, working forward, and
at the great sail crumpled on the deck; we had begun to pitch
violently, and I did not blame him. "What are they doing? Why
are they taking down the mast?"

"I cannot explain now . . . it is for safety. Keep your wits and
stay alert. . . ." I ran forward again, keeping a picture of the
three huddled together in their fright. The mast was down now,
and the men were dragging it aft as best they could, for the
weight. There was a sickening lurch, but we did not go over.
Slowly, lumberingly, as in a nightmare, the ship began to turn in
a spin, pitching and rolling all the while.

I thought the oars might do something, but there was no one to
man them, the men were all flat on the deck, clinging fast to
whatever they could find that did not move under them; some
were sobbing, and one man cried out over and over for his
mother, like a lost child. I had no power to command them, or
even to comfort; I was down flat myself, or I would have been
over.

Slowly, very slowly, I began to inch toward the women,
squirming forward on my belly, grabbing what handholds I
could lay to as I went. As I sighted them, I saw with gratitude
that they had had the sense or instinct to lie flat also. "Are you

holding fast?" I screamed into the howling wind. I had to repeat it three times before it was heard; the din was unbelievable. I could not hear them reply, but when I got closer I called, "Can you swim?" They all nodded, but looking terrified, as who would not? "Good!" I answered. "None of the sailors can. . . . If we should hit, try to jump clear—oversides. Try to get clear!"

My last words were lost in a great grinding and a crash that was louder than any thunder; the reefs had got us, all right. I prayed as a huge wave engulfed me; as I came out of it, gasping, I *heard* my ship breaking apart; I have never heard anything so completely terrifying.

As to the rest, I can recall nothing but sheets of water bearing down, flung spray, the noise of splintering, and a sudden clear minute when I saw the deck, strangely upright, like the wall of a house, and all the sailors on it sliding into the sea. Then came the black that I can recall nothing of; my head must have hit something. But I was unconscious for a moment only, and the instinct for survival works while one sleeps, it seems, for I found myself hanging onto a piece of the mast. I guess it had been shattered; it was the hardest wood I could find, especially brought from Africa, and as big around as a man's waist!

I could see nothing at first but spray, wild, a world made of it. When it stopped swirling, and settled into choppy waves again, I saw that there was nothing at all left of the ship but the mast I clung to, a bit about the length of a tall man's height. I saw some black dots, randomly placed on the water, not far away, really, but for the waves. I kept losing sight of them as they went down behind. I tried shouting; I must have been doing it all along, for my voice was hoarse and the sound little more than a croak.

Not gradually, but as though some god had stretched out his hand, the wind stopped, and with it, the waves. The whole sea stretched before me, like a sheet of hammered silver, barely rippling, empty except for those same black dots. I saw they were, miraculously, the two women and Makro, each clinging to some separate floating thing. Squinting my eyes against the gray glare, I saw the things were Sappho's boxes, with one to spare, spinning slowly by itself, high in the water.

It hit me suddenly; I cried as loud as I could from my tortured throat. "Those boxes will sink! Swim away from them. . . . They are not watertight—they will sink. . . . Try to get here—to the mast . . . the mast will float. . . ." I did not know why, but they always did float; they were coated perhaps, with something to keep out the water.

They heard me and understood. Slowly, unbearably slowly, they kicked their way to me where I hung; the boxes, as I had said, went ever deeper under them. When I reached out, finally, and could touch Sappho, the first of them to get to me, the box had sunk already, and she was about to go under with it. I hung her arms over the mast, and reached for the others, behind her. Soon we were there, and safe, if the gods still were with us, four in a row, clinging to a broken mast from a vanished ship, and looking, spent, across an empty sea. The sky was colored faintly rose by a sun that would set soon, when the clouds lifted. I felt wild laughter rise in my throat, but I kept it down, and said, as matter-of-factly as I could, "A pretty sight, and gentle. But we are facing the wrong way. We must somehow get this lifesaver of ours turned around to shore, or whatever passes for it here. . . ."

Sappho shot an angry look at me, and Praxinoa's eyes were closed; I knew they all, and I, too, would rather have drifted off into eternal sleep. But manage it we did, somehow, kicking and maneuvering until we faced Gyara, no more than a barren rock at best, but now looking like something worse, jagged peaks in Hades. "Cheer up," I said. "It is a shore . . . and we are lucky to have it here. . . . See, to the left, there is the lighthouse." One beam cut through the thickening half-light. We kicked as hard as we could, pushing toward land. At least three of us did; I was not sure that Praxinoa still breathed.

My foot touched rock. "We are there," I said. "But hold onto the mast till we get right in. . . . There are step-offs around these parts—treacherous . . ."

We got in, and sank onto the hard shore, exhausted. I looked around, taking stock; we were all right, except for the freed-woman, who lay quite still. Sappho was staring out to sea, her eyes straining at something. "There! There it is!" she cried. "My box—my box with my poems. . . ." She jumped up, about to leap back into the water. I caught her arm, and she turned a wild face to me. "You cannot go out there!" I shouted at her as though she were deaf. "You cannot go! It will sink anyway! Let it go!"

She shook off my arm. "No—it is copper lined, and that *is* it.

. . . See the copper bands about it? It will float—it is very light. . . ."

"I'll get it, Sappho!" Makro ran to the water before I could stop him and struck out to the bobbing thing afloat there.

I shrugged, a little exasperated, and turned to look at the woman, who had still not stirred. I bent over her, and felt her heart. It was slow, but beating still. I thought she must have swallowed a great deal of water and blocked her breathing. I flipped her over onto her stomach and began to press downward, hard, and in time, on her back, over and over; after a bit it came up, seaweed and all.

The clouds rolled away and the red sun flamed upon us, bathing us in fire. I laughed grimly to myself as I thought of the scene; here was I, no ship and no men, flung up on the unwelcoming shores of nowhere, emptying a servingwoman's body of a salty mess, while the maiden I loved sent a boy to risk his life over again for some scraps of paper!

Behind me I heard, "Here it is, Sappho . . . here are your songs!" And she answered, tears in her voice, "Oh, Makro . . . I shall love you forever!"

I could have cheerfully brained him, child that he was.

Chapter 6

Gyara's folk are few; it is a tiny island and there is not much upon it that will sustain life. There are no houses; the people mostly live in caves, natural openings in the face of the rock. The lighthouse—which I built myself, or rather, ordered built and transported the workers and paid for it all—is the only man-made structure. It is not that the people of Gyara are so very primitive; it is that no simple house will stand against the winds, which blow here with hurricane force, sweeping the place of all growth, and flattening even the sandy scrub that is rooted in the shallows.

It is this lighthouse toward which we struggled, guided by its steady light. I built it ten years ago, to stand forever, or very nearly; odd to think that it had kept away all wrecks until now, and this one my own ship!

It is all uphill; we were not having an easy time of it, for we were all deathly tired. I am the strongest, probably, and I felt as though I had been beaten on rocks, like dirty laundry. Makro and I had to support Praxinoa between us; she would be all right, but she was very weak; Sappho carried her box, staggering with it, light as it was.

By the time we reached the foot of the little knoll on which the lighthouse stood, evening was upon us; I could not be sure of my footing in the dark, so I cupped my hands and called, as loudly as I could, for the lighthouse keeper.

"Ho! Meniskos! Are you there?" I had to call several times, with Makro helping, before the door opened. We saw a lantern held high, and in its light a man, not old, but gnarled and bent as the low scrub of Gyara. "Meniskos," I said, "make haste, man! We are ready to perish!"

He peered at us, wrinkling his forehead. "Master? . . . Is it you, then? I saw the ship—and then suddenly I saw it no more. . . . I feared it might be pirates washed ashore. . . ."

"No . . . it is two ladies, a young lad, and I. Will you light us up the path? As I remember, it is all rocks. . . ."

Inside, the downstairs room, though dark, was comfortable enough; I asked for more light, and Meniskos got it quickly from the tower room. Behind him came a small figure, shadowy; I saw it was his little daughter, a girl called Hero, after the old tale. I knew her very shy, and did no more than nod.

Meniskos came toward me, his knobby features wearing a look more suited to a god. I saw he knew already. I said, low, "Yes, Meniskos . . . they are gone . . . all . . . all are gone—into the sea . . ."

"Oh, Zeus," he said, barely audible. "Pelagon—my only son . . ."

I held him for a moment, clasped to my chest. He gave one harsh sound, deep; these folk here face death every day of their lives, and that was his only sign of grief. Embarrassed, he moved away from me, lowering his eyes. "There is fish broth, Master," he said. "Not much, our catch was poor, but Hero, here, she put in some of the barley you left us last time you came this way. It is nourishing, and still bubbling from the fire." He turned to the small girl behind him. "Bowls for the ladies, child . . . wash them first."

He brought us some sheepskins, cured, to put across our shoulders, for we were all shivering still, more from shock than cold; the sheepskins were some I had brought him long ago, for Gyara has no sheep, having no pastureland. The only animals are a few pigs, that will eat anything, and some poor half-starved dogs. The child brought the broth, steaming, and with a good smell.

"There is no bread, Master, except our flat loaves . . . we have been saving the barley." Meniskos, even in his sadness, gave a little smile; he knew I hated the dreadful stuff that was their subsistence—seaweed pounded to a paste and mixed with salt water, baked hard in flat cakes on the hearth. Still, it is said to be as good as a medicine for certain ills; perhaps it would help near drowning. I took one that he handed out, biting into it with a straight face. It nearly broke the teeth, and had a fishy flavor, but we all felt better after it, what with the heartening soup.

"I had some more barley for you, from Eresos," I said, "and honey, too. But it all went down with the ship. . . ."

Meniskos brought a jug and some wooden goblets, carved

native work. "Here is some of your own Andrian, though, Master . . ."

He poured the wine; Sappho gasped. "I cannot drink it without water," she said.

"They have little water here on the island," I said gently, into her ear. "What little they have is too precious to waste on watering wine—which is precious, too. Come, drink a little, it is very smooth, and will do you good."

Meniskos did not drink; I realized these were the only goblets, and said, "Meniskos, friend—do me the honor," and held out my own goblet. "Let us drink to Pelagon. He was a good man . . . the best."

He took the cup. "To all of them," he said. "To all the lonely dead . . ." He drained the goblet; his face was grim.

Sappho held out her own cup, touching the child's arm. "Come—Hera, is it? Share my cup, and drink to your brother." With her soft dialect, she had promoted the girl from a folk name to the name of full goddess! I did not smile, though; the occasion was too solemn. Besides, though the child stared, I saw she liked it, a more musical sound than "Hero." I had hardly noticed her before; small and thin, with a fugitive prettiness, marred by an odd lack of grace, though I could see no deformity.

We were full exhausted, we survivors; the father and his daughter left us to the room where we were, bringing pallets for sleeping, filled with that same seaweed, dried; some herb must have been mixed in, for there was a faint aroma that came from them, not unpleasant. Makro and the servingwoman fell asleep almost before they lay down, but Sappho and I sat for a bit, staring into the fire, and sipping the wine. I heard her sigh, and turned to look at her; her face shone wet with tears. "The poor sailors," she said.

I put out my hand and covered hers. "Do not grieve," I said, softly. "It was a quick death. . . ." A moment passed; she did not take her hand away. "What of you?" I asked. "You have lost all. . . ."

"I have not thought . . ." She held up her hand; a gem winked in the firelight, and some arm rings clanked together. She laughed a shaky little laugh. "How strange," she murmured. "They are still there. . . . I should have thought to wear them all—these are worth little."

I smiled. "They would have sunk you," I said, "judging from the weight of your boxes."

"I have my poems, at least . . . but not my harp or lyre. And nothing at all to wear, except this." And she looked down at herself. "It is stiff with salt and torn in a dozen places."

"They will find you something here," I said. "Not beautiful— but it will cover you. . . ." I thought a moment. "You must count it all up in your head . . . what you have lost, and its value—so that you may be compensated."

She turned to look at me. "You mean—I will be paid for my loss? Your master must be a very unusual man."

I looked at her full. "I lied to you," I said. "I am my own master. I am Kerkylas."

"Why?" she breathed, staring at me.

I shrugged. "I do not know. It has been my whim always . . . to act the commoner. My men like me for it . . . and it brings us closer."

I saw that she was watching me intently. "And now you are sadder—because you knew those dead men well."

"That is true," I said, nodding. After a bit, I poured what was left in the jug into our cups, and spoke.

"I had planned to tell you at Andros, for that is my home. My mother and father are there, and would have welcomed you. Now it must wait. . . ."

"Will a ship come, then?"

"Yes," I said. "Meniskos will signal . . . with smoke by day, and flares by night. I have a ship due to pass before the week is out, heading down to Crete. She will take us off the island and put us ashore at Andros. . . . I am sorry for the delay."

She shook her head. "Do not be. I am not so drawn as all that to my exile—to Sicily."

"I understood that you had kinsmen there."

"So I have heard, but I do not know them. My mother's people . . . she is long dead. For all I know, they may be also—or they may not welcome me. . . ."

"I cannot believe that," I said, meaning it. She tossed her head a little and sent me a slanting look from her long Eastern eyes; I saw then, almost, what she was like in the normal way of things, and wished to keep her so; she was enchanting.

My Name Is Sappho

"And will you really pay me back—for all I have lost . . . really?"

"If you will reckon it up . . . I will, certainly." I laughed then, and took off the rolled leather belt I wore about my waist. "I could almost pay you now . . . look!" I showed her the cunning contrivance that closed it on the inner side, hiding the gold and silver coins. "Feel!"

She lifted it, whistling like a street boy in soft wonder. "By sweet Aphrodite," she murmured, "I have never seen so many!"

"They are from Lydia, mostly," I said. "They are minting them there by the hundreds."

She handed the belt back to me. "Truly I should have thought *you* would sink. . . . All of my jewels do not weigh so much. . . ."

I smiled, fastening the belt again and clasping it at my waist. "Iron spits are worth more," I said. "But *those* one cannot carry!"

She looked almost merry. "One of the lost chests held two dozen—wrapped all about with bits of clothing. We had dug them up from our garden, Alkaios and I, where my father had buried them for safety before we went to Pyrrha. . . ."

"That was your—first exile? . . . "

"Yes. There were so many of us then. . . ." For a moment her eyes had a soft dreaming look, suddenly stricken. I thought those wild and brilliant tears would flow, but they did not. She lifted her chin ever so slightly, folded her hands in her lap, and said, "Now . . . I am alone."

I have concubines all over the islands, some of them quite highborn; perhaps I might have had her, too, if I had worked at it. But it was then that I decided to make her my wife, without an obol to her name or a shred of silk to stand up in. I do not quite know why; I was twice her age and up to now content with my life, all free and footloose. Perhaps it was that little lift of the chin, so brave.

Even placed as she was, she would take some convincing. Though I was nearly dead from weariness, I did not sleep when I hit my seaweed pallet, but lay awake, planning my campaign strategy.

Sappho slept on the far side of the room, beside her serving-woman. I listened to her breathing, a little, snuffling snore, like a tired child's; it was very sweet.

Chapter 7

It is the custom on Andros to marry at the first Festival of Dionysos, when the grapes are harvested and trodden for the wine; it is a fertility festival, after all, and some not-too-distant ancestor of mine took the sting out of it by making it clean, as it were. Even though the island is small, it is not unusual for upwards of a dozen couples to celebrate their weddings on that night. And so we led them, Sappho and I, as the King and Queen, or the High Priest and Priestess, or whatever you might wish to call us.

It was Sappho's idea; I think she did it to please my old parents, who treated her from the beginning like some adorable little goddess. True, for their wits were straying by now, mother sometimes took her for a great-grandchild, which she might well have been, and father's bleached-out eyes often got a satyr look, remembering some nymph of his long-gone youth. Mostly, though, they knew who she was, my promised bride, and the singer from Lesbos, and they loved her, as did most people. By now I had replaced her drowned lyre and harp with some twenty others, the finest gold could buy, and she was making songs out of the very motes of dust that danced in the sunbeams of my home. I think she was happy, then and after; I prayed that she would always be.

I do not know, truly, why she married me; it is easy to say that, once asked, she had no choice. For most girls it would be true, for I was wealthy, powerful, and respected; quite a catch, even if I had been repulsive to look at, which I am not. But Sappho was a being gifted by a god, or a muse, and unique because of it; besides, her upbringing had not been to the Greek convention, she was more learned than most highborn youths, and with a mind trained to think. I believe she would sooner have jumped back into the sea than wed where the urge did not take her.

She was loyal, though; I liked her for it, even if it slowed things up a bit. When I first spoke to her of marriage, her long eyes went round, and she stared at me. "But I still love Alkaios," she said. "I do not love you."

"You will," I said, and smiled, knowing my teeth looked very white in my sunburned face. It has done the trick before; it took a little longer, but in the end I wore her down.

After some long moonlit nights, and a few caresses where she did not expect them, she gave in, suddenly, as a fish will after it has been on the line a long time. I sensed it, for she was in my arms, and I have been gifted with such love-knowledge besides. Even then, she did not go all limp and giving, but drew away a little and said, with a prim mouth and cool eyes, "You are not so handsome as Alkaios—but you are taller . . . and I think you do not love boys. . . ."

I laughed, and said, "No . . . women."

"You must give them all up," she said. "Every one."

"It is a bargain," I said. I was laughing still, but I meant it.

And so we were wed, to the sound of wild laughter and the shrilling of pipes, with the torches flaring golden and streaming like horse's tails, and the white legs of the village girls flashing in the fire's light, purple-stockinged from the grape vats, and the smell, warm and sweet in the nostrils and sharp along the jawbones, of the spilled juice.

We whirled in the dance together, all the other couples falling away to watch us; between our spinning turns I caught a glimpse of my mother and father sitting at the skirts of the crowd, their dry old bodies touching, their hands held each in each, their old, old love sweet and withered, like an aromatic dried herb, between them.

We were wed to the honor and glory of the wine god, but I knew she would rather it had been Aphrodite to whom we offered. I whispered that we would honor the love goddess later; she cast down her eyes, but her hand in mine burned so that I could hardly hold it.

I saw, before we slipped away to our bride chamber, the freedwoman Praxinoa standing tall and still among those who watched. I think her heart was broken, though nothing showed in her face. I knew, as one knows such things, somewhere within, that she had been my Sappho's first lover. I have never been jealous of woman love, as some men might be; it tunes the strings, so to speak. I felt for Praxinoa nothing but pity; she had lost all.

I had shrugged away the pangs that had come with Alkaios' name, and steeled myself to take his leavings, telling myself that I did not care. But she was a virgin still. What had he been about, all those weeks and months in Pyrrha? I clucked my tongue silently, for I had to start all over again, not wanting to hurt her, but I was glad, really. For myself, of course; we are all human and cursed with the collector's urge. But for her I was glad, too. It is not every man who can take a virgin and make her like it first time.

I think we made the child that night; the timing was right, and the night went on forever, make no mistake. Of course, so did all the other nights for a week, so perhaps it is just my fancy. Still, I like to think it; I am sentimental about children.

Chapter 8

We had got off Gyara as soon as ever we could signal a ship; the place is not worth dwelling on, in body, or even in the telling of a tale. Even so, I saw more of it than I had seen in all my years of trading, for Sappho is the sort that will have to look at everything, and find wonders where others see nothing. It is one of the things that made her such a fine traveling companion. When we finally sailed away, all the folk of the island turned out to bid us good-bye; Meniskos and his small daugher Hero were weeping. For Hero it must have looked like the end of a world, which she hardly knew except for this glimpse; Sappho had discovered that the child had some talent, untaught, for music. Indeed, Hero had pipes of her own making, and even a homemade lyre, rude and rough, and with only two strings; when she played on them, I had all I could do not to clap my hands to my ears, but Sappho said no, the girl had a gift, and could be taught. She spent some time with her while we were stuck on Gyara, patiently guiding her fingers into some semblance of order, and promised to send for her, one day when she was older. The father wept for his son, and for the simple sad lovely words that Sappho had written to hang above his votive offering. I think it was the first such thing she had written; in later years she might have made her living from these epitaphs, had she the need; she could turn them out like a cook woman turns out honey cakes for the hearth.

Well, to shorten a tale grown long in the telling, we were not yet done with Gyara; no sooner had we settled into our wedded state (for I thought it too late in the year to risk a marriage trip by sea) than the child Hero appeared on Andros, brought by one of my own boats, a small one that visited the islands regularly. I was to find this the pattern of our life, for Sappho collected girls as a smear of honey catches flies. It was Fate, as in this case, or a dream that called, or a way of escape, or all three; a maiden's life in this world of ours is none too lovely, for sure.

As I have said, Andros is a grape island; still, there are a few big trees, carefully cultivated. Outside the house I had taken for our own, there grew a very old apple tree; it no longer bore fruit, but in the spring it was a cloud drift of blossoms, and its spreading arms were thick and strong. I had made a swing for Sappho and hung it from one of them; I was getting into my second childhood early, you will say, but she had begged me. Autumn was coming early that year; it was still summer in the air, but the leaves were turning already, casting a rosy glow on Sappho's bronzed, laughing face. (For once she went without sunshades, believing me when I said the sunny look became her.) I pushed her in the swing, and she cried, "Higher, higher!" I had just run under the swing, pushing it at arm's length above me and letting it go, and she was squealing, when I caught sight of the small figure trudging up from the shore. The boat had put in minutes ago, but I had not given my attention to it, letting the men unload the little trade stuffs by their own orders. I had grown a little lax lately, except for important cargoes; I was a bridegroom, after all.

I stopped, shading my eyes, and watching the figure come on, toward us, stumbling in its long black robes. The swing, of course, was still going, but Sappho jumped out before it stopped; I was always afraid she would hurt herself in such ways, but she never did, she was as agile as a boy. She caught my arm. "It is the child of Gyara!"

The child came on, a little awkward, carrying her homemade lyre and several pipes; on her head was a mourning wreath, the leaves gone a little brown and curling at the edges. From her face, I guessed her news before she spoke.

Meniskos, her father, had died in his sleep; they do not live long on that island, and he had grieved sorely for his drowned son as well. She had nowhere else to go, and had come to us. Of course, if Sappho had not held out the promise of a better life to her, she would have stayed where she was as a matter of course, keeping the lighthouse as her father had done. Now I would have to busy myself to find another keeper; not an easy task, for who is willing to bury himself on that lonely rock? I shrugged the selfish thought away, for Sappho was welcoming the little maid with a face wet with tears and shining with tender concern. It was her business, after all, and she could use another serving maid, besides.

The child did not remember her mother; vaguely I called to mind a shadowy figure, glimpsed with a nursing babe, at the time of the building of the lighthouse. She must have died soon after; the child must now be somewhere between eleven and twelve years of age and shy as a wood nymph. Still, she had had the courage to leave her home and enter an unknown world.

She was very ignorant; Gyara has no teachers. Between them, Sappho and her Praxinoa began stuffing knowledge into her as one fattens the calf for the sacrifice. They said she learned quickly; I remembered that her brother had had a good head for figures, once they had been shown to him. It was how he had become my mate; a good seaman must know how to count and to reckon.

After the first fun of it, Sappho left most of the girl's teaching to the freedwoman, except for a few music lessons. I smiled to myself; of course she could not teach the art of sewing, spinning, or weaving, since she was all thumbs at those things herself! But she loved clothes and ornaments, all the pretty girl-things, and gave away to Hero several of her finest bride clothes; they had only to be cut down a little to fit. The girl even had to be taught the draping and girdling, and the ways of binding the hair! I have said before, she was curiously awkward, with a shuffling gait and jerky arm movements. Once, as Praxinoa was patiently guiding her in the management of her skirts, she tripped and almost fell. Sappho murmured to me, "Gods, poor little one—she is almost as rough-hewn as Gorgo!"

I remembered the redhead and the grimacing face she showed me as I walked past her in Pittakos' courtyard; I laughed aloud. At Sappho's questioning look, I told her, "I saw that Gorgo once . . . she made a face at me."

"You got off lightly," she answered. "Gorgo hates men. But I guess she saw you were too big to tangle with. . . ." And, turning, she came into the curve of my arm, her head fitting softly just under my chin.

Often I noticed Sappho as she watched Hero; there was a little earnest frown on her brow. Once, in the night, after we had lain in love, and I was just drifting off to sleep, she sat up suddenly, shaking me. "I see what it is now!" she said. "The poor child has never learned to use her body properly. . . . Gyara is so rocky, there is no flat land to practice on! So all her movements are inhibited. . . . She must be taught to run and dance—don't you think?"

It was an unlikely time to pose such a question, and I did not care all that much anyway, but Sappho was so earnest that I laughed aloud, and clasped her to me. And so I did not get to sleep just then, after all.

Once, at some later time, I read a poem of Sappho's, not a song, but words only, as she sometimes wrote them; it was about Andros and love and our first sweet days together. Somewhere in the middle there was a line that went like this: ". . . and Hero of Gyara, the little maid that I taught to run like a star . . ." A strange simile. I turned to her, and asked, "What do you mean . . . a shooting star?"

"Well, of course," Sappho said, looking surprised.

The thing is, she did not teach her to run like a star or anything else; I did. For I had forbidden Sappho to run and jump or to dance then; she was several months gone with child already. But Sappho's memory is very convenient; it comes of being a poet, I guess, and must be allowed by the rest of the world.

I determined no rough midwife should touch her. We would take ship for the island of Kos, which is sacred to Aeskulapius; there is a priesthood there, under Apollo, in his healer's guise, and those men have much knowledge of medicine and surgery.

As autumn had come early, so had winter, a short winter and easy; spring warmed the land and brought out the tender shoots of the vine. Sappho's time was due in late May or early June; she was restless and nervy, as women are often when they are carrying. I judged that a change would do her good, and the air from the sea was fresh and healthful with cloudless skies and a little skittering wind; I decided to start for Kos ahead of time, and stop at Samos first.

The island of Samos was on our way, and very close, on a direct line with Andros; from there we could cut down to the smaller priest isle, where she would bear our child.

I had spent the winter ordering the fittings of a pleasure ship, fully decked and with a sumptuous cabin below and luxurious furniture, as well. And I would take no chances either; we carried forty oars. It was almost a foolish precaution, but one taste of the Aegean in anger was enough. I would not risk another storm, or an ugly calm. If it is possible to be fully safe at sea—which it is not, of course—well, then we were as safe as could be.

Praxinoa, I knew, was dreadfully frightened, and I thought to leave her behind, but Sappho would not hear of it, and must have her by at the birthing, poor lady. But one must not cross a bearing woman; it is unlucky.

I looked forward to Samos; it was a place of great beauty and refinement, and I had many friends there as well. A marriage trip, with a child at its end, is not given to many; we were happy.

Chapter 9

The isle of Samos is not large, perhaps twice as big as little Andros, but the city of the same name is famous all over our Greek world. It is like a little Egypt, almost, for its busy trade, and its temples rival those of Athens. Being only a mile away by water from the coast of Lydia, it has all the refinements. I knew that Sappho would love it, and bask in its luxuries. It is said to be the birthplace of Hera, the goddess who protects all married women, and blesses fruitful wombs. There would be many like Sappho, on pilgrimage to the Temple of Hera; I hoped she would not be so peevish, among all the other swollen bellies. Poor child, being so small, she looked, already, about to burst, and could not bend over to fasten her sandals.

We had a perfect passage; the weather was delightful, warm in the sun and in the evenings cool enough for a woolen robe. Sappho lay on the deck in a silken sling chair, indolent as a Sybarite, commanding all the attentions of the four of us; her two serving maids and the boy Makro to run and fetch, and myself as well. For once I left the ship's handling to another, and behaved as much like a wealthy merchant as indeed I was. It was rather pleasant, for a change.

The city of Samos stands on the southeastern coast, facing the Lydian mainland across the straits. The sight, as one sails into harbor, is breathtaking. The city is backed by an encirclement of hills, their peaks shrouded in cloud, with the mountain of Ampelos rising above all. An acropolis, gracefully proportioned, stands on the lower foothills, and the houses of the town cluster around it and march all the way up the slopes.

In the harbor itself were four of the famous triremes of Samos, their sails painted with the peacock's eyes of Hera, and their hulls bright red, like blood. Beside me, I heard Sappho draw on her breath; she had left her chair and was hanging over the rail gazing in wonder. "Take care," I said, pulling her back a little. Though, truth to tell, she was far enough away from the edge, with her bulk between her and the rail.

"They are like jewels!" she cried. "The pattern of the sails—so beautiful and wild!"

"Those are peacocks' eyes," I said.

"Oh," she said, sounding a little disappointed. "Just birds' eyes. . . ."

"You will see the real thing presently—at Hera's Temple. They are her sacred birds. . . ." I pointed to a road running westward from the city, its edges flanked by rows of tall cypresses. "That is the sacred way that leads to her temple—two miles long it is, and each foot lined with trees." You would have thought it was my native city, for the pride in my voice. But I had a great love for the place, partly for its newness, there were no ruins here. It had grown, even since I saw it last, not a year ago. One could not begin to count the houses that were new-built along the beachfront, and the city glowed red from the rose color of the tiled roofs that spread throughout.

Sappho pointed. "Are those temples, too? I have never seen so many!"

"Well," I said, "Hera has many kindred . . . and each has a dwelling place." I pointed in my turn. "See that great jutting rock? That is Poseidon's rock, where he sometimes suns himself. . . ."

She clucked impatiently to show her contempt for such folk stuff; she liked to be thought modern.

I pretended not to hear and said, "Of course, he only shows himself to sailors . . ." and squinted far out along the coast.

She looked up at me, pouting. "I never know when you are joking. . . ."

I put my arm around her waist and whispered, "I am joking. But his temple is there, a fine one, all new. And there is Artemis' house, and there Apollo's . . ."

"And Aphrodite?"

"There is no house for Aphrodite," I said gravely. "This is a clean town."

"I am very glad to hear it," she said, in the same tone. "I will let you off your chain for a little then."

"I like my chain," I said, biting her ear.

We had put into harbor just after dawn; we sat on the deck eating our breakfast and watching the busy wharfside. It is truly a sight; every day is like a festival day. There is a long, broad walkway, smoothly paved, and all along it the booths set up with things to sell, with tumbling shows, cockfights, performing animals, and the like. The smells of incense, perfumes, oils, and humanity mingled with cookshop odors, all canceling themselves out, as it were, and producing one odor, the sharp and pungent smell of Samos.

As we looked, another ship of mine pulled in with a cargo from Naukratis, in Egypt, a Greek base not far from the mouth of the Nile. Egypt has traded for hundreds of years with every country, even the remotest; one can find anything there, even tin bangles from the misty northern isles, where the people are colored blue, even silk from the secret Far East places. I had commissioned the captain to find a special robe, a thing that I had seen once on a wealthy Ephesian wife the night before she had been brought to bed of a child; I had not even known the lady was pregnant! I remembered the robe as rich and gorgeous, stiffly standing out from the shoulders, some Eastern ceremonial garment, intricately embroidered, woven of the precious silk. I hoped to please Sappho, for I knew she fretted for her lost slenderness. Even now she was looking glum at a railside message from my friend Iadmon, an invitation to take supper that evening. I saw the panic racing behind her eyes. "I have nothing to wear!" I smiled to myself and whispered swift words to Makro, dispatching him on his errand to my ship captain.

It was a perfect day, cloudless and blinding blue. We hired a chariot, painted all over with those same peacocks' eyes, and drawn by a pair of pretty white mares, and set out along the Sacred Way to see the new temple of Hera. It was still being built when I was last on the island; I knew the architects, brothers, Theodorus and Telekles. The plans had been drawn up some years ago by their father, the famous sculptor, Phoikos, but, upon his death the work had passed on to them; I was most anxious to see the finished building, for it was said to be the most advanced and modern in the world. There were some dozen more of these little chariots, going the same way, and all filled with bulging bellies. It was a sight to make you smile, truly, but of course I would not dare, with Sappho scowling beside me. The chariots had little padded seats for the ladies, and the wheels were leather-wrapped to smooth the going; even the little mares, I noticed, had been taught a special gait, so as not to jounce. No wonder the hiring had been so high! These Samians know how to make money, even off the gods!

The ride was a fairly long one, but pleasant; we went between those cypresses I had mentioned before, making a cool shade; on our left were the grassy foothills, where white oxen, also sacred, grazed, and on our right the brilliant blue of the sea blazed between the rows of trees.

The temple, when we came to it, was a sight to take the breath. I had not been told how large it was, quite the largest temple I have yet seen, traveled as I am. I think one does not notice this, for the design is so spare and clean, almost stark. It seems, from a distance, to be all columns and stairs, with red tiles roofing it, like house tiles, but larger, an innovation. Indeed, there is only one wall, by the mountainside; the rest of it is all open to the sea.

From quite far away one can hear them, the sacred birds; I saw Sappho, beside me, clap her hands to her ears. They have the worst voices in the world, peacocks, for all their beauty; they sound like Harpies.

We could not enter the goddess' courtyard on wheels, but must dismount and walk along the twisting paths. They are all hedged with rosebushes, in full bloom, and the perfume is as heady as wine. "Roses!" cried Sappho, softly. "Already!"

"There are roses all over Samos," I said. "They bloom the year round, for the winters here are nonexistent."

Suddenly, across the path, went one of the gorgeous birds of Hera, kingly, with its tiny stupid head raised high. It stopped before us and spread its great tail in a fan of brilliant gem-colored feathers. "See," I said. "There are the peacock's eyes. . . ."

"Oh-h-h," she breathed. "It is wonderful. . . ." The bird seemed to hear her and turned, cocking his real eye to look. It was a bird's eye like any other, little and glittering like a piece of glass; he fixed us with it for a second, with utter disdain. Then he folded up his tail, and waddled off like a duck. We burst into laughter. Quickly a shaven-headed priest appeared, shaking his head and frowning, with his finger to his lips.

Sappho whispered, "Do you think Hera only likes peacock voices?"

"Sh-h-h," I said, "Miss Irreverence . . . they will put us out!"

I waited till her giggles died down, then I said, "Perhaps she is deaf. . . ." And so started her off again. We were like silly children; often together it was so, in those first days.

"Oh-oh, here they come," I said. "We're in for it!" Two more of the bald ones in their saffron robes were coming toward us, as we came out onto the grassy place before the temple steps.

But they came on with serene faces, bowing as they reached us. The taller of them said, "You may not advance further, master . . . we will escort the lady."

"What is it?" I asked, annoyed. "Some kind of holy day?"

He bowed again, with an oily smirk. "The fruitful womb is sacred to the goddess," he said. *Much you'd know about it, my friend,* I thought. They had, both, the swaying hips, and the soft pale mouth of the eunuch. I reproved myself silently though, as I watched them lead Sappho up the sacred stairs. After all, poor fellows, it is none of their doing!

There were a few stone benches in the courtyard, presumably for those, like me, who were forbidden the sacred precincts; I sat down to wait. The peacocks amused me, after the first shock of their brilliance. There must have been more than a hundred of them; stupid as they were, they looked almost to be trained, for at some unknown signal the whole gaggle of them spread their blazing tails; the very air seemed to shimmer with color, and the grass was hidden beneath the carpet of dazzling eyes.

Then, as if at another signal, all vanished, and there were the silly birds again, squawking and shrieking. There were some peahens among them, quiet and no-colored, smaller, but these stayed at the edge of the spectacle, as if bidden by the goddess. I wondered idly at the ways of nature; so it is with all birds, and, as I reflected, with other animals as well; the male has always the finest plumage, the most luxuriant fur. How is it then, that among the human creatures, it is the woman, as a rule, who goes in the brightest garments and the boldest face paint? I brushed the thought away, leaving it to the new philosophers; they will be at it long after my time.

I saw another man, at a mate to my own bench, a few long paces away. He was not sitting on it, but kneeling before it with his back to me. I was intrigued, and got up, strolling toward him. I saw he had a lump of clay upon the bench and was working with it, molding a shape, intent. He did not hear me until I spoke. "So, friend, you are making a likeness of this noisy bird?"

He looked up, startled, boy more than man; I knew his face, blunt nose and wide eyes set far apart under a shock of stubborn springy brown hair. "You are your father's son," I said. "Theodorus or Telekles?

"I am Theodorus the Younger," he said, getting to his feet. "You know my father, sir?"

"I know both those brothers, yes . . . and have met your grandsire, too, the great Phoikos, when he was alive. I am Kerkylas of Andros."

He smiled. "This clay came in one of your ships," he said. "Babylonian clay."

"Is that the best?"

"Yes," he said. "It takes a better glaze." He looked at me suddenly, a shy small look. "Once I was minded to run away to see on one of your ships. Got as far as the deck, too—dripping wet I was . . ."

"You swam out?" I shook my head; the water in this harbor is very deep, with a swift undertow.

"It was the only way," he said. "The plank was up. . . ."

"What happened?"

He grinned shamefacedly. "A sailor talked me out of it. I was only eight years old. He had a rough speech and peasant's hands, but he was kind, and never told . . . name of Pelagon."

"Pelagon the fisherman," I said softly. "My mate . . ."

"Oh, sir," he said, "greet him for me. Tell him he was right and I am well content. . . ."

"I cannot," I said. "He was drowned last year."

There was a little silence. "That is sad news," he said. I nodded. After a moment, awkward, I stooped to look more closely at the small sculpture. I could not help but laugh. He had made a comic creature; this was the image of the peacock without its glory, the long drooping folded tail, the haughty inane eye, the dumpy partridge body. He smiled, too. "It is just a sketch in clay . . . I cannot waste a bronze casting on it." But one could see he regretted. "I must do another, for I am commissioned by the high priest here. . . . I should be happy, I suppose, for the pay is good, and it is my first commission—it is for the temple, bronze, with the eyes set in with gems. . . ."

"For sure you have inherited the family talent," I said.

He shook his head. "I am not sure. I cannot do the big things, the heroic ones. . . . My talent is small. And then my father says I scatter my skills, as well. For I like planning houses and the decorating . . . and to carve gem faces."

"There is room for all those," I said. "I should like to bring my wife to your workshop. . . . Will your father show us his work?"

"Certainly. Has she seen the temple?"

I laughed. "She is seeing it . . . but I have not—as yet. Some womens' mystery . . ." I took my leave of him, promising to come on the morrow or the day after, and went to meet Sappho, where she walked toward me between the two priests.

"You must see it, my darling . . . the temple is so beautiful— and there is a huge statue of the goddess, and a great bronze cauldron that must be one of the wonders of the world. . . ."

"Another day," I said, for I saw she looked weary, under the excitement. "We must go back now and rest, for we dine tonight in one of the great houses. Besides, I have a gift for you, back at the ship. I trust it has arrived by now."

"Oh—what? What is it?" And she clasped her hands together, pleading.

"You will see."

She pestered me all the way home, but for once I did not give in. I would not hint, even; she saw the robe when we went aboard, glittering like treasure in its box, caught her breath and snatched it up. I was happy not to have spoiled her pleasure in the surprise.

She must try it on straightaway, atop her own garments, though the heat was at its highest. The thing was heavy; her forehead was beaded with sweat, but her face glowed with delight.

Little Hero held a mirror, while Sappho turned about, trying to see all of herself in its small surface. "I think," she said, frowning, "that no one could tell. . . ."

"It is nothing to be ashamed of," I said, smiling. "But it is true. No one could tell . . . except that you are as beautiful as an Eastern princess."

"Truly?"

"Truly," I said. "But you are always beautiful."

"The most beautiful in the world? Say it."

"The most beautiful in the world."

Chapter 10

The house of Iadmon was one of the showplaces of Samos, surrounded by rose gardens, laid out in a formal pattern, with tiled walks winding throughout. Beyond it rose a gradual slope of hills, covered with silver-green olive trees, Iadmon's wealth. Even now, at sunset, there were a dozen slaves tending the groves, their short brick-colored tunics bright among the dusty softness of the leaves. It was a conceit of this man Iadmon that he dressed his slaves always in some shade of red, though he himself wore snowy white. The litter that he sent for us was borne by four slaves clad in the crimson of the Samian ship hulls; these bearers were of a giant size, and lifted the conveyance, with us in it, as lightly as if it had no weight at all.

The ancient woman slave who met us at the door, bowing and offering towels, and the two Nubians who, impassive, held the great bowl of scented water for our hand washing, all were in dark red also. Sappho and I exchanged glances, she wrinkling her nose in distaste. We had come by covered litter and a short way; it was ostentation to proffer the guest bowl as for a wearisome and dusty journey. Besides, she had told me that her father had freed all his slaves, putting them on wages, except for those too old or too dim-witted to understand; I often wished that I had known him, this man Andros whose short name was my island's name.

Iadmon came halfway to meet us, for courtesy, leading the way into the long banquet hall; to my mind it was another form of ostentation, that hall, decorated as it was, like a festival. But then he was an Asiatic Greek; it was to be expected.

Tall slaves flanked the entrance way, and several stood stiffly at attention around the walls, all in the red of his service. The room was brilliantly lit, and flowers made a profusion of color and scent; the tiled floor was spread with exquisite fur rugs. I saw at once they were a hazard, and took Sappho's arm; she was wearing new slippers, with very high wooden heels. It was a fashion I deplored, for it changed the whole rhythm of the walk, besides being dangerous. Of course, I was overprotective; it was my first trueborn child she carried.

There were four places set only, in the midst of all this splendor. I expected the lady of the house to join us; I had met her once, a shrewish, pretty woman. But Iadmon turned to Sappho and said, "My Lady Kleto begs to be excused. She is in the same delicate condition as you, sweet lady, but it does not so become her . . . and she is often sick besides, even though this one is her third." I felt Sappho stiffen, affronted, and gave her hand a gentle pressure. Truly the man was a boor, however rich.

He said to me, "May I congratulate you, Kerkylas, on your lady's fine health, and her youth. . . . May she bear many more as is evident she will, for she carries well, and with unusual poise."

I said quickly, "Her poise is a god-gift, one of many . . . but the most necessary for a performer."

He stared as pop-eyed as a frog, which indeed he somewhat resembled. "Performer!" he gasped, as though I had brought a flute girl into his house.

A voice behind me, rich and full, said, "But certainly. This lady is the Black Lark of Lesbos. Her songs are known to all literate people . . . and soon even you, my master, will have heard them."

The speaker went on one knee before Sappho. "Permit me, Lady." And he took up the hem of her gown and kissed it. "In homage to the Muses," he said, rising. I heard behind the harp of the voice the thin cutting edge of sardony, and looked swiftly at Sappho's face. But she had heard more than that, or seen it in his eyes, perhaps, for she smiled and held out her hand. "You are courteous, sir. . . . May I know your name?"

"It is Aisopos, the freedman . . . now once more enslaved." And he took her hand and kissed it. I turned sharply, for his speech was bold and, I thought, overfamiliar, then the name hit me. This was the famous Aesop, or Aisopos, as he called himself, the teller of tales, the mime, the entertainer, the intimate of all the great leaders of the world. I knew his words then for what they were, the compliment of one artist to another.

I had not yet seen his face, but I heard him, speaking softly, "It is a beautiful robe, Lady Sappho—but it is that which gives you away. They are the fashion now—these Eastern costumes—

among our pregnant women. They hide all . . . but one knows that they are meant to. Besides, my former master is the fool of the world, and must be forgiven."

He turned then, giving me a long cool look. "The wealthy Kerkylas—and husband now to a genius—rich and daily growing richer, master of a hundred vessels, and handsome as a god as well. Lady, you are gifted indeed!" It was as though he were speaking of some fancy boy. The measure of his quality was that he did not offend; behind his manner was a mockery, not of others, but of himself, and of all the gods, and of everything, equalizing all.

It is difficult to describe this man; his features were as ever-changing as the moving sea, and as constant, too, as the ocean in its depths. This is a paradox, but so was this man. The tales I had heard of him were varied, but all agreed on his surpassing ugliness. I assure you this was not so. I had heard him called deformed, lame, twisted, corpulent, hideous, bestial, potbellied, clubfooted; he was made as all men are, and closer to the norm than most. He was neither tall nor short, fat or thin; one would have passed him in a crowd without a second glance, but for his face, and that, too, was unarresting, except upon close scrutiny. True, the chin and nose were long, leaning a bit to one side, and the mouth thin and curling, but no face is like its fellow, except if it be born of one womb. It was a face that, during the evening, as he talked, looked like a hawk, a rabbit, a weasel, or a lion; this was his gift. The eyes did not change; they were the eyes one sees sometimes on a dog, bright with intelligence and deep with old pain. He was the most urbane of men; one could not imagine him in a huddle of peasants' huts or walking behind a plow, though he had been a slave, and sold to it by his poor country parents.

Again, one heard variously that Aesop was an Ethiopian, a Phrygian, or an Egyptian; assuredly he was none of these, being neither black nor swarthy. I place his beginnings, for my own reasons, in Thrace, that country of rock and rock-hard barbarians.

One tale that is told of him is that he had more than a dozen masters, each of whose wives he seduced (this could be true, for he could surely seduce the birds from their nests!), until, in fear and disgust, each master in turn sold him. I cannot go into all the tales, for they are myriad. The story he told of himself has the ring of truth, to my ears. He said that he was sold first, too young even to remember his family, to a troupe of traveling acrobats; they in turn sold him, when he grew too large to fit into their trickeries, to a gymnasium master, to run errands and fill oil cruets, or to strew sand under sweating feet. There, in one of the buildings, was a new school of philosophy, in small attendance, and Aesop slipped away when he could, to listen and to learn. He learned so much and so well that he was bought next as a pedagogue, to teach young aristocrats in an Athenian school. Iadmon's firstborn son, a laggard learner, attended this school, and begged his father to buy its best teacher for his own. And so he had become Iadmon's slave, and his childrens' master; another paradox.

Now, this man Iadmon, being truly one of the most important and successful traders of the world, enjoyed the acquaintanceship of all the great leaders; the new Tyrants that have risen of late have all been guest or host to him at some time or another. His learned and clever slave, Aesop, grew famous through his appearance before these Tyrants and their followers, for Iadmon knew him to be a great asset. Each Tyrant in his turn offered to buy the man, but Iadmon put the price too high, even for them. Finally, and this is quite recent, as I understand it, Solon of Athens, Periander of Corinth, and some others, put pressure upon Iadmon to sell Aesop, as it were, to the world! They pooled their money, tax money from their subjects of course, bought the slave, and manumitted him forthwith, freeing him, as they pronounced "in the cause of humanity"! So Aesop was now paid for such appearances as he was making tonight, and he was well on the way to becoming a man of means himself. However, with no blink of the eye and with a daring candor, Aesop stated that, of course, each Tyrant took a cut! "It is the way of the world," he said, spreading his hands and shrugging.

Sappho, who detested all Tyrants and life under them as it must be lived, spoke up, indignant, calling it an outrage. He listened gravely, a little smile playing upon his thin lips. Then he bowed and said, "Lady . . . you can afford such sentiments. Genius has no masters but the gods. Mere wit must pay its way."

In his case, it certainly did, and more. I have never laughed so hard and so long; even Sappho, whose humor is not her strong point, was holding her sides as if she would burst, tears of laughter running unchecked down her cheeks. This Aesop was the greatest talker of the world, there can be no mistake. Again, it is hard to describe, his talent, compounded as it was of satire, mimicry, and worldliness. His animal tales were already told everywhere, but much simplified. As he himself told them, they were sly jibes at folk in high places. Some of them I knew and recognized, some I did not; it did not really matter, for the stories themselves were brilliant. When one recognized Periander as, say, the fox in a tale, it was only an added spice. His delivery was a marvel as well; he seemed to become these animals, even his face changed. And his voice whined or snarled, grunted or crowed, while speaking each word clearly as a drop of sparkling water. That is the best I can do to explain Aesop's monologues. One simply must hear them for oneself.

After, and at just the right moment, he refused to talk any longer, and asked Sappho for the pleasure of a song. "Just a tiny one, Lady . . . one must not tax the brain of Iadmon. . . ." This was a way he had, of good-humored insult to his patrons; I am told that he spoke in the same manner to the mighty Solon, and received nothing back but laughter!

Sappho said, "Good sir, I have laughed so much I am hoarse. Besides I have not brought my lyre. . . ."

"A hoarse Sappho is still divine . . . and far too good for this house, you may be sure. . . ."

Iadmon, in good humor, implored her also, saying he had many lyres and she might choose.

"Well . . ." she said, "I will try them over. . . ."

Iadmon snapped his fingers, bringing one of the slaves to his elbow. "Have some of the girls—the prettiest—bring in their lyres." He turned to us. "All my girl slaves are taught to play and sing . . . and to dance as well." There was a fatuous look upon his face, pride and avarice as well, as when a merchant shows his wares. I wondered at it briefly; Aesop leaned close to me and whispered, "He hires them out . . . they fetch a higher fee when they can do other things as well. . . ."

I nearly gasped; I had never heard of such a thing, to make whores of your own property. But as I said, Iadmon was an Asiatic, and what could one expect?

Five young girls came in, bearing lyres. As Sappho looked over the instruments, I looked over their bearers; I am a man, after all. They were certainly pretty; Iadmon spoke truth. And one was more, much more. I asked her name.

"Doricha," said Iadmon, rubbing his hands like a Levantine hawker, pleased.

"It ought to be Rhodopis," I said.

"Ah . . . like a rose . . . yes," murmured Aesop. "She is from my own village," he went on. "Perhaps a distant cousin of sorts. Though you would not think it to look at us. . . ."

I laughed. "Well, you said distant. . . ." I was talking partly because I knew that Sappho disliked attention while she was trying out strings and tuning; a thing I understood perfectly, it was like watching a woman paint her face. She was still busy at it, Sappho, though she had chosen her instrument and was tuning it. To keep the idle conversation going I said, "Perhaps the roselike comparison is, in part, due to the rosy chiton that she wears, your little Doricha."

"Well," said Aesop, "they are all dressed alike. No, my own Thrace must take the credit."

The girl was very young, not much older than little Hero; very young and very fresh, with the dew still on her, so to speak. I was still taken with my own image of a flower, and saw her thus. The five girls knelt, waiting, perfectly quiet, before the dais where we sat; to kneel gracefully is quite a feat, they were indeed well trained. All the young eyes were downcast now, the lids innocent and somehow inviting. I had seen earlier the girl Doricha's eyes; large, round, and very blue, almost staining the whites from their color. She was slim and delicate, taller than the others, though not really a woman yet. Her hair was of a red color, a leaf that is turning, or old burnished copper; one would think the rosy gown unbecoming beneath it, but it was not. Her skin and the very flesh beneath wore a glow, translucent, softly glimmering, like the pale inside of a shell, exquisite.

I saw Aesop staring at me. He spoke very low. "Iadmon is considering selling her—for a huge sum, of course, she is still virgin—to a certain Xanthes, who will take her to Naukratis and make his fortune there, where all the merchants and sailors stop. . . . Perhaps you, too, plan to touch down there, at Naukratis, in the future?"

I smiled a little, and dragged my eyes away from the girl. "I

think not," I said. "I am not much for paid love . . . besides, she
is surely too young. . . ."

"Go on, my man . . . you have been devouring her all this
while, like a vulture, but from a distance."

I stirred uneasily; I must have felt the truth of it. To cover my
guilt I said, too loudly, "Yes, she is certainly the most beautiful
creature in the world. . . ." I heard the harsh thwang of a
snapped lyre string.

"None of them will do," said Sappho, holding it out. "I am
sorry about the string—it was poorly strung."

There was a little uncomfortable silence; then Aesop said, "I
have a small Phrygian harp, Lady. Perhaps? . . ."

"Yes," she said, stony. "I am not familiar with it, but I am sure
it will be better." She turned to Iadmon. "You may send your
. . . girls away. . . ."

His jowls fell. "Oh, but, Lady, they are all musical. They want
to listen . . . and to learn."

"I do not teach slaves," she said. "Nor play before whores."

"Sappho!" I cried, utterly aghast. I had never known her
rude—and to insult her host, and in such words! Her eyes blazed
at me, huge and nearly black. Then she said, "Well, perhaps I
will not play. I have said that I am somewhat hoarse. . . . Will
you take me home?"

Iadmon protested then, and begged her, as did Aesop, and
Iadmon motioned the slave girls out of the chamber. Coming
close to me, he said low, "Can you not persuade her? It does not
do to let women in her state remain in anger . . ."

"Please play," I said, "for courtesy. Aesop has given much . . .
can you do less?"

She nodded. "Very well, I will play . . . and perhaps I will
sing one song. . . ."

I know she had never handled the Phrygian harp before, a
triangular small thing with only three strings and a strange high
tone; she did not even try it out, but took it as if born to it and
played—divinely. She did not sing one song, but three; I never
heard her in better voice; but above the harp her cheeks burned
as with fever and even from the distance between us I felt her
anger shimmering like summer heat upon the air.

She did not speak all the way home. It was not till I got her
below deck in our cabin and alone that the storm broke. Her

tears flowed like a fountain, as always, and she cried, "You called her the most beautiful . . . and you said I was! You said I was!" I had forgotten my words.

I made it up to her in bed, but it took some doing. Making love to a woman more than seven months gone with child is not only difficult, but forbidden. However, there is always a way . . . if one puts one's mind to it.

I loved my sweet wild Sappho then as ever.

But Doricha, that I had named Rhodopis, *was* the most beautiful creature in the world. The name I had given her stuck, but I never saw Doricha-Rhodopis again, to my secret sorrow.

Chapter 11

I remember little of the island of Kos or the birth of my daughter there; I was deathly ill and fed with draft of poppy to make me sleep. I had never been sick before except with little fevers or chills that quickly passed and were as soon forgotten. This thing was like a beast of prey.

I do remember our arrival there, at the island, one of the loveliest of the Sporades, with green grass growing right down to the shore, tinting the waters. There is much green there, and little wind; one feels peace, and the gods. The sacred grove of Aesculapius is well inland from the shore, still and hushed. White-robed priests move silently, tending the sick in their leafy tents. There are no moans or cries of pain, no smell of blood; the whole island is a temple. Now and again one hears a soft murmur of voices, or the low consenting bleat of a sheep at the sacrifice; the place is holy.

For the last few days I had been clamping my teeth shut on a mounting nausea, though I had eaten no strange foods, and the crossing had been exceptionally smooth. I had contrived to keep silent about my indisposition, for fear of affecting Sappho; she had not thrown up since the first weeks. There were the first small clawings of pain across my middle, too; I assumed I had drunk some polluted water, though I could not remember it.

When we landed and stated our case, we were given a large and surprisingly well-appointed hut; that is hardly the name for it, but I can think of no other. The roof was low and the sides lightly lashed together; one felt the whole thing might be dismantled in an hour.

There was accommodation for Praxinoa, but we were warned that she could not be present at the birth, though Sappho wished it; these healers would have none about them except professionals. I must say a word here about these healing priests and their calling. The island was sacred first to Apollo, and boasts a very ancient shrine, looking as if it went back to the time of the Titans. Some claims are made that this is the birthplace of

Aesculapius, but they cannot be taken seriously; he was probably born at Epidauros, for the evidence there is much more certain. He was a man before he was made a god, the god of medicine, so he cannot have been in two places at once! The priests both at Epidauros and here are said to be all his descendants; an odd thing, that—for he was celibate! Well, no matter—these are old tales told to impress the faithful. In any case, these men are the most skilled and dedicated surgeons and doctors in the world, no matter what their birth. It is certain the priesthood is not hereditary, as is said, either—for there are priests of every race and color and speaking many tongues. Even with these differences, there is, somehow, a sameness about them; the same serenity laps all their faces, and the same grave light kindles deep in their eyes. They are not eunuchs—or at least I do not think so—but there is no maleness about them. Neither is there any age marking them; the older priests teach only and do not practice, for they hold that vision must be perfect and fingers steady. Yet one cannot see youth anywhere upon them; they are set apart from other men; one feels, beyond a doubt, that they have been molded by the hand of a god.

On the morning when Sappho woke, feeling her first pangs, I was hard put to keep from grimacing; the clawing in my belly was dreadful. They would not let me go with her, but bore her off to one of the sick tents unattended. I whispered to her my love, and bade her have no fear. One always whispered there, at Kos.

I was reminded, when they had taken her away, of that old folk saying, that the husband suffers all the symptoms along with the wife, having some ancient earth-jealousy. I spoke of it to the priest who remained behind to purify the air or some such mystery. As I said it, I tried to smile, though the pain was great. He gave me a sharp look, and did not answer, but bade me lie down.

He examined me at length, probing my abdomen with gentle, seeking fingers, and looking inside my mouth and nose, scrutinizing the whites of my eyes beneath the lids. After, he called in two others and stood talking with them in the shadows; by this time the pain was making me stupid and I cannot recall everything. I do remember that they opened a vein in my arm and took some blood, painlessly, holding it up to the light in a glass vial, and, I think, mixing it with something that turned it muddy. But I am

not very clear on any of that now. I know I was given a draft of
something, a blessed drink, for it sent me out of my senses for a
time. Of the rest, I recall nothing but dreams and intermittent
sharp stabs of agony, and dreams again, until I woke, feeling
weak and weightless, but free of the clawing beast inside. They
told me I had been abed four weeks, and that I had a healthy
daughter.

They let me sit up, and brought Sappho to me. She looked
wonderfully glowing, slender once more, but with a little
plumpness in her cheeks, becoming. "I have grown fat," she said,
laughing a little "Will you still keep me?" But I saw behind her
eyes a leaping fear, quickly stilled. I made myself answer her, in
as loud a voice as I could muster, and smiled at her, making light
of my own weakness.

"Here is your daughter," she said. "I have called her Kleis,
after my mother." Praxinoa had come in, bearing the little
bundle; I had half expected the child to be walking already, so
lost in time I was then! But, though the babe was nearly four
weeks old, she looked newborn to me, still crumpled and pink,
with milky eyes that moved about in her head and saw nothing. I
held out my finger and she took it in a tight little curling fist, that
miracle that shakes the father's heart.

One of the priests came in and told them then that they must
leave me to rest; I recognized him as the man who had tended
me first. I cannot remember when it was they told me what I
had. They must have waited a bit, till I was stronger; and I know
they spoke to me alone, out of the hearing of my poor wife. They
called it the disease of the crab, or cancer, and said there was no
cure.

I lay still as a stone against my pillows, while the words washed
over me like waves, again and again, till I took them in.

Then, "How long do I have?" I asked. The priest said nothing,
looking at me with his young-old eyes, dark with centuries of
wisdom.

"Tell me," I said. "Ten years? A year? A month?"

"A year or two perhaps," he said. "At the most, three."

He was wrong. I lasted four. And every day of every year
counted.

BOOK IV

The House of the Muses

(Told by Sappho, the Woman)

Chapter 1

I had not known how sick he was, my husband. The priests of Kos were grave when they spoke to me of him, but then they always were. They said that he must be easy for a while and let others do his sailing for him; I was pleased at this, to tell the truth, because it meant he would spend all his time with me and with our little darling, Kleis. When I asked what disease he had been abed with for so long, the priests said it was a bowel fever and that he must eat light foods and drink well-watered wine. Again, I thought little of this; I was accustomed to such fare myself, from preference.

We went to Andros for a time, the home of his youth; we were happy there, with his aged, ageless parents, in that sleepy sunny place, watching our daughter change and grow; there was something new about her every day, a delight, like a golden flower unfolding. Kerkylas would lie on a couch, under the trees, in good weather, watching us play on the grass near him; though he was stronger, still he was made to rest each day. Once he laughed, showing his startling white teeth, still beautiful in his sunburned face, and said, "You are like a child with a doll. . . . When will you grow up, little Sappho?" I was startled and a bit affronted, but, thinking back on it, it was true. She was so round and rosy, so perfectly made, with Kerkylas' fine, paler-than-gold hair and his sea-blue eyes. She was a merry little thing, too, and very good, hardly ever crying; when she did, I gave her to Praxinoa to hold, for she could always calm her. Perhaps I should have done it myself; in after years I fretted about this, and other things, wondering if I had erred, made wrong turnings with this, my only child. But we are all as the gods made us, and cannot go back and do it over. I loved my baby, and my darling husband, and I loved my music too; in those days I had all three.

I practiced a great deal, there on Andros, on lyre and harp, perfecting my art. I did not make many new songs, though; perhaps they do not come when one is truly happy. Oh, I wrote some, of course, when there was a wedding, or a funeral, or a god's day, to please the folk of the island; they were good, too, in their way, and put a polish on me, but they did not spring from the heart.

Kerkylas, I thought from his enforced idleness, taught me much of figures and trade, his trade. I always liked to learn new things and tried to learn well, to please him and make him proud. He said I was the cleverest creature in the world and could make my way in merchanting as well as any man. I did not know then the real reason why he had taught me. Even now, with my old, dry eyes, tears flow, remembering how well he hid it from me, his tragic destiny.

Little Kleis was a bright, forward child; she walked and talked early. When she could run about and speak whole sentences, we sailed for Sicily. "It is the hub of the world," Kerkylas said. "We will make you famous there. . . . Besides, we must establish ourselves there—so that Pittakos can know where you are when he sends for you to come out of exile."

"Do you think he will?" I asked.

"I am sure of it."

Sweet Zeus, make it so, I prayed, silently. For Mitylene was my heart's home; even in my happiness I longed for it.

Chapter 2

It was true, what Kerkylas said, that Sicily was the hub of the world, or rather, its great city, Syracuse, was. Vast stretches of that country are empty, or peopled by folk that have not been a half-mile from the places of their birth. When I corrected my husband on this, he laughed and said, "Well, you, my darling, are a poet and precise with words. To me, Syrakuse *is* Sicily." I felt a little dashed and as though I had spoken primly, like a raw girl getting above herself; though I loved him, his light and worldly manner often made me feel so; perhaps it was the great difference in our ages. In all honesty, and, again, looking back, I see that I felt myself above Kerkylas by virtue of my talents, but in all other ways far beneath. Unlike Alkaios, who was my equal in all things, bad and good. We were the same, really, Alkaios and I, except for our different sex, like our little Egyptian cats, that I had named Boy and Girl. Now and then, briefly, I wondered what had become of them—and of him.

It was strange to think that more than two years had passed since I was exiled to Sicily, and that I had not yet seen it! It was a longish journey, too, though we cut across the isthmus of Korinth to save sailing clear around Greece. After our dreadful shipwreck I prayed always to Poseidon, and to Nereus of the Aegean, but especially my own goddess Aphrodite. I thought of her as mine alone, Aphrodite; I had named my first doll after her, long ago. Never mind that it was a boy doll, left over from some ritual sacrifice; children never know the difference. Perhaps there is none, among the gods.

I had not been brought up to believe all the god-tales. Who could believe them all? But, just in case, I prayed, especially at sea. And it worked, for we never had another mischance or fright, even. I was too stupid to pray for the one thing that truly mattered; even when I saw my beloved turn pale beneath his sun-looks, or smelled on his breath the pain-killing laurel that he chewed, a kitchen smell—I put the thought away. Looking back, I think I knew, always, inside myself, that no prayer would help.

We were very gay, Kerkylas and I, in those days; he lounged upon the deck with me, another master at the helm, and called himself, with a laugh, "a man of leisure, for once." The golden days sped past; blue skies and bluer seas and distant misty shores, glimpsed once and gone forever, until we came to Korinth.

The isthmus is there; narrow as it is, still one must dismount from ship and cross on land, an adventure. There is complicated machinery there, pulleys and ropes and wheels, to get the ships across, a long wait, for there are two harbors, both full of shipping; Kerkylas would not go ahead, but must wait to see his own ship safely on its way.

It was a fascinating sight, the huge ships, dripping, lifted in the air to the whine of the machines, and put down slowly, slowly, inch by creaking inch, onto a set of absurdly small wheels, trundling off, wobbly, like a fat lady on heeled slippers. Even Kleis, baby that she was, held her breath, watching, and laughed with joy in the girl Hero's arms. But that was the first ship only, and we were fifth in turn. I stole a glance at Kerkylas, seeing what I feared, the look of strain, hidden, and a little muscle twitching in his jaw. There was a bright-colored cook tent behind us, its insides looking cool and dark under the canvas roof.

"Could we not go inside here for a bit," I asked, gesturing, "until it is our turn? . . ." I meant to plead faintness, for I knew he hated attention brought to his own weakness, but just then Kleis began to wail fretfully, squirming and kicking so that Hero could not manage her and had to give her to Praxinoa. "See," I said, "it is too hot for her, your daughter. . . . Let us go into the shade, get a cool drink perhaps . . ."

He looked at it, grumbling; he was snappish now when he was tired; he hated his own condition. "Anything inside there would poison us, surely . . . it looks a low place." But Makro spoke up, saying that he would fetch some wine from the ship; he always hung about Hero now, she was growing prettier and taller.

And so he let himself be persuaded inside, my Kerkylas, and into a chair; we had to pay three obols each for them, an outrage. I said so, but Kerkylas stopped me, laughing now. "The poor man has to make a living . . . he is in trade, like us." And he took my hand. His ill humor was always quickly over. Kleis was comforted with a sweetmeat and we all sipped the wine that Makro brought, cooled with snow from the mountain, another ten obols. I looked at Kerkylas and said, shrugging, "The poor man is in trade." We burst out laughing. Odd, how I remember the incident, among so many; it had no significance.

The harbors, both of them, were filled with warships, as well as the merchant kind; I remembered that Periander, the Tyrant who had mediated that old war of my girlhood, still ruled here. Those warships were the famous triremes, with three banks of oars, and very impressive; in spite of myself I stared in awe. Everywhere were soldiers, fully armed; we were stopped twice just in the few paces it took to cross the narrow strip of land. Kerkylas, each time, flashed something that he held in his palm, and they stepped back to let us pass, saluting sharply. "What is it you carry?" I asked.

"The great Seal of Periander," he answered.

I gasped. "Where did you get it?"

"He gave it to me, of course." I stared at him, outraged.

"I did him a favor once," said Kerkylas. "A dirty deal, you might call it. . . . But it did no one any harm—and it gives me a hold on him, besides. I always make a good haul at Korinth— whatever cargo I carry. . . ."

He looked at my face, a keen look. "Cheer up, little one," he said. "I shall do nothing to shame you. I do not love tyranny any more than you do. But it is a passing phase . . . and will pave the way for something better, a freer form of government, with fairer laws and more freedom for more people."

I thought a moment. "Father always said that Solon of Athens made many reforms. . . ."

"Yes," he said. "But these things take time to grow . . . even our little Kleis does not reach womanhood in a day . . ." His words trailed off. Before I had time to turn to him, he caught my arm and said, "Look—there is Akrokorinth . . . from its mountain one can see Athens, Sparta, and Arkadia, too!" His voice had lost its somber tone and was light again, almost gay. "We will climb it together."

I did not think he could, but did not dare to speak. He said it for me. "Don't worry, there are surefooted ponies, and trails to the top. . . . It is the finest sight in all Greece."

"I did not know we were going to stay," I said.

"Only long enough for you to sing before Periander," he said.

"Oh, no!"

"Oh, yes!" he insisted. "I am going to make you famous . . . and rich!"

"But we are rich already!"

"In your own right," he said. "Ships can go down . . . as you know. There are pirates—sometimes a bad season. One cannot tell in trade. I would not leave you in uncertain circumstances, when—" His voice was cut off as though by a knife. "Besides," he said, with a little smile, "why not be richer still? We will charge Periander a whopping fee! He cannot refuse!" And he rubbed his hands together like a gleeful miser, mocking, and making me laugh.

So, though I hated Tyrants, I sang before a great and illustrious company at the court of Periander, and won much praise and a huge purse of new-minted coins. Kerkylas had asked for my payment in these, for they had each one a value of one hundred drachmae, and so were very easily carried; after, when I counted them, I found that I had been paid ten thousand drachmae, for one appearance! More than a thousand drachmae for each song! I felt a sudden surge of power such as I had never felt before, and, afterward, a feeling of guilt. Should not an artist give freely to the world? But when I said it, diffidently, to Kerkylas, he laughed and replied that Periander and his like were not the world, and had I seen the colossal statue he had erected of himself, solid gold, bled from the citizens? So I was in part soothed; as he said, men who are artists receive gold for their work, whatever it might be, paintings, statues, temples—or poems—and why should a woman be denied it, if she is their equal? That won me over; I had not thought of it that way.

The coins themselves were very beautiful, and surely designed by another artist; they were delicate thin ovals, stamped with an exquisite image of Pegasus, the winged horse of myth, who was said to have been first bridled at the sacred spring of Pirene, here in Korinth. At least Periander had the taste not to have his own image stamped upon them! Kerkylas did a wonderful thing; he had a goldsmith make a tiered skirt that fell, shining, to the floor, out of these same beautiful coins; it should be my costume, he said, when I sang before the great. A subtle hint, as well, of my worth. In after years, indeed, I was sometimes called "golden Sappho" because of this; it added to my fame. As Kerkylas said, a performer must have such little tricks; it is part of the profession. Odd, how clever he was, and how knowing, who was not himself an artist!

It was he, also, who, at this very first of my paid performances, instructed that all the lights be dimmed except for a ring of candles where I sat, and, when it was over, Hero was sent, summoned from the shadows, to receive the fee purse. "Always keep yourself apart," he said to me. "You are above these mere mortals, rich and powerful as they may be . . . remember it."

At that same evening of my first performance I met again that great teacher of my childhood, Arion, who had devised the now-famous song and dance from which came the Black Lark song. He was court musician to Periander and his success was assured, though he no longer could play any instrument. He had been always a great wine bibber, still was, in fact, though now a sip could make him drunk. A few years ago, full of unwatered Chian, he had fallen down a long flight of marble steps, dislocating his shoulder and smashing all the bones in his harp hand. He could not teach any longer, even, except by lecturing, and dictated all his songs to a scribe. Folk counted Periander kind for keeping him on, but I thought it no more than a genius' due.

He knew me, Arion, after a moment of peering shortsightedly; he himself had aged greatly, and I would not have recognized him if he had not been pointed out. They said he no longer took food, but got all his sustenance from wine; the once-round body was withered to a shade, and the skin hung upon it in folds, pitiful to see. He asked after my father; when I told him of his death, he wept, and I with him. It was a sad reunion; sadder still to hear, a few months later, that that had been his last court appearance. He had been felled by a massive stroke, like a thunderbolt from a god; he never woke from it. Kerkylas said the wine had finally reached the brain. I laid a wreath of laurel on Apollo's altar in memory of a great artist, and put a double portion of water into my wine thereafter.

While we were still there at Korinth, I paid a visit to the famous Temple of Aphrodite; we left Praxinoa with Kleis to spare her the unhappy memory of the place. I do not know exactly why I myself wanted to go, for I was revolted by both the old tales and the new. Kerkylas said that all virtuous women are curious about whores; I opened my mouth to argue, but felt the red flooding my face and knew that he was right. At any rate, that day I got my fill, if that is truly what I wanted; I have never seen so many temple prostitutes, they might have peopled a sizabie town! Indeed, the famous temple and its environs looked like a town, for surrounding the temple itself were dozens of houses, all alike, where these women lived and plied their trade. Though some were shockingly old and coarsened, thickly painted and bewigged, there were even more that were beautiful and just as shockingly young. They were quite brazen as well, and accosted Kerkylas boldly, even in my presence. He declined gravely but courteously, and I stared, amazed. One, seeing me, smiled sidelong, and said, "Perhaps the lady? . . ." I went pure scarlet and hurried Kerkylas away; he made me furious by laughing.

"Do not be so angry, my sweet . . . I thought her very obliging," said he, laughing. "And the goddess makes no distinctions. . . ."

I was still sputtering and protesting. "Did she think I wanted her?" I demanded. "What does she take me for?"

"A lady made for love . . . and so you are. And now, if you do not hush, I will think you rail to cover up. . . ."

That quieted me; I thought about it all the way back to the ship. That particular girl was no more than sixteen, black-eyed and small, as I am myself, and with a lively sort of prettiness, very appealing.

"Your thoughts must be very deep," said Kerkylas.

I started; I had not realized how very silent I had been. I said, not speaking truth, "I have been wondering how they . . . those girls . . . can bring themselves to do it. . . ."

He shrugged. "Well, it is a living, after all. And a better-paying one than most . . . even though Periander takes a big cut—"

That made me quite wild. "They should rise up and kill him . . . as the girls did at home!"

He smiled. "And be killed in turn for their pains? Anyhow, he is perhaps wiser and more generous. There are so many of them, he can afford to take only a pittance from each."

I shook my head. "I shall never condone prostitution—however sacred!"

"It is a necessary evil," he said.

I looked at him sharply. "Have you been to them?" I asked. "These?" he asked. "No. And now," and he laughed, "now I am in no shape. . . ." We went in silence for a moment; he held me close to him. "Besides, I have you."

I did not much like the comparison, but held my tongue. I knew he felt his weakness still, though he made light of it.

Chapter 3

Though we made search for my mother's relatives throughout all Sicily, we never found them; perhaps they had died years ago.

My time in Syrakuse seems very brief, looking back, though we were there for a full three years. They were the busiest years of my life; not an evening went by that I did not sing, somewhere, and my commissioned poems took up many hours of my day. I grew rich, in my own right, as Kerkylas had promised; fame came with it, as it always does. As Kerkylas said, people respect the more the things they must pay dear for!

Syrakuse was built upon a spit of land separated from the mainland by a narrow channel, bridged over so heavily one forgot that it was really an island, called Ortygia. Its bay was the largest and safest in all Sicily. We leased a large house, almost a palace, on the highest ground overlooking it; we could, at all times, see our own ship, idle below us. From our house, too, there was a breathtaking view of Mount Aetna, capped with snow even in the heat of summer; the lesser hills around are heavily timbered, unlike our Greece, which is beautiful but tree-bald. Some of the trees bear flowers, and the hillsides blaze and shimmer like a drift of sun-shot clouds, far away.

Syrakuse has no Tyrant, and is ruled in the old way by a Council of Nobles; I had thought to feel great comfort there, and so I did, at first. There is evidence of great wealth all about, and the aristocrats live in luxury; even the little children wear purple every day (a dreadful expense, for of course they soil it, and the dye is very rare) and everyone wears golden jewels and eats off gold and silver plates. But, after a bit, one sees the other side; there is not a streetcorner that does not have its maimed beggar, or a refuse mound that does not have its starveling children, hollow-eyed and swollen-bellied, fighting over the poor scraps with the swine. Mostly they are so weak that the pigs win, a dreadful thought.

I went, seeking audience, to the Council of Nobles, to attempt to right this injustice; they would not receive me, famous as I am, because I am a woman. All the privileges of women are curtailed here, though at first sight it does not look so; their menfolk pamper them as though they were toys, but laugh at them when they offer serious conversation, or sober thought. In the end I got up a petition; all my patron ladies who could write their names signed, and the others set seal to it; the petition asked only for an audience with the ruling nobles, but they did not grant it. I was shocked beyond belief, for it looked, truly, as though the Tyrants were more just, and this was contrary to all that I had believed, from childhood. Kerkylas said that this government was outmoded now, and, in a way, fighting for its life. "I told you earlier," he said, "all things must change. In past years, the Council of Nobles worked; now it does not. Life is more complex, cities are larger, trade is expanding, new classes are rising. Everything is in foment. . . ."

He formed a committee of men like himself, who thought ahead and deplored injustice and poverty, and went before the council; even they met with evasive answers, taxes were too high, there were too many foreigners, the common folk had too many children, and so on.

"Well," he said to me, returning from this meeting, "there will be a revolt of sorts, in time . . . meanwhile, we can do nothing."

Still, I could not walk abroad in the midst of such misery in the streets. By now, I had much gold, and all of my own earning; I set up a food booth that dispensed bread and broth to all who asked for it. Of course, there was never enough to go around, a heartbreak.

I set up two others, in the poor sections. And I set a fashion. Soon there were these small booths all over town, dispensing alms; they were donated by all the wealthy, idle women who were my patronesses; many of them were wives of those lofty nobles of the council who had refused to hear our pleas! It was their own money they spent, for many of these ladies were greatly dowered. It became the fad to wear the same dress twice, and to boast that the price of a new one, forgone, had opened a new alms booth in the corner of the agora that faces Hera's temple, or at the sacred shrine of some other goddess. They vied with one another for the title of most charitable, rather than best-dressed, and bragged of the austerities they practiced and the amounts of foodstuffs they pilfered from their own kitchens. At one banquet where I sang, the lady of the house proudly served black bread and country cheese, with thin, sour peasant wine. When this fare was brought in on the silver trays and gold dishes and goblets, it got more applause than my songs! And one poor unsuspecting gentleman came home one night to find a camp bed and wooden stools in his personal chamber; his wife had shipped out all his inlaid ivory furnishings to distribute among the poor!

This side of it was a little ridiculous; even I saw that, and laughed with Kerkylas. Still, it was a beginning, and at least some of the starving were fed and clothed; it would take much more than whims to do the whole job, of course, and more than the three years that we spent in Syrakuse to change the order of things.

More important, really, in the long run, was that my vast popularity brought on a desire to emulate. Some women and girls began to make their own songs, those few who could write; others, on the sly, began to learn. Small groups of ladies met, in the afternoons, and I gave lessons on harp and lute, and in metered song. The talent uncovered there was small, though, except for one. It is a strange tale, that.

There was one lady, a cross-grained, thin-lipped person in her middle years, named Pamplona, who sometimes attended our lessons. Her fingers were all thumbs on the strings; she simply could not learn. She was an aristocrat, that was plain in all her bearing, though her robes were simple and almost threadbare. All the other ladies knew her but she was not their intimate; one never saw her head-together, whispering, with any other, or exchanging the small chat that such women love. Still, she was received everywhere; I heard that she was widow to a once-powerful noble who had died suddenly, leaving little but gambling debts; no wonder she looked cross-grained!

The odd thing is that, though she could not play, she would now and then produce a written poem, handing it to me and studying my face. I was astonished, for they had great merit; the words, indeed, soared, and the meter was flawless, in the old, Homeric style. Each was better than the last; I set them to music, and asked her to bring me all she had. There were not many, but all of them were very fine; I was excited and offered to teach her privately, thinking perhaps the presence of others inhibited her learning. There was a strange expression on her face, but she nodded, and told me the way to her house; I promised to come the next afternoon.

The house was in the old quarter; the street was wide and tree-lined, but the paving needed sweeping. Clearly the whole district had come down a bit, selling off its slaves one by one; all the houses wore the thin grime of the servantless. Pamplona's house was in need of whitewash and several of the roof tiles were missing, like broken teeth in a smile.

An ancient slave woman met me at the door, in a mended chiton, and led me to an inner chamber, where Pamplona sat. It had been a gray day, threatening rain, and there was a little chill in the air, but no braziers were lit, and indeed there were no lights burning. I could just make out a shape in the corner; a spinning wheel, and a figure seated by it. "There is your poet!" said Pamplona, scorn roughening her voice; she made a gesture toward the corner.

I was bewildered, and truly it was far too dim to see. "Madame," I said, "perhaps I might have a candle . . . I am a little shortsighted." I said it for courtesy; I have perfect sight.

"Fetch a rushlight," Pamplona said, to the old slave. There was a little nervous pause while we waited; no one spoke, though the figure at the spinning wheel made some sort of movement. When the light was brought, Pamplona took it and, holding it aloft, went close to the wheel. Again she said, harshly, "There she is . . . your poet!"

I gasped. Out of the shadows leapt a white face of great beauty, but bitterer than the face of Medusa. The eyes were huge and dark, defiant under a straight black line of eyebrow; the features were like marble, thin, stern, and proud. Looking closer I saw it was a girl, and very young.

"My daughter, Erinna," said Pamplona. "She will not mind her wheel—so I have chained her to it."

"Gods, woman!" I cried, not being able to help it. "What has the girl done—to treat her so? I cannot spin either! We are all made as we are made, by the gods. And they have given her other gifts—like mine!"

"But you have a husband," said Pamplona. "This one—she will not take a mate!"

The girl gave a strangled sound, half laughter, half cry.

"Three times now she has refused to wed," said the mother.

"She has no dowry . . . she will not learn women's ways. There will be no more offers for her!"

"They were pigs, those suitors!" cried the girl. "Gross and fat—horrible!"

"They were decent men . . . and who are you to choose?" cried the mother. "A pauper—as your father left you—and not even pretty!"

"But she *is* pretty," I said, going closer to the girl. "She is very pretty. . . ." I smiled a little; the dark shadow lifted from Erinna's face and the brow smoothed, the mouth curved. "How old are you, Erinna?"

"Sixteen this month," she answered.

"That is young to wed," I said. My thoughts were darting very fast; one could feel the hatred, like a black mist, between this mother and daughter. And the poems were good. "Can you read and write?" I asked the girl.

She nodded. I heard the mother's voice behind me, waspish.

"Her father taught her—behind my back—the idle fool with his crazy Homer and his empty purse and his hands itching for the luck-throw!" I was sorry for her fallen fortunes but sorrier for the girl. I turned to the mother.

"Pamplona," I said, "I have a little daughter . . . she will need to learn her letters, and I have no time to spare. . . . Can you not let me have Erinna for her governess? I will pay a good wage and her keep . . . and give you her marriage price besides. . . ."

And so, in truth, I *bought* the girl Erinna, as much, truly, as my father had bought the slave Andromeda, long ago.

Chapter 4

Erinna fitted into our household very well, though Kerkylas cocked an eyebrow and said that Kleis would be spoiled with so much service. I looked at him with reproach, for I had related her sad story. "I know, little darling," he said, "you were very sorry for her—but if she had been ugly and could not put one word before another and make a rhyme . . . what then?" He was right, of course; I could never bear to see talent go to waste. Her pleasing looks were just an added thing. I thought a moment, and said, "Well, I would have taken her anyway—even if she had a squint!"

"I once had a mistress who was squint-eyed," he said. "She was charming . . . I never knew where she was looking. . . ."

"Who . . . where?" I sputtered. Then I saw he was teasing. He pulled me down beside him on the couch. "Truly, Sappho, at this rate you will have a ready-made school before ever you get back to Lesbos. The next thing will be that some of your lady pupils will up and leave their husbands. . . ."

"Most of them have," I said, "or as good as . . ." It was a thing that appalled me, the faithlessness of these Syrakusans. There was a constant flutter of intrigue going on, secrets whispered, giggling, and assignations made, slaves sent to summon lovers—and even interrupting their lessons for it! I had spoken of this before to Kerkylas, but he only smiled and shrugged.

"It is high society," he said. "Marriages are arranged—there is no love lost there. . . . And the men do it, why not the women? You are all for equality—you must not be inconsistent. . . ." I saw he was teasing still, underneath; as I have said, I could not always tell.

I said, thinking to tease a bit myself, "Well, then, sir—shall I take a lover . . . when you are feeling ill and are lying abed?" As soon as the words were out I could have bitten my tongue, for his face grew very grave.

"That would make me unhappy," he said. "But I would not

blame you . . . I am not much of a husband these last months. . . ."

I threw myself into his arms and cried, "You are all the husband I want!" But I could not take back my words. He smiled and kissed me tenderly. He smelled strongly of cloves; he must have been sick again that day and chewed the cloves to sweeten his breath. I wanted to weep, but held back the tears; it was a thing I was learning to do.

He still worked very hard at his business, and trade was good; not a week went by that some ship captain did not come to the house with his tally and his price list. Kerkylas lit up like a lamp at the voyage tales; I knew he longed to be seaward, and I ached for him. But he seemed to grow worse instead of better; he had lost flesh and there were some white hairs mixed in with the gold. He had let his beard grow and looked very Zeuslike, but I knew he had done it to hide the thinness of his cheeks.

It would seem that I thought constantly of his health; this was not true, for often I forgot. He was very cheerful and active, for the most part, and I had my own work to fill my days. I grew to be sure mistress of the wedding song; I could turn them out in moments, and each different. They were easy, for the subject appealed. I used to beg off funeral odes, and disliked even to write Adonis laments; these last, though, paid so well I could not very well refuse; Sicily is very strong on the Adonis rites; the women make a three-day festival of it, and go in procession, rending their garments and tearing their faces with their nails. I always felt the whole thing distasteful and a little nasty; go back a few steps further and they would be tearing the chosen bridegroom apart in a frenzy, as happened in the ancient days!

In the meantime, I was extremely successful and imitated by all the women who could play and sing. After a year or two, those who could write made up verses and called them "Sapphics"! Kerkylas said it was an insult, and truly the verses were clumsy. But what could I do? I could not stop them! I simply made sure to copy my own poems out very clearly, several copies of each, and signed them boldly in my own hand. I would not like to be confused with any of those others!

I kept up my charitable works and was glad to be imitated in this, as well. I wrote a good many verses there, some set to music, of a different character, that criticized the government, and took the men to task for their unfair treatment of women. These songs were sung all over Syrakuse; even the prostitutes sang them, I was told, and the hired flute girls at the men's banquets. I was a heroine, truly; whenever I walked abroad, a little knot of women followed me, crying out my praises and running to seize the hem of my robe and kiss it. Sailors coming back from far places told of my songs that were sung in all the islands, and even in Athens itself! I wondered how they had traveled so far, so quickly; Kerkylas reminded me that sailors, in their lonely voyaging, love to sing, and they, of course, go everywhere.

I was, of course, gratified—who would not be? But the other thing that happened, due to my well-known reputation, was simply and truly wonderful—though it made Kerkylas laugh, as most things did; he could always see the comic side.

One evening at twilight, I came in with my two girl pupils in tow, flushed from a successful afternoon of singing and crowned with a wreath of lilies made of gold, my fee-gift. Kerkylas met me at the door. He wore a look I could not read, one eyebrow flying high and his eyes beneath like little wicked flames. "What is it? What has happened?" I cried, for I knew him well enough; it was either a disaster or a joke. I suppose, in a way, it was both. And more, too.

"You are banished," he said, quietly.

"What?"

"I said it—you are banished . . . the Council of Nobles has voted on it. You are to go back to your native city. They will no longer bear your revolutionary incitements of their women."

"You are joking!" I cried, though my heart leapt.

"No," he said, solemnly, and shook his head.

"But—my city! Mitylene! I . . . I cannot!"

"Yes—you can . . . For they have written to Pittakos, and asked him to revoke your exile. I understand he drove a hard bargain . . . two hundred thousand drachmae. . . ."

"Oh . . ." I sighed, "I thought for a moment it was true. . . . Kerkylas, sometimes your jests go too far."

"Oh, darling—it is true! Not the money—I made that up—but the rest! Look, sweetheart, look! Here are the two documents—they arrived together, as it were. The one to banish you from Syrakuse, and the other to terminate your exile. Here they are!"

My hands were shaking as I took the parchments, each bearing their official seals. It was true! I could not care what the Syrakusan nobles said, but tossed that one aside, after a glance. The other I read aloud, wonderingly, as in a dream. "The Lord Pittakos, Protector of Mitylene, extends warm invitation to the renowned Lady Sappho. All the city desires the speedy return of the Black Lark to her home, so long deprived of her genius." I looked up at Kerkylas. "But he did it himself, Pittakos! He exiled me!"

"He thinks best to forget that now," said Kerkylas, smiling at my joy. "It is the way—"

"—of the world!" I finished for him, laughing until the tears came.

And so, feverish, happy, wild with it, we set about preparing for the longed-for journey home.

Chapter 5

"Like the hyacinth—there is a light blinding my eyes. . . . O Mitylene!" As I stood at the rail long shudders shook me and I sobbed aloud. The city, white and shining, still far away as a dream, awaited me at last. . . . O gods—our fast boat is slow! The line of a song ran through my head over and over; it wrote itself, I had not thought it out. If I had—why "like the hyacinth"? Kerkylas always smiled at the strangeness of my comparisons; I blamed it on a god, usually, and would not change the song. I smiled, thinking of him, and turned away from my vision, remembering that he lay below on a padded litter. We were some little distance from port, according to the helmsman; it would humiliate him to be carried ashore, I knew. We had a doctor aboard now, one who had trained at Kos, not a priest, but a dedicated man. He studied the progression of my darling's terrible illness, and wrote down everything in a book; it angered me at first, it was so cold-blooded. But, as he said, sadly, perhaps the knowledge would help some other person someday. I bit my lip and went to fetch him; maybe there was some potion that would strengthen Kerkylas—just so that he might walk ashore with me to my native city.

It had been a long, slow voyage; some days the heat was so heavy I could not move. How much worse Kerkylas! We were becalmed often, an angry bronze sun beating down, and the deck so hot one might fry a slice of lamb upon it. It was the worst summer I ever remember; the grass upon the shores we passed was white-bleached like the rocks, and the sky itself had no color and shimmered in the sight.

We seldom ventured out from under our canvas shelters; the cabin below was cooler, but the air was bad. It was difficult to eat and the wine we sipped all day was tepid. We welcomed a shore, any shore, and did not miss setting our feet to land wherever possible.

I had three more pupils, making now five in all. At Phokia I was sent a formal letter requesting that I take two sisters; it was an intriguing thing, for their father, a musician himself, had lately died, and this was his wish, expressed in the letter. It read that they were proficient in several instruments and had been trained since babyhood; rather quaintly it also asked that I watch over them both and find them worthy husbands, when the time came. Their dowries would be large, and the fee for their keep larger still. "So you will have a school for brides," said Kerkylas, laughing.

When they were presented I was doubtful; they were well-mannered children, but unremarkable, almost plain, though they played beautifully. I took the lady aside, the aunt who had accompanied them; I said I could not undertake to find husbands, for I had long been away from Mitylene and knew no eligible young men. "But you have a school there?" she asked.

"I mean to start a school, yes . . . but for the arts only. They will learn to compose songs and to sing . . . perhaps some dancing, too."

She was a tall, commanding woman, and looked down at me with a smile.

"I think, Lady, you might teach them the wearing of clothes as well, and to make the most of themselves . . . they have never had a mother. . . ."

Well, I took them, but did not promise the husbands. She shrugged and said they could always be sent back to Phokia. "They are heiresses, after all. Their father did not think much of the Phokian men, but he was an artist. Perhaps he felt that on Lesbos all are artists, too."

"Regretfully, that is not so . . . on Lesbos or anywhere," I said. "But I will accept them." So along they came, with all their father's music and several lyres, and one change of clothes each. They were Gyrinna, the elder, and her little sister Timas.

I was much surprised, for almost at every port there was such a request; most of the girls had to be turned away, having no talent or ear, though some were lovely, if I really had intended a brides' school!

Only one other proved worthy after I heard her, a certain Damophyla, from a small Asian coastal town. One could not properly call her a girl, for she was older than I; at first I was uncertain, though her songs were very fine indeed. Kerkylas persuaded me, saying, "The poor creature will never get a man

. . . think of a spinster's life!" It was probably true; she was tall as a man herself, with a little dark growth of hair on her upper lip, and a gruff voice, except when she sang. She was very willful, too, and had a very high opinion of her own abilities. After I had consented I said privately to Kerkylas that I would leave much of her teaching to Praxinoa. He darted a keen look at me and said, "She could always go to Gorgo's!" I laughed. They would be a good match, but who would win? When I voiced this, he said, "Both."

I looked at him blankly; then it sank in. I blushed and said, "You have a wicked humor, husband. . . ."

I found the doctor with Kerkylas; the hum of their conversation stopped abruptly when I opened the cabin door. My heart was sick at this sad and useless precaution between them. I had guessed already, of course, that my husband was afflicted with something dread, and that it would worsen with time. I was a girl no longer and had the sense to hold my tongue. Kerkylas would tell me when he wished, or felt the need; I could not hurry him.

I made myself smile before I saw him, like putting on armor. Each time I was struck anew by the wasted look of him. He no longer looked like Kerkylas; his frame had grown so thin that his head seemed too large for it, as a child's is. Indeed, except for the cords that stood out upon his throat, he looked strangely youthful, his blue eyes larger and brighter than the sparkle of the sun on the sea, and his mocking white smile grown curiously sweet.

The physician had anticipated me; an empty goblet stood on a low chest, and Kerkylas, up from his pallet, sat beside it, draped in a new white robe, his best brooch at the shoulder. He was fastening a sandal, purple-dyed, that I had never seen.

"What beautiful shoes!" I said.

"I have been saving them," he replied. "Lydian work . . . still stiff, they are." And he flexed his toes, testing them. "Fetch me a knife from the shelf there, darling . . . the soles need scoring. I would not want to enter your city on my behind—and the decks are always a little slippery. . . ."

"Have you eaten?" I asked, not being able to help it. I never fussed like this with my daughter!

His bright smile faded, and he waved his hand impatiently. "Later—there is time. . . . Now I await the doctor . . . he will put on his lowly barber disguise." He felt at his chin. "This beard needs trimming. Have you your scissors, sir?"

"I have given up that part of my profession," said the doctor, with a little laugh. "But for you I will do it . . . just mind you do not noise it about, or all of Mitylene will be after me for a haircut!"

"Get out of here, Sappho!" said Kerkylas, laughing. "This is men's business. Get back to your women! Surely you do not mean to step onto the wharf in your Chian nightgown!"

I flushed, looking down at myself; truly I had forgotten, in my excitement. "I have seen Mitylene!" I cried. "That is what I came to say . . . one can see it already . . . so lovely!"

"I will meet you on deck in a half hour or less . . . hurry!" He waved me out.

I was there before him, for once; I had dressed carefully, as always, in my newest and best, a short chlamys, girdled under the breasts and round and round to make a tiny waist, the latest style from Sybaris, in a gauzy stuff colored like a pale new violet. Was my skin too sun-colored for it? My hands shook too much for the binding of my hair, and I let it flow down over my shoulders like a virgin's, though I was wife and mother, and did not paint my face at all. We had no flowers, but Praxinoa plaited some purple ribbons into my hair, with a fine careless artistry. A quick glance in a mirror showed me a girl I had not seen for a long while, breathless and wide of eye.

My girls were all crowded at the rail, little Kleis held up by Hero to get her glimpse of the city. Timas, that shyest of maidens, who hardly ever spoke, stared at me and whispered, "Lady . . . you are so beautiful today . . . as beautiful as the dawn. . . ." Tall Damophyla shot a dark look at me; she was very possessive of little Timas, a thing I had noticed before. This day, though, I had no time to soothe her jealousy with motherly words; my joy was intense as I watched Mitylene coming ever nearer, and felt the little wind of Apollo blow upon my cheeks, as I remembered it all my early years.

We moved slowly, so very slowly; I stretched far out over the rail to meet the city halfway, yearning. I heard Kerkylas' low laugh behind me. "Will you imitate the ship's goddess then?" And he gestured to the huge wooden figure at the prow, an image of Aphrodite, done in the old style, with head and shoulders rising out of curled wood, made to represent the sea-foam; her neck was as long as a swan's. I drew mine in, feeling silly, and turned to come into the circle of his arm.

I looked up at him, seeing him almost healthy; I wondered what the doctor had put into his potion. He could always read me like one of my poems, and said, with his old mocking way, "It was the honey—and the barley gruel. That will always do it." I wondered if he really had breakfasted; one never knew when he was serious.

We were close enough, finally, to see the dock, dark with people, crowded like a swarm of flies. "They are all turned out to welcome you," Kerkylas said. "The whole town is here. . . ."

"Oh, no," I murmured. "It is always this way when a ship docks."

I was still straining to pick out familiar folk, though there was still too much distance. Kleis was bored by now, though, and so were the girls; they began to fight over who should hold her, as always.

"I am taller," cried Damophyla, and grabbed at the child roughly; she began to cry. Kerkylas left me and firmly took our daughter from tall Damophyla. "She is my own, after all," he said.

And so we came in to the dock, the waves barely lapping the hull, and Apollo's breeze soft upon us, and the roar of the crowd swelling like an enormous sigh; myself, my husband, and our golden child, home at last.

Above the shouts I heard the notes of my song, the high wild melody of the Black Lark.

Chapter 6

Mitylene shone around me, but I lived in a world as shadowy as a gray nightmare, and carried a heavy stone where my heart had been.

Kleis was six years old, and did not remember her father, though it was a bare two years back that he had died. I had my school, grown almost too large to handle, and growing all the time; I had my house, a palace really, with a huge wing for pupils and teachers, built at great expense by an architect from Samos, Theodorus the Younger; I had a rosy marble villa in the country, cooled by shade trees and perfumed by thousands of flowers; I was the wealthiest woman in Lesbos, after my hag-aunt, Phaedra. And I had my terrible grief, and nerves that were raw as flayed flesh. It is not pretty to watch a beloved die by inches.

I have not written one poem to ease me of it; it goes too deep. Alkaios wrote the funeral ode; I am told it is unforgettably lovely, but I have forgotten it. I have not even unrolled the scroll to read it now, after all these years that have passed.

Charaxus, my brother, has taken over the trading business; Kerkylas had spent much time with him, teaching him all its secrets, and he did very well, operating out of Mitylene instead of Andros; there was always a ship or two of ours in harbor, loading or unloading, but Charaxus was often away, for he had caught the sea fever. He even dressed in that outlandish sailors' garb that Kerkylas once wore, right down to the gold earrings.

He managed to look quite gay and attractive; he was not as tall, of course, and had not the sea-blue eyes or the white, mocking smile, but he smelled of the sea, and of leather, and of man, as Kerkylas used to do. When Charaxus came ashore, without changing, and stood close to me to point something out or to match up a tally, the tears stung behind my eyelids, and I moved away, my voice gone harsh, to hide it.

My other brother, Larichus, was something high up in the government; he had the title of Cupbearer, but of course he did not carry cups or wait on table, even at a solemn banquet; the title is honorary, handed down from some long-gone sacrificial rite. He prospered under my old enemy, Pittakos, but I shrugged the thought away; it did not seem to matter. I was only not yet twenty-five, but I felt my youth had left me.

It is a time that is difficult to get in sequence, it blurs; but I will try.

I was wild with joy when we walked onto the dock at Mitylene, that day of our homecoming. Kerkylas, beside me, stood tall and walked with something of his old swagger; the sunburn hid the pallor beneath, and the folds of his robe were carefully contrived to cover his thinness; his smile flashed in the old way. I almost believed—against belief—that he had taken a turn for the better. But that triumphal dock walk, slowed by greetings and welcomes, used up all his strength; I think he never again walked, outside our house walls.

We made our home, at first, in my father's house, while our new one was being built. It was a bit cramped; my brothers were there, each with his own apartments and servants, and our own household had grown somewhat large. Still, it was comfortable enough, for the time. Melanippos, our great friend and now our kinsman, my cousin Telesippa's husband, had ordered things well, out of his bounty; I was happy that at last I could repay him for his generosity. They had prospered well, that couple, the plain, shy girl, and the man a "late bloomer," as Kerkylas, smiling wickedly, called him; they had two little girls, both older than our Kleis, and a year-old boy.

Melanippos relayed us all the late news. We exiles had all been recalled, Antimenades arriving first. He had been fighting with the army of Nebuchadnezzar of Babylon, against the city of Jericho, but was wounded early and retired with a pension; a catapult stone had crushed his foot, and, though it had healed cleanly, he dragged it still. He had gone to Pyrrha to work his estates and make them ready for the coming of his brother Alkaios, expected any day on the first ship from Egypt. My heart gave a little leap at the sound of Alkaios' name, but I concealed it, and asked about the other exile, Pittakos' son Tyrrhaeos. Melanippos shook his head sadly. "He is dead. A senseless accident . . ."

"What happened?" I asked.

"He was on his way home, waiting for a ship in Kyme, a town of the Asian coast. While he sat in a barber's shop, being shaved, a drunken brawl started in the wine shop next it. Someone threw an iron brazier; it caught him in the head and killed him instantly."

"Oh, Zeus!" I whispered. "Poor Old Pitt . . ."

"Yes," he said, "he has not had much happiness, for all his success and fame. His wife is no better than she ever was, the talk of the Aegean, and his daughter . . ."

"Gorgo?" I asked. "What of Gorgo?"

"Well . . ." He shrugged expressively. "She will still not take a husband. . . . It is the end of his line. . . ."

"But I have always heard he had children by the dozens!"

"Bastards—yes. They cannot inherit. And Gorgo—she will barely nod to him—never goes near his palace. Though he has done well by her, given her a big house and gardens where she keeps a school for games and dancing . . ."

"It does well—the school?" I hoped not, for I wished to brook no rivals.

"Tolerably," Melanippos said, eyeing me with amusement. "She has had to admit boys to the wrestling part, there were not enough girl pupils. But the dancing division makes up for it. Two of the great teachers of the world, after all—Andromeda and Phaon."

"Phaon!" I was amazed. "He was a slave!"

"Well," he said drily, "so was your Andromeda. . . ."

I thought about it; it did not seem to me to be the same; perhaps I was unfair, but I did not think so. I had never liked him, even though he had helped our cause. For all his beauty, there was a reptile look about him, cold, and his dancing, too, lacked heart.

'Nippos said, "When he appears at a festival—Phaon—the older women send him rich gifts. And the young girls weep and swoon for ecstasy."

"I hope that none of my pupils ever will," I said, feeling my mouth go prim.

Kerkylas said, beside me, "Well . . . he does not merit so much discussion, surely . . . a dancing boy?" And he gestured to the dining couches. "Shall we have a little wine and a bite of food?" His voice was light, but I thought his look fretful; he had risen to greet our guests, and was probably bone weary by now.

Melanippos shot him a quick look, his mouth grave. "Are you in good health, friend?" he asked kindly. "I think you have lost flesh. . . ."

"We had a bad journey—hot and slow. And then I had a fever some months ago . . . it returns from time to time."

"Oh, yes . . . they will." Melanippos nodded. "I had one such; I thought I should never be free of it. It hung on and on. . . . Poor 'Sippa worried. I think she feared I was ready to cross the Styx any moment." He put his arm about his wife and looked down at her, smiling. "But everything passes. . . ."

I thought to myself, *Oh gods—I wish it did!*

My school grew and grew; not only did some girls from Lesbos itself apply, but from other islands, from Athens, and from Lydia. It was impossible to send these wayfarers back by the same boat, it lacked both heart and courtesy; that is how it happened that some of my girls had not a great talent. Strangely enough, they did seem to find husbands, often, even the plain ones. Again and again, after only a few months, this one or that would be sent for, to wed, and off they would go, amid tearful farewells. Kerkylas said, "I told you it would turn out this way! How many parents, after all, know anything of the Muses? They believe that you are grooming their daughters, and pay through the nose for it. And, my sweet, you must admit they go from you a good deal more attractive and poised than when they arrived!"

Such a girl was Anaktoria. Her talent was small, but she had the cleverness to make the most of it. She was a rosy-dark maiden, softly rounded; she would be overblown in a few years, but now the lovely bloom of youth was still on her. Her home was Pyrrha, our old place of exile, though I think she had been born at Miletus on the mainland. I did not remember her from our time at Pyrrha, but of course she would have been no more than a small child then.

Since she lived so very close, she visited her home often, her parents sending slaves to escort her back and forth about every two weeks or thereabouts. She had always seemed a high-hearted maiden, easygoing and cheerful, but I noticed that each time she returned from home she wore an air of unease, almost despondency. Because of my husband's condition, worsening each day, I felt a pall of despair threatening to overcome our household, and threw myself with a kind of mindless fever into my work in an attempt to dispel it. I could very well do without it in my girls! In truth, I am softhearted. It troubled me to catch a glimpse of her at her lyre, her fingers quiet upon the strings, and her eyes large with some vague longing. Such attitudes are infectious, especially among the very young; I resolved to question her. Truly, I was growing so old in those days, with the weight of my inching sorrow, that I felt myself a mother, almost, to these maidens in my charge, and my own Kleis once removed, like a granddaughter!

One morning, at our choral work, she was so very out of tune and meter that she spoiled the whole class. Seeing that wretched look upon her, I held my temper and set her to some writing exercise, in a small room apart from the others. When I could slip away, I went to her; her parchment, a fresh one, was all smudged and blotted, and there was nothing of sense written there. I could not help myself, I began to scold; two tears snaked down her cheeks, leaving pearly tracks.

I pulled the heavy hanging across the doorplace, and led her to a low couch, seating myself beside her, and wiping her cheeks with an edge of my robe. She was so flushed and warm and soft, like a pretty bird, I took her in my arms, kissing her hot cheeks and caressing her softly. "What is it, my little one? What troubles you?" There was a scent of myrrh rising from her breast; another time I would have told her it did not become her youth, being for older ladies, but now it was oddly disturbing.

She twisted in my arms. I could feel her heart, wild, shaking us both; her face was very close, filling my vision, her lips parted and very red, shaped like a bow, and her round chin cleft. I kissed her mouth and held her close, tasting the salt of her tears. I thought of Praxinoa, long ago, and my wild misery that leapt to passion in her arms. I put the girl a little away from me, gently, taking both her hands in mine. "Tell me what troubles you, Anaktoria. . . ." I knew, without thinking, that her feelings were not for me.

It tumbled out, between sobs, released by kindness. There was a girlfriend, in Pyrrha, just her age; they had been friends forever, all their years, close as lovers and more. I had a sudden quick image of little girls, laughing, playing at rolling hoops or dressing dolls, their bright hair falling forward over their eyes and their faces dirt-smudged, and the look between them, fugitive, and as quickly gone. I thought of my own girlhood.

"And now she does not love me, and will not be with me. . . . Oh, she is cruel, my darling!"

I stroked her soft and shining hair and murmured in her ear, sweet soothing words, meaningless. After a while she stopped her sobbing. She sat up straight and combed her fingers through her tangled hair. She smiled a tremulous smile. "I look a mess. . . ."

"No, you look very sweet. . . . There is a jar of rosewater in the corner, and a mirror and comb, and I will leave you. . . . It will all come right, I promise you . . . everything passes, my darling. . . . Soon we will have you married to a fine young man. It is only a girl, after all. . . ."

She shook her head and smiled, an old smile, and sad. "Only a girl! You do not know Atthis, Lady. . . ."

The name struck my heart like a finger pointing to it, a finger of ice. "Yes . . ." I said, slowly, "yes . . . I think I do. Sister of Alkaios and—"

"—and Antimenades, yes, that is the one . . ."

"Yes, surely," I said, as in a dream, remembering, "she must be grown up now. . . ."

I pulled myself together and said some more of prudence to the poor girl, the lovesick one. I did not know then, truly, what ailed me; I thought that my thoughts were of Alkaios.

Often and often I have remembered my foolish words . . . "only a girl."

I put Anaktoria out of my mind, and Alkaios, and his sister, too. It was late afternoon and I went in to my husband where he lay. There was little I could do for him except be with him at odd moments, when he was awake and the drug had worn off; the doctor had promised to stay with us till the end.

This day he seemed a little better, my Kerkylas; his eyes were lively and unclouded by pain, and he asked me for a song. I tried it over a little, for one had been working in my head, and played it, singing it softly; it was about our lovely first days on Andros, with no sadness in it, and all full of joy. He smiled and clapped his hands, though he could not make a sound come from them, they were grown so very weak.

I put down my lyre and slipped to the couch beside him, straining close. He turned his head and kissed my hair. Taking my hand, he gave a little ghost-laugh, and said, "You have been with a woman. . . ."

I opened my mouth to protest; then, remembering how ill he was, lay quiet. "You have been with a woman . . . a girl, I suppose . . . that is all we have here in the house—girls. I smell her perfume on you, myrrh . . . and her own smell, too, stronger than your own. . . ."

"Anaktoria," I said. "I wished to comfort her. . . ."

"Yes," he said. "That is how it will start. . . . Don't do it too often, my Sappho . . . it will make you mannish. When I am gone—"

I put my hand over his mouth. He took it away, finding a firmness from somewhere. "No, darling, listen . . . when I am gone, find another man and marry again. Have another daughter . . . or a son."

I shook my head. "Never. I will never marry again."

Those were very nearly our last words together; he lay day after day in a drug-induced coma, close to death. The chamber, too, smelled of death; the doctor said it was the nature of that dread disease.

Once, he wakened, the look of suffering smoothed out, and asked for our daughter. "I will fetch her, darling," I said. But Kleis hung back at the doorway, holding her nose. I pulled her hand away and hissed a scolding word in her ear; she began to cry.

"Never mind, Sappho," he said, clearly, from the bed. "She is only a child . . . let her go."

When I had done so, and come to him, he gave a little curling smile. "She is growing prettier, our Kleis. . . . Tell her good-bye for me." I started to protest. He shook his head, weakly. "I shall not last much longer, I know it. . . . Promise me something."

I could not trust my voice, but only nodded, holding tightly to his hand. I had to bend close to hear him. "My ashes . . . scatter them in the harbor . . . my home was ever the sea. . . ." He closed his eyes. I thought he was gone. But I had not reckoned with the awful power of the beast that gnawed within him.

It went on and on, his death-in-life. He did not know any of us again, and never spoke, though he moaned. We knew that he suffered agony.

One afternoon, and the sun nearly gone, the room in shadows, the moans changed to groans and then, in a bit, to animal howlings. He still was not conscious, but somewhere he knew the pain, terribly. His head tossed from side to side, and ran with brownish sweat; his legs drew up and his body twisted. I looked at Praxinoa, helpless. We had just given him the draft, a strong one, prescribed by the doctor. I put my face in my hands; I did not think I could bear it.

When I looked up, I saw that Praxinoa held a beaker in her hand, that same beaker that his potion was always put into. Her face was grim, but her hand did not shake. She held it to his lips, her arm supporting his head.

I whispered, "Is it not too much? . . ."

"Yes," she said, and looked at me, a question in her eyes. I nodded.

And that was how he died. I know in my heart that all the gods forgave us.

Chapter 7

Alkaios was late returning from exile. Some said that Pittakos blamed him for his son's death, unfairly, for he was in Egypt all the while. Perhaps Pittakos thought Alkaios ought to have kept an eye out for his son. It was foolish, if so, for Tyrrhaeos was a grown man. But grief deranges, as I well know; one thinks irrationally and does unaccountable things. I myself, after Kerkylas died, in place of the ritual lock of hair laid in mourning upon the pyre, cut all mine off close to the scalp. To my horror, afterward, it set a fashion; all the ladies of Mitylene copied it, and went about with cropped boy-heads. I have even seen my likeness on new-struck coins; one cannot tell that I am a woman in those little portraits. To this day I do not know why I did it.

At any rate, Alkaios did not arrive in the city until the death-day; though he was among the mourners and wrote the funeral song, I did not receive him for close to a month afterward. He came with his brother, Antimenades. I think they must have thought me mad indeed, for I wore black still, like the country folk up in the hills, who hold to the old ways; and harp and lyre lay silent in a corner, wrapped against the dust.

I thought both brothers greatly changed. Only the gods knew what thoughts they had of me, with my pale indoor face, shorn curls, and widow's garb! Antimenades' face, still good-humored, was crisscrossed with old scars, seamed and ridged like a bad seamstress' mended linen. He wore even more now that look of not belonging to houses; his dragging foot made him clumsier still, and I feared for the delicate furniture that Kerkylas had chosen with such care.

Alkaios was as beautiful as ever, but with a difference. He was dressed in the Egyptian style, a short kilt, stiff with gold embroidery, his bared chest covered by a bib of gems and gold beads, and wearing a black wig square-cut at the shoulders. His face was painted, too, the eyes bold with antimony and kohl, and the lips carmined. He affected this look to shock, I am convinced; Alkaios' nature had this in it. But, though he was much stared after in the street, no one copied his way of dress; he did not have whatever it is that others emulate. After a time, he went back to Greek tunics; after all, he liked admiration.

I had become very lax in all things. Praxinoa ordered the wine and food and moved about among the couches, acting as my hostess. She too wore black, her bright hair hidden beneath a drab veil. I caught a look in Alkaios' eye that stabbed me. It was quickly gone, but it had, almost, the glint of Kerkylas' eyes when he was amused. I felt my mouth set in a stern line, and frowned a little to hide the melting within.

They had brought gifts. In spite of my sadness, I could not help being curious, for they bore a large chest between them; bright things from foreign places always have had the power to lift my heart. Alkaios opened it. I gasped.

At the top of the chest lay a glistering thing, gauzy silk insubstantial as a cloud, and looking to be painted all over with the peacocks' eyes of Hera. He held it up and I leaned close, drawn to it. They were not painted, but woven into the cloth, a wondrous thing. It was a garment, scantier than our Greek wear, but a bit like a chlamys. "For you," he said. "No one else could wear it. . . ."

I took it up. My hands I always keep smooth, a vanity; still, my fingers' skin caught on the filmy stuff, fragile as the wings of a moth. "It is beautiful," I breathed. "But I cannot wear it. . . ."

"Later," he said, gently, not like Alkaios.

I shook my head. "It is so thin . . . one can see clear through it."

His mouth indented at the corners, a look I remembered. "With all those peacocks' eyes, one cannot tell what is beneath . . . human eyes fall out trying to tell what is what. . . ." I felt a bubble rise, merry, in my throat, the first in a long, long time. I laid it down, my mouth prim. But I knew I would wear it someday; somewhere a tight string had snapped inside me.

There was a long string of pearls, too, huge and almost black in color, enough to go around twenty such as me; I knew they were very rare. There was a ring, too, bearing the scarab design in onyx, pronged with gold. I drew away. "It is a bug!" I cried.

"In Egypt it is good luck," said Alkaios. "But only Pharaohs and Queens may wear the imaged thing . . . others must wear the beetle itself, gold-painted."

"Truly?" I asked. I slipped it on my finger; I would need all the luck I could get.

The last gift was a little pot, alabaster, showing a rosy color in the light. "Attar of roses," he said, "from Samos." I wept. He pretended not to see, and rummaged within the chest, holding up another pot, its twin. "This is for Praxinoa . . . Nile lilies." He handed it to her with a bow. "I thought the scent suited you." It was the first time I had ever seen her blush.

To cover her confusion and my own tears, I said, "What are all those other little vials?" For the bottom of the chest was covered with them, colored differently from whatever perfumes were within.

"Well, I had heard you had some girl pupils . . . I did not want to neglect anyone. . . ."

I laughed aloud, the first time. "So many! I could not teach so many in a lifetime!"

"Well, keep what you will . . . what you leave over I will take back. Each one will buy a night of love. . . ."

I stared at him. "I had not thought you should need to buy love."

He shrugged, and smiled a little. "Not yet . . . but I am not getting any younger."

I saw he jested, in his way. I was reminded again of Kerkylas; one could not always tell, with either of them.

Suddenly, his face petulant, he reached up and snatched off his wig; it looked like some kind of dead animal in his hand. "Do you mind? It is so hot . . . and I only wore it for the effect."

"Oh, Alkaios—I like this effect better!" He was himself now, except for the paint, damp brown curls plastered to his forehead, the straight nose, round chin and full lips of the boy athlete, that the sculptors love to try for. He helped himself to the wine. I saw, looking closer, faint purplish puffs under his eyes, and the whites veined delicately with red. I remembered my old teacher Arion's wine-death in Korinth and opened my mouth to speak of it. Then I remembered that Alkaios had never known Arion, and that Kerkylas had said always, in his own light, sweet way, to leave my lectures in the schoolroom. I felt my mouth curve.

Antimenades shuffled close and touched my arm. "Sappho . . . I had not thought of gifts . . . and Nebuchadnezzar owes me still for my soldiering, but—" He brought out a large rolled piece of canvas. "I did this from memory, that day long ago on the docks. Perhaps you might like it . . . but perhaps it is no good . . ."

I took it and unrolled it. I looked, and could not speak, for my throat closed. It was Kerkylas to the life, as he had been in his seaman's guise, tall and brown, nearly naked, with the turban on his head, and the blue, blue eyes and the white smile, bold and brave as an army with banners, and shaking my heart.

I looked for a long moment; I still could not speak. I rolled it up, slowly, and held it to my chest, cradling it. I saw Antimenades' face swimming through my tears, and found my voice, low and hoarse. "It is very like . . ."

Afterward Antimenades mounted the painting for me, on hard wood that would not warp, and I kept it, hanging it upon the house wall in a place of honor. I have it by me still.

And the tears that flowed that afternoon washed away my madness. I was sad for a long, long time, but I played again, made songs and sang, taught again, and, after a while, loved again.

Chapter 8

Looking back, I seem to have spent much of my life writing wedding songs. In the two years after Kerkylas' passing, I think there was a new marriage every month. They did not make me sad, as one might have thought, for my own was so very different, there on Andros. There was a dark earth-magic on that vine-island, sweet and heady among the fermenting grapes. These were all of a sameness, gay and light, with processions and laughing faces, and the decked-out bride, maiden-shy, as I had never been. Each one lightened my heart a little. After a bit I became myself again—Sappho, instead of a grieving wraith. Color crept back into my cheeks, and I wore pretty clothes again, and painted my lips and eyes. My hair grew out a little, and I set another fashion, piling it high and off my brow; it made me look taller and set off the shape of my face; I regretted that Kerkylas could not have seen me in this queenly guise.

All sorts of men asked me to wed, drawn by my wealth and fame, though Alkaios said it was my beauty; this was a foolishness, for most of them had never seen me, and courted by letter from far places. Those that were at hand were too young or too old, too fat or too thin, and none appealed. Alkaios did not come forward. I told myself that he feared to be refused, but deep down I knew it was the other way around. He valued his freedom, and so, in a guilty sort of way, did I.

I could lie in a perfumed bath for hours in the evening, and not be teased, ever so charmingly, for a Sybarite; I could putter about my chamber alone with my face in a mud pack and my hair twisted around curling rods, and look ridiculous to no one but myself. Once, though, as I wandered without aim through my empty apartments, humming under my breath, I caught a glimpse of myself in the polished ancestral shield Kerkylas had hung upon the wall. I was naked, and my body gleamed with oil, rare stuff that was said to soften the skin. I could touch nothing, nor sit anywhere for fear of soiling something, until I washed it off. Despair caught me suddenly, and I cried softly to myself, staring in the mirrored brass, "Who are you doing this for, Sappho?" I flung myself uncaring onto the bed, ruining the silken coverlet, and hugging the soft bolster to me; I sobbed aloud, but of course there was no one to hear.

The gods are good, and do not send such moments often, or truly we who are mortal would die before our time. I was content, or almost, with my music and songs, my sweet child, my good friends, and the lovely maidens under my charge. The gifted few among these girls stayed, and learned much, giving lovely songs to the world; it was a joy to teach them. Those others, empty of talent, I clucked my tongue over, and gave up, presenting them with a marriage song at parting. Even so, they profited; many of them had been told nothing by their mothers, and were cold with fear of their wedding night. Imagine! There are still places in the world where daughters are betrothed to unknown bridegrooms and never even consulted. The poor creatures wept to leave Lesbos, as who would not? At least I sped them on their way with the knowledge of what to expect from a man, making it seem easy and a thing of pleasure; I kept my fingers crossed, though, for alas, there are not enough Kerkylases to go around!

And then we had a happy wedding close to home; Antimenades married my cousin Dika. She was a beautiful girl, and clever, though small and dark like me. All the years of his exile she had waited for him, living in her sister's house off Melanippos' bounty, like all the rest of us. Their understanding had been a secret from everyone. She looked to be bursting with joy, no matter that her groom was maimed and poor. I understood how she felt; Antimenades was a man of great heart.

Alkaios gave them a handsome wedding present, his half of their estates in Pyrrha. Alkaios had prospered in Egypt, and had almost as many song commissions as I had, so he could afford it. Besides, he had just acquired Pittakos' great palace, and was making it into the showplace of Mitylene. No one knew how he had come by it; it was worth a million drachmae or more. When I questioned him, he said airily, "My dear, I got it for a song!" Perhaps he meant it literally; his dirge for the Tyrant's son Tyrrhaeos could have made a stone weep. In any case, Pittakos had always hated the place; maybe he was glad to be rid of it. Though it was still half-furnished, the marriage feast would be held there. The dining hall was so large, it could hold half Lesbos, and the list of guests was almost that long. I thought it a foolish extravagance, and said so. "They will need other things more than one great showy day," I remarked to Alkaios.

"It's once in a lifetime—for most people," he replied. "Why not make it something to remember? Besides," he said, tossing his head, "I want everyone to see how rich I am now . . . poor exile that I was!"

"How did you do it, Alkaios? In trade?"

His mouth twitched. "Well . . . you might call it that. . . ." And he sent me a sidelong glance.

Kerkylas would have known what he meant, but I did not. I pretended, though, and gave a little knowing smile. I am not sure that he was taken in by it; his look was quizzical. After all, he knew me very well. I turned the conversation to other things; perhaps I would puzzle it out later. Or ask Charaxus. I had to see him anyway, on a business matter.

Our marriage gift was to be the wedding trip, a cruise among the showiest islands, on a ship of mine, commanded by my brother. After we had spoken of the arrangements, and mapped a likely course, I did mention what Alkaios had said, trying to make it an offhand sort of question.

"Well, surely you know," he said, and explained, lightly.

My eyes nearly popped from my head, and Charaxus laughed. "You mean," I said, when I found my voice, "you mean Alkaios would do *that!* For money! Why—what woman would pay? And where would women get the money—without their husbands' knowing?"

"I didn't say women—silly! You're a big girl now, Sappho!" It sank in then. My face turned scarlet, and he laughed, enraging me. I did not answer him, though, but kept all within, a thing I was learning to do. I composed myself, and bent over the map again. "Here . . . you must stop here—at Samos. It is so lovely. . . ."

"Oh, yes," he said, his face lighting. "She—" He stopped suddenly, and turned away. "I have met someone from there. . . ."

"Oh, who?" I asked.

"No one you would know," he answered. "Someone in trade."

I fancied a strange expression on his face, almost grim, but it was quickly gone, and I forgot it.

I forgot the other thing, too, about Alkaios, until I saw him at the wedding feast, dressed like someone about to be sacrificed, and painted like an Aphrodite girl. He was surrounded by boys just like him, but younger; even the slaves who waited table were pretty boys with slender limbs and delicate faces. I wondered then how I had missed this before; I saw Alkaios nearly every day.

I watched him, seeing how his hand lingered upon the arm of a friend, or among the curls on the head of a kneeling slave. How had I not known? And then, with a little cool chill, I remembered that I *had* known, long ago in Pyrrha, when we were young and lovers, or nearly. How jealous I had been of that boy, my cousin; I had so many cousins, I could not call his name to mind, and frowned, thinking. Why, he was Dika's brother, of course! He was surely here; I searched one face after the other, among those that crowded about Alkaios. Alkaios saw me, and rose, loosing the arm that was entwined about his waist; as he came toward me, I saw his gilded wreath was a little crooked already.

"Who are you looking for so intently, my sweet?"

"Never mind," I said. "It doesn't matter." And I smiled at him, my prettiest smile.

"Sappho, you are still the most beautiful of all the ladies—for me. The most beautiful of all." And he bent down to me where I sat and kissed me in the old way that once had nearly taken my breath away for joy. He held my face between his two hands and stared into my eyes, only a little drunkenly. "When will you marry me, sweetheart?" He whispered it, and bent to kiss me again. There was still some magic left; I felt my knees go like water, and was glad that I was seated. "When, darling?" he breathed in my ear. His eyes were very bright and a little moist; he was remembering, too.

I caught myself up, and sternly locked away the magic, answering him sharply. "When you have given up your fancy boys," I said.

He was not offended; he even smiled a little. "But darling . . . you have your girls. . . ."

"It is not the same!" I sputtered, indignant. "They are my pupils."

"Well," he said, the smile widening, "give it time, dear. . . ." He blew me a kiss, and turned away.

I had been looking in the wrong direction. The boy I sought was not among the crowd of fawning followers at Alkaios' side, but seated upon the couch next to my own, only a few feet away. As I watched him, his name came to me suddenly. Hippias. Then, seeing the line of jaw, sharp and clear, and the skin unshadowed by the beard beneath, I knew this could not be Hippias, for he would be my age at least, by now.

The resemblance, though, was uncanny. I turned to Melanippos, who shared my couch, to ask the boy's name. "Oh, that is young Hermias—out from under his mother's skirts at last—and high time! Phaedra has babied him dreadfully. The boy is as shy as a deer. . . ."

I had to think a little; of course, he was Hippias' younger brother. The last I had seen of him he was not much higher than my waist, for it was long ago, before Drakon's death, before Pyrrha. He had been with his mother all those years, and I had forgotten his existence.

Perhaps he felt my eyes. He moved a little, uneasily, straightening his robe at the shoulder where the folds showed lumpy. I caught a fleeting glimpse of a girl-face beyond his, the profile gem-cut against the torchlight, and a slim bare brown arm, the wrist wrapped in wide gilded leather.

Beside me 'Nippos gave a little exasperated sound, and said, "There she sits—the bad child!" He raised his voice. "Atthis! Please step over here!"

She took her time about it, taking the long way round, behind the dining couches. The boy Hermias followed her with his eyes; I willed mine straight ahead. She stood before us, tall and long-limbed, dressed in a girdled chiton of pale blue like a summer sky. Her hair was darker than I remembered it, colored like amber, and no longer child-silky, but thick and springy, with a deep wave. She wore it unbound and it reached well below her waist. One lock fell forward a little on her brow; she flicked her head to settle it back, an impatient gesture that reminded me suddenly of her brother Alkaios. I saw Alkaios, too, in the slender long fingers, square-tipped, that held her wine goblet. For the rest, she was Atthis only, and wholly divine. The misty, smoky eyes were the same that I had remembered, under the level dark-gold brows; but the girl had grown up to them now.

It seemed an age had passed, though it was no more than a breath. My ears rang, and I heard only the end of 'Nippos' sentence, on a scolding note. ". . . to pay your respects to the Lady Sappho!"

Atthis' eyes were locked with mine; the corners of her mouth lifted in a little curve. "I am sorry for my tardiness, Lady. I was shy. . . ."

I knew it was not true; pride spoke in every line of her. But it did not matter; I was lost from that moment. Perhaps I had always been. Images of her child-face moved behind my eyes as I stared at her, voiceless.

She spoke once more, holding out the goblet. "Will you drink, Lady? I have not yet tasted the wine. . . . We will drink together . . . a wedding wish for my brother's happiness. . . ." She dropped easily to one knee before me, holding the goblet to my lips, and the other hand resting lightly upon mine where it lay in my lap.

I took the cup and drank a little of the strong purple wine, murmuring, "The gods be with the lovers tonight. . . ." It was an old saying I had forgotten that I knew, got from a nurse of my childhood. She showed no surprise, but echoed me, gravely, afterward turning the cup to drink where my lips had touched.

'Nippos' voice was still going on, scolding her now for staying too long, where before he had berated her for her absence. Had he noticed something? Had she been indeed too long? How long?

She smiled, pressed my hand, and rose. "Yes, Uncle," she said, turning to him. "You are right, Uncle." It was gently spoken, but like a little slap, all the same. I knew, as well, that she did not call him "Uncle." Another time, another girl—and I would have sent her from the room for punishment. But this was Atthis.

She had gone back to her couch, greeted by the milky youth. Even from where I sat, I could see his hand tremble as he took hers.

Melanippos was looking at me strangely. "Sappho, are you ill? It is very warm here . . . let me take you outside into the air. . . ."

I heard my voice from far away, like some sound under the

sea. "No . . . no, do not trouble yourself—it will pass. I feel—a little faint." Truly an understatement; I was suffering a sort of small death, sweat pouring down, inside my clothes, and my very blood seeming to course in a panic way within me. I had never felt such a sensation, a kind of dreadful ecstasy. I could not look to the couch where Atthis sat, but stared ahead, unseeing.

"No . . . truly," I heard Melanippos say, "there is no need to sit through all the toasting. We will not be missed. Come." And he led me into the courtyard.

It was dusk, and blessedly cool, the voices and the music from within were faint under the splashing of the fountain. The breeze, like delicate fingers probing, lifted my hair, and the sweat dried cold on me. I shuddered.

Melanippos took my hand. "Your fingers are like ice . . . have you caught a chill? The harbor is full of shipping . . . I always fear diseases from far places—one never knows." He was too kind, and was looking at me too intently. I spoke quickly.

"No, no, friend . . . I get these spells sometimes," I lied. I looked up at him, and smiled. "There. It has passed."

We stayed there for a while, breathing the air, sharp, and laden with a sea-smell, for it blew inland. The fountain played; we listened, not speaking. I caught a movement from him in the half-light, and looked up. He was shaking his head, smiling a little.

"That child . . . that Atthis! She has always been a handful . . . like Alkaios before her. But for a girl, her willfulness is not a good trait . . . it comes from having no mother, and running wild in the country with only slaves to tend her. Well, let us hope young Hermias will settle her down . . . in time. . . ."

I said quickly, "What do you mean? . . ."

He looked down at me, smiling. "Well, is it not a good match? His birth is good, in spite of his mother's morals, and he will have a settlement from Pittakos. . . ."

I stared at him. I had not noticed before how he had aged. He looked now, with his long, high-bred face, like an old sheep. Good friend that he was, my hand tingled to smash itself into that face; I caught my breath, and counted to ten.

"Are they not too young?" I said, carelessly.

"They are of an age, give or take a month or two. And Atthis— At her age you were a mother already, Sappho."

I forced a little laugh, and unclenched my fist, saying lightly, "Well . . . we seemed to grow up quicker, in those days. . . ."

"It is not so very long ago," he said. "You look like a girl still. Exactly as when I first saw you, in your father's house, all nerves at receiving a man. . . ."

"Yes, I was raw then," I said. "But still, however I look in your kind eyes, I am a woman now." *And do not forget it,* I said to myself, and squared my shoulders. I turned.

"We have stayed too long," I said. "My girls will be looking for me to lead the wedding chants. . . ."

I went inside to fetch my little chorus of maidens, with their drums and clappers and baskets of flowers. I did not once glance at the couch beside mine, as I gathered up my things. But, out of the corner of my eye I saw a shape in palest blue, reclining.

Chapter 9

It has been said, and even written, in these last years, that I practically ran every wedding in Mitylene single-handed. This is because often a maiden in my charge celebrated her marriage in my house, among all her companions, with the groom appearing in proxy. The parents paid me to make all the arrangements and to feast the guests. It was cheaper for them, in the end, and easier too, and there was some honor attached to it; my name was becoming famous all over Greece, particularly with those who wanted to be thought more modern. There were many women who threw tantrums if their daughters did not study under Sappho, at least for a month or two, and have a fine marriage send-off at the end. Usually it was their one and only bid for the new woman-freedom that they did not get at home; they were content to let the rest of their lives go. Often I grieved for the lovely milk-white maidens that moved among us so briefly, learning a few soaring notes of song, the lyre scale, and some of their letters, scrawled slanting on the page. Their presences, gone so soon, hung like sweet thin ghosts in my house, dressed in our easy Lesbian chitons with flowing hair tossed with roses. Too soon, too soon came the bridal veils, the jewels, the breastbands and the narrow shifts; too soon the marriage bed, the seeking hands, the bloody sheets. And what was after? The house keys, the cradle, the distaff and wheel, old age and the old, old cackle, the nodding white head, and death. What god made a human soul for this? Or what demon?

I digress, for I am old now too, but differently. It is my favorite disputation, the rights that are owing to women, who are the mothers of all, denied them by the man-world, the war-world, the world that will destroy all if its senseless whirling is not stopped. We have made a start on Lesbos, and the Muses are on our side, and all the goddesses. I pray, and my prayer will be answered, long after me. I have it from the lips of the priestess of the oracle at Eleusis. They rave, these women, but their wisdom is old; beside them the philosophers are prattling babes. I would not have thought this in my youth, but now in my age, I hug my womanhood to me, now that it is in tatters.

I digress, as I have said, but let it stand. I am remembering now that special night of Dika's wedding, the hush while the marriage party put itself in order, and the cicadas beginning in the outside silence, drowned out in the bright clash of our cymbals. I stood at the head of our maiden band; they were all flushed with wine and laughing, and I, beating out the cadence, my eyes were probing, probing, for the one shape I sought.

She came, in her blue, thin gown, veiled in gold tissue stuff all over, the custom for bridesmaids, following behind the bride, walking beside Hermias. He could not keep step, and jostled her, his face dark with shame. She reached out under her veiling, and pinched him. Bridesmaid or not, she was still a child, and cruel. I hated the poor boy, so close to her, but pity moved sluggishly in my breast.

We fell in behind them, for they went, all, on foot, to Melanippos' house. (The streets were too narrow for chariots, for the city was fast-building; sometimes a new house faced its twin across a street's breadth no wider than a wood path.) We played and sang all the way, and the folk lined up to cheer us and shout their bawdinesses.

The party stayed in Melanippos' house only long enough to place their pinch of incense on the house gods' flame, and for the bride to give away her girdle. Atthis, first chosen, ducked it, laughingly, as I had, long ago, at Melanippos' marriage, when my father had given the bride away. There was an odd little scuffle, for Atthis tried to push Anaktoria forward, and got a bitter look. Dika, bewildered and smiling, finally gave the golden girdle to a girl she hardly knew, a new pupil of mine, who could not stop giggling.

We set off again, downhill this time, to the dock, for the bridal bed had been made up on the ship, an innovation; they would sail at dawn. Charaxus was at railside to welcome the pair aboard. I saw with relief that he was not wearing his Kerkylas garb, for once; I think I would have wept.

Alkaios caught up with me and gave me a hand up over the rail. He had lost his wreath by now, and carried a full jug in his

hand, and another, too, inside, by the look of him. He held it to
my lips, and I took a long swallow of the wine; it was a wedding,
after all.

A dozen pairs of hands pushed the couple through the cabin
door, with many rude remarks. I no longer blushed at such
things, but laughed with the rest. Alkaios' face was close to mine;
his eyes were as reckless and wild as a chariot horse's before the
race. He kissed me, hard. "Remember?" he whispered.

"I must have another sip of wine to remember on," I said.

He laughed, and spread his cloak upon the deck, and drew me
down beside him. I beat my drum, and drank my wine, and
kissed him, liking it and feeling a girl again. Someone lit a flaring
torch and I saw, in its light, his eyes half-shadowed, misty;
around the cup he held I saw slim brown fingers, square at the
tips. He drank, and kissed me again, smelling of the wine. I sat
up straighter and said, "Where is your sister?"

"Home," he answered. "She does not much like her partner at
this feast, and begged off. . . ."

"Hermias? . . ."

"Yes . . . I think him rather charming myself, but—" I felt
him shrug. "He bores her, she says. Everyone bores her—my
little sister." He slipped down and laid his head on my lap,
sighing. After a bit I heard him snore. It was the story of our love
life. I sighed in my turn.

I left off beating my drum; there was silence all around. I was
lonely. I slipped out from under Alkaios, letting his head down
gently. When he woke, someone else would be there, in my place;
it was a thing he never lacked.

My eyes had grown accustomed to the dark; besides there was
a moon, reflected in the sea. I looked about at the dark shapes.
Makro sat huddled with little Hero; theirs would be the next
marriage, most likely. I threaded my way over to them.

Leaning down, I whispered, "Will you see me home, Makro?
It is only a step . . . Hero will wait." I might have gone alone,
but someone might see and question me; it was not good
manners to leave before the consummation.

Torches flared in the sconces on my courtyard walls, but the
house was dim and empty; I had given most of the household
leave to attend the feast. Makro looked at me inquiringly; one

could see he did not like leaving me here alone. I smiled, and gave him a little push. "Go back, Makro. Hero will be wondering. . . ."

But I watched him, walking tall in the moonlight, until he turned the corner. He had been whistling to keep up his spirits. When the last faint notes faded into nothingness, I walked through the gate into the court. The statues had a living look, dappled by leaf shadows, and seemed to move; they were the old ones from my father's yard, stiff and wooden. I smiled to myself, thinking that they had never looked so lifelike by day.

I was flushed from the wine, and scooped up some water from the fountain to cool my forehead. A bright fish stopped swimming his endless round and stared at me, caught by my movement. The water felt welcome, a gift from a calm goddess; I raised my eyes and thanked her, whoever she was. There was a glazed clay dipper, old Cretan work, painted with dolphins and sea horses, with a bored hole in the handle to hang it by. The statue in the little pool was a small standing Eros; the sculptor had modestly put a leaf over his private parts. The dipper hung from a point of the leaf. I remembered Kerkylas hanging it there, with a laugh. It had been one of his last days outside the house, and he had leaned heavily upon my arm. I remembered his weight on that arm, feeling it still, my throat full to bursting. I took down the dipper and held it to the pouring spray and drank, taking away the dry taste of the wine upon my tongue.

I went inside, passing through the courtyard and down the darkened hallway, pausing to look in at the nursery door. Kleis was sound asleep, lying on her back, her little arms flung up beside her head; she never slept as some children do, curled like a puppy. I drew the coverlet up to her chin, and blew out the nightlight beside her bed; the wick was sputtering in the saucer. I looked where the old nurse sat in the corner, nodding. Poor thing, she could lie down now, and I whispered to her, smiling to myself that I had to wake her. I made note in my head to retire her and leave a younger in her place; this one was getting too old for the job.

I closed the nursery door behind me and went along to my own chamber, passing the painting of Kerkylas with its three-branched candlestick that always was kept alight. In its flicker he seemed to smile. I turned away my eyes, the first time. The house was still and brooding; the cicadas' song, rasping, was loud outside.

There was no light in my room except the wide beam from the risen moon, that made a path from the window; the servants had all forgotten in the excitement of the feast. The floor was of yellow tiles; where the moon path went they looked blue. Something blue, too, was flung over the standing lightless lamp; a gleam of gold streaked thin like a snake, trailing from it, a girdle. I felt the beat of my heart miss, and then go on. There was a low laugh from the bed.

It was all darkness there, though I could see that the coverlet was rumpled. The path of moonlight stopped just short. In it I saw, clearly, the pale brown dangling wrist, bound wide with gold.

"I thought you would never come," said Atthis.

BOOK V

The Twilight of Lesbos

(Told by Doricha,

courtesan of Naukratis,

later called Rhodopis,

"the roselike one")

Chapter 1

I cannot remember the name of the village where I was born; perhaps it did not have a name. It was no more, truly, than a few mud huts on a hillside, some fields for growing, and, farther up, a grazing place for the goats. My mother's name I never heard either; my father just called her wife. Maybe it was a term of contempt, for she was barren, except for me, and I was a girl. He never beat her, though, as long as she worked from sunup to dark, and lay under his hairy body at night.

The men of the village did not work at all; it was beneath them, for they were hunters, by old tradition. But there was nothing to hunt; all the game had been used up years ago. The hunters sat together companionably in the trodden dirt between the huts and oiled their spears or sharpened the points, drinking fermented barley water.

The village, nameless though it was, had been blessed with a sacred spring, that gushed mysteriously from a fissure in a rock. No one remembered what god it was sacred to, or what goddess, but there was a cave beside the spring where its priestess lived; I learned about priestesses later. When I was a child, we knew her as "the Old Woman," and were frightened of her. Once a year, at the springtime thawing, we had to go to the cave and be washed all over and our heads examined for lice. It was very painful, the wooden comb raking through the tangled hair, the hideous cracking of the red lice in the sharp nails of the old claw-hands, and the icy plunge that took away the breath. The scrubbing afterward, though, was the worst, for the sacred sand took off the skin as well. I cried, the first time, and she slapped me, the Old Woman. After, though, she peered close at me, screwing up her old eyes, I remember thinking that she must not have tortured herself with the water very often, for she smelled rank as a goat.

She looked hard at me, a long look, and kept me back, after the others. I did not know what to expect; perhaps she meant to kill me because I had cried. But holding a bucket under the spring until it filled, she thrust it under my nose. "Look in it, little one. . . ." The ripples of water made everything waver, but after a bit they smoothed out; I saw a milk-white face with red cheeks and mouth, blue eyes, and, above it, hair that was the color of a leaf before it falls. I thought it was the goddess of the water and opened my mouth in amazement; so did she. I closed it; so did she. The Old Woman gave a dry cackle, clutching my arm. "It is you, child. It is you . . . there in the water." I could not understand what she meant and shook my head, seeing the creature in the bucket do it, too.

"Look—" The Old Woman reached down a polished shield that hung upon the cave wall. It was dented, but I saw the same face in it, distorted at the cheek where the shield was flawed. I put my hand out and touched the place, seeing the two sets of fingers meet on the brass surface. Then I knew; the goddess was me. The Old Woman said I was pretty and gave me a twig that had been dipped in honey. It was the first I had ever tasted.

Three more times I went to be cleansed in the sacred water, and each time saw my image, shining and clean, and each time had a taste of honey. In the hottest part of the year after, my mother died, I think in her sleep.

She did not rise with the sun, I remember. I opened one eye and saw her lying there still, on the pallet with my father, and shut the eye again, thankful for the extra moments of rest. I had been set to work along with her lately, and I was always tired. I must have dozed; the next thing I recall were my father's curses and the thud her body made as he dragged it onto the dirt floor.

I got up then and ran to her where she lay, for I saw him kick her. I knelt down and touched her arm; it was stiff and cold. Her face was different, too, all the lines smoothed out, and looking like the face in the sacred water. Her headcloth had fallen back, and I saw that her hair, too, was of my color, but rustier.

My father went out through the doorplace, darkening it, for he was big; he was cursing still. I sat beside her body, crying, not for her, but for myself; I was frightened.

They buried her as they might a dead dog, so that it would not stink, in a shallow grave behind the hut. I knew nothing of funerals or rites, but when they began to shovel the dirt over her, I scrambled down upon my knees and pulled off her headcloth to cover her face.

I did no work all that day, for no one was there to tell me what to do. My father sat with the other men, drinking and talking low, a black look on his face. I was hungry and lit a fire under the porridge pot, but the thin stuff tasted sour and made me sick. When no one was looking, I drank a little of the goat's milk that had been set aside for cheese. At nightfall my father came to the hut and beckoned me out. The men were sitting around a fire, roasting a kid. There was much laughter and the jug went round many times. This only happened on feast days, a taste of fresh meat. Were they celebrating then? "Sit there," my father said. I sat down on the ground, well away from the drunken men.

When they pulled the kid off the spit and began to hack at it, one of the men brought me a hunk of the hot meat. It was charred outside and raw within, and slimy to the touch, but I ate it, being empty. "Well, what do you think?" said my father. They all looked at me; the fire made the night as bright as noon.

"What can you do?" one said, shrugging. "You need someone for the work . . . and the rest of it." And they all laughed loud.

I thought they meant I should have to fill my mother's place, even to lie under him on his pallet, and I was so frightened that I shook all over. But my father, when he led me inside, pointed to my own spot and said, not unkindly, "You can sleep late in the morning." Then he fell onto his own pallet and almost immediately began to snore.

The next day he woke me, holding out a dipper of milk. "Drink it," he said, "and then we go to see the Old Woman."

It was not the time of year for it, and none of the other children were there, but I was washed all over, my hair as well, and scrubbed with the rough white sand. The sun was up and she made me sit in it to dry. Then she washed my tunic, too, spreading it on the rocks beside me. "It will dry almost white," she said. They left me and sat talking together in the cave. I had slept longer than usual, but the sun made me drowsy, and I fell asleep in its warmth. When I woke, the Old Woman was pulling my tunic over my head; it smelled clean, but the water had shrunk it, and it did not reach to my knees. She called my father out. "Look," she said to him, fluffing my hair with her fingers. "She ought to be given to the goddess."

"Do they pay?" asked my father.

"No. It is a sacrifice. But she will feed well . . . in the temple, and wear pretty clothes . . . a good life. The goddess likes the pretty ones. . . ."

"I don't care about that," he said, making an angry gesture. "What will she fetch on the market?"

She narrowed her eyes, looking at me. "The price of six goats and a woman . . . maybe two women."

His mouth fell open; he swore softly and grinned. "They say there are slavers over the hill—in the next town—a day's walk."

She shook her white head. "She cannot walk so far. How old is she?"

He held up his fingers, all five on one hand, and two on the other.

"Seven," said the Old Woman. "She must ride. Do you want to spoil her looks? I will lend you my donkey. Two obols when you are paid. Is it a deal?"

He nodded. "A deal."

She looked sharply at him, cocking her head. "Mind you keep to the bargain," she said. "I have the Cold Curse . . . remember!"

I saw him shiver, as if he felt the curse already. "All right, Old Woman, I'll keep it. Two obols."

The donkey was almost as old as his mistress, and did not like me on his back; he had a wicked eye and kept turning to look at me. I was sure he would bite me, but the Old Woman read my mind.

"He won't bite," she said. "I'll put a spell on him." And she whispered something, close to his long ear. "If he balks, give him a kick. He'll get you there."

We had started down the hill, my father leading the beast by a rope. The Old Woman came running after; she came up to me and thrust something into my hand, wrapped in a broad leaf.

It was a whole honeycomb. I ate it all myself, and would not give any to my father. I had always hated him. And now I knew something else. I knew he was going to sell me.

Chapter 2

I do not remember much of what followed, after we reached the larger town over the hill, where the slavers were waiting. There is much confusion and noise, a whirl of bright colors, strange smells, and many people speaking many tongues. A philosopher who visited me just the other night, a very wise man, and fond of good talk, told me that the brain is very odd; it will block out something it does not want to remember, and hide it away. I think this must be so, though I am sure no real cruelties happened to me, as they do sometimes to others that are made into slaves. I was not cuffed or beaten or starved; I was pretty and they did not want to spoil the merchandise.

There are quick pictures in my mind, like landscapes seen in the flashes of lightning. There is the sea, painfully blue and looking to go on forever; there is a ship, and being sick, crowded somewhere below the deck; there is a huge place, a city perhaps, and standing on a high platform, naked, with many others.

My first clear memory comes here, on that platform. A man, small and thin, with pursed lips and quick little eyes, walked in front of us where we stood, tied loosely together by our wrists, a whole row of naked boys and girls, all young. The man carried a wax tablet at which he glanced from time to time, and a piece of chalk in the other hand. He stopped in front of me, and looked at the tablet, finding something written there. Then, stooping, he marked my feet, on the instep, with the chalk, two marks on each foot, straight lines crossing each other. I heard the boy beside me catch his breath.

The man looked at him and marked his feet also, the same marks. The boy began to wail, high and thin, like an old woman, a wordless sound. The man stepped up and slapped him smartly on the cheek, not really hard, but it must have stung; the boy's crying stopped like something cut off by a knife. The man passed on down the line.

I whispered to the boy, asking what was the matter. I had to repeat it three times, for our dialects were different, though the words were the same, really. We had managed to speak before; he was not as ignorant as I, perhaps because he was bigger. He had told me I came from Thrace, and spoke the Thracian way. "Don't cry—or he will come back," I whispered. "Just tell me what it means."

After he understood, his throat worked a little, and he spoke, low. "The sign of the cross that they marked on us . . . it means they are going to crucify us!" I thought he would cry again, and shook my head, warningly.

"Crucify? What is that?"

"Nail us to a cross to die," he said, his eyes wild. His voice rose in spite of himself. "Nail us to a cross! That is what they do . . . they do it in barbarian places!"

The man with the chalk had heard, and came back. "Be quiet," he said, "or get a slap on the other cheek. You are not in a barbarian place. We are all Greek here. This is Chios." He was smiling broadly, so I knew they would not nail us. And that, too, is how I knew where we were. Chios. One of the great slave marts of the world.

I lost much of my ignorance that day, just through listening, and being silent. It was not long before I learned the crosses were put to show off the best, those who would fetch the highest price. When I told the boy, he did not believe me, and still looked wretched.

I do not know how much was paid for us, but the crowd beneath us gasped at the figure bid, so it must have been high; I knew nothing of coinage then. One man bought the whole lot of us with cross marks; I thought he would be our master, but he was only a slave himself, though richly dressed and wearing gold. When he took us apart and spoke to us, his voice was richer, even, than his clothes; there were so many words in his speech that I did not understand that my head spun and I felt heavy and stupid. Looking around at the others, though, I saw they could not follow him either, and stared like dumb beasts. We were the pick of that day's sale, so none of us showed fear, or perhaps it was because his eyes were kind. How I recognized kindness I do not know; I had never seen it before.

First off, he issued each of us tunics, the boys' rusty-red, and the girls' a rose color. I had never felt anything so soft; the cloth was like a caress. The style, too, was not like the sack thing I had

worn at home, but had to be girdled at the waist and pinned at
the shoulders. The pins were all wondrous things, in gold or
silver, and of many shapes. When the man came to give me
mine, he looked at me and smiled, rummaging in the casket he
carried; I got two golden roses, exactly alike, the most beautiful
things I had ever seen.

He had been talking all the while, but as I said, I could only
understand one word in three. There was a man with him who
drew outlines of our feet on pieces of leather; every one of us,
about twelve in all, had to stand still for it.

"What is it for?" I asked the scared boy, still next to me.

"They are measuring us for sandals," he said, with awe in his
voice.

"See now—what did I tell you?" I whispered. "They are not
going to spend so much on us and then nail us up to die!"

The man heard us, though we had spoken low. He turned to
the boy. "You are from some Ionian colony. Phokia, is it . . . or
Miletus?"

I saw the boy's eyes go round and wide. "Yes—Miletus . . .
sir."

The man's thin mouth twitched. "You need not call me sir. I
am only a slave, like yourself. They call me Aisopos. What is
your name?"

"Milo, sir—I mean, Aisopos." And he grinned, for the first
time, showing strong white teeth; I saw he was pretty, like me.

"And yours, little one?"

I shook my head. "I do not know. They never said."

"Well, you are from Thrace, that is sure. But we must call you
something. . . . What was your father's name?"

I shook my head again.

"Your mother's?"

This time I was almost in tears, but I had to say again that I
did not know. "I don't even know my town!"

He smiled. "Sounds like my own—the one they took me from.
Mud huts, a cave, a spring? The Old Woman?"

I nodded, eagerly. "Yes, yes . . . that's the one!"

"Well, there are probably a number like it . . . but let's say it
is the same. That makes us kinsmen, eh? But what shall we call
you?"

I could think of nothing, never having heard any names at all.

"Cheer up," he said. "I had no name either, until my master gave me the one I bear now. . . . Let me think. You certainly have Dorian blood, by the look of you. . . . How does Doricha sound?"

"Doricha . . ." I tried it over twice, before I got it his way.

"You learn quickly, little one . . . Doricha. You'll do all right."

Chapter 3

We had another sea voyage before us, to the island of Samos, where the man Iadmon, who had bought us, made his home. Aisopos said he already owned more than six hundred slaves; I could not see why he needed any more.

I was not sick this time, for we had quarters on the deck, and the ship, being larger, rode better. It was Egyptian, and carried, besides its human cargo, great rolls of beautiful cloth in many colors, more than I knew existed in the world. But then, of course, I knew almost nothing at all. We were all of us from rustic places where ten miles had been an unheard-of journey before, and most of us were full of fears. To quiet us, the good man Aisopos taught us new words, praising me again for my quickness. At night, before we slept, he told wonderful tales, funny and sad, of animals and birds that talked. For the whole journey I thought that, in Samos, where we were bound, this would be true. Indeed, one of the sailors had a pet bird, many-colored, with a great fierce beak, that spoke, though it did not say anything very intelligent. Still, it held a promise of wonders. I supposed that it was simply ignorant, like myself, and that there were other, wiser creatures in more civilized places. I truly was a little savage, as I look back upon myself. When we landed at Samos, I cried, for I saw right away that the dogs only barked, and even the glorious peacocks squawked hideously and made no sense at all. Imagine crying about such a thing, in a world so full of sorrow and injustice!

Two wondrous ladies met us at the boatside, taking us girls in charge; one of them held her nose, complaining that we smelled.

"Could you not find two tunics each for them, poor lambs—so they could wash and change about?" she scolded Aisopos. He shrugged and sent me a wink. I thought we were all marvelously fresh; we had only worn our new clothes a week!

The sights of Samos are too wondrous to describe; they dazzled. And the house of our master was huge and strange, with ceilings that made your neck sore looking up, and bright painted walls with lifelike pictures, light streaming in from open places, and shining white floors. I did not want to walk upon them in my dusty sandals, but the ladies pulled us along, clucking, and saying they would be cleaned after us. Even as she spoke, folk appeared with buckets, mopping up. We went down a long white hall; in one chamber there were some women spinning, and the clack of a loom; through a great open window some men could be seen, spreading something around a bush of flowers, on the ground, where they grew. I caught a whiff, blown on the breeze, that smelled like goat dung, and said it aloud to the girl next me. One of the lady slaves, for such they were, I had learned, said it was not goat dung, but from the stables. "Everyone knows horse manure is good for roses!" So I learned three more words, just in that one short sentence: *manure,* something like dung; *horse,* a kind of animal; and *roses,* the flowers. I felt very conscious of the gold ones I wore on my shoulders, so small and perfect.

We were led, after a bewildering long walk through halls and up steps, to a chamber that was for washing only. Huge painted pottery tubs stood about, each with its own bucket and spray, and there were serving people standing by to pour hot water and cold; I could not think where it had come from. Later I found it was pumped up somehow—through the walls, unseen!

Each of us girls was stripped and lifted into her separate tub, and washed all over with some wondrous, soft, sweet-smelling stuff, even to our hair. Then we were bade to lie back, up to our chins and soak, while the bath women poured in a creamy liquid, that I later learned was milk of almonds. It was a glorious feeling, like floating on a cloud.

What followed was a wondrous attention and care to make us look beautiful; I could not believe anyone would take the time. In view of the hours I spent at this regime in later years, that morning's ritual was simple to the point of carelessness, but then it made my head spin. Our hands, feet, and elbows were pumiced to make the hard skin smooth, and all the hair of our bodies was removed by a cream made of arsenic and lime, called psilotrum. I was too young still to have more than a fine, fair down, so I was the soonest finished and could watch the others. There was a bigger girl, with an Eastern look, whose arms and legs were covered with dark hair; it was singed off with red-hot pieces of walnut shell. She screamed in terror, and two of them had to hold her down. Poor thing, she thought it was some kind of torture! But truly it did not touch the skin, the bath women were very skilled. She stopped howling and stared in wonder at her smooth self, touching the skin again and again.

They painted the nails of our fingers and toes a bright red color, and touched our lips with pink. After, one of the women pursed her lips, looking at me, and commanded that the lip color be washed off. "She does not need it," she said. And even later, when I reached my full growth, I used paint sparingly; my great attraction was always an untouched, virginal look, an irony, surely, after the first thousand men! We none of us choose our lives, please remember. Perhaps I should have been better off in the mud-hut village, laboring in the fields, bearing nameless babes, and shoveled, at the end, into an unmarked grave. It is all one, or so the philosophers say. I do not always believe this, of course, only when I am sad. Most times I lay the burden of my destiny in the lap of an unknown god; it is an easier way.

Our clean hair was brushed till it shone, and dressed with ribbons and flowers, and we were given new tunics, the same rosy hue, but finer. I was allowed to keep the gold rose shoulder pins.

We had had nothing to eat since our wine-dipped bread on the boat. I was learning some courage, and mentioned this. The lady who had pursed her lips at me said, "Later you will eat. The master does not like to see full bellies and greasy lips." But she gave us each a cup of honeyed wine. Then kind Aisopos came, himself dressed in a fine fresh robe, red also, and took us to the master's hall.

The boys of our group were just leaving as we entered; Milo, the one I felt to be my friend, was taken off alone, escorted by a very fat man; he saw me and tried to smile, but I thought he had a sickish look.

The master sat on a kind of high seat, like a god pictured on a throne. His lady, covered with jewels, sat beside him, holding in her lap a strange little beast, dressed like a man, that Aisopos whispered was a monkey. She petted it, and it flung its tiny arms about her neck, but the face it turned to us was the saddest thing I had ever seen, like a baby that had grown old without living.

By now, I had seen myself in several mirrors, and did not need to rely upon a reflection in water or a warped shield; I had seen that, clean, I did not much resemble other human beings, even the loveliest. I was, as a perfect apple is, or a flower, or a shell from the sea, without flaw. I do not say this from any sense of pride or vanity; it was the simple truth, and a phenomenon like a great talent or a brilliant mind. Men have exploited all three, demeaning the gods' gifts. I am not bitter, for I have been granted a lesser gift, which has served me better: acceptance.

I say this, looking back, as human beings will. That morning, standing with the others before the frog-faced Iadmon and his idle, bored, sulky-faced lady, Kleto, I was a little frightened and more than a little awed. My life lay in their soft white hands.

Iadmon looked us over. His lady did not seem to notice, but played lovingly with her pet monkey, after one first sharp glance.

Iadmon rubbed his hands together; I was to learn it was a habit he had. He looked at Aisopos and smiled; at least, he stretched his lips wide; a frog cannot smile.

"You have done well, my good Aisopos," he said. "As usual. You will be rewarded."

"The task is not to my liking," said Aisopos. "Let my reward be that you take it from me."

"Well, well," said Iadmon, waving one hand in a brushing sort of way, "we will talk of that later." But I saw he was displeased at the answer. He looked at us again, leaning forward. I saw his eyes move over us, coming to rest on me. He opened his mouth to speak, but his lady spoke first, though she did not raise her eyes from the sad animal in her lap.

"I will take that little one, husband . . . the one with the red hair. She will make a good handmaiden, when she is properly taught. She looks clever."

He scowled, turning on her angrily. "What are you about?" he hissed at her, in low tones. "We can make a fortune training her for a hetaera. . . . You can have all the others for handmaidens, a round dozen. This one . . . she is like a chest of gold, and not to be wasted!"

"I do not want the others," she said, quietly. "The red-haired one." She flicked a glance at him, like a snake's tongue, as suddenly gone. "You have enough concubines already. . . ."

"What do you take me for?" he shouted, the cords of his neck standing out. "I am a businessman. I would not spoil my goods. She will sell virgin—and high as a prince's ransom!"

"How do you know she is?" she asked.

His face turned purple. "She is a child! Besides, they have all been examined, before they were paid for." I did not remember any examination; it must have been part of what I had pushed to the back of my mind, in the first days of my enslavement.

They argued back and forth, too rapidly and too low for me to follow. Finally she said, "Half! I want half of the sale!"

He nodded, but I thought he looked crafty. I wondered if she really knew her numbers so well; I had learned already that most women are not taught much of men's knowledge.

And so we were divided. The other girls were taken somewhere else in that vast palace, and I do not remember that I ever saw them again. I was taken to the quarters I would share with four others, picked for the same destiny, to train as strictly as priestesses.

Aisopos was sent to guide me, along with one of the servingwomen, called Phylyra. On the way I asked him what it meant, *hetaera;* I had stored away the name in my head.

"Companion," he answered.

I shook my head; I did not know that word either.

He thought a moment. "You are to be trained to please men."

There is an instinct about such things, or perhaps I heard a note in his voice; I thought of my father and mother on their pallet across the room, and the sounds, brutal and frightening, and the cries she sometimes uttered. "All men?" I asked.

"Those who have the price," he answered.

My father had never had an obol that I remembered, except what he got for me; I let out my breath, for I had been holding it.

We walked a little in silence. Then I said, "What of the boy Milo? He was nice."

His face looked a little hard. "I am afraid they will geld him," he said.

"What is that?"

He explained; I asked if it would hurt.

"They will give him juice of poppy," he said.

"Have they gelded you?" I asked.

He gave a little laugh. "No, for I am not beautiful."

"You are to me."

"Thank you, little one," he said, gravely. "You are the first to say so."

"When I am trained and can please men," I said, "will you come and be pleased?"

He put his hand over his heart, and looked into my eyes. "If ever I have the price," he said. "I will come, surely."

And he did, one day when I was almost as famous as he.

But, by that time, men called me Rhodopis, likening me to a rose. I never knew who said it first.

Chapter 4

Six years I spent in the household of Iadmon at Samos. In the seventh year, when I was about fourteen, I was sold to a man called Xanthes, and taken to Naukratis, in Egypt.

I had learned much; I was far more accomplished than a woman of the aristocracy. I spoke good Egyptian, as well as all the Greek dialects, and a smattering of most of the barbaric tongues, too; I could write a good hand, and read quickly, without moving my lips, scanning the page. When I read aloud, I spoke each word clearly and rendered the meaning of the piece. Numbers were not unknown to me, and I knew the values of all the new coins. I could recite Homer in pure Ionic Greek, all from my head, without looking at the words; I had all the old tales by heart. I could sing the newer songs, too, of Archilochus and Arion, and the popular Aeolian ones that everyone loved, by the Lesbian poets, Alkaios and the Lady Sappho. My voice was small and unexceptional, but I got the cadence right and did well on the lyre. I am not really musical, and the harp was too much for me. I could pluck a few chords as background for my Homer, and I knew the most beautiful harpist posture, one foot extended prettily, arched, head bent pensively to the instrument, and the fingers long and delicate upon the strings; it sufficed.

I had been taught all manner of dancing, too, even the Phrygian, which demands walking upon the hands and bending one's body into a hoop. Of course, I could play upon the flute, but it was not expected that I would ever be called upon to use this knowledge; such was for the taste of common sailors or soldiers.

Every day for six years I had bathed in milk three times; my hair was washed, perfumed, and rubbed with precious silk to give it shine; every inch of my body was tended by no fewer than six body slaves. They were part of the sale; the figure I fetched, with harp, lyre, books, clothes, jewels, unguents, cosmetics, and slaves, was enough to buy Iadmon another palace and three merchant vessels. He had made a good investment; I never knew whether his lady got her share.

I was not sorry to go. What did it matter? The girls I had been trained with had been sold off earlier, for they were older than I; they had gone to other parts of the world, and I would not see them again. I wept each time, but there was no one left to weep for now. Aisopos had been given his freedom, bought by Greece itself, for he was counted one of its wonders. Soon he himself would be a wealthy man!

Milo was bought with me, by that same Xanthes, for there are some men who prefer boys. I suppose Milo's training had been similar, in its way, to my own.

We were better friends now. The eunuchs of the house had been used for us girls to practice the love arts on. We had at first fought bitterly among ourselves, for all of us would have rather had Milo. That was soon stopped, though, and we were made to take turns with all the others, even the oldest and fattest eunuchs. After all, we would not always be getting pretty young customers, and we had to face up to it.

It is not true, as most people think, that these gelded men feel nothing; it was sad to watch the agony of their frustration. I learned some ways to please Milo, secretly, for he was my friend; I would not do it for the others. I am kind by nature, but it was too risky; I might have been caught at it.

I was glad to have Milo with me. On the journey we were allowed to take our meals together and spend a great deal of time in pleasant conversation; he was very intelligent. I thought it augured well, and that I would have him for a friend always, but it did not turn out that way. Boys and girls were kept separately at Naukratis. Once in a while a customer would pay highly to watch; those were the only occasions when I saw Milo, and by then he had lost his taste for women. A good thing, for in this business the pretended thing is always better than the real, and there is no sadness in it.

I was put up for auction, for my first, virgin engagement. Every day for a week I was made to show off my accomplishments, playing and singing, reciting and dancing; my hair was dressed with jewels, and the chitons I wore were almost transparent. The highest bid, finally, came from the agent of the Pharaoh; it was the first time he had ever hired a courtesan, or so it was said. The man Xanthes, who owned me now, told me of it and that I would journey by caravan to Cairo for the assignment. I guess he thought I would feel pride. I felt nothing at all; it is how I have managed to endure until the end.

I went, duly, to Cairo, and indeed there were wonders there; Amasis, the Pharaoh, was not one of them. He was an undersized person with a head too big for his body, like a child's. Beneath his robes of state his body was pitifully wasted, one arm withered and a leg that dragged. It is from the Egyptian disease, when it strikes other nations, the afflicted mostly die. Over thousands of years in Egypt the folk have built up a strength against it; usually they are not even left crippled. But the royal blood of Egypt runs thin, for they have married sister to brother all down the line. Any animal breeder will tell you such a practice makes maimed beasts or mad ones, after a time; I suppose it works the same way with humans.

The morning after Amasis lay with me, Xanthes' agent asked me how many times he had performed the act of love; the agreement, you see, was for the deflowering only. When I answered that that had been all, he looked disappointed. All procurers are greedy.

I was not disappointed, for I had expected nothing, Pharaoh or no. I never expected anything throughout my career, though once in a while, with a philosopher or a poet, the conversation was stimulating.

When love came, I was unprepared for it; my heart nearly stopped.

Chapter 5

Naukratis is a Greek colony, the headquarters of the Greek mercenary troops as well, and, of course, it is a big trading center. From my windows I could see the busy life that teemed in its streets, strange and beckoning, with people of all nations, curiously dressed, different and exciting, and each going his own way, intent upon unknown importances. I would lean upon the sill, though it was forbidden, and gaze, as at another world.

For the hetaerae of Xanthe's house never were allowed upon the streets or in the agora, except once a week to visit the Temple of Aphrodite, and then by covered litter. It was to set us apart, and keep our value high. Friendships, too, were discouraged among us, though we found ways to meet secretly, to gossip and giggle and eat forbidden sweets; one can always bribe a handmaiden, they have nothing of their own.

I never saw a soldier or sailor, of the common sort, except from this distance, for of course they did not have the price. I do not know why they intrigued me from my window. The soldiers mostly were paired off arm in arm, swaying against one another as they walked, and painted heavily as street girls, and the sailors were bearded and hairy like my father, but dressed in outlandish garb, tattered drawers below bare chests, with gold rings hanging from their ears. There was one sailor, though, that was different. I saw him from a distance, walking alone, and coming toward the place where our house stood. He was very sunburned, a deep brown, and not hairy at all; his short drawers were oiled dressed leather and a rolled leather belt, dyed purple, was pulled tight about his slender waist. His brown chest was almost covered by strings of golden beads, and his hair, brown too, but lighter, hung to his shoulders straight as rain.

When he passed beneath the window I hung out to get a better look. He raised his head. Some god must have whispered to him. Our eyes met. A little shock ran through me, such as I had never felt; I do not know how, but I know he felt it, too. There was a long moment while our eyes held; his were some light color, looking lighter against his skin, and with little lines around them from looking into the sun. I fancied in him a look of a Homer hero, though he was no bigger than other men, and his face was just a face, Greek, with a shaven chin. I did not smile, but stared, and he stood very still, with all the folk milling around him. I heard a footfall behind me, and the creak of the door opening. I pulled the curtains together quickly, and turned back into my chamber.

It was the day for our temple worship. I did not dare open the litter curtains, but there was a little tear in the cloth that I had widened with my finger; no one had noticed it yet, and I used always to peep out at the crowds, close to. It was exciting and had a daring feel, for the folk outside could not see me, though sometimes their faces passed, exotic as bright birds in a deep jungle, just inches from my own. I looked this day for my sailor, but the tiny hole did not give me much range, and I did not see him. I thought he was probably back on his ship; perhaps it had even sailed.

But when we came out from the temple, walking two by two and veiled, with our eyes downcast as we were bidden, I felt his eyes. I looked up quickly and saw him, misty through my veil. He had been waiting outside! My heart thumped heavily, with an uneven beat; I was afraid it could be heard, and was glad to reach the safety of my lonely litter.

I had been in the house of Xanthes for almost six years and had earned much more than six fortunes; by now I had certain privileges. I could refuse to entertain more than three nights a week, pleading headache, boredom, or whim. Besides he knew better than to tire out his girls when they began to get old; I was nearly twenty! I gave out that I would sleep alone that night; I wanted, for the first time in my life, to dream.

After supper, which I could not eat, I sent my body slaves away. When I was alone I usually got out my spinning wheel or small loom, or sometimes worked at embroidery; once in a while I baked honey cakes over the coals in my brazier. After a thousand readings even Homer palls, and the new songs were few and got to us late. Besides one does not want to do for pleasure those tasks that have always been work. I liked the baking and spinning and the rest, though of course it had to be put out of sight when I had a customer; it smacked too much of home to them.

That night, though, I could find interest in nothing. I paced the floor, lay down, got up again, sighed, tapped my fingers on the table, snarled my embroidery silks, and let the honey cakes burn. The charred smell was nauseating. I flung myself face down upon my couch and cried.

Someone scratched at the door; I had shot the bolt and went over to it, not opening it and speaking sharply. "What is it? I want to be alone!"

"Please, let me in!" I heard the voice of my youngest body slave, sounding close to tears. I am softhearted. I opened the door.

She stood there looking scared; I have never in my life slapped a servant, and it annoyed me. "Well? What is it?"

"There is someone . . . Xanthes made me ask you . . . someone wants to visit you tonight. . . ."

"I am off tonight . . . tell him tomorrow!"

She stood in the doorway, small and mute; of course she was afraid.

"Where is Xanthes? I'll tell him!" My voice rose stridently for once; I was sick of keeping it soft. I saw a figure some way behind her, dark in the dim corridor. A voice, not Xanthes', said, "Leave us." She darted into the shadows.

The figure came forward, cloaked and hooded; in the light from my cooking brazier I saw light eyes with sun wrinkles at the corners. I caught my breath, and stepped back from the door to let him in.

"How did *you* get in?" I demanded. He laughed; I saw the hooded cloak was purple and bordered with gold, and the brooch that held it set with a precious stone.

"I can afford one night, anyway," he said. His eyes were on a level with mine, for I am tall. "Unless you yourself would turn me away . . . they said you wanted to be private. . . ."

"No . . . no . . ." I said, my breath short. I looked around the chamber. "I am in disarray . . . and—the cakes are burnt."

"I know," he said, smiling. "I can smell them. But I do not want cakes. May I? . . ." And he made to take off his cloak.

"Yes . . . yes, put it here . . . or no—hang it—" I pointed to a gilded hook upon the wall. Beneath he wore his seaman's garb.

"I thought you were a sailor," I said.

"I am," he answered, "in a way. I command a vessel . . . and own a few others." There was a little bravado in his voice; I saw he was young, for a man; about my own age. "Though I am not very rich really. The business belongs mostly to my sister."

That was odd: a woman—owning a business! But I put the thought aside, for his eyes were on me, and his hands upon mine.

"So you are Rhodopis . . . the Rose," he murmured.

I shook my head. "My name is Doricha."

"I never heard it," he said.

"I do not tell everyone."

"I am Charaxus of Lesbos," he said, drawing me down beside him on the couch.

He was my first lover, and my last—never mind all the others.

Chapter 6

Mitylene is a beautiful city, especially when one comes to it a bride and a freedwoman, who had been nothing before.

There are those who would say that to be the most famous courtesan in the world, for I was that, truly, is enough for any woman; I say that all the perfumes of far lands are nothing beside the air of freedom, and chests of gold and silver and sparkling jewels are nothing beside the one you love.

My sister-in-law, the great Sappho, knew it too, and has said it better in her songs. I was only an ignorant hill girl pumped full of knowledge and polished on the outside to please men, and why should Aphrodite have spoken to me? But she did, and while I am alive I have heard her words, and when I am dead, I am dead. But Sappho's songs will live forever, and tell the words to the world.

It took us two years to buy my freedom, for the price was very steep; Charaxus cheated his sister when he could, for which I am sorry, and I cheated Xanthes, for which I am glad.

Long before, when I had first been brought to Naukratis, and given a chamber of my own, I found a secret place, big enough to hide coins and small jewels. We hetaerae were forbidden to keep any presents that were given us, except for perfumes or scarves; everything went to Xanthes, for he owned us. We were searched every morning, quite thoroughly, even inside our ears and jaws and other private places; of course, every inch of our chambers and clothing and chests was gone over with care. But I liked to go barefoot when I was alone, having spent my earliest years without shoes; besides I liked the feel of the cool clean floor tiles against the soles of my feet. One morning, going behind the screen to the chamber pot, a dark corner, my toe was caught by a loose tile, and scratched. It bled a little and I bent down to wipe the blood from the tile. It moved under my hand and I lifted it. I saw that several tiles around it were loose as well and could be easily removed. Under was a space about a half-foot deep above the ceiling of the room below mine. It had been used before, that was clear, and probably for the same thing; slaves must learn some cunning. After that, when I was given a valuable jewel or a coin, I slipped it into the hiding place under the tiles. By the time I knew Charaxus, I had nearly filled the place. Still, it was not enough for manumission, even with what he could come by. I gave him what was there, and began to save again. He, too, put away what he could. Still, it was a long wait.

I knew he hated that I had to be with other men. I said it was like taking a nasty medicine; I held my nose. "Remember that, my darling," I said. Besides, he had to pay Xanthes, of course, whenever he himself visited me. There was no sleep for either of us those nights, I can tell you, seeing that we tried to make up for a whole month of being apart.

I cheated in small ways, too; leaving a stubble on my legs or a roughness in my hair; often I coughed as well, pretending illness. When we finally had the price, Xanthes was not too unwilling to get rid of me.

Our marriage was a simple hand-fasting, and private to ourselves; he prayed to Hermes, his favorite god, and I to Aphrodite. I promised her an offering someday, far off, when I had the means; I prayed to Hera also, for marriage-happiness. I had scant hopes of children, after the life I had led and the strong abortive medicines I had been dosed with.

My manumission fee did not include anything which had been bought for me. I sailed for Lesbos without a handmaiden, and even without cosmetics; Charaxus swore I did not need them.

Word always gets around when people like me go anywhere or do anything; there was a great crowd at the dock awaiting us, all the folk craning their necks for a glimpse of the notorious Rhodopis. It must have been a shock to see an unpainted country girl in rude health, red-cheeked and windblown, in a simple white chiton!

The great Pittakos greeted me in person, presenting me with a wreath of roses, and making a speech of welcome. He was from Thrace himself, so perhaps that was why. I had heard much of this man, some good and more bad, and pictured him such a one as my dimly remembered father; I saw an old man, shrunken and nearly bald, his great red beard streaked widely with gray, and his eyes tired. In his retinue was Charaxus' young brother Larichus, a slim, delicate youth with a priest-look; he was the

City Cupbearer, a title, I learned later, which was more religious than civil, so my impression was not far off. He greeted Charaxus with as little warmth as he showed for me. There was no hostility, only distance; he did not seem to belong to the world.

I met many fine folk that day, friends and well-wishers; I was confused and bewildered, my mouth aching from stretching in a smile. The temple whores were lined up, too, at a respectable distance, most of them with tears in their eyes; my love story was the bright sun of their lives.

There were even some gentle girls, young, fresh as flowers and very wide-eyed. Charaxus said they were Sappho's pupils. One of them held by the hand the little daughter, Kleis, a sunny child. She broke away and flew to Charaxus' arms. She kissed me, too, when bidden, and called me "Aunt"; I loved her at sight.

Only Sappho was not there. She did not come either, to Charaxus' house, though she was always invited whenever we entertained; our feast-day gifts were sent back promptly, unopened, too. She hated me, and her hate lived long. The emotions of an artist run deeper than those of other folk; it is their greatness, and their failing too.

Charaxus said, to soften me, that Sappho was wild with love for a fickle maiden, and could think of nothing else. He was angry with her, and sad, too. I was only sad.

I did not tell him this, but quite by accident I had happened upon some letters she had written him, a little bundle he had kept over the last year or two. They were written like poems and I thought that was what they were, and began to read; after, I could not put them down. In beautiful cadence and perfect sentences she reproached him for loving me. The language was shockingly foul, even to someone like me, who has heard all kinds of obscenities. The mildest thing she called me was "a rooting sow, with a filthy snout"; my face burned. I would have liked to burn them, too, but I did not dare, and put them back quickly, feeling guilty. I tried to put them out of my mind as well, and after a long, long time I succeeded; I am of a placid nature.

There was another thing I did not tell Charaxus. Long ago, in the house of Iadmon, my first master, she had demanded that I be sent from the hall, saying she would not play before slaves and whores. I have sharp eyes, and ears, too; that was not the true reason. Her husband had looked upon me with idle desire, and said something flattering, too, and she was wild with jealousy; she even broke a lyre! I remember her well, as who would not? Especially a slave girl who was set to learning her beautiful songs and could not learn for crying over them.

I remember her sitting there, in Iadmon's house, in a rich Eastern robe, looking, in her smallness, like a little girl who is playing at being with child. Her face, even puffy with her condition, was alive with a sweet, wild glow. Her beauty is not like mine, perfect, so perfect that, like all such perfection, it can tire the eye after a while. No—her face is odd and the features do not match; yet one keeps looking to discover new things, for it is always changing. And this strange beauty Sappho kept all her life, for age makes no mark upon it; it is from within. Her husband I cannot recall; he was just a straight-featured Greek, tall, with corn-colored hair. My impression is of a healthy man, but he died soon after of a wasting illness. They say she grieved to excess, like a madwoman, and would not make songs or play for a long while. I gave thanks that the gods lifted this sickness from her, for she was the wonder of our age, and a woman—another wonder. No one could match her, in my opinion, though Alkaios had great skill, too, and was much admired.

This Alkaios was a beautiful man. One saw his likeness on all the newer statues, and his profile, proud and pure, was stamped on the first Lesbian coins. Charaxus says he was Sappho's lover, long ago, when they were exiled the first time, in Pyrrha. I would not contradict him, but privately I do not think so; Alkaios has the look, unmistakable, of a boy lover. I can always tell, after the life I have led. How happy I had been to open my door to one of them! It meant an evening spent in pleasant converse, music, and dance—and no work at all!

Alkaios is still Sappho's great friend. He visits her every afternoon, just before sunset. They try over songs together and discuss the latest fashions; he is as knowledgeable about such things as she. Often he comes to our house after, dry as a bone and demanding wine; she will not serve him any. She does not drink very much herself and is fastidious by nature; I suspect she lectures him! Of course he is the biggest drunkard of Mitylene, and growing worse every day; one can hardly blame her, if she is really fond of the man. It is on account of Alkaios that Pittakos has passed the new law, making any offense doubly punishable if it is committed when drunk. Poor Alkaios has been locked up regularly in the last years since he returned from Egypt and his exile, sometimes as often as once a month.

We do not refuse him wine; it is no use, and besides, he is very witty after a few cups, and often inspired. His beautiful face is paying for it though; there are tiny veins showing in his skin like a veil of red, and a thickening along the clean line of the jaw. Well, we are none of us what we used to be, and at least he finds pleasure in his life, for he takes it all lightly, wine and boys, too. Sappho is forever in the toils of agonizing love, like a trapped bird. But perhaps that is her pleasure; we are all different.

Chapter 7

In the first years after I came to Mitylene Sappho had many favorites among her maiden pupils, one lovely girl after another, and she has written many a lovely languishing song, all far too good for them. For what are they, all, but pretty mortals?

It is the same song, really, that she sings, with other melodies and other words. And it is the same girl, too, for each new one that she chooses has the look, somewhere, of Atthis. This one will have her huntress' hands and farseeing level eyes, and that one her length of leg; Gongyla has Atthis' hair, dark honey and rippling free.

This Atthis is the young sister of Alkaios. Even he, wild as he is, shakes his head over her. He and his brother, her guardians, have been bringing pressure to bear on her; they want to marry her to the boy Hermias, who has loved her through all her headlong passions. He is not the only one; she has all the beauty of the faithless of the world, and many of the young men of Lesbos have asked for her. She looks at them all with scorn, and has taken up with Gorgo and Andromeda; she lives in the house where they keep their school. The wrestling attracts her; she is very athletic. They say she has started some classes in archery as well; many of Sappho's pupils long to bend a bow, but while they are in her charge she will not allow it, for the dancer Phaon is there, a profligate; he has debauched half the women of Lesbos, and even some of the noble girls, a scandal. He would have been banished long before, except that no charges have been brought; he is the idol of all the great ladies, young and old. He is a manumitted slave, like myself, who has gone far; I should feel some kinship, but I do not. One cannot be cousin to a snake!

These songs that I have mentioned are not among those that Sappho sings in public, of course; now and then she will include, usually at the very end, a small love song that does not name a name. These are always among the most admired of her work; though they are sung only at great houses for the aristocrats, still, a bare week later, they are heard in the lowest wine shops, and whistled in the streets. Indeed, Charaxus says that he will hear suddenly a familiar tune in Crete, perhaps, or Korinth, and stop, listening, recognizing it as his sister's. For, though she is much praised by the nobles, she has that which touches the heart of the lowly folk; often they do not even know her name!

As time passed, she performed less and less in the houses of the wealthy, often sending one of her pupils instead; she herself preferred to honor the gods at their festivals. Of course, these appearances drew huge crowds that filled the agora in front of the temple and spilled out into all the streets. Charaxus said she was getting a taste for applause; he was her brother and felt no awe.

I think, truly, that she did it to help her pupils; she no longer needed the money, and the girls she sent did. The most talented are often the dowryless and poor. Damophyla did very well, for instance; this was a big girl, almost ugly, with a voice like a deep bell. Her songs were intense and almost barbaric, haunting and wild; they were a great novelty to those bored rich folk. She saved the fees, and was able, later, to open a school of her own. Another favorite was Erinna, who wrote in the Homeric manner, for the harp. Her story, was, in its way, as shocking as my own; her mother did not honor the Muses, and kept the girl chained to her spinning wheel, believing that was the rightful place for a woman. Sappho paid a large sum to get her away, recognizing her worth as an artist.

Erinna wrote some popular pieces (all Greece loves the saga-song). The most famous was a long poem that was called, "The Distaff," and rang with high words meant to free women from that very thing, the distaff. It was hummed secretly by all the rebellious girls that were kept in the background of life; often, too, it was sung on a goddess' feast day, sometimes causing small riots. Wives from the hill places, poor drudges all year long, grown bold this one day with free wine and the rousing words of the song, belabored their husbands with the rough side of their tongues and even with their fists. Erinna, alas, died young, before her songs mellowed; she was twenty when she caught the summer fever. Her mother sent her ashes back, saying that Sappho was welcome to them, as she had bought the girl! They are kept in an honored place, beside those of little Timas of Phokia, who died the same day.

That was a dreadful summer. No one understood that fever, and the doctors could not cure it; many died, all over Mitylene. It started with a scratchy throat and swollen tongue, and the whole body hot to the touch. If the fever broke by the third day, they recovered; if not, the end came. The girls of Sappho's house slept four and five to a chamber, for the school was crowded that year; the fever spread there like a brushfire, and many were afflicted.

Sappho was wild with fear for her little Kleis. Ours was the only house of Mitylene that did not have the infection somewhere; she had to let us take her, or risk the fever.

The freedwoman, Praxinoa, who had been with Sappho since her childhood, was very ill; Sappho tended her with her own hands and she recovered. But the illness left her mumbling and weak, old before her time. Her beautiful hair fell out, and the flesh hung pitifully upon her. She lost the use of her hands, that had been so capable, and it pained her to walk. She sat in a corner like an aged crone and could not feed herself, and her wits strayed. She hung on to life for a long while, worsening each day. One morning she did not rise from her pallet, but lay like a stone. She was greatly mourned by all who had known her; Sappho's funeral ode was as beautiful as a love song, and even strangers wept to hear it.

Little Kleis was well throughout, happy and healthy, a joy in our childless home. We kept her until all danger was past, a long time; she cried when she left, for she had grown used to us. I hoped that Sappho would not hear of it.

Chapter 8

After our care of Kleis during the fever-days, Sappho, out of plain courtesy, had to receive us. Our first meeting was a good five years, perhaps six, after I came to Mitylene. She was polite, but distant, her performer's poise serving her well. I knew she was curious about me, but only her eyes showed it.

I had dressed with care, just the opposite of the old days. The latest fashion, which used to be worn only by women of my sort, was for transparent silks and linens, daringly cut. Sappho's chiton was slit on one side halfway up her thigh, and was the color of flame, but showing the pale gleam of the flesh beneath. I had chosen a creamy wool, with an effect of sleeves, pinned at intervals with mother-of-pearl, down to the elbows. I wore no paint at all and braided my hair, winding it into a knot, fastened low. My only jewel was my troth ring, a simple band of pale gold. I saw surprise leap in her eyes, but she made no comment at all, and merely offered us a seat and signed a servant to bring wine. Charaxus took some Chian, but I declined, saying that it was too early. "For me, also," she said. "Perhaps you would prefer beer?"

Now, beer is an Egyptian beverage, not often drunk here in the islands; I wondered, with a little shock, if she meant to insult, but gave no sign. "I have not tasted it, Lady," I said. It was quite true; we hetaerae were trained to refined beverages and expensive foods.

"It is my favorite drink," she said, surprising me in her turn. "This jar has not been broached and is quite cool," she said, feeling it. "Beer must be cool, and it must be bubbly and not flat. Will you try it?"

I liked it, and said so; the taste was sharp and not sweet, a change from our wines.

"I find it more refreshing," she said, taking a long drink, "and not at all intoxicating. . . ."

"Don't you believe it, sister," said Charaxus. "You can get drunk as a sailor on leave if you try. . . ." She set her cup down hard and glared at him. He grinned at her in that superior way men have about them; I mostly shrug it off, but I did not think she would. I did not wish to be caught between brother and sister in this, our first encounter, so I said I hoped little Kleis was about and that we could see her.

She raised her eyebrows; it was a very expressive face, as I have said. "*Little* Kleis can be heard quite easily—in the next chamber . . . hers is the lyre that is off the melody." Her face clouded, and she said, "I had hoped . . ." Then she gave a little, brittle laugh. "Well, she takes after Kerkylas. He could barely get through a tune . . . at least she will have his looks, though at the moment they do not set so well. A man's face, however fair, does not become a girl of twelve . . . or his height either. . . . One hopes she will stop growing." She listened a moment, cocking her head. "There! It is finished. I have instructed her to come in when her lesson is over. . . . Ah—here is the beautiful Gongyla, with my dear big girl. . . ."

The beautiful Gongyla trailed a long garland of roses; it was fastened somehow to her shoulders and made a loop on the floor behind her where she walked. Kleis, too tall and not watching, tripped on it, and nearly fell, looking frightened; the garland broke.

Sappho jumped up and flew to Gongyla. "Oh, darling, your poor garland. . . . I will make you another, yellow roses for tonight. . . ." She kissed Gongyla tenderly, running her hand along her cheek and smiling into her eyes. Then she turned to Kleis, shaking her head sadly. "Do be careful, my sweet. We shall have no house left. . . ." She gestured to us where we sat. "Here they are . . . as promised!" So it was Kleis who had begged!

"Aunt Dora!" the girl cried, running to me and burying her face in my lap.

"Are you hurt, darling?" I asked, lifting her chin with my hand; her eyes were a pure light gray, tears standing in them.

"Oh, no, of course not . . . but I have annoyed Mother! I am so awfully clumsy!"

"You are not clumsy," I whispered. "It was her fault . . . one does not drag garlands about. . . ."

"No—but I always am!" cried Kleis softly. "I break things. . . ."

"You have not grown up to yourself yet," I said. "You will

break hearts soon. . . ." She smiled a little tremulous smile, not sure of itself. Her face was spotty and her yellow hair needed washing; still, she was very fair and would be beautiful. "I have brought you a new cream from Lydia," I said, taking out a little cosmetic pouch, and showing her the jar. "Apply it every morning and every night. . . . And here is some soft soap for your hair—I made it myself."

She shook her head. "Mother will not let me," she said. "I am too young, she thinks."

"One is never too young," I said, firmly. "It is not paint, after all. Here—slip it into your pocket, and say nothing. And mind you keep your hair clean, especially in hot weather. . . ."

She put the little bag into a hidden fold of her skirt, looking guilty. I thought shame that in this household of women there was not one who gave her such attentions. Hero had attended to these matters before, when Kleis was very young, but she was wed now to Makro, who served under Charaxus at sea, and had a baby of her own, besides giving lyre lessons.

I watched as Sappho took tender leave of Gongyla. This girl had a strange, rapt look—half-mad, Charaxus called it; I thought she affected it, to appear Muse-struck. It was rather irritating. She was quite lovely to look at, in a delicate, insubstantial way. Her voice was soft and low, too low for hearing across the room. She embraced Sappho, mothlike, and floated through the door.

"Dear Gongyla begs to be excused," said Sappho. "She has another lesson. . . ." I saw her glance rest, frowning, on her daughter, who was sadly munching her third honey cake. Sappho's mouth opened to speak, but a voice, merry and light, was heard at the hall door, and she turned, alight, to greet Alkaios. I suppose she had invited him to make a kind of link between us all, and very clever it was of her, for at once all eyes turned to him, waiting for the expected quip.

It came. "Ah," he said, "a family party, I see! Is it some kind of god day?" He glinted all over like a sword that has just been polished; it was early still, and the wine had not yet blurred his edges. One saw his youth in him, for a moment, the Adonis that every woman mourns. I saw that Sappho glowed warm in his presence; perhaps she had loved him, long ago. He went right to her, tipping up her chin with one hand and kissing her full upon the lips. "Look what I have found for you, love!" he cried, bringing out the other hand from behind his back.

In it were about five small violets, limp-stemmed and bleached almost white. "The last of the season . . . I spotted them from my chariot and hopped right down, not waiting to call a halt. . . . I nearly broke my ankle, but never mind. . . ." And he waved his hand airily. "Do you like them, my offering? . . . Oh, Zeus—they are wilted!"

"No—no, they are lovely . . . the very last, I am sure. . . . Oh, you *are* sweet! Look—I shall fasten them in my hair!"

"No, dear girl," he said, snatching them out of her hair and tossing them down. "They look absolutely ridiculous!" He shrugged and smiled. "Ah, well . . . it is the thought that matters. . . . and I *did* turn my ankle for you!"

I had never seen Sappho like that, all smiles; she was enchanting. Of course, I had only seen her from a distance at any rate; still, it was another side. I felt myself smiling, too, and Kleis, beside me on the couch, had cheeks as red as roses with excitement; it was plain she adored him, too.

"My dears—" He stood plump in the center of us, making an audience for himself; he never performed in public these days, and I suppose he missed the feeling. "My dears—guess where I've been! I've been to Gorgo's!" I stole a look at Sappho, seeing her still as a stone; I knew that Atthis was there, at Gorgo's house. But Alkaios did not check his speech and left her no time to brood. "Has anyone seen her lately? My dears—she is surely aiming for the Pankration this next year! Except for the beard—one might swear it was Old Pitt himself! But then I expect she shaves it. . . ." He waited, delicately; his timing was perfect. We all burst into astonished laughter. Poor Gorgo is quite a sight, built like a wine barrel and wearing a permanent scowl.

He went on. "And all those girls! They are beginning to get a look of her . . . all solemn and lumbering, like dancing bears from Scythia. . . ." And he struck a ludicrous pose, making us laugh again. "She must have the first obol she ever made, also . . . the place is a shambles, with no one to clean it, the marble stained, and paint peeling from the walls! It simply cannot be believed!"

He told a delightful tale, barbed with a cruel wit, but making us hold our sides. ". . . Andromeda, of course, was nowhere to be seen. . . . I suspect a rift, of sorts. . . ." And he looked at Sappho, a significant glance from under his brows, a private thing between them. I saw a thin wash of color creep over her face, but I could make nothing of it. Was he hinting that Atthis was footloose again? Or did he mean that she had gone off somewhere with Andromeda? The intrigues of these people I could never fathom; artists complicate their lives so.

"I did see Phaon, however. . . . My dear"—he spoke to Sappho now—"you know he has not changed at all! I suspect he dyes his hair—but otherwise . . . he might be sixteen still! One could almost believe the story that is going around . . ." He waited. Charaxus laughed; I saw he had heard it. "What story, Charaxus?" I asked.

"Let Alkaios tell it," he said. Of course it was what he was waiting for, Alkaios.

"Well, it seems our Phaon—when he was ferryman between here and the mainland . . ."

"But that was his father!" Sappho broke in.

"My dear, not even that! His father was the ferryman's slave!" He shrugged. "It is a tale—what do you expect? To do him credit, I don't believe he started it. . . . At any rate—ferrying away one night, business must have been bad, for he had only a single passenger, an old woman. When he held out his hand for the fare, she said she did not have it, but promised, if he took her across, to reward him later. Well, as in all such tales, the hero, being something of a simpleton, believes the old dame, and gives her a free ride. . . ." Here he raised an eyebrow; the double meaning was clear, and we all laughed, except Kleis. "He ferries her over, and lo, as her foot touched the far shore, she turns into a beautiful young goddess—Aphrodite, no less! So for his faith, and his compliant nature, and all that, she gives him a wondrous smile, and a little jar of ointment that will keep him forever young and beautiful! He need only rub a smidgin on each night. . . ."

All the rest of us were smiling, but Kleis' fair brows met in a frown, thinking. "Such a little jar," she said. "How would it last?"

Alkaios raised his eyebrow again. "Well, judiciously applied . . ."

"Yes," said Kleis. "Where was he to put it?"

"Dear girl," said Alkaios, "where do you think? On his—"

"Alkaios!" cried Sappho.

"On his ear, I was going to say," finished Alkaios, and making us all laugh again. Kleis looked miserable, knowing she had missed the point; I resolved to explain it to her later.

Charaxus said, "I heard another version. It wasn't ointment. It was a—"

"Never mind," said Sappho. "Kleis, darling—will you go and tell the girls the lesson is over?"

"It is indeed," said Alkaios, as the girl left, all crimson.

"Well, Alkaios, she is only twelve!" said Sappho, primly.

"Quite old enough," said Alkaios.

"You are not her father!" said Sappho, sharply.

"I know, darling . . . I wish I were," he said quietly. I don't know whether she melted or wilted. Clearly it was the perfect answer.

"A silly story," I said, more to fill in the silence than for any sense.

"Silly, yes," said Sappho, slowly, "but—it might make a song. . . ."

"I was thinking of the sort of thing you did—I never saw it, of course, it was before my time—but the song-and-dance thing you did when Arion was your teacher. The Black Lark thing . . ." Alkaios stopped.

Her face lit. "Yes! It is a colorful tale . . . one can just imagine it . . . torches for stars, and all else dark . . . the boat, and the ferryman with his lantern, and the old woman in rags—she should be in rags, and all bent over, and shuffling—and the song a kind of low mumbling, and then he could sing, pulling on the oars—"

"I don't think Phaon can sing," put in Alkaios.

"No matter," said Sappho. "Other voices can take the melody, somewhere out of sight, while he dances. . . ."

"And then the transformation," cried Alkaios, warming to it, "and Aphrodite throwing off her cloak—"

"And showing up all beautiful and divine!" cried Sappho. She knit her brows. "We could use that new paint with silver flecks in it . . ."

"But who will do Aphrodite?" asked Alkaios.

"Andromeda?" said Sappho, doubtfully.

"My dear, you know Greeks would never accept a black goddess of love—no, it will have to be—"

Sappho whirled to face me.

"Oh, no!" I cried, shaking my head. "I cannot—I am out of practice. And besides—I would be worse. They would never accept someone like me either!"

"No, darling," said Alkaios to Sappho, "it will have to be you!"

Chapter 9

The story of Aphrodite and Phaon was performed at the festival of Dionysos, when there is always much singing and dancing. I had, of course, not seen the famous story of the Black Lark, so the whole thing was new to me. It was, at all events, a new sort of entertainment, difficult to describe, but wondrous indeed and very exciting. The closest thing to it is a certain type of temple rite, but that is always very solemn and slow; this moved very fast and ended too soon. The applause was deafening. Phaon's dancing was very fine; one could hardly believe a human body could achieve such grace. Of course, he is perfectly made and very handsome, too. When he took his bow at the end, there were cries of ecstasy from the women, and one fainted and had to be carried out.

The voices of the maidens were lovely, singing together, and Sappho's was truly glorious. One could swear, too, that she was really an old woman in the first part. When she became the goddess, suddenly, everyone gasped, not expecting it. Even I, who had watched a rehearsal or two, was amazed. Not only was she divinely beautiful, much more so than she is close to, she was also tall! Charaxus whispered that she must be standing on a box, but it was not so; I think she willed it, a kind of performer's magic.

Alkaios had no part in it, and did not sing either, but he ran the whole thing, planning it all and making everything go smoothly. He was ten persons in one that day, giving the signals for the singers, who were in the dark and could not see the action, oiling the hidden wheels that made Phaon's boat glide across the cloth sea, and trimming the wicks of the night stars.

My brother-in-law Larichus, whom I had seen only twice, if that, was there, seated down front in one of the special seats set aside for important folk. He nodded gravely to us, but left before the performance was over. Charaxus shrugged when I questioned him. "No doubt he finds it impious . . . He is of a very holy turn of mind. We were always taught to take these old god tales as we find them, all handed down by men's words and changed in the telling . . . but he was very young when our father died. I remember him as a merry child—but he has greatly changed, mumbling in the Old Greek that nobody understands anymore, and studying the sheep's entrails. . . ."

I shuddered; I have lived hard, but still I am very squeamish. He put his arm around me. "Don't let it bother you, sweetheart. It is his cupbearer's job, after all, to read the sacrifice. . . . I could wish he did not take it so seriously." He looked at my mouth, that was curling in disgust, though I tried to hold it straight. He laughed, and kissed my cheek. "Take heart, darling. At least he washes his hands before he comes to dinner. . . ." I said no more, but resolved to think twice before I invited him, brother or not. I need not have troubled myself; within the year he had taken the celibate's vows at Eleusis, and been sworn to holy silence. We never saw him again.

At the time, though, I remember speaking to Charaxus; his brother's departure had brought something to my mind. "Wonder that it is, this singing show, still—I cannot help but feel it is not wise of Sappho to pair herself with this Phaon. She is a noble, after all, and he but a dancing boy with an unsavory reputation. . . . people will talk."

"They are artists both . . . it is a leveler. Besides, they talk already, in all the ports . . . behind their hands, but I have heard it anyway. It is fame's penalty." He laughed, a harsh sound. "To hear them, one would think Sappho kept a harem full of women, like an Eastern prince!"

"That is ridiculous!" I cried. "There is not one man in Greece—except for you—that does not have his slave boy! And the soldiers swear eternal love, each to each, before a battle. And have you seen the burly athletes, still damp from the baths, jostling each other for a look from the newest thirteen-year-old?"

He looked at me, amused. "I had not thought you loved my sister so well, after her coldness. . . ."

I felt myself flush. "It is not that," I said. "But it is unfair . . ."

He shrugged. "It is a man's world," he said. "Who should know that better than you?"

I kept silent, then. Yet we were both right. Years after, when Sappho's girls were all dispersed, her school closed, and she no longer wrote of love, much less played at it, the tales still grew. Some of the men who talked would not stop with calling her mannish, but gave it out she was a man! They could not bear to think the Muses might smile so sweetly on a woman! As for the Phaon part of it . . . well, the story of Aphrodite and Phaon was performed three years straight at the Dionysia; after that, when it was half-forgotten, I heard it called the story of Sappho and Phaon! An idle mistake, of course, but in view of later events, a bitter one.

I become somewhat confused about those next years; I seem to have thought about nothing but Kleis, and her upbringing. They were feverish years for Sappho; she seemed, in a way, to burn herself up. I think she wrote the greatest part of her poetry then, a new song each day. She had a flow of pupils, too, girls that stayed only a few months, learning scraps, just enough to give a look of polish, and then were whisked home to be wives, and boast of their accomplishments. She had not much help with her teaching, either, Sappho, for most of her most talented girls had gone off to form little groups of their own. For a time Alkaios helped with it, but he was often too drunk, and made the girls laugh and not attend to their lessons. And, of course, with his sort of person, the novelty wears off quickly. He was not much use to her, and she wound up doing all the teaching, even of the slowest and least promising, herself. She grew thinner, and her movements were quick and irritable; I have seen her slap a girl for stupidity!

There was no place for Kleis in her life; the child was not talented enough, a disappointment. Kleis felt it bitterly; I think she was jealous of Sappho's favorites, some of whom were not a great deal older than she was. She came every day to my house, often in tears. I taught her to weave and spin, and to embroider pretty designs. (I think she never told her mother!) And I found ways to arrange youths to keep her company, making her blush and blossom. Oftener and oftener she stayed the night, Sappho having grown used to me by then; after a while Kleis visited weeks and months with us. I looked upon her as my own, and loved her dearly. She was married, finally, from our house.

It did not help that Atthis came back to Sappho; the girl was a born torturer. Strangely enough, some of the most beautiful of Sappho's songs were written then, when she was most wretched.

Her bittersweet passion for this cruel girl served her well; perhaps, deep down, she knew it.

After many a false start, and tearful return, Atthis went forever from Sappho's life. For years the girl's brothers had been urging her to marry the youth Hermias, and always she had refused, with light contempt. When they had nearly given up, Atthis decided she would. I think she was fond of all such games; there was something unstable about her. Who knows—perhaps she tired of Sappho as a victim and looked for another; Hermias was made to order, like a lovesick calf.

Their wedding was celebrated with perhaps the greatest pomp ever seen in Mitylene. Pittakos was the boy's stepfather and used all the city facilities; taxes were fierce that year. He even built them a fine new house, rosy marble from Asia, and his wife, Phaedra, furnished it expensively with teak and ivory. Alkaios said it was in the worst possible taste. "But," he said with an airy smile, "when they fall upon hard times, they can sell it!"

Sappho led the wedding singers, beating her drum wildly. She looked like a white-faced Bacchante. I had never known her drunk, but I swear that night she was. It marked the end of her love songs, too; I think she never wrote another.

Kleis, grown very beautiful and very tall, like a golden goddess, married the next year. Her groom was the tallest youth in the city, and folk marveled to see them, the two young creatures, so fair, and looking to be made for each other, like something out of an old tale. His name was Timotheus and he dabbled in the New Philosophy. They had five tall sons, close together. After the birth of the fifth, Kleis said to me, gaily, "Done. That is all. I will have no more . . . too risky! You have no notion how sick I have been of girls!"

Chapter 10

Sappho was a grandmother twice over when Pittakos resigned from public life; I was about thirty-five at the time, so I place her age at forty or thereabouts. (She was always a bit secretive about her age; it was one of her vanities.) Pittakos had been suffering from ill health for many years; it was probably this which decided him, and, indeed, a short while after, he died, escaping from his nagging wife.

He appointed no successor; his son was dead, and he had no favorites among the city's servants. His retirement was without ceremony; he simply walked into Melanippos' house one morning and handed him a large gold key, saying, with a wintry smile, that it was the key to the city. Melanippos had no desire to set himself up as Tyrant; it was a form of government he abhorred. He called a large meeting of nobles and freedmen, including women, and called upon them to decide on a council of thirty to administrate the city's laws.

I was there, being qualified; it was a large group, as one might imagine, and the meeting was held in the agora. About a hundred names were put up, and the entire body voted for the chosen thirty. It was most interesting how it was accomplished; I do not think that this had ever been done before. A huge bowl was brought, from the temple of Demeter, and set up on a tripod in the sight of all. Each person was given a roll of parchment, long enough to write thirty names. Several demurred, saying this was too expensive, but Melanippos answered that it was worth it, for only in this way would the will of the majority be fulfilled, and make the voting fair. It made sense, and we all applauded. Of course, it could not be accomplished in one day, for they had all to be counted three times over, to make certain of no mistakes. Indeed, the counting took nearly a week; most folk made a holiday time of it, and some even made bets on the outcome!

In the beginning, when names were put up, Charaxus was nominated several times, but refused, saying that his business took him too often away. I was nominated, too, for a wonder. I did not see who spoke, but it was a woman's voice; I blushed for pleasure, feeling I had come a long way, but shook my head and declined.

Several other women, too, including Pittakos' widow, Phaedra, were nominated, but, in the end, only Sappho was elected. There were more women than men among the voters; I can only conclude that women were still so unused to being consulted, that habit prevailed and they went along, as always, honoring the men!

I will not name the thirty, for it would be silly and take up time, but Alkaios was among them, and his brother, Antimenades, too. Melanippos was elected, as a matter of course; he had been for years a prominent citizen. The oldest member of the council was Erigyus, the uncle of Charaxus and Sappho.

The council sat twice a week, determining among themselves the rule of the city; on another day, but also weekly, they made themselves available to the citizenry, to hear complaints and settle disputes. The complainant picked the council member of his or her choice to hear the case; Sappho was the only woman, and women being great complainers, she was very sought after, as one might imagine. Often, on those days, she did not have a moment to take a bite of food or wet her lips with wine, from sunup to evening! I should have thought it extremely fatiguing, but she seemed, truly, to thrive on it, looking younger and livelier every week.

Strange it was. Until this happened she had been dull and listless often, taking no interest in things around her and complaining of feeling tired and ill. Now she was attending to the city's business, entertaining a great deal, and still finding time to write and practice on the lyre, though she had given up teaching by then.

No matter what her day had been like, or what sort of evening she looked forward to, there was one thing that had become, over the years, a twilight ritual. Alkaios, with lyre, presented himself at her door and they two, both dressed to kill, as if for a state occasion, pleasured themselves with gossip, light bickering, familiar jokes, and music. Besides his lyre, and often a new song or its beginnings, Alkaios always brought her a gift. (I rather think he made a ritual of buying it, too, in the agora each morning; I have seen him at it, haggling happily like a marketwife.) It might be an oddly shaped ring, or an ornament for her hair, or a quaint old bit of pottery that had escaped the dealers' eyes. Once, triumphantly, he brought her a little cat, striped like a tiger; she wept. He announced it was the great-great-granddaughter of their little pets of long ago. "I have called her Atthis," he said, slyly, waiting to see how she took it. But she only laughed, like glass breaking, and produced a leather wristband, dyed blue, fastening it around the creature's neck. "I found it a while back, in my clothes chest," she said. "There was no mate—so I never returned it. . . ."

"Well," he said, drawling the words, "my sister has given up wrestling now. She is getting too fat—on her husband's cooking. . . ."

Sappho's eyes glinted, and her lips curved in a little smile. She stroked the cat; I saw that the animal's face wore the same look. I took my leave presently, feeling uncomfortable. Those two singers understood each other too well, making a wall about them.

Age sat on them gracefully, particularly Sappho. Her body had lost the enchanting curves of her girlhood, and from much dancing looked muscular and taut, and the lines of her face were sharper. Aside from that she looked much the same, from a little distance. She painted her face carefully and delicately and dyed her hair. She held her back straight, her neck long, and her chin high; it gave her a look of majesty, and one forgot her small stature. Alkaios' torso was a trifle thicker, and his face puffy from high living, but his look was still bold and merry, and his manner as engaging as a boy's. They both affected exotic dress from far places, such as Egypt or Assyria, costumes, almost; they had given up performing, for the most part, and perhaps they missed it.

When Sappho played at grandmother with Kleis' little boys, about twice yearly, they stared at her, solemn as owls. I suppose to them she looked like a being from another world. After, she enfolded them in great stifling embraces, and they squirmed and pulled away. The youngest, still a baby, wailed until she handed him back to his mother, whereupon Sappho looked down at her lap in distaste, holding her skirt away from her. "Can you not—*pad* him—or something? I am soaking wet!"

"Well, Mother," said Kleis, keeping a straight face, "he is

training and doing very well, as a rule . . . I expect you frightened him."

"I?" said Sappho coldly, raising her brows a foot or so, and looking like an Eastern image. "I have never frightened anyone in my life! You had better have a doctor look at him . . . he seems backward."

Shortly afterward, on Kleis' birthday, her mother very handsomely gave her as a gift the deed to the family property in Eresos, which Sappho had inherited, being the oldest. "It is not in good repair, but it is huge and a fine place for children," said Sappho. "I will send some workmen to put it in order. . . ."

It seemed a very generous gesture, but, I remembered, Eresos was all the way across Lesbos, on the opposite shore, a considerable journey!

Chapter 11

Sappho began, about the time of becoming a councilwoman, to write small treatises, very moral. It earned her another nickname, a new one, "The Wise." I cannot remember them all, or even a few, only scraps remain in the mind; they are not melodic, after all, and do not stir the emotions, as her songs had done. Of course, they were all quite true, but very dull; also, she did not practice what she urged on others! But then the artist cannot be held accountable for his work; the god, or goddess, speaks through him—or her, of course. In this case, it must have been the grave Athene!

Cne treatise in particular I well recall: "When anger rises in the breast, restrain the idly yelping tongue." I thought of those horrid letters she had sent to Charaxus, reviling me. Did Mars speak, too? Never mind, I had grown to love her well, this fascinating, wild, self-centered being. I had not forgotten, either, that all her life she had worked to improve the lot of women.

Indeed, though I traveled much with my husband, to near and far places, only on Lesbos did I see, ever, women and girls (outside of the hetaerae, another thing entirely) taught letters and sums, music and singing. Only on Lesbos did respectable women walk free in the agora, protected by the law. Even the poor hill wives enjoyed a few privileges; for instance, their parents, in famine time, might hire them out to work in some fine house, but there was no more selling into slavery, as had happened to me. As for the prostitutes, they gave only a token sum to the temple, and might leave at any time. This was true, also, of those who lived in brothels; they could not be kept against their will. As for the procurer, he was considered an outlaw; if he was discovered at it, the crime was punishable by death. Of course, all these laws were broken every day, in small ways, and the authorities, being men, winked at it. But one such case was not small, and one of the authorities was not a man—one was Sappho. The story, at the time, rocked the world.

As I have said, the council met on one day of the week to hear complaints and consider them. Often a woman, in this way, by appealing to Sappho, obtained a bit of justice. It might be against her husband, for a whipping, or against a merchant for cheating, or a street girl might have a sailor up for not paying the price.

On one such day, the couple, Makro and Hero, appeared to air a complaint. She knew them both well, of course, and bent her attention to them when their turn came. Hero was living in my house now, for her husband was one of Charaxus' most valued captains; she had a growing family and no longer any duties as teacher, since Sappho's school had been dispersed. She did not speak, for it was really Makro's story; perhaps she thought to lend him extra support.

It really was quite a shocking tale; it seems that on several occasions sailors from Makro's ship had been beaten and robbed while visiting wharfside whores. After, their stories seemed to have more than coincidence, and the descriptions of the ruffians who had attacked them tallied, though the girls used as bait were different. Well, Makro took matters into his own hands. With these men, and some other sailors for protection, he went into one low wine shop after another, seeking a glimpse of the criminals. It took some doing, but the third such venture paid off. The sailors spotted their man, only one, but it sufficed. They waylaid the fellow in a dark alley and overpowered him, taking him on board the ship for questioning. I guess they were quite rough, though they did not kill him. He was made to name the head of these criminal operations. They still held him captive and he could be made to testify. The name he gave was Phaon!

It seemed Phaon had been doing this, on the side, for years. He had always had low connections, from his earliest days; now he was making lucrative use of them. The captive named all the criminals and all the girls, more than twenty. The City Guard was sent to put them all under arrest.

Procuring, by itself, as I have said, was an offense punishable by death; with the other crimes to his credit, there could be no mitigation of the sentence. The accomplices, too, must be dealt with.

The council met in special session to determine the punishments. What was decided had a sort of grim justice. The men who had been doing the dirty work, the beating and robbing, were sentenced to ten years of slave labor on the galley of a warship; since they had preyed upon seamen, it was fitting that they should now serve at the lowest sea job. Most of them would not last the ten years; it was nearly a death sentence.

The girls were another matter. They had all been bought (another piece of lawlessness) from their hill parents, and had no choice but to obey, as it had been with me, but at the very lowest rung of the ladder, all that they earned went to Phaon, for he owned them.

Melanippos suggested that they be given to the goddess, to work at the temple, and have freedwomen's status, keeping what they earned, except for the goddess' share.

Sappho turned on him fiercely. "That is a man's thought!" she cried. "Why not let *them* choose? Let them take other service, handmaidens, cooks, whatever . . . or some might wish to go back to their homes!"

This was agreed upon, for everyone saw the justice of it; sad to relate, each of the girls chose the temple. It was the only profession they knew, after all.

Phaon, of course, must die, but the manner of it must be decided upon. Several of the council wanted the spear-death, or strangulation, and one man even suggested crucifixion. No doubt these were the men whose wives the beautiful Phaon had seduced!

"I think," said Alkaios, slowly, "that we must remember that once, long ago, this Phaon did the city a service. . . . It was to gain his freedom, of course, but still . . . And he helped us greatly during our first exile. I wonder if he should not be given grace to die quietly, by his own hand . . . a draught of deadly poison, quick-acting . . ."

Sappho shook her head. "No, Alkaios . . . that is a statesman's death, or a noble's. Phaon is neither. . . . But he *is* an artist—and we should remember it." She bent her head in thought. "There is a shrine to Apollo of the Muses, at Leukas, on the peak of the highest cliff. Long ago there was a custom—to sacrifice to the god by throwing a victim from the cliff into the sea. Human sacrifice, it was . . . and some say it was voluntary. That of course is lost in the mists of time . . . but now and then a criminal is executed in this way—there at Leukas. . . . To me it seems a fitting end to a life spent in service to the Muses."

And so it was. Phaon was sent to the priests of Apollo at Leukas, at the time of the next Apollo day. The girls and women of Mitylene mourned as for Adonis, strewing flowers in his path as he was led to the ship that would take him to his death-place. There was much weeping and wailing, and many took ship and followed, even some that were wives of respected men. Alkaios swore that he saw Pittakos' widow, Phaedra, among them; I never met the lady close to, so I do not know.

I was not one of those who followed, and did not witness the death. They say, though, that he made a good end, standing straight and proud. When the priest made to bind his hands and feet, as was the custom, so that the victim would not struggle, he shook his head. "I will make the leap," he said. "I go to the god. . . ." And, so saying, he threw himself from that great height into the raging, boiling sea far below. A high, thin wailing rose from the women who mourned, and one rushed from their midst and threw herself off the cliff after him. No one saw who that woman was, for it happened so quickly; the bodies sank like stones and were never found. But, as Alkaios said, the woman Phaedra never came back to Mitylene.

Chapter 12

We all, except the gods, grow old. My sister-in-law, in a poem, said, "The gods are wise, for they chose immortality." I wonder. Myself, I am growing a little tired; I am past sixty.

Charaxus had given up long sea voyages some years before, leaving the captaining to other, younger men. He still was head of the business, though he had been gradually turning over more and more of it to two of Kleis' sons, the eldest and the third; the others had followed philosophy, after their father, and had gone to study in Athens. We had not journeyed together by ship for a long, long time, but it was the year of our fortieth anniversary, and I had promised Aphrodite an offering; I did not want to leave it too late. I said to my husband that I wanted to sail for Naukratis, where we had met, and place my offering at the temple there.

"And I will wait at the temple steps for you, as I did then, long ago . . ." he said, tipping up my chin. "You were so beautiful . . . and you have not changed."

It is not true, of course; I get a shock every time I pass a mirror. That stranger cannot be me! Sometimes I put out my tongue at her; there is little else that I can do.

But time passes, and one cannot hold it back. Melanippos is dead years ago, and his sweet Telesippa also. Antimenades and Dika are gone as well. There are not many of us old ones left. Only Sappho and Alkaios. They are like objects on their own collector's shelves, lovingly preserved.

They still meet at twilight, every day, rain or shine; neither of them ever seems to be ill. She has lately resigned from the council. I think she lies long abed, and spends hours at her beauty rituals; I rather suspect the meeting with Alkaios is the high spot of her day. I know she does little else. She does not sing or play the lyre with any regularity, though she still writes down her songs. She complains of stiff fingers, and a voice that croaks. Alkaios has the same difficulties but takes them cheerfully, hitting a wrong note now and then and grimacing. He seldom comes to council meetings, either, he is probably too drunk; he spends half his day sobering up for his twilight session with his old sweetheart.

Alkaios is almost bald, and his cheeks are jowls. His eyes, sunk into flesh, look little and lewd, but merry, and his wine-flush lends him a look of vigor. He has left off painting his face, and has no hair to crimp. He might be any old ruddy grandsire, but for his golden wreath, which he wears, always, slightly askew.

The poets were presented gold wreaths at the last Dionysia, by the will of the people. His is molded to represent laurel, and hers, violets. She wears hers on hair black as night; one presumes that the dye has accumulated over the years.

Sappho has written a poem describing how she has aged, and lamenting it; strange, she will write it on paper, but she does not let anyone see its effect. The poem says that her hair is white, her face full of wrinkles, her teeth fallen out, and her legs too stiff to dance. Dance! I am hard put to it to *walk* without puffing, for I have grown stout.

The words of the poem are probably true, but she pushes it away while she can, dyeing her hair, and covering her wrinkles with a thick paste, powdered over. From across the room one cannot think her much above fifty. She has developed a masklike look; only her eyes move. But perhaps it is just that she fears to crack the paint. She dresses in rich Eastern robes, which cover all, unlike our Greek dress. Only her hands show the ravages of time; they are corded and knotty and the skin is yellow.

We went to bid her farewell before we set sail for Naukratis. Alkaios was there, of course; it is the only hour at which she receives. She was quite friendly with me, as she has been of late; I suspect she has even forgotten my origins! She asked me for news of Kleis, which we get through her sons, of course. I said that she was well, but that her hair was almost white; Sappho looked startled for a moment, then raised her veined hand to pat a black-onyx curl into place.

She was very arch with Charaxus, calling him "big brother"; he smiled a little but did not contradict her. There was some Egyptian cotton that she wanted, in a rare shade of violet; we promised to look for it. Our conversation ran down, as it does lately; we sipped our beer, still her favorite beverage. The little cat with Atthis' leather wristband about its neck rubbed against me, arching its back. I cannot bear the creatures; they make my skin crawl. To cover my distaste, and for courtesy, I rose, saying we must leave, and make ready for our journey.

"I'll come along, if I may," said Alkaios, as I knew he would. His mouth must have been getting very dry.

We had walked over, as it was not far, but I was glad for a lift in Alkaios' chariot. We went the long way home, for the streets were wider. They were not wide enough, as it turned out, however; when another chariot appeared coming the opposite way, we had to back up into a side path. This chariot was the old-fashioned kind, like a broad-bottomed boat, pulled by two horses, and with a seat big enough for two.

"Zeus!" whispered Alkaios. "It is Gorgo and Andromeda . . . what freaks!"

It was not true, really; they were just two old ladies, dressed a bit mannishly in identical dalmaticas. Indeed, but for their color, they might have been sisters. They had both grown thick and broad; I think they had given up exercise, finally. They did not see us, or did not notice, perhaps. Gorgo was driving; she stared ahead at the road, mulishly. From the other came strange clicking sounds, interspersed with some Greek. We heard Gorgo say, as they passed, "Stop it! You know I can't understand that jungle talk!" The clicks did not stop though, but got louder. Gorgo shook the reins and the horses went by in a flurry. *Poor old things,* I thought, *they are like a married couple that no longer even like one another, but cannot live apart.* Alkaios had the same thought, for he said, tossing his head in the old way of his youth, "Bicker, bicker, bicker—all day long! When one passes their house, one can hear them clear out on the road!"

I said, mildly, "Well, I suppose they have little else to do, now that their school is closed. . . ."

He looked sidelong at me. "You are the best of us all, Doricha. I never hear you slight anyone. . . ."

"Well," I said, after a moment, "perhaps I am the happiest . . . certainly I have gained the most." And I looked up at Charaxus, who bent to kiss me. I caught a glimpse of Alkaios' face; he looked as if he were going to be sick. I suppose to a nature as light as his, the spectacle of old lovers, still at it, is not in the best of taste. But then, I do not care to watch graybeards pawing pretty boys. We all have our prejudices.

Chapter 13

Naukratis had greatly changed, like so many things. Or perhaps it had not, and I simply saw it with other eyes. It had, even though it had grown since my time, a stunted look, somehow; I had thought it the center of the world!

It was still a Greek army and naval base, but most of the soldiers and sailors were mercenaries now, gleaned from all the new colonies. One saw no Greek faces in the waterfront streets, and the shipping, too, looked strange. Most of the boats were galley driven and carried no sail. I had been used to the gaiety and color of painted hulls and bright-dyed canvas. Charaxus explained that the new shipping, especially for war, was painted gray-blue to match the sea, and so remain hidden from enemies.

I wanted, from some perversity, to see Xanthes' house again, though it had been my prison. Of course, it would not be his any longer; he must be long dead. It looked smaller, as did everything, and the street where it stood was shabby and rundown. The house itself was pretty, though, painted pink and the roof gilded, like a child's toy. On an impulse I knocked at the door, smiling sheepishly at Charaxus.

A boy opened it; he had long Eastern eyes and a sulky mouth, and looked to be no more than ten years of age. He stared at me as though I had dropped from the sky. I asked for Milo.

"The master is resting," he said. "And anyway he wouldn't see you . . . we have no need of bathwomen. This is a house of boys. . . ." I smiled. He looked closer, his eyes popping. He did not know what to think, poor creature. He could see now that I did not look for work, being richly dressed and with a stately old gentleman in tow. I had forgotten women's state in other places, having lived so long on Lesbos.

I spoke to him gently. "We are old friends, Milo and I. Tell him Doricha is here."

He did not move. Charaxus reached out and gave him a friendly shove.

"Go now, little one . . . you heard the lady. . . ."

After a little wait, we were led into a small painted chamber; the air was stifling from the heat of a large brazier, and the curtains were drawn. It was dim and I could not see clearly; from a corner came a voice, high and wheezing. "My dear . . ."

I turned. I saw, seated on a low couch, an enormously fat man, completely bald, in a pale pink robe and covered in jewels. "My dear, forgive me that I cannot rise . . . I have grown too much . . ."

I went forward and took his plump, beringed hands in mine, peering close. In the huge pudding of his face shone the black eyes of the boy Milo. The voice went on. "My dear, I would know you anywhere! A little gray in the hair . . . otherwise you have not changed at all . . . still the rose of the world, dear Rhodopis."

"And how is it with you, friend Milo?"

He waved his hand. "As you see, my dear . . . I am my own master now—and master, too, of thirty others. . . . They do well, the little dears. . . . I am very rich, and shall retire soon, and all the little dears shall have their freedom and a bonus. . . ." His face sagged. "To tell you the truth, my dear—I am very tired. . . ."

We spoke for a little and I presented Charaxus. "The brother of the Muse? Ah . . . if I were not at the end of my days! I should go to Lesbos, just for the sight of her! We sing no other songs here . . . only those of the Black Lark. My dear, I heard a sweet tale the other night, from an Athenian . . ." There was a simper on his face; I wondered if he still? . . . "The young man, the Athenian, said that the great Solon of Athens refused to die until he had learned by heart a song of Sappho's."

"Really?" I said. "I shall tell her; she will be so pleased." Of course, the whole world had heard it a hundred times; it was probably just a tale.

We took our leave soon, feeling sad. The poor old thing began to wheeze heavily, and waved us out. "My dear, this bulk . . . you do not know! I must take my medicine now and rest. . . . Come and see me another time. . . ."

I bent and kissed him on the cheek; it was soft and slack. I saw that his round face grew pink as his robe, and his eyes looked moist. "Thank you, my dear . . . may the gods keep you."

I was silent on the way to the temple, thinking of the Fates.

Charaxus pressed my hand; I had told him, often, of the boy Milo, next to me in the slave line, long ago.

"Well, darling," he said, "at least he has prospered . . . and seems good-natured. Some eunuchs are warped by it—if they live so long. . . ."

I was still saddened, but I smiled at him, and said, "Every day I thank the gods for you. . . ."

"And today you are going to pay one for me . . . a goddess, anyway." The litter stopped; we had reached the Temple of Aphrodite. Again, like everything else in Naukratis, it looked small and shabby, even a little poor. "I think," I said, "that Aphrodite is in need of my offering."

"Well . . . it will certainly buy a few new tiles for the roof, and perhaps a coat of paint." He handed me the purse of gold coins; it was very heavy. I had saved it from the housekeeping money of forty years! I had not wanted Charaxus to give it for me; it must come from me alone. I kissed him and said, "I shall not be long. Mind you wait in the shade . . . this sun is fierce." I left him there, for Aphrodite's house is for women only. As I passed through the portal, two young prostitutes jostled me, laughing. "Oh, sorry, grandmother!" said one of them, stepping aside. She was not even pretty. I smiled to myself, a grim little smile, and passed on.

It was quite dark inside. I could just make out the cages of doves, the most popular sacrifice; they looked to be moulting, and their feathers were dirty. When I approached the altar, the old priestess peered at me, screwing up her eyes. I remembered her from long ago, and it seemed she knew me also, for her mouth split in a toothless grin. She had looked old to me then, in the flower of my youth. What age must she have reached by now? "Is it the Rose?" she asked. "I know those eyes. . . . Is it Rhodopis?"

"Yes, Honored One," I said. "But let the sacrifice be marked from Doricha, wife of Charaxus."

She narrowed her eyes, looking sly. "Go on . . . you're never a wife!"

"Forty years now," I said, firmly. Age and freedom had lent me authority. She gave me a little bobbling bow.

"Come this way, then, Lady. . . ."

She led me to a small inner chamber where an image of the

goddess stood, very old, carved in wood, and stiff, wearing a simper. "Make your prayer," she said. "I must have these gold pieces converted into iron spits. . . ."

It was a holy place, so I said nothing; the iron-spit currency had gone out long ago. I guessed they would put some spits at the feet of the goddess, just for show, and spend the money. Well, it was all one. Aphrodite has her priestesses, after all, and they too must live. I raised my eyes to the image and prayed.

As I finished, I saw the old one, with two others, lugging in a great netted bag filled with the spits. The old one looked at me and cackled. "She likes the spits, the goddess does. Shape of—" She measured a length with her hands. I thought it a farfetched phallus image; the spits were cruelly pointed and at least a foot long. I shrugged away the thought; these old women have strange fancies. I took my leave, and they thanked me, almost prostrating themselves, as if I were some Eastern queen. I got away quickly, through the dim, dusty temple chambers and out into the air.

I looked for Charaxus. There was a sacred oak nearby, old, with a vast spread of boughs. I thought to find him there, in its shade, but he stood at the foot of the steps, in the same spot where I had first seen him, all those years ago. I opened my mouth to scold him for risking his health in the heat, but I could not; he looked so happy, with young eyes.

Young eyes, but that was all. Why had I not noticed before the sunken cheeks and the pallor? There were droplets of sweat on his forehead; I wiped them away with a cloth from my sleeve. "Don't fuss, darling—" He pulled away, saying, "Look, here is the litter . . . get in."

I looked in the floor place as I seated myself. "Well, at least there are sunshades." I opened one and raised it, handing him the other. He shook his head. "I will not," he said, firmly. "They are for women and fancy boys. . . ."

"Well," I said, "hold mine, at least. It will cover us both." He took it with an ill grace, unusual for him. Through his thin dalmatica his body felt cold where it touched mine, though the noon sun was high overhead.

We had taken rooms in one of the better waterfront inns, for the ship's cabin was cramped. I said I should like to rest before the midday meal. It was not true, really, but Charaxus had an exhausted look that alarmed me a little, for I had not seen him so before, and he leaned against the door as he held it open for me. I passed through, unclasping my robe at the shoulder and tossing it onto a chair.

I felt, rather than heard, that the door did not close, and turned. He was looking at me, his eyes frightened, as I had never seen them. He stretched out one hand to me. "Dora . . . Oh, Dora . . ." Then he seemed simply to crumple in upon himself. I reached him before he fell. My name was the last word from his lips. I lowered him to the floor gently, but I knew before the doctor came that he was dead.

"A stroke, Lady," the doctor said. "A stroke from a god. . . ."

No, I thought, *from a goddess. . . .*

The journey back to Lesbos was too long. I ordered a pyre upon the wharf and watched the flames rise against the bleached blue sky. We held no service; I would order a memorial day later, when I returned to Mitylene. The sailors from his ship watched with me till it was done, all in silence but for the crackling of the fire.

When I turned, his ashes gathered in an urn, to go aboard, I saw Milo on the edge of the little mourning group, his litter borne by six burly bearers. I went back to him and, stooping, kissed him on the brow. Tears glittered in his eyes. I pressed his hand.

As the wind filled our sail and we began to move slowly out from port, I stood at the rail, holding the casket of ashes. I remembered what Charaxus had told me of Sappho's husband, another sailor, that he had wanted his ashes scattered in the harbor, for he loved the sea.

I opened the casket and emptied it into the bright blue water beside the ship. As we gathered speed, the wind behind us, I watched the white dust sink slowly, slowly, into the harbor waters of Naukratis.

Chapter 14

For the first time since my childhood I was sick on a sea voyage. Our passage was not rough, nor was the air sultry; I can only conclude it was a sickness of the soul. I could not face the prospect of life without Charaxus and put it off as long as I could, lying throughout the voyage in my cabin below.

When land was sighted, I rose, dizzy, for I had eaten almost nothing the whole time, and dressed for shore. I had no mourning black with me, of course; I found in my chest a robe I had not yet worn, in a soft shade of gray. When I looked into a mirror to drape the folds, I saw that it became me well, being the same color as my hair and setting off my skin, still rosy in spite of my grief. I saw, too, that I had lost flesh and looked younger; this was perhaps the saddest thing of all, for Charaxus was not there to see.

Mitylene, the shining city, had no glow for me that homecoming; to my sick eyes it looked green as old cheese. I had sent word ahead, so, in deference to my state, there was no crowd to welcome me, only Hero with a closed litter to take me home.

One must live, somehow, no matter what. The day had to be set for the funeral rites, the mourning wreaths must be hung, and the black robes sewn. When all was settled in my mind, I went, in my new black, to visit my sister-in-law. It was a courtesy; I might have sent Hero or some other to inform her of the arrangements, but I thought Charaxus would have wanted me to go myself.

It was early, not twilight yet, but when I entered the house, I heard voices, quick and high. I had not thought to find Alkaios there before his usual hour, yet surely one voice was his. I followed behind the handmaiden down the corridor, the voices dividing themselves into two and becoming clear.

". . . he was my brother, after all . . . my big brother!"

"My dear Sappho," said Alkaios, silky and slow, "I seem to remember Charaxus always—a child that forever tagged after . . ."

"He was small for his age." Sappho's voice was icy.

"Well, be that as it may . . ." I could almost see Alkaios' hand waving, and slowed my steps, hoping to get the gist of this quarrel.

Alkaios went on. "About this matter of the funeral ode. . . . He was my friend, and co-patriot, and all the rest. I think Lesbos would feel it more fitting—coming from a man."

There was a delicate little silence, vibrant with meaning. *Oh-oh,* I thought, *she is giving him one of her looks!*

She said, slowly, "Lesbos—and the world—honors the name of Sappho."

"My dear," he replied. "No one would dispute it . . . but—I am not unknown either. . . ."

Quiet as I tried to be, my step was heard; and I could not follow so slowly as never to come into the room. I heard myself announced, and must enter. I have walked in a steady rhythm all my life, but now despite myself my feet dragged; I felt all made of earth, and alien, among these two beings of some other element.

Sappho spoke first. "Ah, here is the good Doricha. It shall be her decision."

I made as if I had heard nothing, and busied myself with my widow's garb, throwing back the hood of my black wool robe, and pleating the folds of the gown beneath. Until I seated myself, uninvited, I did not speak.

"What is it, dear Sappho?" I asked mildly. "What must I decide?"

"We have been discussing the matter of the ode . . . the funeral ode for my brother. . . ."

"Yes?" I asked, innocently.

There was a little silence. Alkaios waved his hand impatiently.

"Oh, come now, Dora . . . which of us shall write it? He was my dear, dear friend . . . I saw him every day in these last years—and besides, I feel a man should—"

Sappho broke in, her voice rising. "That is nonsense! Here is his sister, the greatest poet of the world . . ."

"Poet-*ess*," he said, coldly.

I have said only her eyes moved of late, but this once she turned full upon him, glaring. One could feel the sparks that flew between them; I was glad that I was not sitting in the middle, truly!

I could see well that they were both speechless with fury, she white as ashes, and he purpling with choler. I spoke, quietly.

"But that is why I have come. To ask if you will not combine . . . and make the finest and most beautiful song . . . for it will be that, without question, if either does it. How much more if it comes from both!"

They stared at me, like a pair of idols. Even through my great grief I felt a bubble of laughter in my throat. Where had I seen such expressions before? I remembered. Upon the pinched faces of the peacocks of Hera!

I watched as a little color crept into Sappho's cheeks under the paint, and Alkaios' face drained of its purple blood. They looked almost, if not quite, human.

Then Sappho, old Eastern idol that she looked, clapped her hands together like a child, and smiled. The smile was enchanting.

"What a lovely idea! Now, I have been trying over some words . . ." And she reached down beside her and picked up a parchment, holding it at arm's length, for she had grown farsighted.

"I, too," said Alkaios, holding out a scroll. She took it from him, unrolled it, and, holding it away and squinting, scanned it. She frowned.

"Oh, no!" she exclaimed. "It will never do!" She handed it back. "You have written it in Ionian. . . . *we* . . . my brother and I . . . are Aeolian."

"Well, my dear Sappho," said Alkaios, "so are we all . . . but—if the world is to know this piece—then it must be written in the classic dialect."

"I beg your pardon, my dear Alkaios! The world has never had any difficulty with *my* songs . . . and I always write in Aeolian. . . ." She had drawn herself up and was looking those dagger looks again.

I spoke, quickly. "Oh, yes, Alkaios . . . forgive me. I agree with my dear sister." And I caught his glance and sent a warning message through my eyes. "Charaxus—" It was the first time I had spoken his name, and it stuck in my throat, painfully. I went on. "Charaxus would have liked it—in the island speech. . . ."

He tossed his head. "Well, if you say so . . ." He took back his scroll, rerolling it.

Again I ventured something; I feared another freeze between them.

"I know little about such things . . . but—could Sappho, perhaps, read her words, and you take up your lyre and . . ."

"Yes!" said Sappho. "Alkaios—you will listen—and take some chords as we go. . . . That way we may work it out together." She held out her parchment again and began to read, chantingly. He struck a chord or two, tentative. She stopped. "Try it again—shall we? I think a lower note . . ."

They began again. They tried the first three words twelve times, perhaps more, before they both nodded. "Good!" she said. "Let us go on in this key . . ." They were engrossed. I felt as though I might as well be dead myself, for all they noticed me. Well, an ordinary person cannot fathom the soul of an artist. I sighed, softly, so as not to disturb them, and brought my hood up again to cover my head.

As I turned away, I heard a string snap with a sharp thwang; Sappho's voice stopped; the air was vibrant. In the silence I heard Alkaios blow his nose, loudly, and, after, the sound of the string being wound again.

I did not speak, but, as I turned, my eyes down, I saw the parchment, white, with faint ink-scratchings upon it. As I looked, a great tear fell, as large as a gold piece, making the ink run. I heard a low smothered sob; I did not know which one it came from.

I tiptoed out of the chamber, leaving them to their work.

Author's Acknowledgments

For background material and history I am indebted to many authors, among them, E. Abrahams and Lady Evans, *Ancient Greek Dress*; C. M. Bowra, *The Greek Experience*; Will Durant, *The Life of Greece*; Aesop, *The Fables*; Harper's *Dictionary of Classical Literature and Antiquities*; Walter Woodford Hyde, *Greek Religion and Its Survivals*; H. D. F. Kitto, *The Greeks*; Edgar Lobel, *Sappho*; Jack Lindsay, *The Ancient World*; Eugene S. McCartney, *Warfare by Land and Sea*; Gilbert Murray, *A History of Ancient Greek Literature*; Denys Page, *Sappho and Alcaeus*; Mary Patrick, *Sappho and the Isle of Lesbos*; Marjorie and Peter Quennell, *Everyday Things in Ancient Greece*; George Rawlinson, *The History of Herodotus*; David Robinson, *Sappho and Her Influence*; J. D. Symonds, *Studies of the Greek Poets*; William Smith, *Classical Dictionary*; Henry Osborne Taylor, *Greek Biology and Medicine*; Arthur Weigall, *Sappho of Lesbos*; F. A. Wright, *Feminism in Greek Literature from Homer to Aristotle*.

Translations of Sappho's poetry most helpful to me have been Mary Barnard, *The Songs of Sappho*; Willis Barnstone, *Sappho: Lyrics in the Original Greek with Translations*; J. D. Edmonds, *Lyra Graeca*; Edgar Lobel and Denys Page, *Poetarum Lesbiorum Fragmenta*; Max Treu, *Sappho*.

Except for the fragments of Sappho's poems found in an Egyptian tomb, her work has been preserved by quotations from writers of antiquity, among them, Antipatros of Sidon, Aristotle, Catullus, Ovid, Plato, Plutarch, Socrates, Strabo, Suidas, and Vergil. We are all in their debt.